# THE
# LIGHT
## AND THE
# DARK

# THE
# LIGHT
## AND THE
# DARK

## Mikhail
## SHISHKIN

*Translated from the Russian by Andrew Bromfield*

Quercus

First published in Great Britain in 2013 by

Quercus
55 Baker Street
7th Floor, South Block
London
W1U 8EW

A CIP catalogue record for this book is available
from the British Library

ISBN 978 1 78087 105 9 (HB)
ISBN 978 1 78087 106 6 (TPB)
ISBN 978 1 78087 107 3 (EBOOK)

10 9 8 7 6 5 4 3 2 1

Typeset by Ellipsis Digital Limited, Glasgow

Printed and bound in Great Britain by Clays Ltd, St Ives plc

●

I open yesterday's *Evening News*, and it's all about you and me.

It's going to be the word in the beginning again, they write. But meanwhile in the schools they rattle on in the same old way, saying first of all there was a big bang, and the whole of existence went flying apart.

And what's more, supposedly everything already existed even before the bang — all the galaxies we can see and the ones we can't. In the same way that the future glass lives in the sand, and the grains of sand are the seeds of this window here, through which I've just seen a little boy run past outside with a football stuffed up the front of his T-shirt.

There was this bundle of intense warmth and light.

The scientists tell us it was the size of a football. Or a watermelon. And just like in the old riddle about the room full of people, with no doors or windows, we were tiny little seeds inside it. And when everything there inside was ripe and ready, it strained with all its might and burst out.

The primal watermelon hatched.

The seeds went flying off and sprouted.

One little seed put out a shoot and became our tree: there's the shadow of one of its branches, creeping along the windowsill.

Another became the memory of a girl who wanted to be a boy – once when she was still little they dressed her up as Puss in Boots for a fancy dress party, and everyone there kept trying to pull her tail, and in the end they tore it right off, and she had to walk around with her tail in her hand.

A third little seed sprouted many years ago and became a young man who liked me to scratch his back, and hated lies, especially when they started shouting from all the pulpits that there was no death, that words written down were a kind of tram that carried you off into immortality.

In the Druidic horoscope he was a Carrot.

Before he burned his diary and all his manuscripts, he wrote one final phrase, a terribly funny one: 'The gift has abandoned me' – I managed to read it before you tore that notebook out of my hands.

We stood by the bonfire and held our open hands up to our faces to block the heat, looking at the bones of our fingers showing through the transparent red flesh. Flakes of ash showered down on us – the warm, burnt-up pages.

Ah yes, I almost forgot, and afterwards the whole of existence will gather itself back into a single full stop.

Where are you now, Vovka the Carrot?

And now what's going on? Silly little Julie tries so hard, sending him letters, but hard-hearted Saint-Preux fobs her off with facetious little missives, sometimes in verse, rhyming Swedes and centipedes, ammunition and sublimation, shithouse and Mona Lisa (by the way, have you guessed what she's smiling at? – I think I have), navel and God.

My love!

Why did you do that?

The only thing still left to do was choose myself a war. But naturally, that was no great obstacle. If there's one thing that's meat and drink to this unbeaten homeland of ours, that's it – you can't even get the newspaper open properly before friendly kingdoms are spiking little infants on their bayonets and raping old women. Somehow you feel especially sorry for the innocent tsarevich murdered in his sailor suit. The women, old men and children just seem to slip in one ear and out the other, as usual, but that sailor suit . . .

A rousing tattoo on a tin drum, a murky pall hovering over the bell tower, your motherland is calling you!

At the conscription centre the prescription was: Everyone needs his own Austerlitz!

Oh, indeed he does.

At the medical board the army doctor – a huge cranium, bald and knobbly – looked into my eyes intently. He said:

'You despise everybody. You know, I used to be like that too. I was the same age as you when I did my first hospital internship. And one day they brought in a street bum who'd been knocked down by a car. He was still alive, but he'd been maimed very badly. We didn't really make much of an effort. It was obvious no one wanted the old man and no one was going to come for him. Stench, filth, lice, pus. Anyway, we put him on one side, where he wouldn't pollute anything. He was a goner in any case. And when he was gone, I was supposed to tidy up, wash the body and dispatch it to the morgue. Everybody went away and left me on my own. I went out for a smoke and I thought: What do I want with this hassle?

What's this old man to me? What's he good for? While I was smoking, he passed on. So there I am, wiping off the blood and pus – working sloppily, doing just enough to shunt him off to the freezer as quickly as possible. And then suddenly I thought he could be somebody's father. I brought a basin of hot water and started bathing him. An old body, neglected and pitiful. Nobody had caressed it in years. And there I am washing his feet, his grue- some gnarled toes, and there are almost no nails – they've all been eaten away by fungus. I sponge down all his wounds and scars, and I talk to him quietly: Well then, Dad, life turned out hard for you, did it? It's not easy when no one loves you. And what were you thinking, at your age, living out on the street, like a stray dog? But it's all over and done with now. You rest! Everything's all right now. Nothing hurts, no one's chasing after you. So I washed him and talked to him like that. I don't know if it helped him in his death, but it certainly helped me a lot to live.'

My Sashenka!

●

Volodenka!

I watch the sunset. And I think: What if right now, this very moment, you're watching this sunset too? And that means we're together.

It's so quiet all around.

And what a sky!

That elder tree over there – even it senses the world around it.

At moments like this, the trees seem to understand everything, only they can't say it – exactly like us.

And suddenly I feel very intensely that thoughts and words are really made out of the same essence as this glow, or this glow reflected in the puddle over there, or my hand with the bandaged thumb. How I long for you to see all of this!

Just imagine, I took the bread knife and somehow managed to slice my thumb right through to the nail. I bandaged it up sloppily, and then drew two eyes and a nose on the bandage. And I had a little Tom Thumb. So I've been talking to him about you all evening.

I reread your first postcard. Yes! Yes! Yes! That's it exactly! Everything rhymes! Take a look around! It's all rhymes! There's the visible world, and there – if you close your eyes – is the invisible one. There's the branch of a pine tree darning the sky, and there's its rhyme – a conch that has become an ashtray in mundane reality. There's the clock on the wall and there on the shelf is a clump of herbs from the pharmacy for relieving wind. This is my bandaged thumb – the scar will probably stay for ever now – and the rhyme to it is the same thumb, but before I was born and after I've gone, which is probably the same thing. Everything in the world is rhymed with everything in the world. These rhymes connect up the world, hold it together, like nails pounded in right up to the head, to stop it falling apart.

And the most amazing thing is that these rhymes already existed in the beginning – it's not possible to invent them, just as it's impossible to invent the very simplest mosquito or that long-distance cloud over there. You understand, no amount of imagination would be enough to invent the very simplest things!

Who was it that wrote about people greedy for happiness? How well put! That's me – greedy for happiness.

And I've started noticing myself repeating your gestures, too. I speak in your words. I look with your eyes. I think like you. I write like you.

All the time I remember our summer.

Our morning studies in oil, painted with butter on toast.

Do you remember our table under the lilac, covered with the oilcloth with a brown triangle from a hot iron?

And here's something you can't remember, it's mine alone: when you walked across the grass in the morning, you seemed to leave a glittering ski-track in the sun.

And the smells from the garden! So rich and dense, like fine particles saturating the air. You could pour those smells into a cup like strong tea.

And everything all around has only one thing on its mind – I simply walk through the field or the forest and absolutely everyone tries his very best to pollinate me or inseminate me. My socks are just covered in grass seeds.

And remember, we found a hare in the grass with its legs cut off by a mowing machine.

Brown-eyed cows.

Little goat nuts lying on the path.

Our pond – murky on the bottom with blooming slush, full of frogspawn. Silver carp butting at the sky. I climb out of the water and pluck the weed off myself.

I lay down to sunbathe and covered my face with my singlet, the wind rustles like starched linen. And suddenly there's a ticklish feeling in my navel, and it's you pouring a thin stream of sand onto my stomach out of your fist.

We walk home and the wind tests the trees and us to see what kind of sails we would make.

We collect fallen apples – the first ones, sour, good for compote – and we throw these windfalls at each other.

At sunset the forest is jagged.

And in the middle of the night a mousetrap jumps with a snap and wakes us up.

Sashenka, my dearest!

Well then, I'll number my letters to know which one has gone missing.

I'm sorry my scribblings turn out so short – I have absolutely no time for myself. And I'm terribly short of sleep, I feel like closing my eyes and falling asleep standing up. Descartes was killed by having to get up at five in the morning, when it was still dark, to give lectures on philosophy to Christina, Queen of Sweden. But I'm still holding on.

I was in the general staff office today and I suddenly saw my reflection in a mirror, in full dress uniform. It was strange, what was I doing in fancy dress? I was amazed at myself: how could I be a soldier?

You know, there's something to this life after all, always covering off in line with the cheekbone of the fourth man.

I'll tell you a story about a forage cap. A short one. It was filched from me – the forage cap, that is. And falling in without a forage cap is a breach of regulations, in short, it's a crime.

Our chief of chiefs and commander of commanders stamped his feet and promised me I'd be washing out the shithouse from now until doomsday.

'You'll lick it out, you scumbag!'

That's what he said.

Well now, there is something inspiring about military speech.

I read somewhere that Stendhal learned to write simply and clearly by studying Napoleon's field orders.

But the latrine here, my dear, distant Sashenka, requires some explanation. Picture to yourself holes in a floor covered with filth. No, better not picture it! And everyone tries his very best to dump his heap on the edge of a hole, not in it. And everything's awash. Actually, the way the stomachs of yours truly and his fellows function is a separate subject in its own right. In these remote parts, for some reason we always have a bellyache. I don't understand how you can dedicate yourself to Generalissimo Suvorov's science of victory if you're always squatting over a yawning abyss with your insides draining out of you.

Anyway, I say to him:

'Where will I get you a forage cap?'

And he says:

'They filched yours, you go and filch one!'

So off I went to filch a forage cap. And that's not easy. In fact, it's very hard, because everyone's at it.

There I was, wandering hither and thither.

Suddenly I thought: Who am I? Where am I?

And I went to wash the latrine. And the whole world suddenly seemed lighter somehow.

I had to end up here to learn to understand simple things.

You know, there's nothing dirty about shit.

●

Now look, I'm writing to you at night. I nibbled a crust of bread in bed just now, and the crumbs won't let me sleep, they've scampered all over the sheet and they bite.

The window above my head is as starry as starry.

And the Milky Way divides the sky on a slant. You know, it's like some gigantic fraction. The numerator is one half of the universe, and the denominator is the other half. I always hated those fractions, squared numbers, cubed numbers and all those roots. It's all so disembodied, impossible to visualise, there's absolutely nothing to catch hold of. A root is a root — on a tree. It's strong, it creeps and grabs, it gobbles the soil, it's clinging, sucking, irrepressible, greedy, alive. But this is twaddle written with a little squiggle, and they call it a root too!

And what sense does a minus sign make? Minus a window — what's that? It's not going to go anywhere. And neither is what's outside the window.

Or minus me?

Things like that don't happen.

In general, I'm the kind of person who has to touch everything. And sniff.

Yes, even more — sniff everything. Like in the book Daddy used to read to me at bedtime when I was little. There are different kinds of people. There are people who spend all their time fighting with cranes. There are people with one leg, they dash around on it at high speed, and their foot is so big that they shelter in its vast shadow from the sweltering heat of the sun and rest there, as if they were inside a house. And there's another kind of people too, who live on nothing but the smells of fruits. When they have to set out on a long journey, they take these fruits with them, and if they catch a whiff of a bad smell, they die. That's just like me.

You know, in order to exist, everything alive has to have a smell. At least some kind of smell. And all those fractions and all the other stuff we were taught — it has no smell.

There's some kind of night prowler outside the window now, kicking an empty bottle about. The clink of glass on the asphalt of a deserted street.

Now it's broken.

At moments like this at night I feel so lonely and I want so much to be the reason for at least something.

And I long unbearably to be with you! To hug you and snuggle up against you.

Do you know what you'll get if you divide that starry numerator by the denominator? Divide one half of the Universe by the other? You'll get me. And you with me.

Today I saw a little girl fall off her bike – she skinned her knee and sat there crying bitterly, and her long white sock was splattered with blood. It was on the embankment, where the lions are – mouths stuffed full of litter, paper wrappers and sticks from ice cream. Then afterwards I was walking home and suddenly the idea came to me that all the great books and pictures aren't about love at all. They only pretend to be about love, so they'll be interesting to read. But in actual fact, they're about death. In books, love is a kind of shield or, rather, a blindfold. So you don't see. So it's not so frightening.

I don't know what the connection was with that little girl who fell off her bike.

She cried a bit, and now perhaps she's forgotten about it ages ago, but in a book her skinned knee would have stayed there until she died and even afterwards.

So probably all books aren't really about death, but about eternity, only their eternity isn't genuine, it's a kind of fragment, an instant, like a teensy-weensy fly in amber. It just sat down for a moment to rub its back legs together, and it turned out to be for ever. Of course, they choose all sorts of fine moments, but isn't it a terrifying thought – to stay like that, forever porcelain – like the shepherd boy always reaching out to kiss the shepherd girl!

But I don't want anything porcelain. I want everything alive, here and now. You, your warmth, your voice, your body, your smell.

You're so far away now that I'm not at all afraid to tell you something. You know, back then at the dacha, I used to go into your room while you weren't there. And I sniffed everything. Your soap. Your eau de cologne. Your shaving brush. I sniffed the inside of your shoes. I opened your cupboard and sniffed your sweater. The sleeve of your shirt. And the collar. I kissed a button. I leaned down over your bed and put my nose to the pillow. I was so happy! But that wasn't enough! To be happy, you need witnesses. You can only really feel happy when you get some kind of confirmation, if not from a glance or a touch, or a presence, then at least from an absence. From a pillow, a sleeve, a button. Once you almost caught me – I only just managed to run out onto the porch. And you saw me and started throwing prickly burrs in my hair. I was so angry with you then, but what wouldn't I give now for that – to have you throw burrs in my hair!

I remember you, and the world is divided into before the first time and after.

Meeting for a date at the monument.

I peeled an orange and my palm stuck to yours.

You came straight from the clinic, with a fresh filling in your tooth and the smell of the dentist's surgery coming out of your mouth. You let me touch the filling with my finger.

And here we are at the dacha, whitewashing the ceiling, after we've covered the furniture and the floor with old newspapers. We walked around barefoot, with the newspapers sticking to our feet, and got whitewash smeared all over us. We scrape the white out of each other's hair. And our tongues and teeth are all black from bird cherries.

Then when we were hanging the net curtains, we ended up on different sides, and I wanted so much for you to kiss me through the netting!

And then there you sit, drinking tea, scalding your tongue on it and blowing to get it to cool down, taking little sips and slurping so loudly, not at all worried about it being impolite, as they impressed on me when I was little. And I start slurping too. Because I'm not little any longer. And everything's allowed.

Then there was the lake.

We walk down the steep slope towards the waterlogged bank, feeling the damp, spongy path under our bare feet.

We waded out into open water, free of duckweed. The water's murky and full of sunlight. And cold, from the springs that feed it from below.

And then, in the water, our bodies touched for the first time. On the shore I was afraid to touch you, but here I pounced on you and wrapped my legs round your thighs, trying to pull you under. When I was little I used to play like that with Daddy at the seaside. You try to break free, you try to pull my hands apart, but I won't give in. I kept trying to duck your head right under the water. Your eyelashes stick together, you swallow lots of water, you laugh and splutter and bellow and snort.

Afterwards we sit in the sun.

Your nose is peeling, the skin is flaking off the sunburn.

We watch the bell tower on the opposite shore rinsing its ragged image in the water.

I sit there in front of you almost naked, but somehow I only feel shy about my feet and my toes – I buried them in the sand.

I singed an ant with my cigarette, and you came to its defence.

We walk home the short way, straight across the field. Grasshoppers jumping about in the tall grass molest my skirt.

On the veranda you sat me in a wicker chair and started brushing the sand off my feet. Like Daddy. When we came back from the beach, he used to wipe my feet down just like that, so there wouldn't be any sand left between my toes.

And everything was suddenly so clear. So simple. So inevitable. So welcome.

I stand there facing you – in my wet swimsuit, with my arms lowered. I look into your eyes. You took hold of the straps and pulled the swimsuit off.

I'd been ready for this for a long time, I was waiting, but I was afraid, and you were even more afraid, and everything would have happened much sooner, but that time, back in spring, remember, I took your hand and pulled it down there, but you jerked it away. You were quite different now.

Do you know what I was afraid of? Pain? No. There wasn't any pain. And there wasn't any blood either. I thought, what if you thought you weren't my first?

It was evening before I remembered I'd forgotten to hang my swimsuit up to dry. It was lying there abandoned, clumped up, wet and cold. It smelled of pond scum.

I snuggled against you and kissed your peeling nose. There was no one in the house, but we whispered anyway. And for the first time I could look right into your eyes, without being afraid or embarrassed about anything – brown, with hazel and green flecks on the iris.

Absolutely everything suddenly changed – I could touch everything that only a moment ago was untouchable, not mine. A moment ago it was someone else's, but now it was mine, as if my body had expanded and melded with yours. And now I couldn't feel myself except through you. My skin only existed where you touched it.

That night you slept, but I couldn't. I wanted so much to cry, but I was afraid I'd wake you. I got up and went to the bathroom, and cried to my heart's content.

And in the morning, at the washbasin – a sudden surge of foolish happiness at the sight of our two toothbrushes in the same glass. Standing there with their little legs crossed, looking at each other.

The very simplest things can make me die of happiness. Remember, back in town already – you locked yourself in the toilet, and I was walking by to the kitchen and I couldn't resist it, I squatted down by the door and started whispering into the keyhole:

'I love you!'

I whispered it really quietly. Then louder. And you didn't realise what I was whispering to you, and you muttered back:

'Just a moment, just a moment.'

As if I needed the bathroom.

It's you I need, you!

And then there you are, sitting in front of the oven with a spoon in one hand and an open cookery book in the other. Something suddenly came over you – you said you'd cook everything yourself and I mustn't interfere. And I kept coming into the kitchen on purpose, as if I needed something, but really only to look at you. Remember? You were kneading minced meat, and I couldn't help myself, I stuck my hands in the saucepan too – it was so wonderful to knead that fragrant, beefy pulp together, and the mince oozed out between our fingers!

You didn't really get along too well with ladles, oven mitts and frying pans – everything came to life in your hands and tried its very best to wriggle free or pop up in the air or slither away.

I remember every single little thing.

We lay there clasped together and couldn't let go – and that semicircle my teeth left on your shoulder.

Our legs intertwine, our feet nestle against each other, sweet-talking, and our cream-slippery toes slither into each other.

In the tram people turn to look at us: your left fist is up beside my nose, and I'm kissing the first knuckle on the forefinger – the one that's July.

On the way up to your place, the lift seems to creep along so unbearably slowly.

Your shoes under a chair, with the socks stuffed into them.

That was when you kissed me there for the first time, and I just couldn't relax. When you're growing up you know you mustn't touch that place. It's only little boys who think little girls have a secret between their legs, but that place is full of slimy discharges, noxious vapours and bacteria.

In the morning I couldn't find my knickers, they'd disappeared. I searched through everything and couldn't find them. I still think you pinched them and hid them somewhere. I left without them. I'm walking along the street, the wind's creeping up under my skirt, and I have the incredible feeling that it's you all around me.

I know I exist, but I need proofs all the time, I need to be touched. Without you I'm an empty pair of pyjamas, thrown across a chair.

My own arms and legs, my own body, have only become dear to me because of you – because you have kissed it, because you love it.

I look in the mirror and catch myself thinking: that's the one he loves, isn't it? And I like myself. But I never used to like myself before.

I close my eyes and imagine that you're here.

I can touch you and hug you.

I kiss your eyes, and suddenly my lips can see.

And I want so much, like I did then, to run the end of my tongue from one end to the other of the little seam you have down there, as if you were a bare-naked little plastic boy who'd been stuck together out of two separate halves.

I read somewhere that the smelliest parts of the body are closest to the soul.

Now I've turned the light out so I can finally curl up into a tight little ball and fall asleep, and while I was writing to you, clouds have covered over the sky. As if someone has wiped everything off the school blackboard with a dirty rag and there's nothing left but white streaks.

I have a feeling everything's going to be all right. Destiny is just trying to frighten us, but it will preserve and protect us against genuine misfortune.

Sashka, my dear one!

I bluff and bluster, but in reality without you, without your letters, I would have died ages ago, or at least stopped being myself – I don't know which is worse.

I wrote to you about our tormentor, the one I dubbed 'Commodus', after the infamously bloody son of Marcus Aurelius – the nickname has stuck, but the soldiers have shortened it to 'Commode'. No doubt because of his obsession with shit. Today he made a special effort to explain to me exactly how life works. I don't want to write about it. I want to forget, think about something else for a while, about Marcus Aurelius, for instance.

I don't understand what connection there can be between Marcus Aurelius, who died a million years ago, who everyone has heard about, and me, who no one has heard about, sitting here in my prickly official-issue underpants.

But on the other hand, here's what he wrote: No man is happy until he considers himself happy.

Probably that's what we have in common – we're two happy men. And what difference does it make that he died one day, and I'm still here? Compared with our happiness, death seems like a mere trifle. He stepped straight through it to me, as if it was a doorway.

This feeling of happiness comes from the realisation that none of all this around me is real. What is real is that first time I was at your place and I went into the bathroom to wash my hands and saw your sponge there and felt so intensely aware that it had touched your breasts.

My Sashenka! We were together, but I've only really begun to understand that here.

And now I remember it all and I'm astonished I didn't appreciate it all properly then.

Remember, the fuses blew at your dacha, you held the candle for me and I stood on a chair, fiddling with my makeshift repair. I glanced at you, and you looked so incredible in the semi-darkness, with the light from the candle flame washing over your face! And the bright spark of the candle was reflected in your eyes.

Or look at this, we're walking through our park, and you keep running off the asphalt strip of the path, tearing up bunches of grass and bringing different kinds of seed heads to show me.

'What's this? And what's this called?'

You walk on, your heels smeared with mud.

Your poor toe is black and blue – someone trod on it and crushed it in the tram, and you're wearing open-toed shoes.

Then I see the lake.

The water has turned thick, overgrown with duckweed and clouds.

You walked right up to the edge, lifted your skirt and stepped into the water, up to your ankles – to try it. You shouted:

'It's cold!'

You pulled one foot out and ran it across the surface, as if you were ironing out creases.

I see it all as if it was happening right now, not then.

You get undressed, tie up your long, loose hair and walk into the water, checking the bun on your head several times.

You turn over on your back and flail at the lake with your legs, and your heels twinkle pink in the foamy spray.

Then you throw out your arms and legs, lying there like a star, the bun on your head comes undone and your long hair spreads out in all directions.

Later, on the shore, I glanced stealthily – so you wouldn't notice – at the place between your legs where the wet curls were peeping out from under the elastic of your swimsuit.

And now I see your room.

You take off your shoes, leaning down one shoulder, then the other.

I kiss the palms of your hands, and you say:

'Don't, they're dirty!'

You clasp my neck in your arms and kiss me, biting my lips.

Suddenly you yelped.

I was really frightened.

'What's wrong?'

'You caught my hair under your elbow.'

You leaned down over me, touched my eyelids and lashes with your nipple. You drew your hair over both of us like a tent.

I pull off your knickers, they're like a child's – cream-coloured with little bows – and you help me, you raise your knees.

I kiss you on the spot where the skin is most tender and sensitive – on the inside of the thighs.

I bury my nose in the dense, warm undergrowth.

The bed creaks so desperately that we move to the floor.

You groaned under me and arched up in a bridge.

We lie there and the draught feels good on our sweaty legs.

Your back is covered with delicate fluff and patterns from the coarse ribs of the Chinese straw mat. I run my finger along your sharp vertebrae.

I take a pen off the table and start joining up the moles on your back with an inky line. It tickles you. Afterwards you twist and turn in front of the mirror, looking over your shoulder to see how it turned out. I want to wash it off, but you say:

'Leave it!'

'Are you going to walk about like that?'

'Yes.'

You flung your feet up on the wall and suddenly started running across the wallpaper in little steps, you arched up, braced your elbows on the straw mat and froze with your legs up like that. I couldn't resist it, I wanted to kiss you there – you folded up straightaway, collapsed.

I'm leaving, and you've come out to show me to the door – in just a little singlet with nothing underneath. You suddenly start feeling embarrassed and pull down the hem at the front with your hand.

On our last night I woke up and listened to your snuffling.

You were used to sleeping like a chrysalis, you wrapped the blanket round your head and only left a little air hole for breathing. I lie there, looking into that hole. And you're so funny – you've gone to sleep with a chocolate sweet stuffed into your cheek, and there's chocolate dribbling out of your mouth.

I lie there, keeping watch over your breathing.

I listen closely to your rhythm. And I try to breathe together with you. In . . . out, in . . . out. In . . . out.

Slowly . . . slowly. Like this.

In . . .

Out . . .

You know, I'd never felt so light and easy as at that moment. I looked at you, so beautiful, so serene and sleepy, I touched the hairs peeping out from your blanket cocoon, and I wanted so much to protect you from that night, from any drunken night-time yelling outside the window, from the whole world.

My Sashenka! Sleep! Sleep well! I'm here, I'm breathing with you.

In . . .

Out . . .

In . . .

Out . . .

In . . .

Out . . .

●

I peeped in the letter box – again nothing from you.

I have to prepare for a seminar tomorrow, and my head's empty.

I don't care. I'm going to brew some coffee, pull my feet up on the armchair and talk to you right now. Listen.

Remember how good it felt telling each other things about our childhood? You know, there's so much I still haven't told you yet.

But now I'm chewing on my pen and I don't know where to start.

Do you know why I was given my name?

When I was little I adored all the lovely different little boxes and caskets in the bottom drawers of our sideboard, I spent ages rummaging through the things my mother kept there – bracelets, brooches, playing cards, postcards, everything on earth. And then in one box I found a pair of child's sandals – all tiny and shrivelled, small enough for a doll.

It turned out that I had an older brother. When he was three, he fell ill and was taken into hospital. And what they said about him was really terrible – they said he was doctored to death.

My parents decided straightaway to have another child. To take his place.

And a little girl was born. Me.

My mother couldn't accept her child, she wouldn't feed me and didn't want to see me. They told me all this afterwards. It was my father who pulled me through. Me and my mother.

In my little cot three of the wooden bars had been sawn out so I could crawl through. But it was his cot, the other child's. Only I couldn't understand then that the hole was for him. That he used to crawl through it. I liked scampering through it as well, but I was really only repeating his movements.

For me that boy had been left behind in some unimaginable life before I was born. If it ever existed, then it had faded into some kind of prehistoric age, but for my mother it was right there beside me, all the time, it never went away. One day we were going to the dacha on the train and a child was sitting opposite us with his grandmother. Just a normal child with a squeaky voice and runny nose who couldn't pronounce his r's properly. He kept pestering his grandmother for something. And she kept snapping back:

'Just calm down, will you!'

And I remember the way my mother flinched and shrank when the old woman said:

'Sasha! We're getting off here!'

When we got off the train, my mother turned away and started rummaging desperately in her handbag, and I saw the tears pouring out of her eyes. I started snivelling and she turned round and kissed me with her wet lips, trying to reassure me that everything was all right, that it was just a midge that had flown into her eye.

'But everything's all right now!'

She blew her nose, touched up her mascara and snapped her powder compact shut. And off we went to the dacha.

I remember that was when I thought: It's a good thing that child died. Otherwise, where would I be now? As I walked along, I repeated what my mother had said: 'But everything's all right now!'

I couldn't *not* have been born, could I? Everything around me, everything that was and is and will be, is simple and adequate proof of that, even this small window frame with its mouth wide open, and these flat pancakes of sunshine on the floor, and the cheesy flakes of curdled milk in this mug of coffee, and this faded mirror playing at stares with the window to see who'll blink first.

As a little girl I used to spend hours gazing into the mirror. Eye to eye. Why these eyes? Why this face? Why this body?

What if it's not me? And these aren't my eyes, or my face, or my body?

What if I – with these eyes and face and body that I just glimpsed

– what if all this is just a memory of some old woman I'll become some day?

Often I used to pretend there were really two of me. Like twin sisters. Me and *her*. Like in the fairy tales: one bad and one good. Me the well-behaved one, and *her* the hooligan.

I used to wear my hair long, my mother was always nagging at me to comb it. And *she* took the scissors and snipped the plait off out of spite.

We used to have theatre shows at the dacha and, of course, *she* played all the leading roles, and I opened and closed the curtain. And then once, in the course of the action, she was supposed to kill herself. Just imagine it, she says her final words with a knife in her hand, then swings and hits her head as hard as she can, and suddenly she's covered in real blood. Everybody jumped to their feet in horror, and she's lying there dying – in the play, and from sheer delight as well. Only I knew that she'd grated some beetroot, taken a hen's egg and sucked it out through a little hole and used a syringe she took from Mummy to squirt the juice into the egg and hidden it in her wig. She jumped up, all covered in beetroot blood, squealing in joy at having fooled everyone:

'You believed it! You believed it!'

You simply can't imagine what it's like having to put up with her all the time! You can't imagine what it's like to wear her castoffs after she's done with them. They always bought beautiful new things for her, that princess without a pea, and I got the same things, already old and disgusting, to wear out. They deck us out for school after the summer holidays, and she has nice new shoes, but I have to get into her old raincoat with holes in the pockets and a stain on the lapel.

She tormented me all my childhood, whenever she fancied. I remember I drew a white chalk boundary line on the floor, divided our room in half. She went and rubbed it out and drew the line so that I could only walk round the edge from my bed to the table and the door. It was pointless complaining to Mummy, because with Mummy she was an absolute angel, but when we were left alone, she started pinching me and pulling my hair until it really hurt, so that I wouldn't snitch on her.

I'll never forget the time I was given a wonderful doll, a huge talking doll that closed and opened its eyes and could even walk. Just as soon as I turned away for a moment, my tormentor stripped her naked, saw there was something missing, and drew it on. I started crying and went running to my parents – they just laughed.

It was impossible to come to terms with her! I suggest something, and she stamps her little foot and declares:

'Things will be the way I say round here, or else there won't be anything at all!'

Her eyes narrow, looking daggers at me, and her upper lip twitches too, exposing her sharp little teeth. She's going to grab me any moment . . .

I remember how scared I was when Mummy asked me who I was talking to. I lied:

'Myself.'

I realise that it used to happen when I wanted to be loved. She appeared when I had to fight for other people's love. That is, almost all the time – even when I was on my own. But never with Daddy. With Daddy everything was different.

He called Mummy and me the same name – we were both bunnies. He probably enjoyed shouting: 'Bunny!' – and we would both answer, one from the kitchen and one from the nursery.

When he came home, in order not to let any strangers in, before I opened the door I had to ask:

'Who's there?'

He used to answer: 'A sower and mower and tin-whistle blower.'

Even when he wiped his feet on the mat in the hallway it came out like a dance.

He liked to bring me strange presents. He used to say:

'Guess what!'

But it was absolutely impossible to guess. It could be a fan, or a tea bowl, or a lorgnette, a tea caddy, an empty scent bottle or a broken camera. Once he brought a Japanese Noh theatre mask. He even brought home a genuine elephant's foot from somewhere, hollowed out for umbrellas and canes. Mummy used to rant at him, but his presents made me feel absolutely happy.

He could suddenly say, out of the blue:

'Forget that homework!'

And then we would put on a concert. We loved humming on combs wrapped in tissue paper – it tickled my lips terribly. An empty cake box became a tambourine. He used to turn up the corner of the carpet and rattle out a tap dance on the floor, until the neighbours started banging. Or grab the box of chess pieces and start shaking it rhythmically, so that everything inside it rattled about.

He made me play chess with him and he always won, and when he got me in checkmate, he was as delighted as a little child.

He knew all the dances in the world and he taught me to dance. I don't know why, but I really loved the Hawaiian dance – we used to keep our hands in our pockets when we did it.

One day at the table he told me to stop being so silly and stubborn or he'd pour a glass of kefir over my head.

I said:

'No you won't!'

And suddenly I was covered in white kefir goo. Mummy was horrified, but I was cock-a-hoop.

I never had to fight for his love.

But when Daddy wasn't there, that other me persecuted me incessantly.

I always suffered agonies with my skin, but hers was smooth and clear. Skin isn't just a sack for your insides, it's what the world uses to touch us. The world's feeler. And skin problems are just a way of protecting yourself from being touched. You sit there, hidden away, like inside a cocoon. But she – the other me – didn't understand any of this. She didn't understand that I was afraid of everything, and above all of being with other people. She didn't understand how, when we went visiting and everybody was enjoying themselves, I could lock myself in the toilet and just sit there without even taking my knickers off. She didn't understand how I could learn the theorems of Pythagoras off by heart, but freeze up in terror beside the blackboard, leave my body and float round in the air, watching myself from the outside – helpless, pitiful, desolate. The only fact about Pythagoras that remained in my head was how when he was a child and his parents showed him the basic forms through which the invisible manifests itself to human beings on a little table – globe, pyramid, cube, scraps of wool, apples, honey cakes and a little pitcher of wine – and named them all, Pythagoras listened to their explanations and then knocked the table over.

I always wrote her compositions for her. And I always got 'D'. And even worse, the teacher used to read them out in class and sigh:

'Sashenka, life is going to be hard for you.'

She gave me a D, because I always wrote about the wrong thing. We were given three subjects to choose from, we had to write about the first one, the second one or the third one – but I always wrote about God knows what. God knows what was more important to me.

I was a monster from a species of gill-winged, brachiopod moss animals. But she was the Dance of Mahanaim, with eyes like the pools in Heshbon, by the gate of Bath-rabbim. I remember how shocked I was by the way our PT teacher looked at her during class.

One day I was getting changed after school and I noticed someone spying on me through binoculars from behind the curtain in a window of the house opposite. I squatted down below the windowsill in horror, but she started putting on a full-scale performance.

When I was little, to frighten me at night she used to tell me she was a witch and she had power over people. And her proof for that was her eyes – the left one was blue, and the right one was brown. And she told me she used to have warts, and when we stayed the night at someone else's place, she washed herself with the sponge in that house, and her warts disappeared, but they appeared on the child who lived there. But the main argument, of course, was her eyes. She told me she could put the evil eye on anyone she wanted. The other girls weren't exactly afraid of her, but they were wary. She could definitely charm blood – she only had to lick a cut and whisper something, and the bleeding stopped.

Even now she won't leave me in peace. And you can never tell when she'll appear again. She can disappear and be gone for months, then suddenly – Here I am, surprise, surprise!

She mocks me because in the library, out of pity for the dead authors nobody wants, I take the most neglected books – otherwise no one will even remember about these writers. Such a slovenly trollop, she says, but you underline the ideas you like so neatly with a comb. She strikes a pose and lectures me, like an older sister: You can't live your life like a wishy-washy dishrag, you have to learn to be pushier than a lamb and louder than a mouse. Remember the seventeenth rule of Thales of Miletus, my little sister: It is better to arouse envy than pity!

And how viciously she used to tease you!

Remember, we were sitting on the veranda, eating strawberries – sour and unappetising, we were dipping them in sugar. And she got the idea of dipping them in honey. She pours some honey out of the jar into her saucer and licks the spoon. And she looks at you. And checks her expression in the mirror. I know that expression only too well, with the gleeful malice blazing in that odd pair of eyes.

She licked the spoon, took the end of it between her finger and thumb and flung it through the open veranda window behind her.

And she looks at you.

'Fetch!'

I tried to shout out to you: 'Stop! Don't you dare do that!' But I couldn't force out a single word.

You got up and went to look for the spoon – and there were thickets of brambles and wild raspberry bushes out there. You came back all scratched, with beads of blood on your hands. Without saying a word, you put the spoon on the table – with the earth and dry grass sticking to it – and turned and walked away.

She simply pulls a wry face at the dirty spoon. Then, as if nothing has happened, she carries on dipping strawberries in honey and biting them with her little teeth.

I couldn't stand it, I dashed after you, grabbed hold of your arm, tried to lick your scratches the way she did, to stop the bleeding, but you shoved me away.

'Go to hell!'

And you looked at me with such contempt.

You got on your bike and rode off.

How I hated you then!

That is, I hated her.

Both of you!

And I really, really wanted something to happen to you, something bad, terrible, evil.

I told myself I wouldn't go to you.

And I went running to you the very next day.

I see it all again, as if it's happening right now, feel it on my skin: It's been drizzling since morning, the mist has clambered up the fence, all the paths are drowned in puddles. I'm walking to your place with an umbrella over my head, and on the bridge across the ravine the rain starts coming down even harder.

There's a small stretch of forest between our dachas, all the footpaths there have dissolved into mud, and all the greenery sprouting there is nameless – it was only you who gave the plants their names.

I walk past your neighbours on the corner, peep over the fence at the roses – huge and heavy, like heads of cabbage. They're even more fragrant in the rain.

I felt afraid to walk up the steps onto the porch, I folded the umbrella and sneaked across to the veranda windows. I went up on tiptoe and saw you there inside the rainy window panes. You're lying on the divan, with your bandaged foot up on its back, reading some thick volume.

You see, I wished you ill, and you fell off your bike into the ditch.

Now you know why you twisted your ankle that evening and ended up lounging about in bed.

I stood there in the rain and looked at you. You sensed something, looked up, saw me, smiled.

■

Yes, Sashenka, my dacha girl, how long ago that was, and in some quite different, faraway life.

It was so good to lie there and write all sorts of nonsense in my diary, listening to the rain rustling on the roof and the mosquitoes buzzing on the veranda. If I look out of the window, the apple trees have no feet in the mist. The clothes pegs on the washing line are soaking wet and the water is dripping off them.

The rain makes it dark for reading – I switch on the light in the middle of the day.

I set a huge tome of Shakespeare on my knees – it's convenient for putting my notebook on when I write.

Do you know what I was writing about then? About Hamlet. Or rather, about myself and how my father had died, or maybe he hadn't, and my mother had married someone else, who was blind into the bargain, but I absolutely can't understand why everyone has to harass each other and run each other through with pointed instruments – and it doesn't even flood the stage with blood. What if they all die without any contrived acts of dastardly villainy and subtle scheming, just like that, all by themselves, after they've lived their lives – does that mean it wouldn't be Hamlet any more? Why, it's even more frightening. His father's ghost – so what? A bogeyman for little children.

And as for that poison poured into his ear!

And why does all of it only start when he comes back to his father's castle, wasn't he Hamlet before all that? Even before anything has happened, before the curtain has opened, before

Bernardo and Francisco have started squabbling – all that may be specified precisely in the general service regulations, but he's already Hamlet, isn't he?

And that's the most interesting thing of all, surely – what happened to them before all these encounters with ghosts, poisonings and stupid theatrical tricks, like hiding behind the arras?

He was just getting on with life – the way I live. Without any deathbed monologues in verse.

And his life before that should be written. For instance, how he played at postmen when he was little – he used to take an armful of old newspapers and stuff them into all the postboxes. And how during the breaks between lessons at school he used to hide away with a book in the cloakroom and the library – the weakest and most cowardly boys used to taunt him, getting their own back for what they had suffered from others. By the way, do you know what was the first thing that disenchanted me with literature? I'd read how the medieval jesters used to ask their lords tricky questions and the lords tried to answer them with painstaking correctness, and every time they just made fools of themselves, so during the break I tried asking my tormentors something artlessly ironic, but they just slapped me round the ears without even bothering to listen to me!

And in addition people ought to be told about the time when one day Hamlet was bathing in a lake and this man swam up to him and said: 'You swim quite well, boy, but your style's a bit messy. Let me show you!' And then this swimming teacher supported him from underneath with one hand and his other hand kept slipping down off the boy's stomach, lower and lower, as if by accident.

And about the dovecot. In my childhood, when we still lived in the old apartment, our neighbour had a dovecot in the courtyard, and when he was waiting for his pigeons to come back from a flight he didn't look up into the heavens, but into a basin of water – he could see the sky better like that was how he explained it.

I also wrote that I wanted to become myself. I still wasn't me. It wasn't possible that this could be me. I wanted to break out of the calendar.

And look, now I have.

It's a good thing you can't see where I am now and what I'm surrounded by. But if I don't describe it, it's as if it doesn't exist at all.

Remember those beautiful stones you had on your shelf, the ones you brought back home from the seaside once upon a time? One day you took a round pebble and put it in your eye, like a monocle. I took that pebble away and it used to lie on my windowsill, watching me all the time. Then suddenly I realised that it really is the pupil of someone's eye. And it can see me. And not only me, but absolutely everything. Because before that pebble can even blink, everything will flash past in front of it and disappear – me and this room and this town outside the window. At that moment I realised the absolute insignificance of all the books I had read and all the notebooks I had filled up with writing, and I felt very upset. I was seized by this terrible anxiety. I suddenly realised that in fact that pupil simply couldn't see my room or me and couldn't have seen them even if it wanted to, because for it I would flash past so quickly, it wouldn't notice a thing. It's real, it exists, but do I really exist for it?

Do I even exist for myself?

What does it mean to exist? Is it to know that you were? To demonstrate your existence with your memories?

What are my arms, my legs, my moles, my intestines gurgling with pearl barley, my bitten fingernails and my scrotum to this stone? My thalamus? My childhood memories? One New Year's

Day I woke up early in the morning and ran to the tree in my bare feet to look at the presents. There were guests sleeping all over the room, but there was nothing under the tree – the presents had been bought, but after the champagne and vodka they had simply forgotten to put them out. I went to the kitchen and cried there until my mother got up. Is that stupid?

Probably, in order to become real, you have to exist, not in your own awareness, which is so uncertain and subject to the influence of sleep, for instance, when even you don't know if you're alive or not, but in the awareness of another person. And not just any person, but one for whom it is important to know that you exist. You know that I exist. And here, where everything is topsy-turvy, that makes me real.

When I was still a child I avoided death by a miracle – I got up at night to go to the toilet and the book shelves collapsed onto the bed.

But I only started thinking seriously about my own death for the first time at school in a zoology lesson. We had an old teacher, an invalid, and he warned us to put a tablet from his pocket in his mouth if he ever fell unconscious. We put the tablet in, but it didn't help.

He always used to wipe his glasses with his tie.

At first he taught us botany and I took such a liking to him that I was always collecting herbariums, but later I decided to become an ornithologist, like him.

It was very funny the way he used to lament the disappearance of various plants and birds.

He stands there at the blackboard and shouts at us, as if we're to blame for something.

'Where's the shady crocus? Where's the weak sedge? Where's the caldesia? And the summer snowflake? And Dubyansky's

cornflower? Well, say something, will you? And the birds? Where
are the birds? Where's Steller's sea eagle? Where's the bearded
vulture-eagle? Where's the glossy ibis? I'm asking you! And the
crested ibis! And the marbled teal! And the shikra! Where's the
shikra?'

And when he asked this, he himself looked like some sort of
bird with ruffled feathers. All the teachers had nicknames, and he
was called Shikra.

Do you know what I used to dream about? About how some
day sooner or later I would meet my father and he would say:

'Right, show me your muscles!'

I would bend my arm and tense my muscles. My dad would
put his hand round my biceps and shake his head in surprise, as
if to say: 'My, my, aren't you something!'

But I understood all about the invisible world when Granny
got a job for the summer working at a dacha for blind children
and she took me with her.

Ever since I was little I'd been used to her having all sorts of
blind things at home. For instance, she would lay out a game of
patience with special cards with holes pricked in the upper right
corner. For my birthday she gave me a chess set, a special one,
with the figures all different sizes – the white ones bigger than
the black ones. And she whispered to Mum, but I heard her:

'They don't play there anyway.'

It was strange at first at that dacha, but then I actually got to
like it – it felt as if I'd become invisible.

There's a boy with a watering can in his hand, feeling the kerb
of the path gingerly with his foot, and I walk past him and he
can't see me. But that was only the way it seemed to me. Often
they would call out:

'Who's there?'

It's actually very difficult to hide from a blind person.

In the morning they had P.T. and after that the whole day was study and games. At first it felt odd to see them running out for P.T. in a chain, each one holding on to the shoulder of the one in front.

There were rabbits living in a cage in the yard, and they looked after them. It was a great tragedy one morning when the cages were found empty – the rabbits had been stolen.

They did a lot of singing there. For some reason blind people are thought to possess exceptionally keen hearing and they're all supposed to be born musicians. It's nonsense, of course.

Every day they did modelling. One little girl modelled a bird sitting on a branch like a person sitting on a chair. I remember how amazed I was that in their lessons they had to dip their hands in the aquarium and feel the fish. I thought that was really great! Afterwards, when there was no one else in the room, I went over to the aquarium, closed my eyes, rolled up my sleeve and lowered my hand into the water. When I touched the beautiful goldfish, it felt slippery and disgusting. That was the moment when I suddenly felt afraid, genuinely afraid, that I might go blind some day.

But being blind wasn't frightening for them. A sightless person is afraid of going deaf. He's afraid of darkness in his ears.

Blindness was basically invented by the sighted.

For a blind person, things are what they are, he lives with that, that's his starting-point, not something that doesn't exist. You have to learn how to suffer over something that doesn't exist. We can't see the colour to the right of violet in the spectrum, but that doesn't bother us. If we feel unhappy for some reason, that's not it.

Granny pitied all of them, and they clung to her. I sometimes thought she loved them more than she did me. It's nonsense of course, but I wanted her to stroke the back of my head like that too, hug me against her immense breasts and sigh tenderly:

'There now, my little sparrow!'

She never used to thrash them with a withy, but I got plenty of that.

I always wanted to ask her about my father, but I was afraid to.

She didn't tell me very much at all. I learned one family story from her when I grew up a bit. Her own granny had a child when she was still a young girl. She claimed she had conceived without sin, but no one believed her. They hadn't heard about partheno-genesis in those days. The ice on the river had just started to break up. She went down there one night and put her little bundle on an ice floe.

I remember I couldn't get that picture out of my head for a long time – night, the ice floe drifting along and that little bundle squealing.

But I was consoled when I read Marcus Aurelius many years later. The way he put things there was like this: imagine a piglet is being carried on its way to be sacrificed, the piglet's struggling and squealing – but what is it squealing for?

You know, every living creature and every thing struggles and squeals like that every moment. You just have to hear that squealing of life in everything, in every tree, in every person on the street, in every puddle, in every murmur and rustle.

●

I want so much to cuddle up tight against you and tell you some-thing terribly stupid and terribly precious.

I remember the first time my parents took me to the seaside — perhaps it wasn't the very first time, but it was the first time I can recall the booming of the breakers drawing me in and grabbing me in its fist and carrying me like that for the whole summer — held tight in its fist.

I remember so clearly how we started walking down through the crooked little streets, with the sea shouldering aside the horizon as it rose higher and higher, all covered in little pricks of sunlight, and the way it breathed its scent of salt, seaweed, oil, wood-rot and vastness straight into my nose.

I ran out onto the jetty and it exploded into breaking surf — and immediately I got a wet slap on the face from the sea.

The seafront is paved with wooden boards, transparent to the spray, like holes in the sky, with reflections of seagulls in the planks.

A breakwater white with bird droppings.

Seaweed like tattered rags.

A log scoured smooth by the sea.

A sail lying low, flush with a wave.

Every day the beach, with people airing their armpits.

What happiness to run through the shallow water, raising clouds of spray that glitters in the sun!

The gravel is incandescent, sizzling in the foam. The waves beat against my ankles and pull me back into the deep with them, they clutch at my legs, trying to tumble me over and drag me away.

Nimble black flies skip about on clumps of eelgrass thrown up by a recent storm. Waves creep up skew-wise, sending the startled little flies darting up into the air again and again.

Pieces of bottle glass are the sea's sugar candies — it has already given them a good sucking and spat them out. I gather them up and give them to my parents as a treat.

Daddy starts building a castle with me out of little stones and sand, we build walls and towers, he gets carried away, flies into a real passion. I decorate the towers with pieces of broken shells and flags made from sweet wrappers, and he shouts at me not to interfere. I resent that – it's my castle he's building, isn't it, for me? Then suddenly a wave comes along and wrecks everything. I burst into tears and Daddy's really upset too. Then in his despair he starts smashing everything that's left. And I join in. We skip about on the remains of our castle, laughing happily again. He rakes me into his arms and drags me into the sea, we fall into the breaking waves. He clowns about, diving in and folding his hands together before every dive, as if he's praying.

The water's so transparent, I can see the scarlet nails on my toes – I painted them with Mummy's varnish. I pinch my nose shut and duck under the water, head and all, Daddy holds me, I swim, my ears are blocked, there's an abyss of turquoise below me, the stones down there on the bottom are overgrown with woolly fleece that stirs about. I surface and the booming surrounds me again.

We swim as far as the wooden jetty. Over the long sea years a pillar has sprouted a beard of seaweed and frightens away the small fry with it.

A broad hairy back swims past.

I keep wanting to get as far away from the shore as possible, go out deep – Daddy doesn't let me, I start ducking him, I grab his shoulders, pull his ears and his hair – he fights me off, grabs hold of the slimy pillar, surfaces and snorts, drops of water glitter on his eyelashes, he's laughing. We climb out onto the jetty and walk over the boards, trying not to get splinters in our feet from the rough wood corroded by salt. We run to Mummy, both of us shivering, wrap ourselves in towels with our teeth chattering.

Daddy keeps asking me:

'What time is it?'

He's given me a little watch – not a real one, a toy, with the hands painted on. I look at it proudly and reply:

'Ten to two.'

The watch always says ten to two.

The salt smarts on my skin in the sun.

Mummy is sunbathing on a broad towel, she slips off her straps so her shoulders will tan evenly and asks Daddy to unfasten the clasp on her bra. A man with sturdy footballer's thighs is lying on the gravel nearby and he looks at her.

Mummy pretends not to notice anything around her.

The man lifts himself up on his elbows to peep in there, where the towel is pressed down by her round, heavy, wide-set breasts.

I still didn't understand anything then.

Or rather, I already understood everything.

My father catches these glances. The gratification of ownership shows in his eyes. He likes the feeling that he has something others dream about.

Several times we saw a very strange couple on the beach. Young, handsome, in love. She was missing one leg below the knee. I remember her sunbathing with her legs spread apart – ten to two. The whole beach watched them when he took her in his arms and carried her into the sea. They splashed about and squealed, swam a long way out, all the way to the buoys. When they came back and clambered out of the water, she laughed and tore herself out of his arms and hopped to her towel on one leg. People gazed at them, transfixed either by horror or envy.

Straight out of the water, I throw myself on Mummy. Icy cold, with wet sand sticking all over me, I climb up on her, shuffling my chilly knickers across her hot back. Mummy squeals, flings me off and gets ready to go for a swim – in the same painstaking way she does everything. She fastens her bra without hurrying, twisting her arms behind her back. She straightens her straps, puts on her white rubber cap, takes a long time tucking her hair under it. She walks down to the water slowly, as if she's checking every step of the way. I skip round her, showering her with spray, she squeals and shouts for me to stop, tries to slap me on the bottom. In the bathing cap her head is suddenly very small.

I remember her once squatting down in the water, raking it towards her with her boneless hands – under the water arms and legs looked boneless – and suddenly in the transparent water I saw that she was peeing. That seemed very strange to me then, but I was too frightened to say anything.

She used to swim very far out and her rubber cap bobbed up and down on the waves like a ping-pong ball.

Daddy and I sat in the breaking waves and watched Mummy. Everything was so wonderful! I sit there, stirring the water around with my toes, the waves move my legs apart. All around me there's nothing but happy people, happy voices shouting, happy waves, happy legs.

It was only later I realised that my father couldn't swim at all. Mummy used to go for long swims, and every time I started worrying about her, but Daddy only laughed.

'What could happen to our swimming bunny? Nothing will ever sink her!'

There's Mummy getting out and drying herself off – and that man with the footballer's thighs watches her again as she dabs with the towel, blotting the swimsuit over her breasts, on her stomach, under her arms, between her legs.

Mummy lies down on her stomach, slips off her bra straps again and reads a book. I sit down beside her and start plaiting her hair.

As the sea water dries out, it leaves little crystals of salt on her skin.

Seagulls scud by above us and for me they're plaiting the wind's hair.

Then I lie down at Mummy's side and close my eyes. The rustling of the waves is like someone endlessly turning pages.

And I fall asleep happy.

I'm woken by thunder. Darkness all around and sharp, cold gusts of wind. The deluge is about to start at any moment. Everybody runs off the beach. The first drops strike my bare body as if someone's throwing pebbles.

We grab our things and run. The wind is so strong, it tips the deckchairs over. Semi-naked people dash along the beach, trying to catch their parasols, towels and skirts that have gone flying away. The sea is already grey, restless, driving in tumultuous waves. We just manage to run to our house before the deluge begins. I get into the shower with Mummy – she unravels my plaits to wash the salt out of my hair. I snuggle against her cold skin, it's puckered up into little goose pimples.

Afterwards I sit on the sofa, wrapped up in a blanket, and wait for Daddy, who has promised to read me a book, and he's getting washed in the shower and singing some aria or other.

Papa was an orchestra conductor then.

I didn't think that was anything so very special.

He told me how his father, my grandfather the violinist, used to rehearse at home, and when he was a boy Daddy used to take two sticks and repeat the movements while his father played the violin.

I remember when I was still very little and loved to spin round on the adjustable stool, Daddy used to play the piano with me: clusters of bass notes sustained by the pedal represented dark storm clouds. Abrupt high sounds, clipped short by the pedal, melted in the air like scattered snowflakes. And summer rain was made with just the index fingers – one hand on the black keys, one on the white – skipping as fast as could be from one sound to the next. He had a broad hand – it spanned one and a half octaves.

Another thing I remember is how he once opened the lid, showed me the instrument inside and said:

'See how strangely it's all arranged – in everything complicated and incomprehensible there's something simple: all we're doing is tapping away with felt hammers.'

He forced me to practise, and in the end I came to hate our Rënish piano.

I practise at home, I play endless scales and arpeggios, and he tells me:

'Don't frown!'

The tension made me develop a wrinkle between my eyebrows – exactly like him.

When my father wasn't there, I used to cheat. I put a book on top of the music on the music stand and read it, playing endless exercises without looking. One day he caught me doing this and he swore terribly. He started running round the apartment, shouting that I had a tin ear and what had he done to deserve this punishment. He said that nature takes a break with the children of geniuses. That set me choking on my tears and I started playing even worse. He had never shouted at me before. It was as if someone had taken my daddy away and put someone else in his place. I couldn't understand it then. But he'd got into the role and simply couldn't get out of it.

While I was playing he squatted down to see if my hand was slack, a false note made him shudder and groan as if he had bitten his tongue and once, when I thought he wouldn't notice and I played a trill with my second and third fingers instead of the fourth and fifth, as required, he got so furious, he almost beat me with our tattered copy of Czerny.

Eventually Mummy glanced into the room with a wet towel on her head and demanded silence. I don't know if she was really suffering from a migraine or it was simply her way of rescuing me.

I remember him coming back home late in the evening, furious, blowing his nose and complaining that he had been struggling with a cold in the head all the way through the concert. And upset because he had played the wrong piece for the encore. Even his tailcoat, which Mummy hung up to dry on the balcony, just couldn't calm down, it carried on conducting.

And I remember how he used to rehearse at home, in his underpants, to a record of some symphony or other that he put on. I watched through a crack in the door as he conducted the table and chairs, the bookshelves, the window. The sideboard was the percussion section. The carpet on the wall was the wind instruments. The cups on the table with the breakfast that hadn't been cleared away yet were the violins. He jabbed his baton at the sofa and it responded instantly with the bass voices. He darted his fingers towards the table lamp – and a distant horn started playing. He waved his arms and writhed about so hard that drops of sweat ran down his face like hail and flew off his nose.

Mummy glanced in and said he would do better to change the burnt-out bulb in the chandelier, but Daddy just rolled his eyes up and kept on shaking his head about, then slammed the door right in her face.

At the end he grabbed all the sounds together in his fist under the chandelier and strangled them.

When he wasn't at home, without asking permission I used to take the case in which his director's baton was kept, put a record on at full volume and start conducting for myself. I used to go out on the balcony and conduct our yard, and the nearby houses, and the puddles, and the dog with its leg cocked up against a tree, and the clouds. But the bit I liked most was strangling the music in my fist at the end.

Then I would sit down at the piano and start hammering out Mendelssohn's 'Song Without Words' once again, always fluffing it in exactly the same places.

Later on Daddy became an Arctic pilot, and I liked that better. His long black raglan coat had such a glorious smell!

The fur flying-suit, the high fur boots, the helmet with a microphone made him seem like a completely different person. I used to take the high boots, squeeze both my legs into one of them and hop around the apartment like that – like those people with one foot that he had told me about.

He used to bring back little figures carved out of walrus tusks, jewellery made of teeth strung on twine, jars of cloudberries, a reindeer skin.

As he put me to bed, he would tell me how as a child he had dreamed of being a flier – one day he had seen a plane make a forced landing in a field beside their village.

As an ordinary village boy, it wasn't easy for him to achieve his goal – he had to study a lot. And in general life in the flying school – he used to call it the 'boot camp' – wasn't easy. There was an infantry college there too, and there were always terrible fights between them in the town when they had leave. They used to fight with their belts and Daddy almost had his eye put out by a buckle – he used to show me the scar on his forehead and I pitied him and stroked the white bump with my finger.

One day in his boot camp he was placed under arrest – put in choky, he said. And this is what for. In the winter he was supposed to stand watch with his combat weapon and guard the planes. He was walking round the hangar and he thought he caught a glimpse of someone in the darkness. But there was no one around, just darkness, with everything dripping and breathing in the thaw. He put his finger on the trigger, peeped out cautiously round the corner and was immediately struck a heavy blow to the head. The trigger squeezed itself. There was the crash of a shot, everything was thrown into turmoil, the officers were woken up and came running – and it turned out the wet snow on the roof of the hangar was melting, and at the very moment when Daddy stuck his head out, a big chunk had fallen on it.

He taught me to fly – we were playing, but it all felt as if it was real to me. We're not on the sofa, we're in the cockpit. The technician takes hold of one of the propeller's blades and spins it hard.

'Contact!' he shouts and jumps back from the engine.

I shout back briskly:

'We have contact!'

The engine sneezes several times, coughs out a cloud of blue smoke and picks up revs. They pull the chocks out from under the wheels. We taxi to the start. A wave of the starter's white flag. Daddy gives it full throttle. The swirling eddies driven by the propeller set the plane quivering and it starts to move. A furious, headlong run-up, faster and faster. On the uneven field the plane waggles its wings over the small tussocks, like a tightrope-walker waving his arms to keep his balance.

Daddy draws the joystick smoothly towards himself and the tail lifts off the ground, levelling up. He pulls the joystick towards himself more firmly, the plane is already hanging in the air, and I can feel us gaining height with all my body. The ground slips away from under my feet and I get a cold feeling in my chest.

Down below I can see the plane's shadow chasing after us. The roar of the engine becomes softer, the hangars and garages on the airfield below us get smaller and smaller until they look like children's bricks scattered across the field, like little houses from my construction kit.

Daddy presses on the pedal, pulls the joystick right or left and the plane promptly gyrates, flipping into a right or left roll. It's as if the plane isn't spinning, but the earth and the sky are spinning round it.

We climb up above the clouds and fly under a glittering sun and our shadow, diving into the holes in the clouds, can barely keep up with us.

I look at Daddy as he shifts his intent gaze from dial to dial and confidently steers our plane into the breaks between the colossal, shapeless masses of clouds and I realise I love him more than anything else in the world, more than Mummy, more than myself.

Daddy used to tell me about his comrades who had been killed.

He said:

'Everyone wants to live, but not everyone comes back from a flight.'

His friends' engine cut out on a steep turn and they heard the silence that airmen fear so much. In front of their eyes the glittering disc of the propeller disappeared and its three blades stuck out like sticks. The fliers couldn't hold on as far as the airfield and they started trying to spot a suitable landing place. The pilot asked the navigator:

'What do you think, old chap, will we make it?'

The navigator answered:

'We've got to! Otherwise my theatre tickets will go to waste.'

There was nowhere to land, they had to jump with their parachutes. But there were villages all around, with people living in them. The airmen could save themselves, but where would the abandoned plane crash and what damage would it cause?

The pilot ordered the navigator to jump, but he didn't abandon his friend. They didn't jump and tried to steer the plane as far away from the houses as possible.

The shattered plane and its dead crew were only found the next day. Scattered wreckage, twisted wings, bent propeller blades, a tail pointing up at the sky. Something had obviously gone wrong with their elevation rudder. They had both grabbed hold of the joystick in a vain attempt to straighten the plane up.

Daddy took me to the cemetery, there were lots of graves there marked with propellers instead of crosses. Handsome young faces looked out from the photographs in their hubs.

One day Daddy was given a special assignment. He had to pick up a woman who was expecting a difficult birth from a remote weather station and deliver her to hospital. A snowstorm blew up and he had to make a forced landing on the ice of a frozen river. And one of his plane's ski props was broken too. Daddy showed me with his hand how he landed on just one ski. The aircraft skidded across the ice as if it was performing an arabesque. As it lost speed, it stopped responding to the controls, the wing with no support dipped down and scraped on the ice, the plane swung round sharply, like the leg of a compass, and stopped dead. The blizzard started covering them over with snow, Daddy made something like a cave under the wing and they sat there for two days until they were found. The woman kept screaming all the time, and then she started giving birth and Daddy had to deliver the baby.

Every time Daddy flew away, he stuffed my old mitten into his pocket, that was his good luck charm. He told me that on that flight when they were waiting for help on the river and didn't know if anyone would come or not, it was my mitten that saved him.

When he flew away, if I saw a plane in the sky I always thought: What if that's him? And I used to wave to him. But the plane was way up high, like a spider in an invisible web.

I was never afraid for him – what was there to be afraid of, if he had my mitten? It would preserve and protect him.

He used to tell very interesting stories about the life of the Evenks. They call themselves 'chavchiv' – the reindeer people. Several times he had to stay in genuine *yaranga* tents and he was amazed at the way these reindeer people could build themselves a warm, comfortable house of whale ribs and reindeer skins anywhere at all in just a few minutes.

I remember, when my father was telling me about how he had to spend the night in one of these *yarangas* in the tundra and he was offered a marrow bone to gnaw as a special treat, Mummy looked out of the kitchen and asked if it was true that according to the reindeer people's laws of hospitality, the host offered a guest his wife for the night. I thought I heard a strange note in her voice, as if she doubted the truth of his stories, and I felt terribly offended. But Daddy laughed and said of course the host had offered him his wife, but she was old and covered in sores, her hair was matted together into felt and it was teeming with parasites, which is hardly surprising, since the reindeer people never wash even once from the cradle to the grave.

Sometimes Daddy flew away for a long time, but when he stayed at home he used to read me something every evening at bedtime. I had my favourite books about various amazing countries, but my most favourite was about the kingdom of Prester John. I could listen to it over and over again.

When he read, he was transformed, as if he wasn't reading a printed book, but runes on palm fronds and sheep's shoulder blades. He tied my pullover round his head like a turban, sat there cross-legged and spoke in a voice that wasn't his.

'It is I, Prester John, Ruler of Rulers, King of the Naked-Wise, Lord of all Lords. I dwell in the Capital of all Capitals, the paramount city of all lands, inhabited and uninhabited, and my palace is an immensely high tower that astrologers ascend at night in order to learn the future. I travel across my lands in a small tower on the back of a she-elephant. And the rivers here flow one way during the day and the other way during the night.'

He didn't even need the book, he already knew everything off by heart, and he made up even more – and every time I listened to those strange and amazing words with my heart in my mouth.

'In my country there are born and do live camels with two humps and with one, hippopotami, crocodiles, metagalarinariae, giraffes, panthers, onagers, lions both white and black, mute cicadas, gryphons and lamias. Here also are born imperishable people, the unicorn beast, the parrot bird, the ebony tree, cinnamon, pepper and the fragrant reed. And I have a daughter, the Queen of Queens, the Empress of Life. And my kingdom is her kingdom.'

When he spoke these words, everything around me – our room, and the chandelier with the bulb that was always burned out, and the pile of newspapers on the windowsill, and the noisy town outside the window – all of that became unreal, but Prester John's country was real, and Prester John himself was real, he wasn't sitting on the edge of my little bed any more, he was in a small tower on the back of a she-elephant, surveying his domains with a regal gaze.

And the kingdom of Prester John really did stretch out on all sides as far as the eye could see and in it there lived imperishable people and mute cicadas.

■

My Sashenka!

Don't be angry, there was absolutely no time to write.

So, at last nobody wants anything from me. I have a moment all to myself.

Why are kisses always saved until the end of a letter?

I kiss you immediately, and everywhere, all over!

All right, I'm pulling myself together.

Yesterday there was shooting practice, and you can't possibly imagine what a long face our Commode pulled when the flagmen signalled that three of the five bullets I fired had hit the 'head target' from four hundred paces!

In a case like that, how can I help thinking about chance?

After all, everything in the world consists of chance events. Why were we born in this century and not, say, in the thirty-fourth? Why in the best of all possible worlds and not in the worst? And perhaps right now, at this very moment, there's a man sitting somewhere, reading a book about bell-ringing. Why didn't the bullets go flying into the past or the future, instead of into that unfortunate target's head, already full of holes? After all, if

There, you see, Sashka my dear, they didn't give me a chance to finish, and now I have to hurry to let you know that I'm not just anybody any more! See what a high-flier I am! From now on

I'll be polishing the seat of my pants in staff headquarters, writing out orders and death notices. The old man dumbfounded me completely. He summoned me and appointed me general staff clerk, since I'm schooled in reading and writing. I draw myself erect, raise my elbow so it juts into that sunset of ours in the dusty little window, with the tips of the fingers in the side-lock of my wig:

'Your commandership!'

'Well, what do you want?'

'I won't cope. My writing's incomprehensible.'

But he says:

'Well now, Sonny Jim, you don't need to write comprehensibly, just sincerely! Do you understand?'

He pours a glass of vodka.

Hands it to me.

'To your new appointment!'

I drink it.

He gives me a piece of black bread with some herring and onion.

'When I was your age, Sonny Jim, that was when I suddenly understood everything. And ever since I've spent my whole life trying to understand what it was I understood then. Take some of the fatty bacon, it's superb! And remember: any word is smarter than the pen. And don't let the death notices upset you. The clerk before you kept getting upset all the time. When he drank a lot, he used to slump on my shoulder and cry like a little kid: "Kolya, I'm sorry I haven't been killed, I haven't been on the front line even once in the whole war . . ." He was asking me to forgive him, but it was more like he was talking to everyone whose death notice he'd ever had to write.'

●

Guess where I am right now.

In the bathroom.

Remember how King David arrived in the bathhouse and suddenly saw that he was naked and there wasn't anything there.

Well, now I'm naked too and there isn't anything there.

I'm lying here contemplating my own navel.

What a wonderful occupation!

Your belly button's a knot, I remember.

But mine's a ring.

Mummy's is a ring too.

A ring in an endless chain. And it turns out that I'm suspended on this chain of people by this ring. Or, rather, this chain carries on further, doesn't it? In both directions. And everything is suspended from it.

It's so strange that this little ring in my belly really is the navel of the world. And the chain that runs through it is the axis of the Universe, with all of creation moving round it – right now, at a speed of millions of dark years.

No, he might have been naked and there wasn't anything, but I've got the whole of creation from beginning to end in just my belly button!

And another thing I've remembered is, when I had chickenpox as a child and my whole body was covered with little pimples, Daddy said:

'Just look at all the stars that have come out on you!'

And I played a game that the rash on my stomach was a constellation and my belly button was the moon. Many years later I saw that was the way the ancient Egyptians used to represent the sky goddess, Nut, who had obviously come down with my starry chickenpox.

And now I suddenly want our child to creep in under this heavenly firmament. Is that stupid? Too soon?

It feels so good to think that the two of us sat in this bath – you remember, face to face, we could barely fit in. I washed your feet with my hair, as if it was a bath mitt. Then you took hold of my foot and bit the toes, exactly like Daddy, he used to do that to me sometimes when I was little, growling and threatening me:

'Now I'm going to eat you up!'

And he would bite my toes. It tickled me and scared me – what if he really did bite them off!

And after that I climbed behind your back and stuck my legs through under your arms, and you soaped them up with the sponge and scrubbed my toes and in between my toes, and I loved it all.

I really loved that, the way you lathered me absolutely everywhere!

My love, why aren't you here now, so you could see my short gold fleece shimmering and shining in the water down there . . .

Sorry! I'm a fool.

Can you believe that between the sixth and eighth months a child is covered with fur that drops out afterwards? They showed us a child like that in the hospital after a premature birth – it's horrible!

And do you know why people lost their fur and became naked? They told us at the lecture yesterday. After all, fur is such a useful thing! Look at a cat! Soft, comfortable, beautiful, so good to stroke! Can you imagine a naked cat? What a catastrophe! Well, the reason is that the flood happened. All that stuff about Noah is made up – no people were really saved. But some monkeys survived, because they started living in the water. For thousands of generations we were water monkeys. That's why our nostrils face down and not up. And the dolphins and seals lost their fur too.

That's me – a water monkey. Sitting here and dreaming that you'll come back and we'll get into the bath together.

I look at myself and feel worried because I've got so much hair in the wrong places. You said you liked it, but now I think you simply didn't want to upset me. Tell me, how can you possibly like it if I have hair here, and here, and there, and even down there?

I sit here pulling the hairs out with tweezers. It hurts!

Then I start imagining some cave girl pulling out her hairs with two seashells instead of tweezers. And she scrapes away the hairs under her arms and on her legs with blades made from flint or animal horns.

Yanka's lucky, her hairs are light-coloured and small everywhere.

My love, what am I talking about? Why am I saying this? Here I am talking nonsense, and you put up with it all.

Yanka sends you her greetings, she called in yesterday.

She told me about her new beau, it was very funny. Can you imagine, an old man has fallen in love with her and proposed!

He tells her:

'My dear child, I was falling in love with women before your parents were even born.'

Yanka showed me the way he went down on his knees in front of her and asked her to marry him, grabbing hold of her legs and pressing himself up against her, and she looked down on his bald head: one side of her felt so sorry for him she could have cried, but the other side really wanted to give him a flick with her finger and she only just managed to stop herself!

She refused him, naturally, but she's beaming as brightly as if she'd won a medal.

He worked all his life as an engraver and he entertained her with stories about all the inscriptions he had made on watches and cigarette cases.

Just imagine what he gave her as a present! He hands her this little case, like one for a ring. She opens it — and there's a grain of rice inside! He'd written something on that grain for her. He said:

'Yanochka, my dear! This is for you, the most precious thing that I have!'

Afterwards at home, she took a magnifying glass to read what he'd written, but the grain of rice slipped out of her fingers and skipped off out of sight. She searched and searched but couldn't find it. So she still doesn't know what he scratched on it.

What do they all see in Yanka? She has an overbite like a rabbit. And jug ears. She hides them under her hair.

I'm writing this to you now in the room, I've wrapped myself in a blanket and I'm sitting on the divan.

You were the first to tell me I was beautiful. Well, apart from Daddy, of course. But I didn't believe him. I believed Mummy. She called me her 'fright-face'.

She used to wear her rippling, shimmering Chinese silk gown with the sky-blue dragons. We would pull our feet up on the old, deep sofa, make ourselves comfortable and whisper together. We talked about everything in the world, she told me about everything. How I was born, for instance — I didn't want to come out, and they had to do a Caesarean section. I touched the hard scar on her stomach with my fingers and it was strange to think that was where I'd come from. It still feels strange even now.

And we talked about the first time too.

'It has to happen beautifully,' she said. 'And only with someone who is worthy of it. The most important thing is you mustn't regret that it happened. Perhaps you won't marry him, perhaps you won't stay together afterwards – anything can happen, but you mustn't regret that night.'

I believed in 'fright-face' more than what Daddy said, even though she was always constantly abusing me and kept saying I had no taste, I dressed badly, I made conversation badly, even laughed badly. I always felt guilty with her. I could never even imagine that she was being too strict or unfair with me. He saw the virtues in me and she saw the shortcomings.

Daddy never even slapped me once, but I got the belt and slaps from her right through my childhood. One day they were arguing, and I came up to her from behind to put my arms round her, but she was taking a drink to wash down a tablet and I accidentally jogged her elbow. She spilt the water on herself, then went for me and started beating me and couldn't stop. Daddy pulled me away.

They used to argue because of me.

Daddy shouted:

'Why are you always picking on her?'

She answered:

'What will she grow up like otherwise?'

She went away somewhere for a few days and when she got back she kicked up a fuss because everything was a mess. The next time I tidied everything up before she got back, made everything all bright and shiny, but she was still dissatisfied, in fact even more. Maybe she sensed that Daddy and I could get on perfectly well without her, that when she was away life at home carried on quite normally.

She always kept repeating something she'd read somewhere about life not being a novel, that it wasn't all a bowl of cherries, in life you couldn't just do what you wanted and, in general, we weren't put on earth just to have a good time.

She didn't like it when I went out, she didn't like my girlfriends, she hated Yanka. She thought everything bad about me came from her.

Daddy always stood up for me:

'But she needs friends!'

It all ended with Mummy crying and saying:

'You always take her side!'

She could feel that there was more between me and Daddy than there was between them. Probably both of us felt that I meant more to my father than she did.

One day I realised exactly what it was I didn't like about her. She was a woman who had everything right in her life – everything exactly as she wanted it – and it simply couldn't be any other way. She had always known what she wanted and how to get it. It was the same with furniture and with people. In school she was a star pupil. Her women friends were all miserable, she was always telling them how to live their lives. And inside she despised them because they couldn't live the right way, because everything about their lives was wrong. And she always stuck photos of our holidays in albums that were logbooks of happiness. She wanted to make me and my father fit her photo-albums. But it didn't work.

Offers for my father to play parts in films became less and less frequent. He took it hard and went on binges. He didn't drink at home, but he came home drunk more and more often.

I ask him:

'Daddy, are you drunk?'

And he answers:

'No, bunny, I'm pretending.'

They quarrelled as if they didn't know that angry words can never be taken back and forgotten. They didn't know that people quarrel with all their strength but only make up half-heartedly, so every time some love is sliced away and there's less and less of it. Or they did know, but they couldn't help themselves.

I used to lock myself away from them and simply die from this non-love.

The worst thing of all was the mirror. That non-face, those non-hands. Those non-breasts, untouched even by a suntan, promising to exist, but still not arriving.

And I couldn't understand how it could have happened that Mummy was a beauty and I was like this.

I used to think how strange it was that this thing was called me.

And what a misfortune it was to be this.

Yanka had already had her first love ages ago, and her second, and her third, and I already believed that I would never have anything. I used to howl silently, staring at the wallpaper.

And then he appeared in our home. He and Daddy were friends from their young days. And now he was a film director and he took Daddy to play a part in his film.

He had ginger hair, and his eyelashes were fiery-red, long and thick. Like ginger pine needles. His hair was monstrously thick in general. If it was hot at the table, he unbuttoned his shirt and rolled up his sleeves, and I could see powerful biceps, covered in freckles. And red wisps stuck out through the open shirt collar on his chest.

I remember he said he'd just got back from the seaside, but his fair skin didn't tan, it only turned pink.

He started coming often.

Daddy showed me a photograph of them fooling about, hanging upside down on a crossbar, I looked at those little boys and even then I thought: before he became a father, was my daddy already my daddy? And was that ginger-haired boy already *him*? And who was that?

He was an old bachelor, and Mummy and Daddy were always joking that they ought to marry him off. Once he said:

'Once you've seen one woman's breasts, you've seen them all.'

But Mummy objected that, far from it, women's breasts were like snowflakes, no pair was like any other, and they laughed. I found all this strange and unpleasant.

He used to call me Sasha-the-smasher. I felt terribly self-conscious when he was there. Or rather, I divided in two again with him, but the one who was afraid was here and the other one, who wasn't afraid of anything, used to disappear at the most inconvenient moments.

He would drop into my room, glance at the cover of my book and ask:

'How's Troy getting on? Still holding out? Or have they taken it already?'

I plucked up my courage and asked what he wanted to make a film about. He answered:

'Well, for instance, you've been drinking kefir and you've got a little white kefir moustache left on your face, and outside in the street – they've just written about it in the *Evening News* – a bus has run into the stop where a lot of people were waiting for it, and they've been killed. And there's a direct connection between the little kefir moustache and these deaths. And between everything else in the world too.'

I fell head over heels in love with him.

When he was visiting I used to creep out surreptitiously into the hallway to take a sniff at his long coat, white scarf and hat. He used some eau de cologne that I didn't know and the smell was ravishing – astringent and manly.

I couldn't sleep. Now I was dying of love. I wept into my pillow all night, night after night. Every day I wrote in my diary: 'I love you, I love you, I love you . . .' – I covered pages and pages.

It was so painful. I didn't know what to do with it all.

Mummy saw everything and she suffered with me. She didn't know how to help. She hugged me and comforted me, stroked my head as if I was a little girl and tried to bring me to my senses.

'You're still nothing but a child. You have an intense need to be loved and to give love. This is all wonderful. But who can you love? Your boyfriends have only just stopped playing with toy soldiers. That's the reason for all these tears cried into the pillow, the envy, the fantasy, the daydreams, the resentment against life, the anger with the whole world, with the people dearest of all to you. As if the people dearest to you are to blame for everything. And then you start inventing everything for yourself.'

She tried to convince me that it was too early for love, that none of it was real yet. I blubbered and asked:

'And what is real?'

She said:

'Well, like me and Daddy.'

Daddy used to come into my room, sit on the edge of the bed and smile guiltily for some reason. As if he was to blame. As if it was some serious illness and there was nothing he could do to help me. He sighed and said:

'Bunny, I love you very much. So why isn't that enough?'

It used to make me feel so sorry for them!

I started writing him letters. I sent them every day. I didn't know what to write, I just sent whatever was a part of me that day in the envelope – a tram ticket, a little feather, a shopping list, a piece of thread, a blade of grass, a fireman beetle.

He answered several times. He wrote something humorous and polite. And then he started sending me stupid things too: a broken shoelace, offcuts of cinema film. Once I took a paper napkin out of the envelope, and wrapped inside it was his tooth that had been pulled out the day before. On the napkin he wrote that if it had really been love on my side, he hoped that now it would definitely pass off. The tooth really was horrible. But I took it and stuck it in my cheek.

One time he came and spoke about something for ages with Mummy and Daddy behind a closed door, then came into my room. I stood at the window as if I was paralysed. He wanted to come closer, but I pulled the curtain shut and hid behind it.

He said: 'Sasha-the-smasher! My poor little lovesick girl! How can you possibly fall in love with such a monster? Listen, there's something important I have to explain to you, although I'm sure you already understand everything anyway behind that curtain. You don't love me at all, you simply love. These are two quite different things.'

And he left.

He didn't come to our place when I was there any more after that. And he didn't answer my letters.

One day I played truant from school. I just decided I wouldn't go – and I didn't. I wandered about in the rain, not even noticing that it was pouring from the heavens, the way that cows don't notice rain.

I was holding his tooth in my fist in my pocket.

The only thing I remember is the smell of a burned rubbish bin that got stuck in my nostrils. And a sugar-coated pair of newly-weds in the mud-splattered window of a photographer's shop.

I was chilled to the bone and soaked to the skin. I trudged back home.

I open the door of the apartment and there's someone's huge umbrella standing open on the floor.

I catch a familiar scent in the hallway. A long coat, a white scarf and a hat are hanging on the hallstand.

I hear water running in the bathroom.

The bedroom door is open. Mummy glances out with her hair in a mess. Pulling on her Chinese robe with the dragons over her naked body. She asked in fright:

'Sasha? What's happened? What are you doing here?'

■

Today the chief of chiefs and commander of commanders summons me and says:

'Sit down, write an order.'

I sit down and write:

'Brothers and sisters! Soldier boys! Contractors, peacekeepers and assassins! The fatherland is disintegrating like blotting paper in the rain! There is nowhere to retreat! Not a single step backwards! Whoah, take a look at that! Did you see the butt she has on her? No, not that one! She's already turned the corner. Cross that out about the butt. Right, where were we? Ah, yes! Right then. Wigs to be woven into a hairy braid from the centre of the crown of the head and thereafter plaited into a braid woven with a ribbon. No toupees to be worn. All men to arrange their temples in identical fashion, as is presently established in the regiment, to one long pigeon-wing, but brushed out and backcombed smartly so as not to droop like an icicle, and in frosty weather to be made wider so as to cover the ear. This drill will preserve the men from the idleness that is the source of all soldiers' wanton antics. Which seems reason enough to keep a soldier practising it constantly. Boots to be of each man's correct size, neither too broad nor too narrow, such that in frosty weather straw or fibrous material may be inserted into them, nor too short, such as not to chafe the toes in walking, owing to which a soldier on the march often cannot keep pace with the fleet of foot, but to sit straight on the foot. Also to be kept always faultlessly repaired, cleaned and greased and changed daily from one foot to the other so as not to wear out and not to damage the feet during marching and walking. Shaving shall not be neglected. For the slower of wit I explain: the wearing of a beard may connote defeat in hand-to-hand combat, because it is easy to grab hold of it and defeat the enemy. We march out tomorrow. Our road is long. The night is short. The clouds are sleeping. First we shall march through the friendly kingdom of Prester John, whose great might is the talk of the whole world. It says here in the *Evening News* that he defeated Genghis Khan himself in a war of attrition. This terrain is difficult and most savagely savage. I most stringently recommend all gentlemen commanding regiments and battalions to expound and impress on their men that as they pass through the townships, villages and taverns they must not wreak even the slightest devastation. Local inhabitants are to be calmly spared and in no wise offended in order not to harden the hearts of the people and thereby earn the vicious reputation of marauders. Houses are not to be run into, enemies begging for mercy are to be spared, unarmed men are not to be killed, women are not be fought with, minors are not to be touched. To save the bullet, with every shot every soldier must aim at his own enemy, in order to kill him. The blessings of the heavenly kingdom on those of us who are killed, and to those who live – glory! Fear-mongers and cowards must be eliminated on the spot. Follow me into the attack, hurrah! Press on, press on! Attack! Fix bayonets! Rifles to the fore! Stab, shoot, finish them! Drop them where they stand! We'll kill, drop, capture the lot of them! Chase, stab! Slash, beat! Hoik, skrike, dreck, doom, hell!'

He broke off to get his breath back, unfastened the button of his collar and walked over to the window. Blotted the sweat off his forehead with the curtain. Took a cigarette case out of his pocket. Tapped a *papyrosa* on the lid. Broke a match on the sodden box. Then another. Lit up with the third. Took a deep drag. Breathed a thick stream of smoke out through the open window frame.

For a brief moment he had the feeling that all this had happened before: this ink-stained youngster who reminded him so much of his own dead son had sat in this room in exactly the same way. With the milk not yet dry on his lips, and women still seeming mysterious. That long-cold teapot with the broken spout had existed before. Everything was exactly the same as then: this wall-paper with the pattern of small red flowers, like a rash – as if it had caught chickenpox from the draught. This bundle of dried fish hanging on the window latch threaded through their eyes. That man who had just walked past, shuffling his feet, with both of his jacket pockets weighed down with bottles. That sign oppo-site, 'ARMY STORES', which someone had altered with mud, so that it read 'AMY SCORES'. From somewhere round the corner he heard the rattle of a child clattering a stick along a picket fence.

Running his hand over his chin, he heard the stubble rustling. That definitely had happened before – him running his hand over it and it rustling.

He reflected that the secret of déjà vu was probably that in the book of life, of course, all this was only written once. But it came back to life when someone read a page that had already been read before. And then it all lived again – the stick on the picket fence and the fish that smelled from close up, hanging on the window latch, and the rustling of this stubble and the teapot full of cold, strong tea, and women were still mysterious.

So it was simply that someone was reading these lines at the moment – that was the entire secret of déjà vu.

He flicked his butt out through the window and it went spinning through the air.

He sucked bitter, cold tea out of the broken spout of the teapot. Wiped his lips on his sleeve.

Carried on dictating.

'In the third place, and perhaps most important of all – do not kill without need. Remember – they are human beings like us. This will be tough, lads. And we'll have to go a long way, to the ends of the earth. Even further than Alexander the Great went, he only reached the border, where he ordered a marble column to be erected with a line of verse written on it: "I, Alexander, did reach this point". You don't believe me? I'll show you it. The cacti there have prickly pricked-up ears and the people are naked-wise. Alexander the Great was greatly surprised when he saw them and said: "Ask for whatever you wish, I will give it to you!" They replied to him: "Grant us immortality, which we desire more than anything, and we do not need any other riches." But Alexander said to them: "I am mortal, how can I grant you immortality?" And they said to him: "If you consider yourself mortal, then why do you roam and wander through the whole world, doing so much evil?" See what a smart lot they are. Turn your back for a moment and you'll get a bullet in the back of your head. First we'll travel by railway and then by sea. And we'll know we've arrived as soon as we see people with dogs' heads. And when we carry oars, they'll ask what kind

of spades we're carrying. In that place there are also public lupa-
naria with effeminate men and innumerable other abominations, so
always keep your guard up! For us peace is a process, for them it is
a result. They believe knowledge is remembrance. Everyone knows
his own future, but he still lives his own life. So it turns out that
lovers love each other even before they find out about each other,
get to know each other and get talking. And they don't pray for
themselves, because we ourselves don't know what we're good for.
Their gods are simple, but there are as many of them as there are
birds, trees, clouds, puddles, sunsets and us. Concerning the existence of other worlds they are doubtful, but consider it madness to
assert that apart from the visible nothing else exists for, they say,
there is no nonexistence, either in the world or beyond it. They
acknowledge two primary physical elements of all earthly things:
the sun-father and the earth-mother. They regard the air as a rarefied
section of the sky and all fire as deriving from the sun. The sea is
the earth's sweat and a link connecting the air and the earth, as blood
connects the body and the spirit in living creatures. The world is
an immense living creature and we live in its belly in the same way
as worms live in our bellies. However, whether a worm is happy,
we do not know, but a man is born, lives and dies happy, only he
keeps forgetting this all the time. These naked-wisemen have
unscrewed all the nuts off the rails. And not even for sinkers for
fishing lines. Blast them for wreckers! The railway lines spoil the
feng shui, you see! All these scumbags are to be exterminated merci-
lessly. Like mad dogs! Wipe the entire pack of these rotten hounds
off the face of the earth! Remember, someone has to do the dirty
work too. Men! We will avenge ourselves for our comrades and
friends in battle, who are still alive, see them there, smiling among
us, but very soon now. Most important of all, remember we have
truth on our side and they have untruth! But perhaps vice versa.

For is not light the left hand of darkness and darkness the right hand of light? And does the Sun not strive to burn up the Earth, and not at all to generate plants and people? In this life there are no victors, all are the vanquished. Especially since when you stab them with a bayonet, they'll still think like this: "To be concerned about what will happen to you after death is like asking yourself what will happen to your fist when you open it, or to a leg bent at the knee when you unbend it." And most important of all, my lads, take good care of yourselves! Don't fire until the order is given! Do you remember Pythagoras's hippopotamus? Ah, you scatter-brains! You did it in school! It just flew in one ear and out the other! It's pointless teaching fools like you anything! The only thing on your mind is skirts. What did Pythagoras teach us? Pythagoras taught us that when your destined time comes to die, as soon as your soul leaves behind the sublunary world and the light of the sun, direct your steps to the left through the sacred meadows and groves of Persephoneia. And when they ask who you are and where you've come from, you should reply: "I am a goat kid and I fell in the milk." Well, now I think that's all. Ah yes, one more thing. Please don't spit in the bowl with the general staff clerk's porridge. Just leave the holy fool in peace, will you! What if he does scribble out death notices with his little pen? Who's he bothering? He doesn't want to pray for the tyrant-tsar? Well, who does?'

I'm back from the clinic now and I still can't pull myself together.

After all, I went to study because I wanted to help give life, but now they're teaching us curettage.

I actually wanted to be a veterinary surgeon at first, but when I saw that they sterilised dogs simply for people's convenience, I was so outraged that I left.

Now I'm going to write to you, then sit down to carry on studying. If you only knew all the things we have to take on trust!

Have you ever thought where clothes came from? Just imagine, the reason isn't the cold or a sense of shame. It's walking upright! When we stood up on our hind legs, the need arose to cover our sex organs. But not out of shame, oh no – animals don't have any sense of shame. To show their sex organs and demonstrate preparedness for coupling, monkeys have to assume a special pose. But people are in that pose all the time! They have to do the opposite and cover themselves to signal their unpreparedness!

It really is so off-putting to know that there's an explanation for everything. For maternal love, for instance. Do you know why it's stronger in humans? Because in comparison with a little monkey, a child is born so very prematurely. To appear in the world as mature as that, it would have to spend twenty months in the abdomen. That is, to be born as it will only be at the age of one year. So the woman goes on carrying the child – only not inside, but outside. And then there's no way she can let go of it. The child grows up and the mother keeps clinging to it, she can't part with it.

When I was a little girl I couldn't possibly have imagined that the day would ever come when I would want to puke my mother up out of myself like vomit.

When there was no one at home, I took her grand-gala photo album and started pulling the photographs out of it, tearing them into little pieces and flushing them down the toilet.

And I started smoking – but only because my mother forbade it.

I come back inside and she runs a check. She knows where to sniff. She doesn't say: 'Breathe!' – no, she realises that after just one sweet there's no more smell left. She sniffs my hands. Your clothes and your hair get impregnated with smoke if someone smokes beside you. But your hands only smell if you hold a cigarette yourself.

I didn't try to hide – I smoked openly, to spite her.

Daddy used to say to me on the quiet:

'Childy, why do you go asking for trouble? Hide the cigarettes, don't have them brazenly sticking out of your jacket like that!'

My mother rants at me and I say to her:

'I'm bad? All right, so I'll be even worse!'

We upset each other so badly, we start crying and get hysterical. I probably needed it all for some reason – the tears, the shouting, the stamping, the tearing of pillowcases. One time I locked myself in and started tugging on the curtains so hard that the curtain rod came down with a crash. She hammers on my door and says that she's my mother and because of that alone she deserves my respect, and I shout that I didn't stuff myself into that egg cell and I never asked her to have me anyway, so I don't owe her anything.

Another time she rants at me because I took her manicure set and didn't put it back and I wonder what will happen if she finds out I've started stealing money from her. I don't even need it – my father always gave me some for cigarettes or whatever else. But there was some kind of line I had to cross.

It was disgusting to watch her getting dressed, sprucing herself up. I could always guess where she was going from the blowsy, slippery look in her eyes.

I used to imagine her getting undressed in front of her lover, carefully removing one piece of clothing after another, straightening it out, folding it neatly.

I was sixteen then and I felt the change in myself without the slightest transition – one moment I was a child, then suddenly I was a very lonely woman.

I left home then. I shouted that I would never come back to them and slammed the door. But I had nowhere to go. I went to Yanka's place to spend the night. She only had her mother and grandmother, and she called them her parents.

My father ran round everywhere looking for me until late at night, although he could have guessed straightaway where I was. He came and started demanding that I go home immediately. I felt embarrassed in front of Yanka's parents. I told him:

'All right, I'll come back. But what can I do about the fact that I don't love her or you any more? I despise you – what can I do about that?'

I thought he was going to hit me. He didn't. And he didn't say a thing all the way home, just sniffed as he walked along.

I don't know why I've remembered that now.

My only one, how much I miss you!

I read every letter you write over and over again and put kisses where the full stops are.

I walk past the monument, it's still there, but where is our date?

And I keep trying all the time to find some justification for you not being here beside me. Not an explanation, a justification. After all, if that's the way things are, it must be necessary for something. And this is the idea I've had. It's like when you're a child – if you have something, you have to share it. You've been given some sweets, but the others don't have any. And you have to share. Or else they might simply take everything. So in this life you have to share what is most precious to you. And the more precious it is, the more you have to give away. Share what you love the most – or else it will be taken away completely.

I kiss you, my love! Be well, take care, my happiness! I fall asleep and wake up with the thought of you.

If you weren't there, I would drown, floundering in the void of myself, unable to find any foothold.

And I'm so afraid that something will happen to you.

Now for some reason I've remembered you telling me about some kind of birds that make love on the wing. I can't remember what they're called.

Do you know what I want right now more than anything else in the world? To be pregnant all over from you – with my mouth and eyes and navel and hands and every opening, my skin and my hair, everything!

They brought up the railway carriages. Forty men, eight horses, one hamster. How strangely everything in this life is arranged! Men become brutal with other men so quickly, they turn icy cold and cruel – and they thaw out and become human with a little animal that lives in their pocket. They feel compassion for it. They are suddenly transformed when they stroke its back with their finger.

A long day in the carriages.

We're probably travelling through the kingdom of Prester John.

Telegraph poles, bridges, wooden bunkhouses, brick factory buildings, rubbish dumps, railway sidings, warehouses, grain elevators, fields, forests, more railway sidings, goods depots, water pumps.

The train is barely crawling along. Wagons stand behind a closed boom at a crossing. A pregnant pointswoman scratches the back of her head with her small, rolled-up green flag. A goat tethered to a stake watches intently.

In open areas the smoke of the locomotive trails low across the ground, clinging to the withered grass.

At some station yesterday there was an accident – I saw a coupler crushed by the buffers.

Now we're picking up speed again – down below, where the rails are, everything has blurred into a rapid flow.

They looked for proof that the earth turns on its axis – well, there it is, outside the window.

We've just passed a half-hamlet with a half-dozen columns of smoke and a half-dozen souls.

I think about my mother a lot. She came to see me off with her blind man, although I asked her not to.

It has suddenly occurred to me that I'll only be able to love her properly when she's dead. Who was it who said that blood kinship is the most distant? How cruel and how true!

I remember them walking away – him taking one step for two of her short, little ones.

What a strange word – stepson.

My mother met my stepfather through Grandma. How old was I then, eight? He came to visit us several times, Mum gave him tea and made silent, threatening gestures across the table at me, so that I would sit quietly and behave myself. I found this man disgusting from the very beginning.

He spoke to me in the cheerful, bantering tone that people use with children, all the while watching me with his shaggy ear. I didn't answer his stupid questions, and Mum said affectionately:

'Come on, darling, answer when you're asked a question.'

The falsehood in that affectionate voice was obvious to both of us and it hurt me very much.

To spite him I muttered something even more stupid and his face blossomed into a grimace — that was the way he smiled, it was very hard to get used to that smile.

Sasha, my dearest, is it all right for me to write to you about this? The two of us never spoke about him.

You know, when I tried to imagine his world, it made me feel queasy. The life of a blind man seemed to me like the life of a shrew that burrows its lairs and tunnels through darkness as dense and heavy as damp clay and then runs through them. All of his black space was crisscrossed with these passages. And Mum and I were in one of them. Especially at nights he would steal into my brain with his blindness and I couldn't scrape him out of my head no matter how hard I tried.

I remember Mum completely flooring me when she said she was going to marry this man and she loved him very much and asked me to learn to love him too. I was astounded by that phrase — 'learn to love'. Learn to love him? I simply couldn't get it through my head that she could bring this weirdo with the terrible hollow eyes and greenish, protruding teeth into our home.

Mum asked me to let the blind man touch my face. Even now, after all these years, I remember it with a shudder.

Can you believe that I even made some kind of childish plans to do something that would spoil their wedding — cut Mum's wedding dress to pieces with the scissors, lace the cake with laxative or something else of the kind — only there wasn't any wedding as I imagined it. They simply moved into our place and started living there.

I simply couldn't understand why Mum needed this invalid. And the smell! You would have understood me. He gave off the thick, heavy odour of a large, sweaty body. It puzzled me why

Mum put up with it – could she really not smell it? I simply couldn't believe that she didn't notice that odour.

Sometimes he gave me presents. I remember he brought a little box from the cake shop and it had my favourite cakes in it – rum truffles. Two truffles with an intoxicating chocolaty scent. I wanted to eat them so much! But I sneaked the cakes out when I went to the toilet and flushed them away.

He was delighted when he heard we had the special chess set for blind people that my granny had given me, but I flatly refused to play with him, although I would have been happy enough to play with the mirror before that.

When the three of us walked along the street, people turned to look and I felt terribly ashamed. I remember that at the very first opportunity – for instance when they stopped in front of a shop window or went into a shop – I tried to pretend I was simply strolling about on my own. I invented the most impossible excuses in order to avoid appearing in public with them.

When they took me to the cinema, Mum used to whisper in his ear what was happening on the screen and people kept shushing her all the time, and I had to take him to the toilet. He had a problem with his bladder and he went to the toilet almost every hour.

It was the trivial little things that annoyed me most. I couldn't just leave anything anywhere I liked – every item now had to be in its own set place. I couldn't leave a door half-open – it had to be closed or opened completely. When he lay down for a rest, everything in the house had to fall silent. He put a box of matches in the toilet and struck a match every time after he went – and demanded that everybody else do the same.

I couldn't bear to watch his hands fumbling around on the table, searching for the sugar bowl or butter dish.

When he fell into thought, he often used to tilt his head back and press his thumb in under his eyeball.

And I can see him now, shuffling along our corridor, staring hard with his outstretched fingers.

It offended me to see Mum take off his socks and rub his feet in the evening. And it offended me even more – I don't know why – when she called him Pavlik, like a child.

Sometimes it seemed to me that he wasn't blind at all and could see everything. One time I accidentally glanced in through an open door – my stepfather had just come in and he was getting changed, taking off his shoes by standing on the heels, and he suddenly shouted at me harshly:

'Shut the door!'

When Mum couldn't take him somewhere, she used to ask me. My stepfather held on to my forearm. I was astounded the first time, when he said:

'Don't be afraid, it's not catching!'

Everybody looked at us, and I couldn't bear those glances of sympathy, those comments with sighs: 'How terrible!' or 'Lord spare us!' And he had to be led along smoothly, with no sharp movements or jerks, otherwise he would start scolding me angrily and squeezing my arm painfully. You had to know how to help him. He got furious when tender-hearted people wanted to help and grabbed at his hand holding the cane. And what a chore it was leading him past all the puddles when it was raining!

My stepfather always carried around a small iron tablet in a cover with little square windows in it. As we were walking along, he would suddenly get some idea and want to write it down, so we stopped and I waited while he punched holes in thick paper with a blunt awl. People walking by stared and I wanted to disappear, I felt so ashamed.

However, he walked through his familiar tunnels and passages quite confidently on his own, tapping briskly on the pavement with his white cane.

We kept a suitcase full of old things in the cupboard up under the ceiling. Mum sometimes sorted through them, and one day she took out a big sweater, measured it against me and said I could wear it when I grew a bit more. I realised it was left over from my father. And then suddenly I saw my father's sweater on the blind man. Somehow that made me angrier than anything else.

They used to hire a boat on the pond in the park, my stepfather took the oars and mum would steer. They couldn't understand why I didn't like boat rides, when everyone else did. They really enjoyed themselves – he would start catching crabs with the oars and splashing us, Mum squealed and broke into peals of laughter, but I sat there wet and angry. And when I scooped up a handful of black, weedy water and splashed it into his face, Mum shouted at me and slapped me on the cheek. I'd never been slapped by her before that.

She wanted me to apologise to him, but I was stubborn:

'What for? What did I do? He was splashing us!'

Mum burst into tears, but my stepfather wiped the duckweed off his face and smiled with that grimace of his.

'Never mind, Ninochka! It's all right.'

But I knew that he hated me too.

Some students went sailing past in a boat, one of them whistled and said:

'Look, it's Charon!'

They laughed so hard, their boat almost capsized.

I already knew who Charon was. I laughed too.

Afterwards, when we were alone, Mum said to me:

'Forgive me, please, darling! Try to understand. And have pity.'

It seemed so strange to me then that I ought to have pity on Mum for something and not the other way round.

I never could forgive her for that slap.

Once he went out alone and fell, he came back all bloody and dirty, with his shirt torn. Mum burst into tears and rummaged in boxes, looking for sticking plaster and iodine, while my stepfather dripped blood on the parquet floor. I remember that I didn't feel sorry for him at all.

On Sundays Mum strictly forbade me to wake them early and came out of the bedroom looking pleased and humming some tune, with red blotches on her neck – irritation from his stubble. It grew so fast that my stepfather sometimes shaved twice in one day, if they were going out somewhere in the evening. He didn't need any light, he often sat in the dark and even shaved in the dark – by touch and the sound of where the razor scraped most.

Once there was a very muggy night and I was lying under the open window, unable to get to sleep. It was very quiet and I could hear every little rustle outside in the street. The window in their room was open too, and I could hear them talking, certain that I wouldn't hear anything through two closed doors. He was purring about how firm her breasts were and her nipples were like thimbles. About how she had tropical jungles under her arms. And she liked all this, she was giggling.

How I hated him at that moment, and how I despised her!

Then the bed started creaking. I wanted to jump up and do something to spite them. But I just lay there listening to them wheezing and the sweat squelching between their stomachs. And then she started crying out in a muffled voice:

'Yes! Yes! Yes!'

Afterwards she went dashing to the bathroom at full pelt, with a patter of bare feet.

Some way station or another. We're stuck. I've decided to write another couple of lines.

Sashenka, why am I telling you about my stepfather? I don't understand why myself. To hell with him!

I should tell you about something interesting instead.

How amusing it is that for Democritus the body is only divisible as far as the soul – the soul is the final, indivisible item, like the atom. There's always a space between atoms. 'If atoms touched, they would be divisible, but they are indivisible by definition: for it is only possible to touch with parts.' That is, bodies can touch, but there will always be a gap between souls, a void.

I'm hungry.

Rooks – black and glossy, like locomotive seeds.

People are probably simply divided into those who understand how it's possible that here I am, about to drink tea at ten minutes to two, and at the very same time the Earth is spinning, and they don't see any contradiction in that, and those who can't understand this at all and never will.

We're standing at a water pump – the locomotive is about to drink its fill of water.

I sit at the window and stare at a little old shunting engine. It goes puffing past, giving off heat and sticky steam.

It's got dark and we still haven't budged.

It's actually cold here at night, I have to wrap myself in my greatcoat in order not to get frozen.

There's a little man with a hammer on a long handle walking along the rails for the full length of the train and tapping every axle box. He hears some special sound that no one but him and the axle boxes can hear.

The rails in the sidings are rusting.

Then suddenly I understand a very simple thing – that this railway halt, this lamp, the blows of the hammer on the axle boxes, the chirring of grasshoppers from the window of the telegraph office, the smell of smoke and the hot locomotive breathing steam and grease, and the call that locomotive gives, hoarse and weary – it's all me. There is no other me anywhere and never will be. And all the assurances about eternal return are just fairy stories. Everything is only once and now. And if we start moving this moment, the railway halt will drop out of sight and I'll disappear.

The locomotives have started bellowing for some reason. Perhaps we'll move on soon.

Or perhaps they're simply calling to each other, males and females, in their low chesty voices. Searching for each other in the night. Locomotive love.

And now there's someone calling all alone and no one answering. For them, perhaps, that's a very tender voice.

In Dostoevsky's *Brothers Karamazov* Grushenka had a special 'curve' of the body. I keep wondering what kind of curve that could be.

●

My love, I feel frightened.

In every unguarded moment the thought comes that something might happen to you. Then I take a grip on myself and I know that everything will be all right for us.

The longer you're not here with me, the more you become a part of me. Sometimes I can't tell where you end and I begin.

Everything that happens to me is only real because I think of how to write to you about it. And without that, even when things are good, I can't feel any joy. I have to share it with you for it to happen.

For instance, yesterday we agreed that I would call round for Yanka, but I got there early, their classes hadn't finished yet, and I decided to wait inside, so as not to hang about on the street, this summer's not very summery, it's cold and windy. They're having repairs done, and some painters were just getting into their cradle by the entrance — one of them, with a huge unripe strawberry of a nose, winked at me and joked that he was going to pour paint on me from his bucket. I laughed. How little I really need to feel happy – if I can tell you about it afterwards. Otherwise, you know, none of it exists. Including the painter with his strawberry and his battered bucket of ochre paint.

I walked along the corridors for a while, the whole place felt uncomfortable, with a draught from the windows, the smell of paint from all sides and the stink of the toilets. I found the room from the timetable. I glanced in. They're doing life drawing. I slip inside and sit down. No one even looks at me, they're all busy, concentrating. Trying hard. There's a woman standing on a dais, naked, and all those young men around her don't even see her. Or, rather, what they see is something else.

The scraping of pencil leads in the silence, charcoal rustling over paper. One kept holding his pencil out at arm's length and screwing up his eyes to measure some part of the woman.

The professor strode around from one student to the next, tapping on their drawings with a big door key, as if to say: That's not right and this here is wrong. He told someone haughtily:

'Distinguish the half-tones!'

He didn't even glance at me.

Yanka called him 'our Chartkov', after Gogol's character in *The Portrait*.

There was a heater on the floor in front of the model, but I could see that she was chilly – she kept sniffing all the time as if she had a cold.

And the way she was standing wasn't really feminine either, with her arms and legs spread wide. As empty as a vase – her body was there, but she was somewhere far away.

There was something unreal about all of this – about that non-woman and those non-men.

And then that painter suddenly appeared in the window. He saw her and froze with the roller in his hands.

She noticed him too and covered herself at once. Such a womanly gesture, one hand up here, the other down there. She suddenly became real.

And I suddenly wanted so much to draw her!

At this point everybody started gathering up their things, she threw on a robe and darted behind a screen.

And again I thought that I would tell you all about it.

And there, now I have.

But today I woke up and lay there without opening my eyes, just listening to all the sounds around me, so alive and simple, part of my life – the sewing machine that has been stitching away somewhere since early in the morning, the lift droning, the door of the building slamming, a tram rattling past at the end of the street, some bird chirping through the open window – you could have looked at it and told me what it's called.

It's impossible to believe that there's war somewhere. And there always has been. And always will be. And they're really maiming and killing people there. And death really does exist.

Believe me, my dearest, darling love, nothing will happen to you!

■

Received from the port as provisions for the company: sugar 19 poods, 5 pounds, 60 zolotniks; tea 23 pounds, 1/3 zolotnik; tobacco 7 poods, 35 pounds and soap 8 poods, 37 pounds.

Sick men: two sailors and 14 soldiers of Line Battalion No. 4. Water in the hold 5 inches after pumping.

The afternoon of the same day. A light wind, clear, barometer reading 30.01. Taken ashore on today's date: crate of ammunition – 1 off; barrels of meat – 4 off; hemp 25 poods; rye flour 29 poods; grain 4 poods; crate of (illegible) – 1 off; cartridges – 2,160 pieces; cast-iron cauldrons – 3 off; ropes – 5 poods, 20 pounds; sheet iron – 50 sheets; seine net – 1 off; horse – one off and bulls – 2 off. Water in the hold at 12 o'clock – 24 inches.

Days under way – 193, days at anchor – 102.

Today the company was given maggoty meat – and it was all right, they scoffed it down. No mutiny.

After four months we reached a flat featureless island about one mile in length and disembarked from the ship to cook food for ourselves. As soon as the fire was kindled, the island sank under the water of its own accord and we ran back on board ship as fast as we could, leaving our supplies and pots behind. They told us that it wasn't an island, but a fish by the name of Jaconious which felt the fire and sank under the water, taking our supplies with it.

Having sailed further to the north, for six days we journeyed between two mountains hidden in fog. On approaching close to an island, we saw there various rare animals and forest people without any clothes. We sailed on to an island on which there live dog-headed people and monkeys the size of a yearling calf, where we stood at anchor for five months owing to bad weather that prevented us from sailing further. The local inhabitants here have the heads and teeth and eyes of dogs. If they catch foreigners, they eat them. And the fruits here are not the same as ours.

It is very hot here. The sun burns so fiercely, I can hardly bear it. If I lower an egg into the water, before I can pull it back out it is cooked. There is much olibanum growing here, only not white, but brown. There is a lot of ambergris here, they have bombazine and lots of other goods. Huge elephants are born here, and also the unicorn beast, the parrot bird, the ebony tree, the red sandalwood tree, Indian nuts, cloves, the Brazil tree, cinnamon, pepper, mute cicadas and the fragrant reed. Peafowl also live here, they are bigger and more beautiful than ours and look quite different. And the chickens they have are not the same as ours.

There is much ginger and silk in this part of the world. There is so much wild fowl, it is quite amazing. For one Venetian farthing you can buy three pheasants. The people here are spiteful; robbing and stealing are not considered sinful, there are no greater jeerers and bandits in the world. Idolaters live here, they have paper money and burn their dead, they have plenty of all sorts of victuals, but they eat mongooses.

They pray to various different things. When someone gets up in the morning, he prays to the first thing he sees.

The Pole Star is not visible here at all, but if you stand on tiptoe, it rises up a cubit above the water.

They burn their dead, so they say, for the following reason: if dead bodies were not burned, worms would appear in them and those worms would devour the entire body and when they left it there would be nothing for them to eat and they would all die, and that would be a grievous sin on the soul of the person whose body it was. Worms have souls too, they say.

I walk along with an oar and someone passing by asks:

'What's that spade you're carrying?'

Just imagine, my Sashenka, first there was the Brazil tree, and only afterwards was there Brazil.

I went out on deck, there was no one in the bow, I sheltered from the wind behind the windlass. It's cosy in behind the canvas cover, I can smoke up my sleeve.

The sea and the sky – how strange that somewhere they can exist apart.

It will start soon. Sashenka, perhaps I'll be killed. That's still better than coming back a cripple. And God forbid that I myself should have to kill.

You know, I'm ready for anything.

I look at the waves, at the dark clouds. There's a vague jolting under my feet. The rumbling of the engine room.

The wind seems to be trying to stuff the smoke back into the funnel. It's wasting its damn time, though.

A seagull froze, motionless, in the sky – lost in thought. Then suddenly it remembered something important, perhaps that life is as short as a blink, and went dashing off at full pelt.

Why am I lying to you and myself? I'm not ready for anything at all!

They've thrown a vat of waste overboard – the seagulls are going wild.

You know, Sashka, the way it is is probably this: the corporeal, visible shell of the world – the material – gets stretched and greasy, chafed and worn into holes, and then the essence pokes out, like a toe sticking through a hole in a sock.

●

My darling, dearest, only precious one!

Listen to what happened.

I rode my bike to that forest of ours, then walked to the abandoned aerodrome. Do you remember?

Everything was overgrown with grass, there was a rubbish dump on the landing area, the hangars were empty, with piles of shit inside them. Thickets of rusty barbed wire everywhere.

I think: Why did I come out here? All I've done is get my legs stung by nettles. And my socks are covered in grass seeds.

And the sun is going down.

Then I go back to my bicycle and I see a bundle of barbed wire as tall as I am that is grown through with goosefoot. Lit up by the sunset, it starts glowing red, burning like a bush.

And suddenly it says:

'Stop!'

I stop.

It doesn't say anything else.

I ask it:

'Who are you?'

The blazing bundle says:

'Why, can't you see? I am Alpha and Omega, Gog and Magog, Eldad and Medad, dexter and sinister, apex and root, inbreath and outbreath, seed and weed, udder and rudder, if I knew where the ace was, I'd scoop the pot. I am that I am. Sower, mower and tin-whistle blower. Do not fear me. It is simply that I talk differently to different people. For we live in a world where every snowflake is different from another, mirrors do not really reflect anything and every mole and freckle has its own person unlike all the others. Speak!'

I ask:

'What should I say?'

'Say: Everything around me is message and messenger at the same time.'

I say:

'Everything around me is message and messenger at the same time.'

The blazing bundle asks:

'Well, so what's the problem?'

I say:

'Everybody tries to explain to me that you don't need anyone else for love. They tell me Plato said: Love is present in the one who loves, not in the beloved.'

It says:

'What's that got to do with anything? What does it matter who said what? Why do you listen to them all?'

I ask:

'What should I do?'

It says:

'Take a look at yourself!'

I ask:

'Do I look terrible?'

It says:

'That's not what I mean. Those grass seeds on your socks. They're the messenger and the message too. A special dispatch. About life.

About victory. It's the same thing. In this life there are no vanquished, everyone's a victor.'

I say:

'But I want to be with him!'

It says:

'Say the words!'

I ask:

'What words?'

It says:

'You know.'

I ask:

'I do? How would I know them?'

It says:

'Think!'

I ask:

'What then, is the servant of God Vovka the Carrot getting married to this woman? And shall I step on his foot too, to be the boss in the kitchen?'

It says:

'No, no, not that!'

I say:

'But I can't guess!'

It says:

'No need to guess. You already know everything. Look, there's a mosquito. There's a cloud. There are your fingers with the hangnails and the scar right beside the nail on your thumb.'

I say:

'I think I'm beginning to understand.'

It says:

'There's the visible world. And there – close your eyes – is the invisible one.'

I say:

'I understand!'

It says:

'Well then?'

I say:

'I understand everything.'

I understand everything. We are already husband and wife. We always were. You are my husband. I am your wife. And that is the most wonderful rhyme in the world.

■

Dear Such-and-Such!

I greatly regret to inform you that your son.

Well anyway, you understand the whole thing already.

Bear up.

I understand how you feel at this moment. There are no words that will help or console here.

Believe me, it's not easy for me to write all this either. But that's life. Duty to be done. No such thing as 'I don't want', only 'you have to'.

May it serve as at least some consolation to you that he did not die for no particular reason, but for something good and great. For what exactly? Well, let's say at least for that Motherland of ours.

I understand. That's no help at all.

In short, he was killed in battle.

In what battle?

Suffice it to say that your son did not return from a certain undistinguished war, as the poet T. put it. So what difference does it make? For the Whites, for the Reds, for the Hellenes, for the Hebrews.

What difference does it make which undistinguished war you die in?

I understand, it's important to you to know exactly which hostile empire's fields will be fertilised by a drop of your blood. But does that really matter? The Celestial Empire is as good as any.

Kutuzov came to beat the French and your son, as our lower ranks joke, came to kick the Chinese in the bollocks. Well, here's the result. Sign on receipt.

By the way, they've written about our prodigious heroes in the newspapers too! Look here, in yesterday's *Evening News*, on the third page: 'Hard is the soldier's path to the Order of St George'.

I enclose herewith.

'It is a sad fact,' our special correspondent reports from the theatre of military operations, 'that the experience of the first days of war has demonstrated that no other way is possible: we have tried being merciful and received volleys of gunfire from thickets of kaoliang – Chinese sorghum – in our rear. And take a look at their proclamations, nailed up on every joss house!

'There are no rains,
The earth is drying up:
The foreign devils have disrupted the universal harmony.
The wrathful heavens
Have sent down to earth
Eight million celestial soldiers.
Now we shall give the foreign devils short shrift,
We shall destroy the railroads:
Rain will pour down in heavy torrents,
People and spirits will be revived,

Cockerels and dogs will be pacified.
So kill one when you see him,
Kill him straightaway!
As often as you meet him,
Kill him every day!


'The foreign devils, dear reader,' the reporter continued in his report, 'are subhuman heathens with dogs' heads. *We* are the foreign devils.

'We have disrupted the universal harmony. We are like holes in a perfect universe, through which warmth and meaning escape and an icy cosmic draught blows in. Call the universal harmony feng shui if you wish, call it the general service regulations, it makes no difference, the important thing is that it contains everything in plenty: life and death and – most important of all – human warmth.

'Let me try to put this more simply. The universal harmony is the general service regulations, which are intended to teach new recruits that everything rhymes. Kasha and Masha, love and blood, snow and water, some such-and-such and her son.

'The Celestial Empire is celestial because people there die, but they carry on living. Here everyone carries on living in the same houses, speaking the same words that are too inadequate to express anything, watching the sunset in the same old way as it tries so hard to please, trimming their toenails in the same old way after soaking their feet in a basin of hot water. Everyone is still where they were before. And their houses, their roads, their land, their sunset, their toenails must not be taken away from them.

'In these regulations it is written: you must understand that you live on their land and walk their roads. And if you wish to hammer a nail into their wall, you must first ask permission. And when you build a house, you do not build it for yourself, but for everyone. For everyone living and not-living. For all the sunsets and toenails.

'It is not even a matter of the sleepers and the rails, but that it was done without so much as a by-your-leave. It touches a raw nerve. A celestial nerve.

'The foreign devils have disrupted the universal harmony, it must be restored. Therefore the foreign devils must be annihilated. We must be annihilated. We are the dog-headed ones, we must be put down like mad dogs. We are the ones ruining life for everyone.

'The heavens themselves are outraged and have sent a celestial army to fight against our sons.

'We are fighting against the heavens.

'You should see them, dear reader, these celestial warriors!

'They are mere children!

'And all little girls.

'They believe that uttering special words, celestial incantations, will make them invulnerable. They believe that a transparent golden bell will manifest itself around their maidenly bodies and protect them like armour against a bullet or a bayonet. And they also believe that they can set fire to houses with a single touch or glance, disappear and reappear in the most unexpected place, become invisible, hide under the ground and fly through the air. And in their hands even a kaoliang stalk becomes a weapon. They need only point it at a foreign devil for him instantly to be torn apart by invisible claws.

'And they take no prisoners. The cruelty with which they treat their victims is distinctly unmaidenlike and they feel obliged to abuse the lifeless bodies. They dismember them, feed them to pigs and eat the hearts themselves. But this is not simple barbarity, it contains a profound meaning. These little girls who can fly cannot imagine that even without all this someone's son will not be resurrected anyway, that he will never come again – neither on the third day nor the one hundred thousand and third.'

But let us return to our sheep, as the French say.

I return.

According to an instruction from Somebody-or-Other appended to the Letter-Writing Manual for General Staff Clerks, the present death notification should recount in brief the circumstances and causes of your son's death, such as that he died, faithful to his oath, in the performance of a combat mission assigned by a boneheaded commanding officer, having demonstrated fortitude and courage or – if you prefer: Faithful to his oath, in the performance of a combat mission assigned by a boneheaded commanding officer, after having demonstrated fortitude and courage, he was seriously wounded and died. Another version is also possible if your boy died as a result of the careless handling of a weapon, illness or other causes, for instance, if he expired as a result of bloody diarrhoea – as you understand, we can't write that to you, so it becomes: In the performance of a combat mission assigned by that same bonehead, faithful to his oath, he was taken seriously ill and died.

I recount herewith.

Your son was killed near Tongzhou on the banks of the Pei Ho river.

Or, rather:

Your son was killed, but he is alive and well.

But everything in due order.

We disembarked at the Taku Forts, which had already been taken by the allies.

●

Volodenka!

How much time has passed by already?

Your mum phoned me then, but she couldn't tell me. Your stepfather took the phone. He told me everything.

I lay down for two whole days without getting up. Why bother?

Everything turned to ice. My soul and my feet.

Then I got up and went to see your family.

You mother looked absolutely terrible. Her face was all swollen from crying. She looked at me as if she didn't know me.

We sat down at the table. Pavel Antonovich stood beside her and kept his hands on her shoulders. Then he said he would make some tea and went into the kitchen.

She said:

'If there was a coffin, if there was a grave, but there's nothing – a piece of paper . . .'

She held out the notification to me.

'Look, there's a piece of paper, there's a seal, there's a signature. But where's my son?'

Then her feelings overcame her, and so did mine. We wept our eyes out.

She kept repeating:

'But why was he killed? What for? They could have crippled him, left him with no arms or legs, but alive. He's mine, isn't he! He belongs to me!'

Then we drank tea with ring-shaped cracknels. Your stepfather poured for everyone and I noticed the way he poured – until it reached his finger.

You know, this is probably the way it is: there's a threshold of pain, a person loses consciousness in order not to die. And there's a threshold of grief, it suddenly stops hurting.

And you feel nothing. Nothing at all.

You sit and drink tea with ring-shaped cracknels.

And another thing – there are lots of people around, but when something happens, they disappear. I read somewhere that there used to be prohibitions on associating with widows or widowers, because grief was thought to be infectious. People probably still think that. Or perhaps it really is infectious.

Today I walked through our park, just as they were boxing up the statues for winter with sheets of plywood. As if they were nailing them in their coffins.

One of them was in that natural pose, as if she'd just seen the painter.

I stood and watched. I simply couldn't leave. I got frozen right through.

I was the one they were nailing in.

I'm the one in the coffin.

My Sashenka!

We've been unloading all day long and I've only just found a moment to write to you.

Do you know what is the most difficult thing for me now? It's explaining to you the very simplest things, what I'm surrounded by here. It's impossible to describe. Colours, smells, voices, plants, birds – everything here is different.

And today I also recorded my first death. A soldier was killed in a very stupid way: he was standing right under the windlass when something broke loose and he was crushed by falling crates.

I thought it would be special somehow, but my hand traced out the terrible words as if it was nothing out of the ordinary.

Maybe this is the beginning of what I wanted so much to happen inside me?

All my life, over and over, I have kept asking myself the same question.

And now sometimes it seems that I am getting close, not yet to the answer, but to some kind of understanding.

How I used to hate and despise myself – the person that I wanted to scrape off, like a tight shoe that had rubbed my foot raw! How I wanted to become like all of them: never despondent, mean, jaunty, rugged, never asking questions – everything's already clear anyway. To learn to cling to life. To step beyond everything inessential, incidental, learned from books. To learn not to think about the fear of death or, rather, not to ponder on it. To learn to hit out when a blow must be struck. To take joy in what is and not rack my brains over what it's all for.

There, I've written a report of a man's death and my hand didn't even tremble. Good.

Now in brief about these first two days.

Yesterday we reached the Taku Forts. The roadstead was already crowded with ships sailing under every possible flag, but the bay is shallow and large ships cannot enter the Pei Ho estuary. So we transferred onto barges first, and I felt rather queasy as I watched the horses being lifted and lowered down on the ships' windlasses.

They neighed in helpless fright, as if they had resigned themselves to their fate, and their long legs dangled hopelessly in the air.

We dropped anchor in the bay in the early evening and carried on unloading until late at night. When it got dark, the lights were lit on all the ships – entire constellations of electricity on all the masts and yards. You know, it was very beautiful! At first I regretted that you weren't here with me. The reflections of the portholes in the black water, the lights of the launches and lifeboats. Every now and then the beams of the searchlights flared up, thrusting into the clouds and leaving patches of moonlight in them. I watched these illuminations and thought about you. There was a warm, light wind blowing from off the shore, bringing new, unrecognisable smells. I felt glad for some reason, and a bit afraid. The beams kept flashing on and off. I imagined that was how ships talk to each other, they send signals via the clouds.

It was already dawn when we were towed into the estuary of the river. On both sides of us were long, low lines of forts. Everything empty and dead. The forts had only been taken a few days earlier. Here and there on the walls we could see the marks left where shells had exploded.

I don't know what they hauled on that barge before, but it was dirty and slippery, and my feet stuck to the deck.

You know, apparently in translation the name of the river means 'White'. But the colour of the Pei Ho is reddish-brown with an ochre shimmer. And it carries along everything that can be carried from hundreds of towns and villages – refuse, planks, watermelon rinds, a hotchpotch of absolutely everything.

Sashka, I'll never forget the way everyone fell silent the first time they saw a dead body float by, right up beside the barge, bloated, face downwards, we couldn't even tell if it was a man or a woman – with a grey plait.

Rushes, scanty willows, murky waves, a sandy plain all the way to the horizon. This desert view was relieved by heaps of sea salt and banks of earth – graves, it was explained to us later. Sometimes we saw deserted villages. We didn't come across a single living creature, apart from a pack of dogs. And black pigs also caught our eye, grubbing about on the silty banks of the river.

Soon Tong Ku appeared. From a distance we could see little yellowish-grey adobe houses, then large customs depots hove in sight, and warehouses, workshops, and a wharf cluttered with crates and bales.

We spent all night entraining right there on the wharf. Now they'll move us out. I don't know when I'll be able to write to you next. A fiery glow hangs over the town all night long. The air is filled with the smell of burning. They say the inhabitants are setting fire to their own homes, but they accuse the foreigners of doing it, to provoke greater hatred for them. Half of Tong Ku is already burnt out, but the fires are still burning, especially since no one is even trying to extinguish them,

Do you know what part of the body is the worst afflicted? The nose. Even now the repulsive smell of burnt reeds is wafting on the air, together with an odd, unfamiliar aftertaste on the wind that makes me feel nauseous. I think I've already learned to distinguish that special, sickly-sweet stench.

●

Volodenka!

My beloved! My joy!

I've got frozen in the coffin, my feet are blocks of ice.

How can I explain it to you? I eat, change my clothes, go shopping. But wherever I might be, I'm still dead.

I did my practical training too, in the emergency department – I saw all sorts of things.

But today's a day off, dark and frosty, I don't have to go anywhere in the morning. The heating is poor, the room is cold. The windows are iced over. I lay there under two blankets and thought about you. How are you over there? What's happening to you?

Then I forced myself to get up and did a bit of housekeeping. I could smell the rubbish bucket already starting to pong a bit and decided to take it to the tip.

A frozen yard. Trees covered in hoarfrost. Steam coming out of my mouth.

I went out and walked to the big rubbish skips. Steam coming out of their mouths too.

New Year trees draped in tattered tinsel, dumped in the dirty snowdrifts.

No one anywhere around.

I ask:

'Is that you?'

It says:

'Yes.'

I ask:

'The message and the messenger?'

It says:

'Yes.'

I say:

'Go away!'

It says:

'You don't understand.'

I say:

'I understand everything. Go away!'

It says:

'It's not even properly light yet and here's the sunset already. Look at what a crossopterygian it is, with that webbing on the winter branches! And the moon there's got out of the wrong side of the bed. Do you hear that music and laughter from the open window on the first floor – a feast in the time of head colds? And there's a pram on that balcony, the baby's woken up and it's bawling. Only just been born, and already kicking against the pricks. You know, I'm the one who made you love this world.'

I say:

'Yes. You made me love this world. Is that all you can do?'

It says:

'I know it's hard for you right now.'

I say:

'Can you do anything at all?'

It says:

'I know the names of all things and I can't do anything.'

I say:

'Why not?'

It says:

'The answer's a lemon. Didn't they teach you anything at all in school? Didn't you learn that there's a past, an absent and a future? In physics class you probably read thick novels under the desk, right? It's all a matter of light. That's what everything's made of. And warmth as well. And bodies are bundles of warmth and light. Bodies radiate warmth. A body can lose its warmth and become cold, but warmth remains warmth. Don't you understand that? For instance, you once had a date by a monument. But it's really a monument by a date. The monument's been whisked away, but that date's still there.'

I say:

'I can't live without him. I need him. Why isn't he here?'

It says:

'You said yourself that you have to share things. If you've been given something, you have to give it away in order to keep at least something. And the more precious someone is to you, the more you have to give away. And in general, it's only casual passers-by who stroll along, believing that everything terrible is already behind them. In one of those thick novels that you read under the desk, remember, the hero and heroine are somewhere close to each other all the time, but they don't meet and they suffer because they simply can't manage to meet and then, when they finally do meet, they realise they weren't ready for each other before. They still hadn't gone through all the suffering that was in store for them. Well, you're not ready for each other yet – you still haven't really suffered to the full. It only seems complicated, but it's actually very simple. Like those felt hammers.'

I ask:

'Simple as in easy?'

It says:

'Don't cavil over words. It's only a translation. You know that words, any words, are only a bad translation of the original. Everything happens in a language that doesn't exist. And those nonexistent words are the real ones.'

I ask:

'What do you want from me?'

It says:

'Take a look around. Everybody repeating their own selves, droning on about the same old thing, amazed that anyone can be Persian. There are whole lives with nobody alive in them, not even the people living there, they'll die without ever hatching out. Is that what you want then?'

I say:

'Yes.'

It says:

'But they walk along without even seeing that they're barely knee-high to a snowdrift.'

I say:

'But they know the most important thing.'

It asks:

'What? That a person is not obliged to be happy?'

I say:

'Yes. They know it. But I don't. I want to know that too.'

It asks:

'What is this, mutiny?'

I say:

'Yes.'

It says:

'Don't be silly.'

I say:

'I'm very tired of being myself.'

It says:

'It's just that you still don't know the way things happen. You forget your umbrella in a cafe and go back for it – and life takes a different turning. Remember, you went to that park of yours. It was snowing – small, dry grains that skipped about. You thought there was no one in the park but you, as if it was your own property. You walked up to a bench, brushed off the snow with your glove and sat down. And that boarded-up statue was there, right opposite you. When the blizzard howls on winter nights, she has time to think about what she did wrong. She stands there in her coffin – one hand up here, the other down there – and she changes. Becomes more herself. And she knows she'll get out soon. They'll open the lid, and there she is as if nothing has happened – one hand up here, the other down there. Here I am! Glad to see me? How have you been without me? What's new with you? Have they taken Troy yet? The same, but different, she's understood something over the winter. And this dog came running up to you. A spaniel, it sniffed at you, let you scratch it behind the ear, wagged its tail. And you sniffed at it, breathing in that delicious doggy smell. Then a girl with a lead appeared and told you straight away that she's taking ballet classes now and she knows all the positions, and you mustn't give Donka sweets, or she might get diarrhoea. The little girl has attached earlobes. And a slight squint. Then Yanka's professor appeared, and you recognised him immediately, but he didn't recognise you. He has big, fleshy ears, with tufts of hair, and the lobes hang right down to his collar. At first you thought the little girl was his early granddaughter, but he spoke to her the same way your father did to you – called her "childy". He had a child's enema bottle in his hand. He flung it and the dog chased after it through the trees, barking. Then he sat down beside you on the bench, clasping his hands together on his knees, and his fingers were strong, with peeling skin, corroded by solvent, and there were traces of paint on his nails. The little girl ran after the dog, and he said he hadn't read anything for a long time because writing should be done with the vigour of life – with tears, blood, sweat, urine, faeces, sperm – but they write with ink. And even then you wondered how many foolish girls he had told that to in his long life.'

I ask:

'So what?'

It says:

'Twists of fate should be given a helping hand.'

I ask:

'What for?'

It says:

'A twig in a bottle of water puts out roots. There's nothing for them to take hold of and they start clinging to each other.'

I say:

'I'm frozen.'

■

Sashenka!

My wonderful one!

How I envy them. Tired out after the day, and now they're sleeping. Snuffling, snoring, dreaming about their loved ones. I'm terribly tired too, but first I'll write to tell you what happened today.

We have been sent to Tientsin, that's halfway to Peking. There's still no telegraph connection. A detachment made up of soldiers from various countries set off to Peking under the command of the English admiral Seymour, including two Russian companies who went with him, but there's been no news at all from them.

Everyone here assumes that all the people besieged in the diplomatic quarter of Peking, who we are on our way to save, are no longer alive. There is, unfortunately, no one left to liberate. Those who have managed to break out say there was a massacre in the city, no Europeans were left alive and the missions were razed to the ground. The European detachment is still holding out in surrounded Tientsin and there is heavy fighting there. We have been sent to help them. We'll probably get there tomorrow or the next day.

There's a railway line running from Tong Ku to Tientsin, but it's in dismal condition – the sleepers have been burned, our linesmen have to dig the rails up or search for them in the villages where the peasants have hidden them.

A section of the dismantled line has been repaired after a crude fashion. We took a heavy jolting over the joints of the rails. There aren't enough sleepers or enough spikes to fix them with, so they lay one sleeper instead of three or four. The rails buckle and shift about. We rode along, expecting to end up at the bottom of the embankment at any moment. The telegraph poles along the line have been cut down to stumps. And the water pumps don't work – the soldiers had to fetch water for the locomotive from an abandoned village.

My Sashenka, you can't even imagine how dreary all this is. The region is a desert – the local inhabitants have hidden away, the houses have been reduced to rubble, the fields have been burned and trampled.

We travelled about halfway there. Then we stopped. What was repaired the day before had been rendered useless again overnight – the rails had been scattered about, some carried away altogether, there was no sign at all of any sleepers. We disembarked at some station or other or, rather, where there used to be a station. Not only had all the station's brick buildings been destroyed, even the stones of the foundations had been dug up and smashed into fine rubble. That's how much they hate everything of ours.

We marched along the road bed all day in tactical formation. The line follows the course of the river. The Pei Ho meanders along here, but we could still make it out in the distance all the time from the clumps of trees.

I was very thirsty, but there wasn't any water. The wells in the villages were poisoned and the river was polluted. On the first day our poor horses only sniffed at it and didn't drink, but then thirst got the better of them and now they drink this glop that looks like thin meat jelly.

So we have to treasure every sip.

And the little local mosquitoes never stop biting – my hands and neck have come out in big red blisters that itch unbearably. But that's only a small matter, of course.

The advance detachment has been ambushed twice, fortunately no one was killed, there are only several wounded, and then only lightly.

As we marched past the site of a battle, I saw the signs of war for the first time: dead horses, a broken rifle, an abandoned forage cap, bloody underwear.

What else is there in store for me to see? Is there anything in store for me?

I've become friends with an interpreter seconded to work with us. He's a student from the Faculty of Oriental Studies at Petersburg University by the name of Glazenap. His rucksack is crammed full of books, scrolls and proclamations that he picks up everywhere and holds right up to his nose to read. He has poor eyesight and spectacles with immensely thick lenses.

In one village we went into a joss house, already ravaged quite badly. Soldiers were ripping up books for the soft paper and our interpreter objected to this barbaric behaviour but, of course, he got nowhere.

It was a depressing sight – the large painted glass lanterns hanging in the shrine of the joss house and outside on the porch had all been smashed. The figures of the Chinese gods were sprawling on the floor with their stomachs and backs ripped open. Someone had told our men that the local people were in the habit of hiding gold and precious stones there.

I walked round and looked at everything, it was interesting. Full-length idols with ugly faces were still standing in some places at the sides, with pots of ash in front of them for sticking little candles into. The shrine was empty, the main idol was lying on the floor, with its head chopped off. I stood in front of the head for a moment. It lay on the nape of its neck, gazing at the inverted world with love and forbearance from under half-lowered eyelids. Blue dragons with gaping jaws twined around the columns with their gold scales glittering.

There were huge gongs there, and the soldiers started beating on them with big wooden hammers. Glazenap dashed over to take the hammers from them. He explained that it was bad to summon the spirits in vain and that dragons were a symbol of benevolence. The soldiers burst into raucous laughter.

I'm glad that this young man with his ecstatic love for the language of Confucius, Li Po and Du Fu has appeared in our detachment. He reminds me in some ways of Jules Verne's hero Paganel from *In Search of the Castaways*. Paganel was probably like that in his young days – awkward and lacking in confidence, but still a spunky little know-all. Today he taught us how to drink the brackish, slimy water from the Pei Ho by mixing it with the Chinese vodka, *huang jiu*.

Well then, Sashenka, I'll try to get to sleep now, although the blisters from the bites are itching terribly.

It's hard to believe that tomorrow there will be a battle in which I shall be killed or maimed.

You know, a man is constituted in such an incredibly strange way that he can easily believe in death all around him, but not in his own.

And another thing, very important. Perhaps it's because I'm waiting for my first experience of combat, I don't know, but I feel everything here more keenly, and everything around me, the entire world, is more honest with me – if that's the right word – more adult, more manly. I see everything differently, more clearly, as if some kind of veil through which I used to look at life before has fallen from my eyes. All my feelings are heightened, I hear the night around me with piercing clarity – every murmur and bird call and rustle in the grass. As if I had been living in some unreal world, but now I am beginning – the real me.

Without this feeling there would probably never be any wars.

In actual fact what I wanted to say was that I love you more and more every day. I just don't know how to write what I feel. If only we were together right now, I would take your face in my hands and kiss it – and that would be much more than I can write on these pages that I'm finishing off now without really having said anything.

Haven't I told you again and again that I love you? But now I feel as if I'm telling you for the first time. Because now I love you quite differently. The words are the same, but they mean far more to me.

I feel at ease now and glad, because I know that you will wait for me, no matter what happens!

I love you.

●

Volodya!

My darling! My only one!

I'm so happy that I have you!

You know, don't you, that the moles on people's skin wander about, appearing and disappearing, and can even switch bodies? I found one of your moles on me, can you imagine? Right here, on my shoulder. It's so wonderful!

I tired myself out running around town today and I can't get to sleep. You know how it is, tossing and turning, trying to find a cool spot in the bed, then it gets warmed up and you start looking for another one. So now there isn't even a tiny little island of coolness left, and there's still no sign of sleep.

Snatches of something or other in front of my eyes, whether they're open or shut. At two in the morning it's all the same – the visible world or the invisible one.

Or is it three already?

My thoughts run through time as if it was grass. Time doesn't grow evenly, there are bald patches in it. As if I'm walking to a watering place, always trampling the same spot.

The same pictures come to mind endlessly, always the ones I don't want.

I forgot my change in the shop and they came running after me, shouting:

'Miss, miss! Come back!'

In the tram someone sat down beside me and trapped the edge of my skirt, I had to pull it free.

Then this old couple got in, with their heads shaking – his saying no-no and hers saying yes-yes.

Yanka told me she and her beau went to a restaurant and left small change for a tip, and the waiter flung the change after them as they left.

I'm walking along the street and there's somebody's hand in an open window – either beckoning me in or driving a mosquito out.

The newspaper said that up in the North they found a plane with a broken ski prop and the frozen pilot with his fur boots burned – before he died he stuck his frozen feet into the fire to warm them up. But when his watch thawed out, it started working again.

And this scene is from my childhood – Daddy and I have been walking in the park, our shoes are all covered in mud, at the entrance he scrapes his sole against the edge of the pavement and the grass, and just for a moment it seems to me that he's trying to free himself from his shadow.

And here's Mummy making me my favourite milksop. She cuts the bread into little cubes and throws them into the bowl of warm milk, then sprinkles them with sugar and my throat suddenly contracts at the thought that she will die some day and this is what I'll remember – her making me milksop and sprinkling sugar from a teaspoon.

Chartkov invited me to a concert at the home of a female pianist he knows. She's tall and her legs are so long that she sat at the piano with them splayed out wide. Our seats were almost directly behind her, so we could see the reflection of her hands in the lid of the piano, as if she was playing a four-hand duet with herself. And her cheeks kept shaking all the time.

On our way back there was an accident, someone had been killed and was lying on the pavement with a newspaper over his face.

And now look, it's back again, the time I worked in an ambulance.

A woman who was trying to hang curtains fell and broke the same leg that she had already broken several times before.

A man who was tending a campfire snagged his foot on a branch and fell – they took the skin off his hands like gloves.

Another man's trouser leg got caught in the chain of his bike, he fell off and smashed his head against the kerb so hard that his eye was dangling on the nerve like a thread.

A child was eating ice cream on a stick, he started running, tripped and the stick pierced his larynx.

And on and on like that every day.

How can I escape from all this?

I was out walking with Chartkov and his little Sonya, she's so funny – she took pity on someone's old shoe that had been thrown out because now it couldn't walk any more and had to look at the rubbish tip all the time, and she moved it somewhere else so that it would have a view of lilac bushes. Then we reached the studio and she started drawing my portrait in profile: she sat me down sideways-on to the wall, pointed a lamp at me, pressed a piece of paper against the wall and started tracing round the shadow with a pencil.

Something should be done about her squint. I move my finger about in front of her little nose, one eye watches the finger, but the other pupil wanders.

Donka keeps trying to chew on my shoelace. I shook her, and then my hands had that delicious doggy smell too.

The studio always smells of paint, turpentine, charcoal, wood and canvas. The pictures stand facing the wall in the corner, as if they are being punished. Easels, stretchers, boxes of paints, oily brushes, palette-knives. Floors covered with bright splashes of colour. Unwashed dishes in the dirty sink. Mouse droppings in the corners.

The second time I came, he sat me on a splotchy, splattered stool, then took a piece of charcoal and set to work. Looking at me over the top of his spectacles. Sniffing, biting his lip, sticking out his tongue. Humming, moaning, whistling. Whispers, groans, sighs. The rustle of charcoal over heavy paper.

The sudden sound of a bell from the window – his place is opposite a school.

An old man with a broom in the schoolyard – he doesn't understand a thing, just like me.

It's so strange to pose. I'm just sitting there, looking out of the window, and the irrelevant and transitory becomes relevant, important.

And then some boys came running into the yard and started playing football with a doll's head. Lanky beanstalks. They're probably skipping physics or something – they'll miss something important, for instance, the Universe stopped expanding a long time ago and it's contracting at the speed of darkness. The doll's head somersaults, smacks against the asphalt with a hollow, ringing, joyful sound. And it jerks its plaits perkily as if to say, never mind, we'll break through, we're not done for yet, keep your pecker up!

He started telling me how he made sketches of his dying mother.

He says the primary canvas is a person's face, their expressions. Then the body. And then comes stone.

It's really the woman who inseminates, and the man who carries and gives birth.

The Houses of Parliament in London were burning, people were dying, but Turner tried to capture the colours of the fire in watercolour. Nero was no artist, but every artist is Nero.

We talked about Job too. He's not real, because he really didn't exist. But every living person is real. First everything is given to him, then everything is taken away. And without any explanations.

Yesterday I walked in and he was working in oils. I wanted so much to squeeze a living worm out onto a palette. So I stood there and squeezed one, then felt it with my finger.

Suddenly he said:

'Yes, paint has to be felt with the skin.'

He ran his palm across the palette and pressed his paint-smeared hand against my face.

My Sashenka!

I don't know when I'll be able to send this letter, but I'll write it anyway. So many different things have happened in recent days and it's only now that I can have a quiet talk with you. I'll tell you what's been happening to me in a moment, but first the most important thing – you are very dear to me. And the longer we are not together, the more powerfully I sense you.

I feel you beside me so strongly, it seems impossible to me that you can't feel it.

We're in Tientsin. How long have we been here already? Only three days. But it feels like three years. Or thirty-three.

Now I'll try to tell you about everything that's happening here. Our detachment has combined with Colonel Anisimov's detachment, who managed to hold out until we arrived. They have many casualties. The wounded are a really terrible sight.

The soldiers, absolutely exhausted after their time under siege, were led out from under the bombardment to our bivouac. For the first time since they set out from Port Arthur they were given a chance to catch up on their sleep, have a hot meal and take a wash. You should have seen how happily they washed their own underclothes in the murky waters of the Pei Ho.

We encamped on the left bank of the river, outside the city's earth wall, on a level, open area, but when grenades started flying in from the Chinese positions in the suburbs of Tientsin, we were ordered to move the camp further away. Our tents are pitched a verst from the Pei Ho and two versts from the settlement – that's what they call the European part of the city.

There's still no news from Seymour's combined detachment. He took with him to Peking about two thousand Englishmen, Russians, Germans, Americans and Italians. They set off along the railway, repairing the line as they went, but they have been surrounded somewhere, the lines have been cut off and ruined again.

As for the foreign embassies in Peking, it is already known for certain that they have been destroyed and the entire European population, together with the Chinese Christians, has been slaughtered. A Chinese who worked at the German embassy managed to escape by a miracle and told us what happened to the Russian legation in Peking; they burned the church and the church mission with its library, hospital and school. Their hatred is so strong that they even desecrated the Orthodox cemetery, dug up all the graves and scattered the bones about. In front of his very eyes they slit open the stomachs of a Russian family living at the mission and decapitated them.

There are various other rumours going around, each more terrible than the last. Nobody knows anything for certain.

I haven't been involved in the present battle yet and haven't seen the enemy from close up, or rather I've only seen bodies. The soldiers have a strange uniform – blue jackets, over which they wear sleeveless jerkins with red trimming and gilded buttons. And on their backs and their chests they have circles of white oiled cloth with black hieroglyphs on them that say what unit a soldier belongs to – they take the place of our epaulettes. On their legs and feet they wear breeches and cloth boots with thick felt soles. But it's rare to see anyone lying in full uniform – more often I see the corpses semi-naked. And for some reason all their mouths are open. I walk past and clouds of flies shoot up into the air.

The weather is unbearably hot, and everyone is tormented by the shortage of water. The soldiers have started digging wells, but there isn't enough water, the wounded suffer especially badly.

Yesterday they transferred the Russian infirmary to us from the besieged city. It used to be in the French hospital. Their tents are right beside ours. I can hear someone groaning at this very moment. And the doctor swearing at him. Our surgeon is called Zaremba. He often swears at the patients, but that's just for show. He tries to seem coarse, but in reality he's a warm-hearted man – he has shown everybody a photograph of his wife and son. He is simply very tired.

All day long they kept bringing more and more wounded on stretchers, I thought there would never be any end to it. Swarms of flies hovered over every one of them. There were no faces – they had sunk deep into the canvas. And all they could see from there was the sky. Many of them groaned at the jolting and one kept repeating over and over, just like a child:

'My leg, careful with my leg!'

How terrible that at any moment I could find myself being carried like that.

I've spoken with the wounded, they tell me appalling things about what happened here. One officer – Rybakov, both of his feet are crushed – has been here since spring, and he said that even before the start of events, Tientsin was teeming with Yihetuan, or 'Boxer Rebels', who organised clamorous meetings and pasted up exhortations to give short shrift to foreigners everywhere. Neither the army nor the police did anything to stop them, although until the allies took the Taku Forts by storm, the government was officially pursuing the rebels. In the Chinese section of the city marks made in blood appeared on houses in which Europeans or Chinese Christians lived – they slit dogs' throats, plastered their entrails on the gates and threw them in through the windows. Chinese who worked for foreigners started asking to be allowed into the concessions with their families, but they were not admitted at first. The gates were only opened to them after the Yihetuan started butchering entire families in the night. Sometimes they spared the children, but they cut their hands off. That was probably to intimidate others.

Sashenka, I realise I shouldn't write to you about all this but I'm sorry, I can't help it. I saw one boy myself – he had attached himself to the French hospital. They gave him a dry biscuit and he was sucking on it, clutched between his bandaged stumps.

Well then, on the very first night of the disorders, this Rybakov and his men were on duty in the gatehouse, defending the French concession. They heard a loud clamour from the Chinese section of the city and a bright glow filled the air there – that was the Catholic cathedral blazing. Frightened people started running towards their gatehouse. The Yihetuan had started setting fire to the houses of the Chinese Christians, hundreds of people had been killed. The senior priest of the cathedral managed to flee to the French concession. That same night brought the first attempt to storm the settlement, but it was beaten back.

It was already impossible for the European population to leave the city – the railway had been cut off, hundreds of women and children were besieged. In addition to Russians, Tientsin was defended by Germans, Englishmen, Japanese, Frenchmen, Americans, Austrians and Italians. Not even a thousand fighting men in all. This mere handful had to stand against tens of thousands of Yihetuan and a regular army. They couldn't withdraw, either to retreat or simply to move out of shelling range. The inhabitants of the concessions who were left in the city had to take up arms and defend themselves. Trenches were dug everywhere, streets that were being bombarded from across the river and from the direction of the Chinese city were barricaded off.

The Russians found themselves defending the railway station on the left bank of the river – the most unfavourable position of all. It had been decided to hold the station at any cost, because if it fell the Chinese would take the entire left bank and would be able to bombard the concessions, hiding behind the mounds of salt that cluttered the approaches, and the defenders wouldn't have held out even for a day.

Rybakov and his men spent several days at the station, where the fighting went on day and night. They made sorties to prevent any weapons that could fire directly over open sights from being brought in, and during one of these sorties he was wounded. He says he had already chosen the moment to shoot himself – he was terrified of being taken prisoner. But our men rescued him and carried him out of the line of fire.

Sashenka, I've seen that railway station through my binoculars – all that's left of it now is a scorched, bullet-scarred ruin.

The bombardment of Tientsin has not stopped even now, we can hear explosions in the city as the Chinese army shells the European quarters. The French concession has suffered worst of all – that was where the Catholic missionaries hated so much by the Yihetuan lived. And that was where the Russian consulate was located, and the Russo-French hospital.

The shelling comes from the outskirts of the city and the artillery school, located on a high embankment by the river opposite the German concession. They say about three hundred young Chinese officers were studying there, the Germans had supplied them with the very latest guns. The European instructors fled, but one who tried to damage the sights was torn to pieces and his head is still displayed on a bamboo pole. That is what they say, at least, and the head could be seen through binoculars only yesterday. Today the Germans and the English took the school by storm. Our allies and the Chinese both suffered heavy losses.

Another wounded man, by the name of Verigo, spent all this time in the concession. There was incessant fighting there too. People kept their clothes on night and day and barely slept at all. They couldn't set up a camp – as soon as they pitched the tents, shells started falling on them. The firing was directed from the city – the Chinese there signalled to their men where to fire. People and horses had to be hidden behind walls, along the streets and in the buildings, and spread out as thinly as possible. But even then they suffered almost as many losses as when they were in battle position, because in all the concessions there wasn't a single corner that wasn't covered by artillery or small-arms fire. The buildings provided poor protection. Bullets flew in through the windows and doors and shells pierced straight through the walls. Women and children hid in the basements.

Both of Verigo's hands are strapped to his chest. The unfortunate man can't do anything himself, his wounded comrades help him, but still he jokes about his helplessness. He was wounded by a burst of shrapnel on the bridge.

Surprisingly enough, the Chinese have better weaponry than we do. Here is what Verigo said, word for word:

'They have the latest artillery and a large stock of shells, supplied by the Germans, and we have obsolete guns. We fired only one shot in reply to five of theirs. And as for rifles, now every coolie has a Mauser or a Mannlicher!'

The railway station is connected to the city by a floating bridge that is made out of wooden barges so that it can be opened up to allow junks through. The bridge was bombarded constantly and many of our soldiers were killed there. Every day burning boats loaded with dry reeds were launched downstream against it, and the barges had to be moved apart under fire.

The nurse who was caring for the wounded Russians in the French hospital has come to our field infirmary with them. She's a Parisienne and they call her simply Lucie. Very pleasant, straightforward and competent, with her hands all red from mercuric chloride. She seems frail, but she can easily change a bed under the wounded man lying in it. She has a large, ugly mole on her neck, which she feels embarrassed about. She keeps putting her hand over it without realising. I don't know how she came to be in China. She speaks almost no Russian, but everyone here has really fallen in love with her.

Last night one soldier in the infirmary started screaming despairingly. Our tents are very close by. It was impossible to sleep and I went out to see what was happening. The unfortunate young man screaming had had both legs amputated the day before. They tried to calm him down, but he only yelled even louder and lashed out, so that he had to be restrained by force. They gave him an injection of morphine, but he didn't settle down and he woke all the wounded men. Dr Zaremba flew into a fury and stalked out, saying:

'Let him scream. He'll soon stop when he gets hoarse!'

Then Lucie sat down beside him, took his head in her arms and started comforting him, in French at first, and then she repeated the few Russian words that she knew:

'Yes? No? Good! Good! Papa! Mama!'

The poor legless man, who had probably never been caressed by any woman's hand before, apart from his mother's, gaped at her with his insane eyes, then calmed down, fell silent and went to sleep.

Every night someone dies in the infirmary. They are taken to a separate tent, but in this heat they don't keep them there for long. Today they buried eight men. I saw two of them alive and well only yesterday morning, and in the evening they were brought back on stretchers: one had been hopelessly wounded by a bullet that passed straight through his throat, and the other in the stomach. The first one died that evening, but the second, Captain Popov, carried on suffering until the morning, groaning and wheezing both when he was delirious and when he came round. He had got married recently.

There were no planks for coffins — they were buried in sacks. The soldiers carrying the dead men hid their noses in their forage caps. One of the sacks looked too small — after the shell exploded, only the shoulders, arms and head were left intact, everything else had been blown to pieces.

They buried them half a verst from the camp on a low hill. Nailed together one cross for all of them and stuck it in the dry clay. The grave the dead were buried in was shallow — the men didn't have the strength to dig a deep pit in the blazing-hot sun.

You know, Sashenka, as I listened to the muttering of the funeral service and looked at the soldiers shooting over the grave, thoughts that were quite inappropriate to the moment crept into my mind. The American Indians fired arrows into the air from their bows in order to drive away evil spirits, and we call shooting our guns at military funerals a farewell salute. But it's the same ritual that the Indians observed when they shot arrows into the sky. And the men lying in the sacks under the clay don't need any of it.

We walked back in silence, every man thinking the same thing: perhaps tomorrow he would be carried off in an empty oats sack and the soldiers would hide their faces from the stink in their forage caps.

While I was just writing these lines to you, my comrade Kirill Glazenap came into the tent. He is totally despondent. He told me that he had interpreted at the interrogation of a Chinese captured by our soldiers in a nearby village. The man had protested to them that he wasn't a Yihetuan, but he had just been shot all the same.

Sashenka, I have to get used to everything here.

Now everything all around has gone quiet, I can't hear any more shots or explosions. Only someone groaning in the infirmary and snoring from the next tent. A mouse gambolling about in a crate of provisions.

It has got dark, but even now it is still hot and stuffy and the mosquitoes have launched their attack again. I'm bitten all over from my head to my feet. There's no comparison with our simple mosquito, who warns of his approach from a distance. These are invisible and inaudible, just a sudden bite. No escape. And they transmit malaria. They gave out special nets today, but they turned out to be too small. Now the soldiers are sitting and sewing themselves canopies out of two nets each, so that they can sleep under them.

My dearest, I'm not complaining, don't think that, it's just that I'm very tired after these last days, because in the daytime I'm always thinking of staying alive and at the same time I desperately want to sleep – I sit down for a moment and I start dreaming – but at night, when I lie down to rest, it's impossible to free myself of the impressions of the day.

I close my eyes, but I still see that boy with the stumps, holding them out to a mug of tea that has been offered to him. I turn over onto my other side, and the bridge leading to the ruined railway station is there in front of my eyes again. I was there yesterday and I saw them open it to let through the dead bodies that had accumulated overnight. I don't know what's happening there, upstream, but the current brings an endless procession of dead. One had his hands tied behind his back. I only saw the twisted fingers, I thought they were moving, but that was the effect of a wave.

My darling, forgive me for having to describe such sad and terrible things. But this is my life now.

I long so much to get away from all of this, to hide somewhere, lose myself in something else – to remember something from my childhood, my room, the books, you and me. To think about something good and dear to me.

There now, I started rereading my letter and it has made me sad – there is so little tender feeling for you in it and I have so much in me.

Now I reproach myself because when we were together I had so many opportunities to show you my love and I didn't think about it. And now you are so far away that I can't do anything for you – I can't hug you or kiss you or run my hand over your hair. Love requires demonstration, not proof. How I long to buy you flowers! I never bought you any, did I? Only once, remember, I picked some lilac for you in our park. And I want to go with you and buy you something unnecessary, feminine – a ring, a brooch, earrings, a handbag. I always used to think all that was stupid nonsense, only now have I realised how important it is and what it's all needed for. Only here has the understanding dawned of why unnecessary things are so essential!

Now that I've mentioned how essential unnecessary things are, I've remembered a neighbour I used to call round to see when I was little. She seemed a hundred years old to me then. Probably she was. She had thick, bandaged legs, on which she could barely even walk, leaning on the back of a chair. She pushed the chair forward and then dragged her legs up to it. Mum said she had water in her legs, a bucketful in each one. I can see her as if it was now. The pins sticking out of her grey bob of hair, her eyes watering, her trembling fingers, swollen at the joints. Her ears were huge, with the lobes stretched from wearing earrings, and there was always cotton wool sticking out of them, because they suppurated. I wasn't afraid of her, she always had a sweet or a honey cake ready for me, but what I really went there for was the chemist's rubber bands from the potions and powders – she kept them for me on the window handles, and I needed them for the catapults that I crafted out of bobbins and pencils.

She was strange and she always spoke about things that I didn't understand. She used to sit down slowly on her chair in front of the mirror and start telling me that in there, in the mirror, she wasn't real, but once she had been real and pretty. I nod, but she can see I don't believe her and she starts showing me old photographs. But the only thing I remember from them is the gondolas. She used to tell me how a gondolier guides his gondola though a narrow channel and pushes off from the walls of the houses with his foot.

One time she said:

'I forget what I ought to remember, but that gesture, the gondolier pushing off with his foot, I remember that.'

She often used to tell me something and then add:

'You won't understand now. Just remember it.'

And look, I've remembered about the gondolier's gesture and only now realised how important the unnecessary things are.

And I also remember that I asked her about something and she answered:

'That's why!'

She pulled me towards the mirror and pressed her cheek against mine.

I don't remember the question at all, but her answer has stuck in my mind: We both look in the mirror and I see my seven-year-old face and her wrinkles, the old, flabby skin, the hairs above her lips and on her chin, the bushy eyebrows, I catch her unpleasant, old woman's smell and try to break free quickly, but she's holding my head tight.

I came back home after the summer holidays and she wasn't there. They told me she had gone away. I believed them then.

But I've just thought: Where are those two bucketfuls of water that she carried about in her bandaged legs? Perhaps they have mingled with the waves of the Pei Ho?

I just read that again and wondered: How did this old woman, whom probably no one remembers apart from me, end up here with me and you? It isn't important.

The only thing that is important, my Sashenka, is that we are together. And nothing can separate us.

I'm responsible for you, after all! That means I can't simply disappear – someone has to take care of you, love you, think about you, share everything with you, delight in your successes, share your misery. There, you see, I absolutely cannot disappear!

It's only now, so far away from you, my darling, that I realise how little I told you about my love, about how much I need you! I cling to you as I do to life itself. It's hard to explain, but the very fact that I still breathe and see – all that is only because I love you.

●

Volodenka!

I can't really think how to explain this to you, but I know you'll understand.

I'm getting married.

He proposed to me today.

It was very funny, we went to a restaurant, and he let me go through the door first – they have revolving doors there – and I wanted to say something to him, so I leaned my head back, but just at that moment he leaned down towards me, and I hit him on the nose with the back of my head. Poor thing, he started bleeding. He sat right through the grand festive dinner with his head held back and bloody cotton wool in his nose.

He said he had already applied for a divorce.

He checked to see if the bouquet of flowers in the vase was real or paper and then asked:

'Yes?'

I nodded.

And went out to the toilet.

The window was open there and I could hear the sound of rain, it had been threatening since the morning. As I washed my hands I thought: 'What am I doing? What for?'

Then a woman about forty years old came in and started putting on eyeliner. Muttering to herself:

'I don't want to pull myself together.'

Then she started putting on scent: she sprayed it up into the air from the bottle and stood under the cloud.

She put on her lipstick, squinting at me in the mirror. And probably she read in my eyes who she was for me – an old, fading woman whom no lipstick in the world could help any longer.

I went back to the table and everybody – especially the waiters – looked at us with mocking eyes.

He talked about homelessness and asked what was the point of painstakingly decorating a compartment in a random railway carriage where you would only spend the night between points A and B.

I smelled of the fragrance of that other woman in the toilet, and he decided he wanted to give me a present, so after the restaurant we went to buy perfume. He probably tried everything they had in the shop, spraying my wrists, pulling up my sleeves and then, when there was no more free skin left on my arms, he sprayed my neck and then himself, and every time he wrinkled up his face and said it wasn't my scent but some other woman's. So in the end he didn't choose anything. And I walked down the street in a thick fur coat of fragrances and started feeling nauseous.

I still haven't told you the most important thing – I'm expecting a child.

Now that I've written those words – I'm expecting a child – I want to write them again.

I'm expecting a child.

All the time I imagine what it's like. The size of a pumpkin seed. Or an earlobe. Or a thimble. Or a scrunched-up stocking. Nine centimetres, forty-five grams. I examined a photograph in a book – the spine is already clearly visible, you can even count the vertebrae.

Mummy told me that when she was carrying me, she had a craving for everything bitter – Daddy said she had a bitter tooth. And I strike a match on the box and lick its hot emery-paper side. We used to do that when we were children. Is that terrible? I guzzle halva too. I open a pack and an instant later there's nothing but crumbs.

And I also suddenly had the thought that this was why the world could not have been created. I mean from the way that I or, rather, someone inside me, wants to sniff into herself the smell of a match after it has scraped along the side of the box. No imagination would be enough to create that, there has to be knowledge. And only I can know this. You understand, there are details that no creator could invent. They can only be seen, experienced, remembered.

I have a ferocious appetite, but everything is vomited straight back up. In the morning, as regular as clockwork, and sometimes in the middle of the day at work. I can smell my own bad breath all the time now. Once I didn't get to the bathroom in time – I held my mouth shut with my hand, but everything broke out and spurted through my fingers. I felt terribly ashamed, although what is there to be ashamed of in this?

Female animals don't have nausea and vomiting when they're pregnant, though – only humans do. We're unfortunate animals altogether, in every way, even this one.

It's so exhausting that sometimes I simply lie down for hours with a basin beside the bed, waiting and feeling afraid.

I store up the flesh inside me and count the moons.

I feel myself becoming different. Smooth movements. Glistening eyes. A sweet lethargy. Graze directed inward. Why do I need the visible world, if the invisible one is ripening within me? The visible is receding, shamefaced. Preparing to give way to what is still invisible.

I have an amazing feeling, as if I'm involved in the formation of a new planet that will bud off from me when the time comes, as if I am life's sister and a close relative of every tree. I tousle the hair on Donka's shoulders and think: my doggy, you and I have a common albuminous ancestor, do you understand? She does understand! Look, she has a navel and so do I. And we are linked together by those navels. I scratch her belly and she wags her tail happily. And I'm chock-full of happiness like her, only I don't have a tail for thumping so joyfully on the parquet floor!

Donka's funny and silly. I point to something in the distance and she looks at the finger. She also likes it when I pull my sandals off my weary feet and lie down for a moment, then she arranges herself beside me and licks my toes. It's so ticklish! And her tongue's rough.

But the most important thing is that inside this blob inside me, the next life is already maturing, and the next one after that and so on without end. I'm simply stuffed full of future lives! In school I couldn't imagine infinity at all – but here it is, under my hand.

I look at the women around me and it seems strange that, when they have an opportunity like this, they walk about empty.

And another strange thing – I'm different, but it's the same familiar reflection in the mirror. And my stomach hasn't started growing yet.

But at night I wake up sweating in fear that I might give birth to something wrong. I lie there, trying to forget how they showed us a lump of meat with fur and teeth or a half-child, half-flounder with both eyes on the same side of its head.

And these fears make me look terrible in the morning. But this is what Mummy said to console me, she'll always find something good to say:

'The meaning of a flower, any flower, is only to wither and leave behind a plain seed box.'

My father, when he gets drunk, calls me and asks me not to hang up and rejoices that he's going to be a grandfather. He babbles all sorts of nonsense.

'Look here, if I feel like it, I'll have kids too, and I'll have a grandson older than my own children! You have a boy for me!'

I say I've got no time to talk and hang up.

Mummy has also given me a bra with a big hook and a suspender belt to go with it, with a fastener that moves along as the time advances.

She gives me advice all the time:

'If you notice cloudiness in your urine, go to the doctor straight away! When I was carrying you, I had albumen in mine.'

I started thinking about something and biting my hangnails, and she gave me a loud slap on the hand, like she used to do when I was little.

It's strange, when she starts reassuring me that everything will be all right, it only makes me feel more anxious.

His studio is now our shared homelessness.

I walk around, learning everything all over again – here are the teaspoons, here's the teapot, but where's the tea? To be precise, I'm domesticating his non-residence.

I wander through the drawers of the kitchen buffet – on my honeymoon trip.

And every forty-five minutes I hear the school bell from the yard.

There's also a sound of banging all the time – a sculptor works in the next-door studio. Hammering on his chisel with his mallet from early in the morning. He borrowed a book to read and gave it back covered in stone dust.

Sonechka comes to us twice a week. He's told her that soon she'll have a little sister or brother. She's decided it's a brother. And every time she asks:

'How's my little brother doing?'

I laugh.

'Fine!'

He takes her to ballet school. The last time I went with them. She holds his hand, but she won't give her hand to me. She asks him:

'So aren't you and Mummy ever going to get married again?'

He explains to her that now he's going to live away from home all the time.

And she says:

'But I'm still your very best girl, aren't I, Daddy?'

'Yes.'

And she looked at me with a triumphant air.

I went there with them for the first time in early spring, there was already a hint of damp in the wind, but it was still getting frosty by evening time. We step on ice-crusted puddles and the crunch is joyful. But before it cracks, the thin ice whines.

We arrive at the dance class from out of the frost and the ballet shoes are cold. He lifts them up to his mouth and breathes into them, warming them up.

And suddenly I wanted so much to take ballet classes too. Oh, why didn't Mummy put me in a ballet school when I was little!

The sound of shuffling feet and rustling muslin. The girls sit in rows on the floor in the corridor, pulling on woolly leg-warmers over their stockings. The teacher – a former ballerina – manoeuvres along the corridor with a straight back, stepping between their legs. Parents and grandmothers in fur coats take seats along the walls. The accompanist warms his hands on a radiator.

'Chin up, higher! Stretch that instep! The instep! A straight back! The legs must be as straight as a compass! The back! The head! Don't stick your tongue out!'

Five positions – five chords. They froze in the fifth position.

Looking at them, I felt such a burning desire to be small and light and do exercises at the ballet barre, starting with the basics, all the positions, the plié, the préparation! I'll definitely send my child to ballet classes. Perhaps it will be a little girl. But what difference does it make! I love him or her already.

All the girls there especially liked doing curtsies.

Yesterday he worked with her at home and explained perspective, he's really good at explaining everything.

'Look, the world is held up by perspective the way a picture is held up by a string hanging from a nail. If it weren't for that nail and string, the world would fall and smash to pieces.'

And then I watch as she takes a picture in some magazine and draws pencil lines from everything along a ruler – back to a single point. Strings running from every chair, flower, hand, foot, eye and ear to a single small nail. I walked over to her and said:

'You do that really well!'

And she answers:

'Do you know what a Chinese burn is?'

'No.'

'Shall I do it?'

'Go on then.'

She took hold of my wrist with both hands and suddenly twisted them hard in opposite directions. I almost howled out loud from the pain. A red welt, my skin's burning.

I smiled at her.

It's her fighting me for him.

My Sashenka!

What a fine, warm feeling I have now that I've written your name on the first line – Sashenka!

How are you getting on? What's happening with you? I think

about you all the time. And I feel so glad to know that in your thoughts you are always with me.

I know you think about me and fret. Don't be anxious, my darling! Look, if I'm writing these lines, it means that nothing has happened to me. I'm writing, so I'm still alive.

Only when will you get this letter? And will you get it at all? But you know what they say: The only letters that don't get there are the ones that are never written.

You're probably trying to imagine what's happening with me, what I look like now, what I eat, how I sleep, what I see all around me. Well then, while I've been granted a free moment, I'll try to describe our life here to you.

During the first few days, as I wrote to you, there was constant fighting, but now there's a calm, only sometimes I hear exchanges of artillery fire.

The unbearable heat is still tormenting me as badly as ever, but now a strong wind has blown up, a genuine sandstorm. It brings fine sand from the Gobi desert and every single thing is covered with a layer of this yellow dust, it insinuates itself into the tents, my food grates on my teeth all the time. Dust in my eyes, in my ears, inside my collar, in my pockets – it's disgusting.

We want rain, but it's not subject to the general service regulations. Everyone here is dreaming of rain – then we could collect some clean water. After our men bathed in the Pei Ho, they came out in a rash all over their bodies. The doctor said it was caused by corpse liquor. There's not much water in the wells that have been dug, and even that's bad. They leave a guard on every well at night – out of fear that they'll be poisoned.

New units keep arriving all the time and our camp has already stretched out to a verst in length. It was set up in fields of kaoliang, but that has all been trampled down now.

Now I'll describe our surroundings to you.

To the south the ruins of Chinese villages are visible. The inhabitants have fled and pigs and dogs wander among the charred walls – sometimes our men hunt them. The dogs are the worst, they've turned completely feral and attack everyone with vicious fury. The villages here are generally dirty and poor.

In the foreground there are several clumps of trees. The whiteness of the tents, set out in straight rows, contrasts with the green background. The horses stand in a long line along the hitching rail, shaking their heads – there are clouds of flies hovering over them.

The staff headquarters tent is noisy. The mats were dragged in from a ruined *fanza*, or Chinese house, nearby. Instead of desks there are empty shell crates. They've just boiled up some tea, they say it's the only thing that helps to survive the heat.

And right there in front of me is the infirmary. I've already written to you about this grim propinquity.

On the left between the tents I can see the range-finders bustling around their prismatic telescope on its tripod.

At a slight angle to my right, soldiers are cleaning their rifles under a canvas awning. I catch the scents of lubricating grease and hear the metallic scraping of cleaning rods and brushes being pulled through barrels.

Further away is the kitchen. Today they killed a cow when I was there. A whole heap of innards came tumbling out, and I was amazed at how they could all have fitted inside it. Are there really all sorts of entrails inside us as well? Inside me? They buried it all – together with the eyes. It turns out that cows have huge eyes, the size of an apple.

But more often we eat horseflesh. It tastes rather like beef. At the very edge of the camp they are digging new pits, further away.

They set up the toilets without thinking about it properly and the wind brings in an incredible stench from them.

My Sashenka, I don't expect you find all this interesting. But now this is me.

In the middle of the bivouac, where the kitchen and the large tent allocated for the officers' mess stand, there's a large burial mound, with lower mounds scattered all around it. You'll smile, but we are living in a graveyard in the most literal meaning of the word.

Their burial mounds are everywhere here, they cover the whole area surrounding Tientsin. Kirill Glazenap told me all about them. The fact is that they don't have any graveyards like ours, but in every field cultivated by each family a corner is always given over to the ancestors. They don't bury their dead, on the contrary, they make a small pile of earth on the ground, on which they stand the coffin, then heap earth up on top of it. This produces a cone-shaped mound, the size of which depends on the size of the coffin and the importance of the deceased. The outside of this mound is plastered with a mixture of clay and straw to produce something that looks like a Kirgiz nomad tent. They believe that ancestors help their grandchildren. And so they do – our soldiers dislike these mounds very much, because every one of them is a ready-made hiding place for a marksman. We have to be on our guard all the time.

The soldiers who spend hours at a time in covert posts also say that there are many snakes here, but I haven't seen a single one of the vile beasts so far. I don't remember if I told you or not that when I was a scruffy little boy, I grabbed a bundle of kindling for a campfire, and a viper slithered out of it and plopped down onto the ground. I've had the jitters all my life after that. There are more than enough petty nuisances here without any creeping reptiles – I reach into my pocket for a lump of sugar and it's full of ants.

Alas, this is a lull for us, but not for death. We have to carry on burying just as before, almost every day, but now we don't put up any crosses and we try to make the grave inconspicuous. The first mass grave that I wrote to you about was dug up at night by the Chinese, the bodies were mutilated and scattered about. That's how much they hate us. It was noticed in the morning because a sentry from one of the outposts spotted a dog with a gnawed human hand in its teeth.

A tug has gone off downstream to Taku with two barges full of refugees from Tientsin. Exhausted women and children, plus their belongings.

The railway lines are being hastily repaired so that it will be possible to bring in munitions and men. The locomotives have all been damaged and the Americans and our railway engineers are trying to get them into working order. The telegraph team is restoring communications, but everything is in short supply, especially poles, and instead of insulators they use bottles.

Sometimes we mingle with the allies – there are new units arriving here every day. Yesterday our officers invited the Japanese officers to be our guests. When the difficulties of fighting the Yihetuan came up in conversation one Japanese, who spoke fairly decent Russian, declared:

'The valour of the Chinese consists in the following!' – and he set his hand down on a table dotted with flies, which all flew away, of course.

'You see, and now I've taken my hand away, the flies have come back. The Yihetuan are the same as these flies. They kill us from under cover, and when we move into the attack, they hide, only to come back again later.'

Then he swatted several flies very deftly with his open hand.

I must say that the exceptional discipline and fatalistic courage of the Japanese is very impressive. Perhaps this is why they have the very heaviest casualties. They are commanded by General Fukushima, famous for riding from Petersburg to Vladivostok on horseback. The Japanese march in a very funny manner, with a cramped sort of stride.

All in all, we make up a very picturesque company here.

The Americans' soft, wide-brimmed hats make them look like rakish cowboys. They fight well, too, but their discipline is not outstanding. Watching them I feel as if I'm in one of Mayne Reid's novels.

There aren't many genuine Frenchmen here, only Zouaves brought in hastily from Indochina. They're not much like regular troops and are very belligerent.

The English have Sepoys here – tall and clean-limbed, in yellow-and-red turbans. There is always an English officer in command of each company and the Sepoy officer, who is sometimes three times the age of his commander, carries out the duties of a subaltern. I don't think the English could rely on them entirely. The Sepoys salute by pressing their hands to their turban and their chest.

There are only a few dozen Austrians here, but their national flags are so large that one would cover all of them at once.

Italy is represented by a company of Bersaglieri – alpine marksmen. They all look as if they came straight out of a picture in the *Pictorial Review*. Hats with cock's feathers, naked calves, with small carbines in their hands. They smile at everyone.

Today I saw some Germans in their awkward brown jackets. One of them had been taken ill in the blazing sun, his comrades had dragged him into the shade and were fanning him. In general, men often collapse from the heat here.

Sometimes all this reminds me of a strange kind of masquerade – all these uniforms, fine outfits, helmets, turbans. People used to dress up for carnivals in order to thumb their noses at death. Is that what we're doing here?

Another point worth noting is that the relationship between the allies is extremely amicable, even among the men. But how could it be otherwise when they have to share the same deprivations and dangers and come to each other's aid in battle?

Do you know what is really remarkable? Mingling here with our forage caps are the white helmets of the English, the round blue headgear of the French, the German helmets, the turbans of the Sepoys, the rakishly downturned hats of the Americans, the small white kepis of the Japanese – and I get the feeling that a genuinely united human family does exist and all the wars that were fought by our ancestors have retreated into the past. We are probably in the last war.

Sometimes, when I'm not on duty, I drop into the wounded men's tents to sit and listen to their conversations for a while. Today in one of the tents they were discussing the artillery. The commander of the second battery, Anselm, whose elbow had been shattered and his nose mutilated by shrapnel – he had effectively been left with one arm missing and a disfigured face, but was still delighted to have got off so lightly – well, he told us that the Chinese were firing from the very latest Krupp guns with smokeless powder, from positions completely concealed by railway embankments and outside the city's earth wall.

It is amazing to see a man with a bandaged face, who is going to be a disfigured freak for the rest of his life, not giving way to dejection, and even finding the strength to laugh and support the other wounded men. I can't help thinking: Could I do that?

The Cossacks display exceptional endurance when they are

wounded. One Amur region Cossack, Sergeant Savin, had his jaw shattered and his tongue has swollen up so much that it won't fit in his mouth, but he still tries to smile at the fact that he has been bound up like a woman.

You remember I wrote to you about Rybakov, whose feet had been crushed? One of his legs has been amputated at the knee. He says he can still feel it. And when I was thinking about him I imagined that after death a man can probably still feel his whole body, which doesn't exist any more.

They bring new wounded every day. Today is a happy exception. The living are still alive and the unharmed still unharmed. But yesterday they brought in a courier who had been sent to us, they say he came under fire accidentally – in the darkness a frightened sentry took him for a spy. There weren't any stretchers, and they carried the poor man in on a door taken from a ruined house. He was wounded in the groin and is in terrible agony. His suffering is only increased by the thought that he might die from one of our bullets and not by the enemy's hand. They are afraid that he might develop blood poisoning. Men die from that more often than from their actual wounds.

I have really taken a liking to the fiery Zaremba, our surgeon. When he is in a good mood, he starts making everyone laugh with his stories about how he worked for several years at our mission in Peking. He understands a little Chinese. Today over tea he recalled how a young Chinese once came to him and explained about his mother's illness. Zaremba gave the young man some medicine, but he didn't take it to his mother, instead he swallowed it himself there and then. It didn't seem at all strange to the young man that his mother was supposed to be healed by medicine that her son had taken! This gives some idea of the level of development of the Chinese.

The surgeon has a great deal of work to do. He has just gone to perform an operation now – they've brought a soldier from a team of sappers who has developed gangrene. He begged them to leave him his leg. I heard Zaremba cut him short:

'I never amputate unnecessarily.'

And he ordered the chloroform mask to be applied by force. You know, the other day I sniffed the mask, out of curiosity – tasteless, warmish air with a smell of rubber.

Sometimes I manage to exchange a quick couple of words with Lucie. Yesterday evening she was helping the surgeon's assistant change a dressing, they had to pull off bandages that had dried on to the wound. In his pain the patient clung tightly to her arms. Lucie showed me her wrists with a smile – they were black and blue. She is proud of those bruises.

It turns out that Lucie became a nurse out of necessity. She tried to leave the city with the last train of refugees that set out from Tientsin to Taku, but it came under fire and the unfortunate people – the carriages were crowded with women and children and wounded – had to turn back, the railway line had already been ruined. They were all obliged to stay in the besieged city and endure the ferocious bombardment. She couldn't simply stay there and do nothing, so she went to the hospital to help as a volunteer. She could have left with the other refugees now, but for the time being she has decided to stay in our infirmary. Indeed, Lucie, with her warmth and affection, is needed by the men every bit as much as their medicine.

When I talk to her, my eyes involuntarily attach themselves to that incongruous mole, she notices my glance and covers it with her hand, and that makes things awkward.

The men are drawn to her. That's quite understandable. So many men, torn away from home, from their nearest and dearest. Every one of them wants a drop of tenderness, a human word, human warmth. But Lucie is equally affectionate with everyone and doesn't allow anyone close. I think the only exception made here is for Glazenap. I often see them together, discussing something animatedly. The nurse has a light, agreeable laugh. Now Kirill has just come back from her to our tent and collapsed onto the camp bed and is sighing silently. He wipes the sand dust off his spectacles, with lenses as thick as the bottoms of water glasses. I tried looking through them once – it only made my eyes hurt.

The thick darkness is advancing rapidly here at this moment. The crickets and frogs have started up their evening songs. And the mosquitoes are back again already. I can hear cursing and slaps on all sides.

I wait for darkness, so that things will become at least slightly more comfortable but, on the contrary, the wind dies down, the earth gives out the heat accumulated during the day and the air becomes absolutely stifling.

Today's sandstorm has left a coating of sand on everything. It even grits on my teeth. I want to rinse out my mouth all the time. But the worst thing is the thirst. I constantly raise my flask to my lips although, to be honest, this water only makes me feel worse. My face and my entire body are streaming with sweat. And the dust sticks to my skin, covering it in a thick, sticky film. Well, that's enough complaining from me. This is all trivial nonsense, believe me!

And another thing I know now, my Sashenka, is that war is not only battles, explosions and wounds, no, it is also endless waiting, uncertainty, boredom. And this is where Kirill's companionship is my salvation. We talk about everything under the sun and sometimes argue or even quarrel and get angry with each other, but not for long: afterwards we forget that we quarrelled and start talking about something again.

I'm sure you would like him. Although Glazenap does have certain habits that I find irritating – for instance, waving his arms about vigorously during a conversation and grabbing the other person by the sleeve – I feel close to him and find him very likeable. I like his judicious voice and his intelligent eyes, shrunk by the lenses of his spectacles. He can only sleep if he puts a little embroidered Chinese pillow under his head – it's stuffed with a special kind of tea and has a little hole for his ear. And the aroma of that tea, so he claims, is very good for the eyes.

He always tells me such amusing things! For instance, how do you like this story? The vital energy that permeates and connects everything all around us is called *chi* by the Chinese. And the *chi* can be influenced by music. In former times, in order to determine if an army was ready for battle, a musician would stand among the soldiers and blow into a special trumpet, and he drew his conclusion from the sound. If the trumpet sounded feeble, then the martial spirit was likewise, which augured defeat. In this case the general ordered his army not to join battle but retreat. Did you smile?

When the opportunity offers, Glazenap practises calligraphy. He has a whole set of brushes. And the ink is in briquettes – sticks that he grates on a stone ink slab, in a hollow with water. But there isn't very much paper, and he often writes on a board or sheet of canvas, dipping the brush into plain water. Several hieroglyphs, written from the top downwards, make up a poem. As he finishes writing the poem, the beginning is already starting to disappear in the sun and the wind. Sashenka, if only you could see how wonderful that is!

You see, sometimes we have quite a good time here.

I'm sorry, I tried to joke, but it turned out stupid.

It's just that I grab at every opportunity to take my mind off things.

Today Kirill was practising his calligraphy and I wanted so much to try that I couldn't resist and made a few strokes myself. Glazenap remarked condescendingly that my stroke looked like a section of bamboo, and I felt inexpressibly proud, but that proved to be a mistake. Just imagine, a brushstroke should not resemble the head of a sheep or the tail of a rat or the leg of a stork, or a broken branch, that is, anything real at all. I know now that a horizontal stroke is like a cloud that stretches for ten thousand li. I've decided not to practise calligraphy any more.

Apparently the ancient writing began as a record of the procedure for offering sacrifice. The pictures showed scenes of the rite with the participants and the ritual utensils. That is all very understandable. But then something amazing happened! You see, it turned out that the mystery had become accessible to everyone who looked at the picture. A dog was a dog, a fish was a fish, a horse was a horse, a man was a man. And then they started deliberately complicating the writing, so that only the initiated could understand it. The signs started freeing themselves of the tree, the sun, the sky, the river. Previously the signs had reflected harmony and universal beauty. Now the harmony shifted into the act of writing. The characters no longer reflected beauty, they were beauty itself!

How clear and familiar this all is to me!

Kirill is sad because he won't get home for his sister's wedding. He says his mother didn't want to let him go, she was terribly worried that he would be killed. He said:

'I've never been afraid for myself, but now I'm afraid with her fear.'

I didn't say anything. I know my mum is afraid for me in the same way.

When we said goodbye at the railway station, she cried and reached out to kiss me, but I felt embarrassed and kept trying to break out of her embrace.

And then her blind man suddenly wanted to hug me too. He scratched me with his stubble.

At the parting she said:

'Well, say something to me!'

But all I could manage to force out was:

'Go! Everything will be all right! Go!'

You see, Sasha, I had convinced myself that I didn't love her. No, of course you can't understand that. And to be honest, now I don't really understand it either.

I close my eyes and see that world which is no longer visible – our old apartment, the wallpaper, the curtains at the windows, the furniture, the parquet flooring. The mirror in the dresser that I used to make faces into, trying to get to know myself. On the sofa there's a cushion with a peacock with a button-eye that I can twist. That cushion was embroidered by my granny. The button kept coming off again and again, with some help from myself, of course, and then it was sewn back on again, which changed the peacock's expression – sometimes he squinted in fright, sometimes he stared at the ceiling in amazement, sometimes he sniggered gleefully.

I see marks on the doorpost – mum used to measure my height by putting a book on my head. But she refused to measure herself, no matter how much I asked.

You know, once again in my thoughts I fly far away from this sultry heat, the wounds and the death, and I feel so good!

Ever since I could remember, there was a cross-section plan of an ocean-going steamship hanging over my bed and I used to gaze endlessly at the cabins, stairways and engines, the captain's bridge, the holds and the little figures strolling around the deck or dining at the tables in the restaurant, the sailors and the stokers – there was even a little dog stealing a sausage from the cook. I was sure my dad had hung that steamship above my bed. I loved to imagine that life – what the captain was shouting through his megaphone, what answer the redheaded cabin boy clambering up the mast was giving him. I used to invent what the sailors were saying as they scrubbed the deck. I made up all sorts of stories about the passengers and gave them funny names. Sometimes I used to draw in the missing little figures myself, for instance, a sailor hanging from a rope like a monkey, with a bucket of paint, and he's painting the anchor.

And it was interesting and strange to wonder who I was for them.

And did they even suspect that I existed?

When we went to the dacha for the summer, I used to pick the thumbtacks out of the wall carefully, roll the picture up into a tube and not let anyone else have it. I travelled with it all the way, gazing thorough it into the distance, as if it was my telescope. Mum kept that picture with my childhood drawings for a long time until I threw the whole lot out myself.

All that was left of my father were a few patchy memories. I don't even know how old I was. We go to the railway to meet Mum. It's very crowded there, Dad puts me on his shoulders and tells me not to let her get past, or we'll miss each other. I remember holding on to Dad's neck and staring hard into the crowd. I feel anxious and afraid that we might not find each other. Suddenly I see her and shout loud enough for the whole station to hear:

'Mum! Mum! We're here!'

A visit to the photographer is another thing that stuck in my memory. Obviously because of my disappointment that the promised birdie didn't come flying out of the box. The photos taken then with my father in them disappeared somewhere, Mum probably destroyed them. The only one that survived showed me on my own with a guitar, which I was holding like a double bass.

And here's another absolutely stupid memory: in frosty weather I touch his nose, as red as a clown's.

I'm so glad that I can share all these things that nobody needs any more with you!

What else can I remember?

For a whole year Mum took me to special exercise sessions, in order to stretch my spine and neck – the doctors had told her I had bad posture. They used to fasten my head into a sturdy leather collar with straps for my forehead and chin and hoist me up almost all the way to the ceiling. There were other boys and girls with bad posture dangling beside me, hanging there like sticks of salami in a shop. I hated those exercises, and Mum as well, for making me go there, no matter how stubbornly I resisted.

And here's something else. I remember that visitors came and I hid in a cupboard and sat there in the stuffy darkness until I was missed and they ran outside to look for me. They told me off and asked why I had done it. I didn't know that myself, but now I realise that I simply wanted them to look for me, find me and be glad that they had.

You know, when I was a child sometimes the strangest ideas would come into my head. Or perhaps not all that strange. Someone gave us some French biscuits in a beautiful tin, and I started wondering what I could do with that remarkable box. Then I thought of something – I could put all sorts of things in it and bury it, and someday someone would find my box and learn all about me. I put in my photograph, some drawings, stamps, various bits and pieces from the clutter in the drawer of my desk

– stones, tin soldiers, pencils and other similar nonsense that was important to me then – and I buried it at the dacha under a jasmine bush. And then it occurred to me that many years from now, when that box was found, I wouldn't be here any more and neither would Mum or anyone else. I had to put something in the box from Mum too. So I secretly pulled one of her photos out of an album and buried that as well. And then I was struck by the thought that I possessed amazing power – the only people who would remain were the ones I took into my tin box with me!

I wonder where that box is now? Is it really still there, under the jasmine?

Mum was always driving me outside.

'Why are you sitting there with your books again? Go on, go and play with the children!'

But I didn't like playing with children, they had cruel games and endless tests that you had to pass. For instance, they would hold a stretched catapult up to my eye, to see if I would blink or not.

When I was a child I really wanted to have a dog, and once I brought a stray puppy home from the street. We fed it. But when mum saw it being sick and immediately licking up its own vomit off the parquet, she wouldn't let me keep it, no matter how much I begged her.

What else?

Granny had a box of buttons and I love playing with them – they were my army. The small white buttons were the infantry, the others represented cavalry and cannons. I remember a huge mother-of-pearl one – that was a general, who always fought against the army of another general – a tarnished copper buckle. I staged entire battles – the buttons rushed into the attack, shouted, grappled hand to hand with each other, died. I raked the dead ones back into the box.

My Sashenka! How good it is to talk to you about all these things that have disappeared!

One day Mum took me to a performance by a conjuror. There was probably nothing special about his tricks, but at the time I was completely mesmerised by it all. Objects appeared and disappeared, one thing turned into something else. The ace of spades became the queen of hearts. The conjuror put a coin on his palm, closed his fist, opened it – and there was a white mouse. He cut off a gentleman's tie with a pair of scissors, then joined the two halves together and the tie was intact and quite undamaged.

Then he called volunteers to come up on stage and started hypnotising them. Mum couldn't resist this, although I grabbed hold of her and didn't want to let her go. It was eerie and enthralling to watch real live people suddenly turn into lunatics right in front of me and move about with their eyes closed. He told Mum that a flood had started and the water was rising in the room, getting higher and higher – and she started pulling up the hem of her dress. But afterwards she said she didn't remember anything.

I saw a conjuring set in a toy shop and cajoled Mum into buying it – she gave me it as a birthday present. What a miraculous box that was! Everything needed to amaze and delight an audience was in there. That was probably what I really wanted – not the actual tricks, but for people to love me.

What remarkable little balls made out of sponge there were in there, and silk handkerchiefs, and ribbons, an egg, a flower – it all looked real, but everything had a trick to it! Special laces, 'Chinese rings', a thumbstall – a thumbnail with a wick in it, as if anyone could possibly believe that my thumb was burning like a candle!

In the library I found a well-thumbed book about various great magicians, hypnotists and conjurors – I liked the idea that a man could be put in a coffin, then buried, and the grave piled over with rocks, and then the coffin would turn out to be empty! And the man who had been buried would be sitting at the table at home, waiting for everyone!

I also dreamed of becoming a conjuror and hypnotist, and I was surprised that Granny didn't like my magnificent idea at all, she just sighed and said:

'Monkey business!'

She wanted me to be enthusiastic about something serious.

The conjuring set had detailed descriptions of all the marvels, I tried to follow the instructions precisely, but my tricks turned out silly anyway. Or rather, when I practised in front of the mirror, everything worked, in fact the hardest thing was to learn to make the passes for distracting people's attention, but when I showed my wonders to our guests, they didn't so much admire my magical art as laugh at my clumsiness. The moment came when I was transfixed by the painful thought that for them I wasn't a magician at all, but a clown. In the end I came to hate magical tricks.

But here's something else that happened involving those tricks.

My granny fell ill. Or, rather, in the winter she slipped on the icy ground beside the post office, fell and broke her hip. She didn't get up any more, just lay in bed for months, getting weaker. I remember Mum sighing and saying that Granny was 'on her way out'. And I also remember the sight of Granny's hand and head shaking and Mum brushing her hair. My granny was very beautiful when she was young, she had a long, thick plait, as thick as my arm. The plait was cut off once when she was ill and kept by us as a family relic. But by the time she was old Granny's hair had grown long again.

One day I came home very late from grammar school. I had picked up a lot of D's in my marks and I didn't want to go home because I was sure I was in for another scolding. I had wandered around somewhere until it was late, and now I knew I would get it for that as well. So I arrive home, prepared for the very worst, but instead of scolding me, Mum hugs and kisses me. I didn't understand what was going on, and then I realised – the doctor came out of Granny's room and washed his hands thoroughly, every finger separately. Mum had a word with him, then she pressed my head against her chest and said that Granny was already at death's door. She took me in to say goodbye.

Shortly before she died Granny became hideous, lying there dishevelled and shaking all over, especially her hands.

I don't remember what we were talking about, but she suddenly asked me to show her a magic trick. I shook my head. I couldn't. It wasn't that I didn't want to – I couldn't. But it was impossible to explain that to anybody.

Mum started coaxing me:

'Volodenka, come on, please! Granny might never ask you for anything again. Why is it so hard?

But I couldn't do it. I tore myself out of Mum's arms, ran off as far away from everybody as I could and burst into tears.

Before the funeral I was astounded by her calm hands in the coffin. Mum sat there brushing the dead woman's hair.

At the cemetery they pushed me forward to kiss her and throw the first handful of earth. I resisted in stubborn silence. I wasn't afraid, but I felt uneasy somehow.

I remember that when the lumps of earth started thudding down gently onto the lid of the coffin, for some reason the thought came to me: If only I could open the coffin now, and it's empty – and Granny's waiting for us at home!

They buried her and smoothed out the ground like a flowerbed. And it was absolutely impossible that Granny could have turned into a flowerbed.

The funeral went on for a long time, I wanted to go to the toilet very badly – Mum let me go to the cemetery's little hut with a hole in the floor. Standing there over the pit that reminded me of the grave, I felt very acutely that Granny couldn't be waiting for us at home, that she was there, in her coffin under the ground, because death was real, as real as this putrid, stinking hole.

Granny's death left me with a feeling of childish horror. Only somehow I just couldn't get the fact that I would die some day too into my head. I didn't become really frightened of that until much later.

But now I listen to the wounded men's groans coming from the infirmary tents and I think: What a marvellous death that was! How wonderful to live your life right through and die of old age.

There, you see how the concept of happiness changes here.

Do you know what has just occurred to me? That I haven't given anybody anything in life. I don't mean the trivial things, but for real. Everybody gave me something, and I took. But I didn't give anybody anything. Especially Mum. And not because I didn't want to – I simply didn't get round to it.

Yet again these simple ideas come swarming in as if they were revelations.

And now I've realised that I want to give so much – warmth, love, thoughts, words, tenderness, understanding – and everything can simply break off before it has even begun, tomorrow, in five minutes, this very moment! It hurts so much!

That's all, I'll finish for today. My hand's tired. And my eyes ache – I'm writing to you by the light of a night lamp.

My Sashenka, I want so much for everything to be well with you.

I know we'll meet again.

What for?

I keep asking myself that question: What for?

Why did I have to be punished in this way? In this particular way.

I was going somewhere in a tram. A sudden pain below my stomach, acute and unbearable. I felt frightened and understood everything straight away, but I tried to persuade myself that it wasn't that at all. I didn't know what, but not that. I started bleeding.

I should have gone straight to the hospital, but I went home, to him. I dragged myself in, he started scurrying about, running round the flat and babbling:

'Tell me what to do. Tell me what to do.'

I never thought I would see him in such a panic. He didn't even know how to call an ambulance. He was more frightened than I was. I start trying to reassure him that it's really nothing terrible, but I understand that if the bleeding from the womb isn't stopped, I could die from loss of blood, and it won't stop on its own.

We waited an eternity for the ambulance.

It felt like my stomach had been stuffed with stones and was being squeezed in a vice. My toes go numb. I'm covered in perspiration and trembling all over. I howl, the pain and the insult are making me hysterical, and he keeps pouring himself cognac, glass after glass, to calm himself down. The pain is hellish. Everything starts going dark, the room is slithering about. Several times I think I'm blacking out.

Straight onto the operating table at the hospital. Anaesthetic. Curettage. My child came out of me and I didn't even notice. I was bleeding torrents of blood that flowed in clots.

Everything inside has been scraped raw – my soul and my womb.

Now that there is less of my flesh, I seem to collide with everything in the world: a door, people, sounds, smells. Everything is a collision for me. Everything has become noisy, petty, irksome. Unnecessary.

How could it happen? Only the other day I stopped to examine a shop window full of things for children and was amazed at how much of everything this little mite needed, and now I'm already alone.

When Mummy found out, she said:

'Cry! That's what you need right now – a good cry.'

But Yanka said:

'You should have had an abortion straightaway, then you wouldn't have suffered.'

We rented a flat with a nursery for our future child – and now Sonechka stays in it overnight.

I was recuperating in bed after the hospital and Sonya asked her usual question:

'Well, how's my little brother?'

I smiled at her and answered:

'Fine.'

'But why are you lying in bed?'

'I've got a bit of a cold.'

I turned away, pretending to cough into the pillow, so she wouldn't notice that I was blubbering again.

And yesterday I took her to the bathroom and started undressing her, but she wouldn't let me, she turned sulky, the high and mighty madam. To coax her along, I started playing with the clothes pegs, snapping at her, but got too close and pinched her skin just a little. I handed her a clothes peg:

'There, you pinch me too!'

She takes it and pinches me really hard, so it hurts. I wash her and she yells that the soap's going in her eyes and her mummy does everything a different way.

Then I rub her down with the towel, and her clean-washed hair squeaks loudly. When I was little my mummy always said that hair had to be washed squeaky-clean.

I'll have a child some day, I will definitely, and I'll wash my child's hair squeaky-clean.

I only realised later why Sonya was so very reluctant to stay the night with us. She still wets the bed. Someone has to get up in the night, check if her sheet's dry and change it if it's wet. She knows all this about herself and feels terribly ashamed.

Today I took her to the dance class instead of him.

As she was changing her shoes she suddenly stuck her ballet shoe under my nose.

'Breathe in it!'

I took the shoe and stuck it under her nose.

'You breathe in it!'

She flashed her eyes at me angrily.

Sasha! Sashenka!

My wonder! My glorious one!

I know I'm not there with you, and it's hard for you. I wonder all the time how you're doing there. What's happening to you? What are you doing right now? What are you thinking about? What's worrying you? How I long to walk up to you this very instant, stroke you, hug you, press your head against my chest. Please, hold on! You've got to hold on!

I'll come back, you'll see, and everything will be all right.

We only parted so very recently after all, but the time has stretched out for years.

Especially since I ended up here, time flies by quickly and imperceptibly or, on the contrary, it stands completely still, and I can't really tell if it exists at all. It's probably just that behind all the events, time seems to become invisible, but if I remember the day when I tore myself away from you, I realise that an awful lot of it has gone by.

You can't even imagine how much you help me, simply because I can write to you! It's my salvation. Don't smile – it really is my salvation!

What have I written? Smile, Sashenka, my wonder, smile.

I woke up early – that's the best time of the day here. It was only just light, the morning breeze was still gentle and fresh. Hours like that are the only time it's possible to live here. Even as I rejoice in the coolness I can already feel the horror of the heat foretokened by this immense red sun clambering out of the haze above the fields of kaoliang. Soon the sun will turn golden, then white. The haze above the fields will evaporate, the morning breeze will fade away and hell will begin again. The heat here can bake your brain in the most literal sense – many men collapse from sunstroke.

Now I'd like to record the impressions I have accumulated during these days here. Forgive me, my dearest, if I have to write about unpleasant things.

I won't write about things because they are important, but simply about whatever comes into my head first.

Yesterday an officer called Vseslavinsky got drunk on *huang jiu* and started pestering everybody with his smashed binoculars. That was actually the reason why he got drunk – a bullet hit the binoculars hanging on his chest and he escaped with only a bruise. He showed everybody the binoculars and the bruise. I used to think that fortunate accidents like that only happened in books. He went completely to pieces, he burst into tears like some little boy and kept on and on drinking. It's strange, because before all this he gave the impression of being a very cool-headed and courageous man. And this morning he was found drowned in a pond. Near a ruined *fanza* close by here there's a little pond in which even a child couldn't drown. He probably slipped. He was completely out of his mind, after all. When we got him out, streams of dirty liquid flowed out of his mouth and his nose. They tried giving him artificial respiration – it was useless. The surgeon's assistant stuck his fingers deep into his mouth and pulled out something sticky.

How stupid it all is!

And his family will receive notification of a heroic death.

On the other hand, what else can we write to them? The truth?

The truth is that we suffer losses every day but, as you see, by no means all of them in battle. Accidents and sunstroke are more common. The heat is still as unbearable as ever.

The men aren't the only ones to suffer. Here is what happened right in front of me only the day before yesterday. The second artillery battery was moving out into position. The road ran down from a slight elevation, the horses were moving at a trot. Suddenly the horse that the guiding soldier was riding fell. Fortunately the soldier managed to jump out of the way, but the gun crashed into the horse and broke both its hind legs. It was whinnying pitifully. They shot it.

But here's some good news – the remainder of Admiral Seymour's expedition has returned. They couldn't break through to Peking, the line had been dismantled ahead of them. They couldn't leave enough men everywhere to guard it and the railway stations behind them had been occupied by the Chinese army, so there was nothing else they could do but fight their way back. They came back empty-handed. That is, with two hundred wounded. They buried their dead, when they were able, on the spot.

Two companies of Russian sailors under the command of Captain Chagin had left with this detachment. Only half of them came back. Our sailors spent two weeks in constant action in extremely difficult conditions. I heard Chagin tell the officers that at one point they had to withdraw briefly and leave some of the wounded in a ruined station, and when they won the station back, the wounded men had all been hacked to pieces. The cruelty here is incredible. And our men didn't take any prisoners either. Chagin did at least try to prevent his subordinates from torturing anyone they captured, but he wasn't always successful. And it's precisely the wounded and helpless who are captured. Men go berserk when they see what is done to their comrades.

Our situation here hasn't changed much as yet. Every now and then fighting flares up around the railway station, by the earth wall of the city and further away, by the Lutai Canal, but it's not extensive. Did I already tell you that a canal that was dug a thousand years ago and stretches right across China flows through Tientsin?

So far both sides are marking time, but the bombardment of the city continues ceaselessly. The Chinese turn out to be incredibly punctual. The shelling of the concessions usually takes place from three in the afternoon until eight in the evening, and then again from two until ten in the morning.

Sashenka, I've listened to that ceaseless rumbling for so long now that I can distinguish our shots from the Chinese guns and even tell the calibre. The Chinese fire from the forts with six-inch Krupp cannon and Hotchkiss rapid-fire guns. Naturally, you'll say: What kind of connoisseur of calibres are you! Well, no kind at all, of course! But the ears just get used to it. And I'm changing here too. I'm becoming someone else. It's impossible not to change here. But that's exactly what I wanted, isn't it?

I had to break off. I'm writing to you the next day.

Yesterday I went into the city to carry out an assignment. I was glad to go, I'm stuck in the camp all the time otherwise. At least it's some kind of change, although there is the risk of getting caught in the shelling, but I tell you straightaway, Sashenka, that not a single shell fell in those districts where I was while I was in the city. Don't worry!

You know, on the way to the city there's a small swamp. In general there are lots of ponds and pools around here, but they seem to have died in the drought and now they're putrefying in the heat. Well, several times I saw snakes tracing out the letter S. It's the first time I've seen these creeping reptiles that everyone here talks about.

Tientsin and the entire valley, bisected by the mustard-coloured ribbon of the Pei Ho, appear quite picturesque from a distance, until you see all the signs of devastation.

The railway station and its buildings are in a terrible state — platforms pitted by shells, heaps of rubbish and broken brick. The iron roofs of the goods shed seem to be made out of metal lacework, they have been riddled so badly by bullets and shrapnel. The burnt-out carriages still haven't been cleared away.

Our sappers have reinforced the bridge with new decking. There are no longer as many bodies as accumulated here a couple of days ago, but they are still arriving on the current. While I was there the soldiers were trying to push something blue and bloated between the barges.

I was there with an officer from Anisimov's detachment, who has the strange surname of Ubri. He first saw the city before it was devastated and now he laments continually as he looks at what Tientsin has been transformed into during the siege. Ubri has shell shock and his hearing is poor, when I talk to him I have to shout.

He showed me the settlement. Immediately after the bridge comes the English concession. The main thoroughfare is called Victoria Road. It stretches along the river and runs straight to the Chinese forts, so the grenades fly unhindered along the street, which is now pitted with craters.

All the walls have been scratched and scraped by shrapnel, many of the buildings have been destroyed – charred ruins, broken windows. At the crossroads on all the streets there are barricades made of bales of wool, lampposts and bricks. Everywhere is littered with furniture, rubbish, roof tiles. The streets are silent, there are no pedestrians to be seen, only patrols of various nationalities in front of buildings that have been converted into staff headquarters, infirmaries, storage depots.

Just imagine, there are still posters on the advertising columns, urging people to go to a circus. An international troupe pasted up posters all over the town before the siege, but instead of the anticipated takings from the public, the artistes had to settle for the relief of managing to escape on the last train that broke through to Taku.

Ubri and I went into Gordon Hall, the town hall of the English concession. He told me that during the siege women and children took shelter in the basements here and food was cooked for them in the neighbouring Astor House hotel. The Russian consul Shuisky and his family also spent the siege in those basements. His seven-year-old son was killed in the bombardment.

The hotel was damaged too, although it is still obvious what a magnificent building it is, with balconies, verandas and a tower. The large, beautiful windows with sun-awnings are now blocked off with sandbags. Ubri told me that inside there are marble baths, electric bells, luxury and every possible convenience. But all that is in the past – from the very beginning of the siege neither the electricity nor the water supply have worked in the concessions.

In general even now it is clear what a beautiful, even foppish city this was! How very comfortably the Europeans had arranged their lives! A beautiful riverside embankment, immaculate broad streets planted with poplars and acacias, gardens, the picturesque Victoria Park, elegant houses in the English style, clubs, post office, telegraph, telephone, drainage system, lighting. Several large, brilliant shops, now ruined and burnt out.

But now this European city in the centre of Asia is an appalling sight. Not a single building or villa has been spared by the flames or the shells. Nor was it only the Chinese who demolished them. In the outermost concession, the French, Ubri showed me a huge city district populated by Chinese Christians, right beside the hospital, that had been totally destroyed – the French consul ordered it to be burned to the ground because he was afraid of arson and an attack from the direction of the Chinese city.

For a distance of two versts there is nothing to be seen except charred walls, solitary chimneys, heaps of stones, rubble and charcoal. The Chinese houses that survived the fire have been looted. The yards are littered with heaps of plain or expensive silk clothing, all sorts of furniture and tableware, junk, sumptuous Chinese embroidery work, porcelain vases, pictures with magnificent inlay-work, clocks – everything smashed and trampled.

The soldiers of the allied nations have already run riot in all the abandoned houses. Unfortunately, there was not a single detachment whose soldiers did not rummage through these mixed heaps of valuable possessions and garbage. There was no supervision in the Chinese quarter, and in any case it was quite impossible to protect the Chinese property lying about in the yards and the streets, nor was there any need to do so.

Ubri showed me the place where the shell exploded when he got his concussion. His comrade, who was standing beside him and took the full force of the blast, had both his legs torn off and died a few hours later in terrible agony.

A regiment of Indian Sepoys has set up camp in the garden of the International Club – when we walked by, there were fires burning there, they were cooking food, playing on their little fifes and bagpipes. Streams of the stinking contents of human stomachs were flowing out into the streets but that didn't bother the soldiers in turbans, although Ubri and I had to pinch our noses shut and slip by as quickly as possible.

While we were there the English forces caught a Chinese spy. He was a mere boy. The Sepoys led him from their headquarters to the square in front of the Astor House hotel, to execute him. We spoke with an English officer who said they had seen the lad waving a handkerchief to someone after climbing up on a roof. The Chinese, of course, know all about everything that is going on in the concessions.

The lad was very thin, nothing but skin and bone. And his head had been completely shorn. As he walked past me our eyes met. His eyes were full of horror and despair. He kept hiccupping, probably out of fear. I can still feel that gaze on me even now.

Sashenka, I thought they would shoot him, but the Sepoys cut his head off. There was a photographer there too, with his camera, some American. Someone will look at those photographs, examine them. The Sepoys posed proudly, smiling.

I tried to make myself watch it, but I couldn't, I closed my eyes at the crucial moment. I only heard the sound. You know, it's like the sound of secateurs. Then I opened my eyes and saw his head on the ground. How many times I have seen severed heads in various different pictures, for instance, on a dish, that favourite subject of artists – there was something horrible in that, but also something exalted and beautiful. But here the thing lying in front of me was small, smeared with black blood and caked with sand. A distorted mouth with a bitten tongue, one eye rolled up and back. The body without a head looked impossible somehow, docked short. A dark trickle flowed out of its neck.

How strange it is. It turns out that it is possible to see all this and not go insane.

And it is even possible to eat the same day. And talk about something else, something not here, far away, human. For instance, today I told Glazenap I had been at an execution and it only served as a pretext for a conversation about the transmigration of souls.

How could anyone here be surprised by someone being executed if everyone knows why it is happening and what for! By killing them, we save our own lives. It's all as simple as that.

Kirill believes in the transmigration of souls. Or at least he says that he does.

I asked why in that case we aren't surprised not to be Napoleon or Marcus Aurelius any more, or even an executed Chinese if it comes to that, but instead some provincial Dobchinskys or Bobchinskys out of Gogol's *Inspector General*, who fear dying more than anything else in the world. But he replied that we are not surprised by anything in a dream when we find ourselves in some absolutely impossible situation, surrounded by people who died long ago.

'You see,' Kirill declared, 'we lived before in a different world and a different time, and we woke up here and carry on living without being surprised by anything, accepting everything as given. And afterwards we'll wake up again somewhere else.'

He really is quite impossible, that Glazenap.

But though I may laugh at him, that Chinese boy – if not his soul, then at least his head – has found a temporary refuge in me. I don't even have to close my eyes in order to see it there on the ground, surrounded by the trampled mud – caked with blood and sand, the white of an eye with no pupil, a black tongue bitten by brown teeth.

Forgive me, my dearest, forgive me!

But I won't cross anything out.

You can simply skip over these lines, not read them.

I want so much to write to you about good things!

My Sashenka, I broke off again for a short while, but I'm continuing now. And do you know why I broke off? It's so stupid, but I'll explain anyway, after all, I want to talk to you about everything. The Cossacks and the artillerymen were cleaning their horses at the tethering-rail and swapping obscenities. It's quiet now, the wind is blowing from that direction, bringing the smell of horses, their sweat and urine, but these are all really such human, heart-warming smells! It's the people here who give off repulsive animal odours, but with the animals, it's just the opposite. Anyway, they were telling each other dirty stories, laughing loudly and coarsely. I tried writing my letter to you with that conversation in my ears, and gave up. I felt as if their words could besmirch my letter simply by being spoken over this sheet of paper.

I went for a short walk. I looked at the horses, standing so sweet and clean in their stalls. Breathing out their delicious animal aroma on me. Twitching their muscles as they tried to drive the flies off them, snorting and shaking their muzzles about. Squinting sideways at me with their sad, docile eyes. They're chaste and virtuous somehow. How good I feel with them!

I am continuing after the soldiers have already gone. What else can I write to you about?

Today Lucie told me the miraculous way she managed to escape when the Catholic mission somewhere to the north of Tientsin, where she had found herself a year ago, was sacked. In general the story of how she came to be in China remains a mystery to everyone, but Kirill told me in the strictest confidence that she told him she came to China for love – she abandoned everything at home and set out to the end of the world to find the man she loved. But he proved to be a scoundrel – the usual business. She couldn't go back home and she found herself a job in the Catholic mission. Well anyway, let me get back to her story.

The things that little woman has been through!

The crowd broke into the grounds of the mission and no one had time to get away. The peasant rebels found glass jars of pickled onions in the kitchen buffet. They started showing them to the entire village as proof of the foreigners' perfidious treachery – they had mistaken the onions for Chinese eyes. It was already impossible to stop them and a massacre started.

They tore out the Catholic priest's eyes with a fork. They decapitated his housekeeper – she was holding her son's hand at the time and they killed him immediately after her. Lucie told me all this without any agitation in her voice, in a strange, dry manner, as if all of it had not happened to her, as if she had died and this was all about the sufferings of some other woman.

Lucie had a small revolver, but she couldn't bring herself to use it. She says that at first she tried to shoot the attackers, but she couldn't take aim at a human being. Then she decided to shoot herself so as not to fall into their hands, but when she saw what these people had done to people dear to her, she started firing at them. And she says she had only one desire – to kill as many of them as possible.

She survived by a miracle – she locked herself in a shed and fired to keep them away, killing several people. And she was saved by a small detachment of the Chinese regular army – at that time they were still punishing the outrages committed by the Yihetuan and the governor of Chili province had even introduced rewards for the capture of insurgents.

After her story everyone sat there in silence for a while. I couldn't raise my eyes to her face – I was watching her hands. It was amazing that those same hands, which pitied, caressed and cured, had also killed.

Afterwards Lucie said that she was willing to kill again. She hates them.

Sashenka, how incredible, incomprehensible and barbaric all this is.

I feel such pain for her. And I start to hate them too.

When the two of us are left alone, Kirill talks about her with great tenderness. You know, he told me that he loved a woman in Petersburg, but she laughed at his feelings and left him for some worthless nonentity. And now it seems to him that he has found something real in life.

Sashenka, it's so wonderful to watch their feelings maturing right in front of our eyes – in the midst of blood and death and wounds and pain and pus and filth. Everyone notices the way they are reaching out to each other and watches them with a smile. Of course, people envy them. No, that's the wrong word. People are glad for them. So much brutality all around, so much cruelty – and it is such a joy that tenderness is still alive at least in these two.

People probably look at them and remember their own loved ones.

My distant Sashenka! You are so close to me now, as if you are standing beside me, leaning over my shoulder and looking at my skipping lines of words.

I kiss you very tenderly.

Goodnight, my love!

You and I have been one whole for a long time. You are me. I am you. What can separate us? There is nothing that could separate us.

●

There's an anthill in my leg. It's gone numb.

Since morning two showers of rain and one student have passed by outside the window.

Glassiness, tinniness, woodenness.

Days skitter and scurry past like lizards. If I try to catch one, all that's left in my hand is the tail – that's this line.

Bell. Break time. Children's shouts from the schoolyard.

I suddenly thought that those children's shouts during the break will still be exactly the same in a hundred years. And in two hundred years.

Donka clatters her claws on the parquet. She has thrown her front paws up on my knees and glanced imploringly into my eyes. She's asking me to go for a walk.

Apparently ballerinas pour warm water into the heels of their ballet shoes so that their foot will sit more firmly.

I go walking with Donka and we've met Sonechka's ballet teacher several times in the park, she has something from the canine genus too, but the size of a slipper. The disparity of size doesn't prevent them from sniffing each other under the tail.

She told me about the ballet. She fell at a concert, while performing a pas de deux – her partner's mistake. She still hates him to this day. On stage he liked to mutter nonsense through his teeth with a stony face, in order to make her laugh.

At first they didn't want to take her into the ballet at all, supposedly because of fallen arches, but really because of the large breasts that were already beginning to form.

Her teacher at the dance class told her: imagine a five-kopeck piece and squeeze it tight in your backside right through the lesson, so that it won't fall out!

She's having an affair with the orthopaedist who treats the ballet dancers. He keeps promising to leave his wife, but he can't – she's not well, the children, and so on. The usual business. She got herself a dog to combat the loneliness.

For a dancer, the resistance of her medium is the earth's gravity.

When she was a child she wanted so much to go ice-skating, but she couldn't even think of skating or skiing – she was afraid of turning her ankle.

She says that Sonechka has good aptitude for the ballet, but she warned me:

'Ballet girls are usually backward – no time for reading.'

She also said that when you go out on stage, the audience are like stuffed decoys, and you have to make them real – make them fall in love with you.

He usually takes Donka for her walks and Mummy has told me several times that she's always seeing him with this ballerina woman.

'Don't be a fool! Keep an eye on him! A husband has to be fought for!'

Poor Mummy. I already have a home of my own and she keeps on pestering me with exhortations, advice and reproaches. She's lonely. I'm sorry for her. After my father left her, she switched her attention to me. I'm afraid of these rare visitations. Now I have to justify and explain everything I do again. And I do everything wrong, and there's dirt and clutter everywhere, and in general I'm ungrateful.

She's always trying to educate me. I bought a raincoat and showed it to her: the colour's wrong, it's a bad fit, you've thrown your money away. When will you ever grow up? she lectures me. Since I don't want to listen to her, it means I don't love her. She's absolutely insufferable and yet I have to feel sorry for her.

Mummy's always saying she wants me to be happy, she wants me to get on well with him, but what she really wants is for me to come back to her and be a little girl again.

He's a terrible hypochondriac, he takes my textbooks on illnesses and discovers he has everything except the woman's ailments. But what he's really afraid of is that he'll inherit the illness his father had – at the end of his life he developed dermatosclerosis.

Sometimes he suddenly starts telling me about himself. His father was a professor, who had an affair with one of his students. Then *he* slept with the girl, to show his father what she was really like and prove that she didn't love his father at all. His father couldn't forgive him. And when he had his first exhibition, his father said something so humiliating that they stopped talking to each other altogether.

His father died a terrible death – when he was on his way home late one winter night he was robbed, and they fractured his skull.

Now he feels guilty because his father died then, and he never told him he loved him.

He smiled and said:

'I condemned him then, because he wanted to leave my mother for a younger woman. But now I've done exactly the same thing. I wanted to prove something to my father, but now it turns out that he's proved the opposite to me from the other side. It's so strange, when I married Ada, you were still building sandcastles somewhere.'

Sometimes he forgets and calls to me:

'Ada!'

He doesn't even hear what he's saying.

I answer:

'Who do you want?'

'You, of course. Who else?'

And then he says:

'You know, Ada was an absurd mistake that I've put right now. You are my destiny.'

That's how he talks about the woman he lived with for eight hundred years. This is what he says:

'What do you expect? Do you want me to free myself from her all at once? We lived together for eight hundred years.'

And another time he said, about himself and her:

'It was a different kind of loneliness.'

Then again, about Ada: at first he wanted to tell her about his women – after all, they'd agreed to be honest and open – then he realised that, on the contrary, he shouldn't say anything. You shouldn't humiliate someone who loves you. He started lying to her.

'And she trusted me completely! But it's absolutely impossible to deceive someone who trusts you!'

Once he said:

'When you live with someone, you have to scour your feelings for that person with sand and pumice every day, and there isn't enough strength or time for that.'

Then he added that he meant himself and Ada, not us.

On the day he decided to leave Ada, a boy selling newspapers in the street called him 'granddad'. It felt catastrophic, he had to do something. He used to talk about it as if it was amusing.

But then, he goes running back there just as soon as she calls him to come and hang the curtains. He explains that a family that lasted a whole lifetime can't suddenly stop existing, just like that.

While I was cooking flapjacks for Sonechka, she announced:

'Mummy says you stole Daddy from us.'

'And what else?'

'That you don't take proper care of me.'

'What else?'

'That it's your fault we're not going on holiday. We don't have any money now.'

Once there's a sudden phone call in the middle of the night: Sonya has a fever. He gets ready to go. I say to him:

'Wait, I'll go with you!'

He's wary of the idea.

'You know, she's convinced it's something you overlooked when Sonya was with us.'

I went with him. We took a taxi. We didn't speak at all the whole way, looking in opposite directions. The taxi driver kept blowing his nose all the time and sneezing so hard, we almost crashed into a tram.

It was the first time I'd been at their home.

All the walls are covered in pictures. He did a lot of nude portraits of her. In this pose and that pose. Standing, sitting, lying. And then she walks in, and I'm astounded by the disparity between the young body in the pictures and this blowsy old woman in a faded housecoat and worn-out slippers.

The child has a temperature of over 102. She's soaking in sweat. The roof of her mouth and her tongue are covered with little white dots. Her face is flushed, with a whitish triangle round the mouth. A rash – grainy in her crotch.

Ada flung herself on me, saying her daughter had come back from us with wet feet, she'd been running through puddles, and I hadn't checked her shoes. There were tears in her eyes.

'What if it's laryngitis again?'

I interrupted her:

'I'm sorry, are you a doctor?'

'No . . .'

'Then I'm not interested in your opinion.'

And I explained to them that it was scarlet fever and the rash would pass off the next day.

I went to wash my hands, he brought me a towel, and without thinking I asked:

'How old is she?'

He replied, embarrassed:

'We're the same age.'

I went home alone. He said he had to stay there until the morning.

'You do understand?'

I nodded: I understand everything.

Three weeks later the skin came off Sonechka's hands.

At night we lay there in each other's arms and he said:

'Look here, I was born, and I'll die – that's clear enough. It's not nice, but it's clear. It's frightening, of course, but it's explicable. But what about my daughter? She already exists, and one day she'll die – and that's really terrifying. I never knew before that anything could be so terrifying.'

He spoils her, and she exploits her power over her father shamelessly.

He thinks he has to take her somewhere all the time – to the circus, the zoo, a children's matinee show. After she's been here there are sugary sweets, chocolate and paper wrappers all over the flat. He buys her all sorts of rubbish – he's simply afraid to say no. And what lies behind this avalanche of generosity is the fear of losing contact with her.

She acts up at the table – I won't eat this, I won't eat that. And everything's different at Mummy's place, it all tastes better. And I can't say a word, he lets her do whatever she likes. And I stupidly feel anxious that she'll go hungry.

She takes my clothes out of the wardrobe without asking, takes my brooches and beads from the box beside the mirror, my scent and nail varnish. He shrugged and said I should talk to her about it myself. But when I started the conversation, he stuck up for her, started defending her, as if there was something unjust in what I was saying.

I'm brushing her hair, and she won't sit still, she keeps fidgeting and if the brush snags in her hair, she howls and says I'm hurting her on purpose.

On Sunday morning, when we can sleep in for a bit, she jumps up at the crack of dawn, runs into our room, climbs into the bed, sits astride his chest and prises his eyelids open with her fingers. And he puts up with it all.

I went with him to buy presents for her birthday. He wanted me to help him choose dresses and shoes. But he didn't remember about my birthday. In fact, even I've forgotten I was ever born.

She eats her favourite currant bun, puts a crumb on her hand

and holds it out to him, and he has to peck at it — take it with just his lips.

Or they sit down shoulder to shoulder and draw in a sketch-book — a tree on one page and a fox on another.

They're happy together.

Do they need me?

At night he gets up to check if her bed's wet. He takes her out of the cot and carries her to the bathroom, dangling drowsily in his arms and muttering in her sleep, and sits her on the loo, and he sits on the edge of the bath beside her, so that she can put her head on his knees, and waits patiently until he hears the gurgling sound.

Sometimes she wets the bed anyway, and he puts a new nightie on her and takes off the sheet and folds it in half, with the dry side upwards. He puts her to bed and scratches her back until she falls asleep.

Before she goes to bed, she's used to having her bottle of 'Mummy's sleepy water'.

Her friends stay over with each other for the night, but she's afraid they'll find out and make fun of her, stop being friends with her. She invents excuses to avoid staying overnight when she visits them.

She feels ashamed with me too, and I tell her it's nothing to worry about, all children wet themselves, but when they grow up, it passes off, and they can sleep without a rubber sheet.

Afterwards I wash her things separately.

Sometimes I think we'll never really be able to love each other. But then sometimes, on the contrary, she suddenly presses up close against me and I'm engulfed by a feeling of tenderness for this awkward creature.

We've taken her to various different doctors for her squint. And they've prescribed special glasses for her to wear, with only one lens and the other eye covered over with black. She's terribly shy about her spectacles and always tries to take them off – she's terrified the other children will laugh at her.

She may be lively at home, but at school she's quite different. We went to a school concert at which she was supposed to recite a poem on stage. When she came out in her spectacles, one of the boys laughed, she forgot the words, got embarrassed and ran off. She cried her heart out.

But she gets her own back at home. She's a queen, surrounded by her subjects, who only exist on this earth in order to dance to the tune of her tin whistle.

I watched her drawing with a pencil and noticed that when she thought a drawing was wrong, it simply ceased to exist for her, she didn't see it any more, she drew another one on the same sheet of paper – she didn't notice the old lines, she only saw the new ones.

That's the way I should learn to live.

But most of all she likes painting with Daddy's paints. I put his old shirt on her, so that she can get it messy. He tried to teach her how to do something properly, but it's too soon, she's not interested.

Once she sheared off a lock of her hair with the handiwork scissors and stuck it on her chin with glue – like Daddy.

One evening as he's putting her to bed she cries into her pillow.

'What's wrong, my little wonder?'

And through her sobs, she says:

'Daddy, you're going to die! I feel so sorry for you!'

She's only just started becoming really aware of herself. When we were watching the sunset at the pond, she suddenly said:

'That trail of sunlight there, it's not the sun, it's me, isn't it?'

We went to the children's theatre to see *The Snow Maiden*. I walked along, thinking: what a strange thing for them to do, sculpt a little girl out of snow. After all, it's not like just building a snowman out of big balls of snow – you have to sculpt the hands and the feet, every finger and toe. But Sonechka didn't see anything unusual about it, the question never even arose for her:

'But she's real, isn't she? Alive!'

He bought her an adult wristwatch. Sonya winds it up, holding it close beside her ear, and says delightedly:

'Can you hear? It sounds like grasshoppers!'

He cobbled together a kite for her, and we all went to launch it, but the kite only flew as far as the nearest telegraph pole and got tangled in the wires. When we walk past, we wave to it – there's nothing left but ragged scraps, and it waves back to us with them.

She likes to take my phonendoscope too, and listen to absolutely everything. Herself, Donka, the wall, the chair, the windowsill. She presses it against the glass and tells the world outside the window in a serious voice:

'Breathe! And now hold your breath!'

I read to her at bedtime, and she listens, spellbound, focusing on something inside herself and licking the little hairs on her arm just above the wrist – first one way, and then the other. She peeps into the book when I turn the page, to see if a picture has popped up.

She has to be checked all the time. She goes to bed, she's already slipped under the sheet, but her toothbrush is dry. Up we get! Into the bathroom! But she'll still come up with some bright idea – she holds the brush still and runs her teeth over it, shaking her head from side to side, in a kind of protest.

I feel that she's afraid to love me, because that will mean she's betraying her mummy. She's afraid of treachery and betrayal. I tried to talk to her and explain that there's nothing wrong, and if she really loves two people it doesn't mean she's betraying one of them.

I think we're going to manage all right. Sometimes we feel so snug and comfortable together. Just last Sunday I was putting her to bed and she asked me to sit with her for a while in the twilight. She's afraid to sleep in the dark, she begs me to leave the light on. I leave her the nightlight, covered with a gauze neckerchief. The shadows are different every time. She lies there, imagining who it is up on the ceiling.

And she always asks me to stroke her with a brush – like Daddy.

I run the soft squirrel hair over her arms, her legs, her back, her bottom. It tickles her, she laughs happily and wriggles about.

I kiss her goodnight and whisper:

'That's all, now curl up tight and warm!'

My Sashenka!

There is so much death all around! I try not to think about it. But I can't help myself.

They've repaired the road to Taku, and new detachments of allies are arriving from there every day, they're preparing for an offensive. So there'll be even more death.

Kirill said a man should die easily, like Louis XVI – when he mounted the scaffold and saw the executioner, the first live human being with whom he could exchange a couple of words after his dungeon, the king asked him:

'What news of La Pérouse's expedition, brother?'

Only a few minutes before he died, he was still interested in geographical discoveries.

And I'd like to go like that too – as easily as if I've just shown up for breakfast.

But for that you probably have to be very strong.

Am I strong?

Sashenka, I saw an ideal death here. A man, young and handsome, with white teeth – although he'd been complaining about his teeth all day long, walking around, almost howling out loud with the pain of an abscess – disappeared in a single instant. He took a direct hit from a shell. I wasn't there at the time of the explosion, but afterwards I saw his arm, tossed up into the crown of a tree.

That's my ideal.

But what if it's not like that?

Every day I see wounded men, and despite myself the thought comes that tomorrow I'll be one of them. Unfortunately, the probability of a direct hit on my skull is equal to zero. But being maimed and left writhing in agony is only too probable.

A bullet or piece of shrapnel could hit me in the knee, couldn't it? Or in the palm of my hand. Get stuck in my kidney – the left one or the right one. Tear open my heart sac. Puncture my bladder. But why list everything? A man is such a vulnerable creature altogether. I've seen more than enough here already.

I look at a wounded man and can't help thinking of his wound in my body.

One soldier was shouting 'hurrah!', and that very instant a bullet pierced through both his cheeks and knocked his teeth out. And for some reason I imagine myself in his place. And I can't stop doing it.

At night I went out, half-asleep, to relieve myself, and heard someone pleading pitifully in the big infirmary tent:

'I can't find my bunk. Someone help me find my bunk!'

It was a young man with his eyes swathed in bandages, feeling his way along the aisle between the camp beds. He'd gone out in the middle of the night too, but got lost on the way back.

They'll bandage me up, operate on me, saw through the bone, amputate the putrefying remains of this right leg of mine. Or my left one?

It would be unbearable for me to hobble about for the rest of my life on one leg, or with no legs at all.

And perhaps tomorrow Lucie will be washing my blood off the white oilcloth on the operating table.

But perhaps, contrariwise, that will be the very time I decide I want to go – easily. When was it, now? The day before yesterday. The surgeon's mate came out for a smoke and walked over when he saw me. Probably he just wanted to talk to someone, let off a bit of steam. Everyone addresses him formally by his forename and patronymic, as Mikhal Mikhalich. I like him, he always has a genial air, with the grey remnants of a student crew cut on his head – he left university without ever graduating – a respectable moustache, a round pot belly, walks with little old man's steps. He has a funny, spongy nose, decorated with little blue and red veins. We sat in silence for a while, then he sighed:

'Lord, all the things you see in this infirmary! This morning they brought in a young fellow just like you, so badly mutilated, he tried do away with himself. I held him until the doctor gave him an injection.'

He finished his smoke, slapped me on the shoulder as if to say: Bear up, we're not done for yet – and trotted back into the operating tent.

Death. The number of times I've heard that word, or spoken it myself and written those five letters, but now I'm not quite sure I really understood what it means.

Now I've written that sentence, I've started thinking about it. Do I understand now?

Sashka, the most important thing here is not to think. But I think all the time. And that's wrong. After all, so many generations have thought about this and come to an immensely wise conclusion – you shouldn't think. Why do they always give soldiers something to do, any task, even the most meaningless, just in order to keep them busy? So they won't think. It's profoundly good sense for a man not to think. He has to be saved from himself, from thoughts about death.

Here you have to know how to forget yourself somehow, do something with your hands – so they make them clean a field gun, or tidy up their uniform, or shovel something about. They invent jobs for them.

And probably that's why I also invent something for myself to do – writing to you at every single opportunity. That is, making letters on paper. And that's how you save me, my darling!

Sashenka, my sweet, my dearest, I'm not complaining to you, no, I know you understand that.

I think about death all the time. It's all around here. From early morning until late at night, and even in my sleep. I sleep terribly badly. I suffer from nightmares and perspiration. Sometimes the way I perspire is really atrocious. Usually I don't remember my dreams, they evaporate a few moments after I wake up – the way breath on a mirror evaporates in a draught, without a trace. But I remember what I dreamed about today.

In my dream I was back at the conscription centre, standing naked in front of the military medical commission – a rather humiliating ritual. It was all as real as if I was awake, and I wasn't at all surprised to be going through the examination again. I stand in the queue, covering myself with my hands, and I can't help inspecting the scars and bruises of the men standing in front of me, their hairy and smooth buttocks, their pimples and warts. All this is degrading, especially when the doctor feels everyone's crotch, and then you have to turn round, lean over and spread your buttocks. And then my turn comes, and the doctor turns out to be Victor Sergeevich, my old schoolteacher who died during a lesson. He wipes his spectacles with his tie and looks at me. I start trying to tell him that I looked for those tablets he'd told us about, but I was so nervous, I couldn't find them.

'Victor Sergeevich! That time in the classroom, when you were lying on the floor by the blackboard, I rummaged through all the pockets in your jacket, but the tablets weren't there! Word of honour!'

But he shakes his head and carries on wiping his glasses with his tie.

'They weren't there . . . But then the headmaster came running in and found them straight away! This is where they were, right here! I showed you!'

And he slaps his pocket.

After that I just couldn't stand any more, and I woke up.

Sashenka, I never told you about that, did I?

When our Shikra had his attack during the lesson, I dashed over to him, to save him, but I couldn't find those tablets. And when they gave him the medicine, it was too late. I know I'm not to blame, but even so I still have to explain that to myself over and over again, even now.

You know, I really loved him, and it used to offend me when they called him Shikra. And during the breaks I liked to drop in to see him on any trifling excuse, I really loved all those glass drawers of butterflies, and the old cupboards of nature specimens, filled with huge ostrich eggs, starfish and stuffed animals.

I remember he came to one botany lesson with wax copies of different sorts of apples on cotton wool in boxes. I wanted so desperately to take a bite out of them — they were so beautiful and juicy, so real!

The assignment he set us for summer was to collect a herbarium — how hard I tried! But what I enjoyed even more than picking plants in the ravines and drying them in volumes of the *Brockhaus Encyclopaedia* was writing the labels for them afterwards in neat writing: 'Dandelion, *Taraxacum*' or 'Ribwort, *Plantago*'. It was amazing that a common ribwort could be such a solemn and beautiful word — 'plantago'. The words probably fascinated me more than the actual dried, boring leaves did.

When Victor Sergeevich started teaching zoology, I developed what I thought of as a serious interest in ornithology, and even at lunch, when I ate my chicken leg, I put the gnawed bones back together to see how the joint worked — the function served by this little bone, or that piece of cartilage.

In fact, to be quite honest, I don't know if I really loved all of this before him — the plants and the birds. It seems to me that I didn't notice it at all. But I came to love all these living things with his love.

Or was it so that he would notice my efforts and praise me?

But then, even before the grammar school, there were a few instances of my love for feathered creatures — I remember I found three little jackdaws in a nest in a birch tree and climbed up there several times a day to tip little pieces of meat rissole into their gullets, and I poured water in too, from an old thimble that I'd begged from my grandmother.

But the real test of my love for nature came a couple of years later, also at the dacha and also with a nestling. The neighbour's boy ran up, bawling his eyes out and choking on his tears, entirely unable to explain to me what had happened. I followed him at a run, and what I saw on the pathway leading to their porch really was no sight for a child's eyes. A nestling had fallen out of the nest at a bad spot, beside an anthill, it was completely smothered with ants, squirming in silent agony, and I was at a loss, I didn't know what to do. It was already impossible to save the nestling, but I couldn't just stand there and watch its suffering either.

You know, Sashenka, I think that was the moment when I really started to grow up. I realised that from somewhere inside me I had to find the courage to do good. And at that moment, 'good' most likely meant putting an end to this suffering. I got a spade, told the boy to go into the house, went over to the nestling that had been transformed into a writhing black clump, and sliced it in half with the blade of the spade. Both halves carried on writhing – or it seemed to me that they did, because of the ants. I took the little ant bundles over to the fence and buried them. But that boy saw everything from the terrace window, and he was so upset by what I'd done that he couldn't forgive me.

Another reason why I liked Victor Sergeevich was that he knew how to make familiar things seem unusual. In the literature class, we laughed at the caustic report written by the young Pushkin when he was sent to deal with a plague of locusts:

The locusts came, flying and flying.
And then they stayed, sitting and sitting,
Till nothing was left there for eating.
And off they went, flying and flying.

Well, it really is funny, isn't it? But Victor Sergeevich made it into something quite different. Pushkin was an official for special assignments and the energetic, bright young man was sent to deal with an important issue. People had suffered a disaster, they had no means of subsistence, they were expecting help from the government.

I think my teacher simply took offence at such an arrogant attitude to insects, which for him were every bit as complex, important and alive as we are.

Everybody at the grammar school used to laugh at him, even the other teachers, and I resented that very much. But what could I do about it?

I could only love what he loved – the plants and the birds. Later, of course, after he died, my enthusiasm for all these gymnosperms, neognaths and ratites passed off. But the names have remained in my memory – and it was so grand not simply to stroll through the wood, but to know – that's lovage, that's costmary, that's orchis, and that over there is pigweed. You walk along the forest path, and all around you there's buckthorn, helleborine, codling, field scabious! And there's marsh marigold, sow-thistle, gentian! And the birds! There's a chiffchaff, there's a black woodpecker, and this is a booby!

It really is grand to walk along the forest path and know why the willow herb likes the sites of old fires!

And all this gives you an incredible sense of life that will never end.

After his death I started thinking seriously about my own for the first time.

Of course, you'll say that every adolescent boy experiences those fits of horror, those paroxysms of fear, and of course you're right, all this is absolutely normal. I realised that perfectly well myself. But that didn't make me feel any better.

My mother used to tell me that when I was five years old I heard the grown-ups talking about someone's death and I asked in a frightened voice: 'Am I going to die too?' She answered 'No'. And I stopped worrying.

When I was little and I played at war with buttons, I used to imagine myself as them on the battlefield, running into the attack, shouting 'hurrah' – and flinging my arms out and falling down dead. Then, after lying there for a moment, I jumped up and ran on as if nothing had happened – alive, eager for the hand-to-hand fighting. Slash, kill, stab!

One day I got so carried away with my game that I didn't notice my mother standing in the doorway and watching me. She said:

'Do you know that every button that's killed has a mummy too, and she's waiting at home, crying?'

I didn't understand her then.

I remember that after my grandmother died, I tried to imagine myself dead – I lay down on the divan, folded my arms across my chest, relaxed all my muscles, squeezed my eyes shut and tried not to breathe for a long time. Just for a moment I even thought I could stop the beating of my heart. And what happened? I simply felt incredibly alive. Some power in me that I hadn't been aware of before forced me to breathe. My will didn't even exist as far as it was concerned. I didn't move a jot closer to understanding death that time, but I did sense very clearly within myself what life is. It is my breathing. It is my master.

I didn't love my body and despised it, I think, from that same time in my boyhood when I realised that I was not entirely it, and it was not entirely me. I found it strange, at the conscription commission's medical examination, that someone was interested in my weight and height and my teeth, like my mother when I was little, and carefully noted down on paper all these figures that had absolutely nothing to do with me. What is all this for? Who needs it all?

Do you know what made me feel afraid the first time? When I was fourteen or fifteen – it was a realisation that suddenly hit me: My body is dragging me into the grave. Every day, every moment. Every time I breathe in and breathe out.

Isn't that alone already a good enough reason to hate it?

I remember, I was lying on my divan and running my eyes over the exposed entrails of the steamship on the wall, and the idea came to me that this huge vessel would sink straightaway if it ever sensed the fathomless depths beneath it.

My body sensed those depths.

And time and again new reasons to hate came along. The time to shave arrived. You know what my skin's like – hideously lumpy, with boils and pimples – when I shave I cut myself all the time, and it bleeds. I tried growing a beard – it didn't grow properly, a miserable excuse for a beard. And I remember one time I cut myself yet again as I was shaving, and I was paralysed by the thought that right now, this very moment, as I press this scrap of newspaper against the cut, this abhorrent sack of skin stuffed with entrails is already foundering and dragging me down with it. And it will drag all the years of my life under before it finally sinks.

Everything became unbearable. Simple objects seemed to have conspired to hammer home a single idea: here's a three-kopeck piece – it will still be here when I'm gone; there's a door handle – people will still take hold of it; there's an icicle outside the window – in three hundred years' time an icicle will still be glittering and shimmering in the noonday sunshine of March.

And at daybreak the mirror suddenly changed from an innocuous object into what it really was – the throat of time. Glance into it after a minute has passed – and it has already gobbled that minute down. And my life has grown shorter by that minute.

And another depressing thing was that everyone around me was so sure of their own existence, but I sometimes seemed so unreal to myself and didn't know myself at all. And if I wasn't sure of myself, how could I be sure of anything else? Maybe I didn't exist at all. Maybe someone had invented me – the way I used to invent the little men on the ship – and now he was torturing me?

I was sinking down into a bottomless black whirlpool, I was disappearing, ceasing to exist. In order to exist, I needed proofs. There weren't any. The mirror reflected something, but, just like me, it had no notion of what I was. It could only swallow everything down indiscriminately.

I wasn't able to do anything, everything I started doing – things that in normal times used to amuse me, bring me joy, those books, for instance – couldn't keep me afloat any longer, everything was overlaid with a clammy layer of pointlessness, like a coating of grease.

And the blind man was especially annoying. I'm lying there in my little room, huddled up in the corner of the divan, hiding under the pillow and trembling in horror at the darkness and emptiness, and he shuffles cheerfully along the corridor, whistling, living a full life that doesn't seem dark and empty to him at all, despite his blindness! What is it he sees with his blind eyes that I can't see? What sort of invisible world is it?

My mother got the worst of it. I used to lock myself in my room and not come out, or eat, or talk to anyone.

Of course, it was pointless talking to my mother. She thought I was just having the usual *fits* for my age. I heard her explaining about me to a friend of hers:

'The painting fad has passed off, now it's the meaning of life fad. But that will pass too! At least he hasn't got himself snared by some goodie-goodie young madam yet. You know what they're like nowadays!'

I was terribly afraid of girls. Not exactly afraid, but so shy that it amounted to panic. One day I was riding in the tram and a girl with wonderful hair sat in front of me – a whole tubful of wavy chestnut hair! Every now and then she gathered it in from the sides with her hands and tossed it back over her shoulders. And I wanted so badly to touch that hair! I saw no one was looking and I touched it. I thought the touch was too gentle to feel. But she felt it and gave me a mocking sideways glance. And I was so embarrassed, I shot out of the tram like a bullet.

After something like that, you start despising yourself even more.

It seems funny to remember it now, but my mother was so worried about me that she searched my things in secret, in case I might have some poison hidden away – or a revolver.

One day I heard whispering outside the door – it was her begging her blind man:

'Pavlusha, have a word with him, please, you're a man, you should understand each other better.'

He shuffles his feet and knocks.

I shout back:

'Leave me alone, all of you!'

I take a book by some wise hermit or other, hoping to find, if not the answer, then at least the correctly phrased question, and in a single voice all the wise men exhort me to live in the present, delight in the transient moment.

But it's not that easy!

How can I rejoice in the present, if it's pointless and worthless? And everything makes me feel sick – the wallpaper, the ceiling, the curtains, the town outside the window, all of it that's *not me*.

And I make myself feel sick, because I'm *not me* too, like all the rest of it. My short, squalid little past, composed entirely of stupidities and humiliations, makes me feel sick. And the future, in particular, makes me feel sick. Especially the future – after all, it's the road that leads into that stinking hole in the graveyard shithouse.

And then, before that hole – what's it all for? What did I choose? The flesh? The time? The place? I didn't choose anything, and I wasn't invited anywhere.

And just when it got really bad, when I really was thinking I could take the blind man's razor from the bathroom, when I was choking on the impossibility of taking another breath in, and then a breath out, then a breath in again, and another breath out, when my skin was covered with perspiration, my heart was aching and I had the shakes – somewhere in the tips of my fingers an incredible vibration would suddenly start up.

An incoherent but confident humming came rising up from somewhere in the depths. Swelling upwards in a wave. Forcing me to run round the room, jerk open the windows that had been glued shut for the winter with a crack and tattering of paper, and breathe in the street. The hum grew louder and stronger, filling me to overflowing. And finally this incomprehensible, overwhelming wave scooped me up from the very bottom and tossed me up to the surface, towards the sky. I was brimming over with words.

Sashenka, this is impossible to explain, it's something you have to experience.

The fear dissolved, evaporated. The world that had disappeared returned to itself. The invisible became visible.

All of that *not me* began responding, humming back to me, acknowledging me as its own. You understand what I mean, don't you? Everything around me became mine, delightful, edible! I wanted to feel it, sniff it into myself, try the taste of the wall-paper and the ceiling, and the curtains, and the town outside the window. *Not me* became me.

I was only alive at those moments. I looked around and couldn't understand how others could possibly manage without this. How was it possible to live without it?

And then the words went away, the humming disappeared, and the fits of emptiness started again, genuine seizures – I shivered and shook, I spent days sprawling on my divan bed and didn't go out anywhere – I couldn't explain to myself why I needed to go out. Who needs to go out? What does that mean – go out? What am I? What is 'what'?

And the most terrifying thing was: What if the words never come back again?

A moment came when I sensed the connection very intensely: This frozen cosmic void that I simply couldn't drag myself out of could only be filled by that miraculous humming, rustling, booming, swelling tidal wave of words. It turned out that the present moment, the transient, only becomes joyful and mean-ingful when it passes through words. And without that, the joy in the present that the wise men exhorted me to experience is simply impossible. The entire present moment is paltry and useless if it does not lead to words and if words do not lead to it. Only words can somehow justify the existence of the existent, give meaning to the momentary, make the unreal real, make me *me*.

You understand, Sashenka, I was living in a state of detachment from life. The letters of the alphabet had grown up like a wall between me and the world. I viewed what was happening to me exclusively from the viewpoint of words: Can I take this onto the page with me, or not? Now I knew what answer to give those wise men who had rotted so long ago: The transient acquires meaning if you catch it on the wing. Yoo-hoo, wise men, where are you? Where is the world that you can see? Where is your transient moment? You don't know? But I do.

I thought I had discovered the truth. I suddenly felt strong. Not merely strong, but all-powerful. Yes, Sashka, laugh at me, do – I felt all-powerful. What was hidden from the ignorant had been revealed to me. The power of the word had been revealed to me. At least, that was how it seemed then. I had become the final link in a very important chain, perhaps the most important chain of all, running from that real individual, who may have been sweaty, with bad breath, left-handed or right-handed, suffering from heartburn – that's not important – but just as real as you and me, who once wrote: 'In the beginning was the word'. And look, his words are still here, and he is in them, they have become his body. And this is the only true immortality. There is no other. Everything else is down there, in that pit overflowing with graveyard excrement.

There was something that extended through the word from that man to me, something that is stronger than life and death, especially when you realise that they are the same thing.

Imagine the amazement with which I watched the people around me. How can they exist? Why, if they aren't suspended on this chain above death, don't they fall? What's holding them up?

To me it was obvious that the most ancient primary substance was ink.

The silver tongues of all ages and all peoples had affirmed that writing knows no death, and I believed them – after all, it was the only means of communication between the dead, the living and those yet to be born.

I was convinced that my words were what would be left after the fleeting present of today had been dumped in the cesspit at my grandmother's cemetery, and therefore what I had written was the most important part, the primary part of myself.

I believed that words were my body, for when I didn't exist.

Probably no one could have loved words more than I did. I loved them to distraction. But they were winking at each other behind my back.

They were mocking me.

The more of myself I transferred into words, the more obvious it became that words were powerless to express anything. Or, rather, it's like this – words can create something of their own, but you can't become words. Words are cheats. They promise to carry you off on the voyage into eternity, and then they set out in secret under full sail, stranding you on the shoreline.

But the most important point is that reality doesn't fit into any words. Reality strikes you dumb. Everything important that happens in life is beyond words.

There comes a point when you understand that if what you have experienced can be expressed in words, it means you haven't experienced anything.

The way I'm saying all this is probably very muddled, Sashenka, but never mind, I have to get it all out. And I know that however confused I might get, you'll understand me.

I mean the futility of words. If you don't sense the futility of words, then you don't understand anything about them.

Let me try to explain it like this: remember I wrote to you about the time, during a break between lessons, after I'd been reading about the way medieval jesters used to bait their bone-headed liege lords with trick questions, I tried to mock my tormentor from the senior class in the same way, but he just slapped me round the ears as usual, without waiting for me to complete my flowery phrase. Well then, all the silver tongues, with their confident hope of extending themselves through time, are the same kind of stupid, bookish boys as I was, spending their whole lives trying to get the best of death with flowery disputations, but in the end it just slaps them round the ears anyway, without bothering to hear them out.

Remember, there was no way I could convince you that any book is lies, if only because it has a beginning and an end. It's dishonest to put in the final full stop, write 'The End', and not die. I used to think that words were the supreme truth. But they turned out to be a kind of sleight of hand, a fraud, unreal, a despicable surrogate.

I vowed to myself that I would never write again. I thought that was a worthy response.

And Sashenka, no one explains, do they, until it's suddenly revealed in some inappropriate place, that there is no answer to the question: Who am I? – because it's impossible to know the answer to that question, you can only be it.

You see, I started wanting to be.

I was not myself. The words came – and I felt strong, but I couldn't tell them: Come! And they left me empty, useless, used up, they tossed me out onto the rubbish tip.

I hated myself when I was weak, and I wanted to be strong, but it was words that decided the way I would be.

Sashenka, understand me, I couldn't carry on like that! You always thought it was something to do with you – no!

I had to liberate myself from them. To feel free. Simply alive, without any reason. I had to prove that I exist in my own right, without words. I needed proofs of my existence.

I burned everything I'd written – and I don't regret it for a moment. You scolded me, but you were wrong. My dearest, don't scold me, please! I needed to change, to be different, to understand what everyone apart from me understood, and see what any blind man can see!

I can't die and be born different – I have only been given this life. And I have to become real in the time I've been granted.

And you know, it's strange – those notebooks were reduced to ashes ages ago, but only here and now am I beginning to burn the old self that I used to be.

You know, I was the one who was blind. I saw words, but I didn't see through the words. It's like looking at the glass in the window, not the street outside. Everything that exists and is transient reflects light. This light passes through words like glass. Words exist to let the light pass through them.

You'll smile: of course, it's so typical of me – I swore never to write anything again, but now I'm thinking that when I come back, perhaps I'll write a book – or perhaps I won't. It doesn't matter.

What I am experiencing right now is far more important than hundreds or thousands of words. Tell me, how is it possible to express in words this readiness to live that fills me to overflowing?

My Sashenka! I've never felt so alive before!

I glanced outside for a moment – a moonlit night, a clear sky, starry and looking very much like happiness. I went for a little stroll, rubbing my tired fingers.

A magnificent night. A moon so bright you could read by it. It glints on the bayonets. The tents are aglow with moonlight.

The silence is wonderful, not a sound.

No – there are sounds from all sides, but such peaceful, marvellous sounds – a horse clopping its hoof, snoring from the next tent, someone yawning in the infirmary, the cicadas chirring in the poplar trees.

I stand there, gazing at the Milky Way. Now all of a sudden I see that it divides creation on a slant.

I stand there under this universe, breathing and thinking: Look at that, it turns out that the moon is enough to make a man happy. And I spent so many years searching for proofs of my own existence!

What an impossible fool I am, Sashka!

To hell with the moon! To hell with proofs!

Sashka, my darling! What other proofs do I need of my existence if I'm happy because you exist, and you love me, and you're reading these lines right now!

I know that once a letter has been written, it will reach you somehow, no matter what, but if it's not written, it will disappear for ever. And so I'm writing this to you, my Sashenka!

●

Yesterday as I'm walking away from the tram stop, I see her – coming towards me.

I cross over to the other side – and so does she.

She comes straight towards me. We halt face to face.

Well-groomed, with her hair styled, she looks a lot younger. Like a different woman. Her hair is brushed back and up and I can see her ears – with attached earlobes.

She doesn't say anything. One of her eyelids suddenly starts fluttering nervously.

I say:

'Hello, Ada Lvovna.'

The eyelid twitches.

'Alexandra, I need to talk to you. You have to listen to me. I have to tell you.'

But I say to her:

'Don't.'

Don't tell me anything, Ada Lvovna!

I know everything.

Husband trouble.

And many years before all this, this husband's wife used to think: Who needs me like this?

When the swelling started around your nipples, you were delighted, after all, you had shot right up already and there was still nothing. You looked like an eight-year-old female Gulliver.

You started thinking about Gulliver – how did he defecate? And what did the poor Lilliputians do with all that stuff? He pissed once, and it was enough to extinguish a major conflagration. What mountains all those bulls, cows and sheep every morning must have been transformed into! You suddenly sensed some big lie, but not because there aren't any people that big.

Your mum's second husband was a failure. Failures always marry a widow with a child.

Once, in the distant days of his youth, he had sent his symphony to a famous composer and got no reply. Later, at a concert, he recognised his own music in the master's new work. After that he took his revenge on mankind by doing nothing. He earned a bit of money as an accompanist at a dance class, warming his chilly fingers on the radiator.

He always used to read out intriguing facts from the newspapers and he loved figures. Say, for instance, in the last five thousand years a certain number of people have killed themselves. No one knows exactly how many. But in actual fact the figure is real. It exists. It's alive. Objective and independent. The way undiscovered America used to exist once upon a time before Columbus.

If we don't know something, if we can't feel it or hear it and we can't taste it, that doesn't mean it isn't real.

According to the statistics, suicide occurs most often at two or three in the afternoon and eleven or twelve at night.

The failure thought that by getting married he had acted nobly and in return had received only ingratitude. When he fell in love, he said to his beloved:

'I'm so glad that you appeared in my life – my salvation.'

But many years later he thought:

'Can a woman really be your salvation? If you're swimming, she'll help you keep on swimming – if you're drowning, she'll only help you to drown.'

You kept expecting your mum's husband to start looking at you in a non-fatherly way, but he never did.

Your mother tapped away the whole day on a typewriter. Calluses on her fingers, hard fingertips. Wills, letters of attorney, bills of sale, legal inventories, notarised translations. Every time she lost her job when the boss, glancing into the neckline of her blouse, kept her behind after work, locked the door, took out a bottle of wine and two glasses and assured her unctuously:

'I know you love your husband and things are hard for you, I could help.'

She declined help, twisting a sheet of paper into the carriage with a single deft movement.

She started working from home. With her head aching all the time, stupefied by tapping away like that hour after hour. She put the typewriter on a cushion. A ribbon tattered and full of holes. Carbon paper shot through and through. When she stuck her head out of the window to have a smoke, the starry sky looked like used carbon paper to her.

Immediately after your mother died you moved out to live with your grandmother and grandfather, in order not to be left alone in the flat with the drunken failure.

Granny said to you at the funeral:

'Don't spoil the grief – cry!'

They said your mother died of a weak heart. Her heart couldn't take the strain.

It wasn't until you were sixteen that you were told your mother had killed herself. They showed you the brief suicide note: 'Adochka, without true grief the soul doesn't mature. A human being grows through grief.'

In actual fact the way your mother died was this: she tipped her remaining sleeping tablets out of the little bottle onto her palm – no one counted them, but that number exists somewhere, it's real, alive – and tossed them into the kitchen mortar. Ground them up with the pestle. Poured rowanberry liqueur over them. It made a kind of wet paste. She stirred it with a spoon. Poured in a bit more, to make it thinner. Drained it into a glass. Drank it down in one and listened closely to how she felt. Then she shook the box of medicines out onto the table and started swallowing all of it, one thing after another: out-of-date pills for the heart and indigestion, for asthma and the liver.

Your mum's husband came home late, saw his wife sleeping and didn't wake her up, although he was surprised that she had gone to bed without getting undressed.

Your mum didn't want to die at all, she wanted to be saved and loved.

Three years later you wrote a postcard to the old folks: 'Dear Grandma and Granddad! I've got married. Ada.' And although you didn't write it, you thought: 'There's just one thing I can't understand – what have I, who know myself as I really am, from the inside, done to deserve such happiness?'

A young husband, still unknown, a fire-breather with tender hands.

He told you about being gifted: it doesn't come from the parents, it's an awakening.

You had nothing to live on, he refused any help from his father, the professor. In fact, he didn't even talk to him. You sold your only treasure, your mum's wedding ring, and he went out at night to work as a dock labourer, on Sundays he washed the windows in empty offices and institutions, sometimes even shop windows.

You learned to weave a nest in rented rooms, succeeded in loving other people's scuffed furniture.

You went to work so that he could study. Living on your money was a torment to him. But you told him:

'Don't be a fool, saying things like that! We're husband and wife, aren't we?'

When you were on the second shift, you made his breakfast and brought it to him in bed, in order to lie beside him a bit longer and snuggle up to him. You heard what his mum used to cook for him and entered into secret competition with her, but his mum's pies were still always best.

Leafing through an illustrated book from the library, he jabbed with his finger:

'Ada, look, that's us.'

A bald lady with a tame unicorn.

You asked:

'When did you realise we would be together?'

'When you took off your glasses. If was as if you took off your clothes. Strange – you simply took off your glasses, and I realised I loved you.'

He used to trim his fingernails with a pocket knife before, but now you did it for him with a little pair of crooked scissors.

You accepted money in secret from the professor. Scruffy and unkempt, with bad breath – complete absorbed in his scholarship. Already sick, with patches of moribund skin on his hands. Every time he told you:

'Only don't tell him this money is from me. He'll be hurt.'

Buildings were being demolished all around, your husband brought home things that had been thrown away: chairs, framed photographs, bronze window catches. Once someone died on the next stairwell in your building, the flat was cleared out, every-thing was thrown onto the dump, and he brought back a bundle of letters. You found all the terms of endearment repulsive: Kitten! My darling! My sweet! My precious Tanechka! That was because the letters were someone else's.

He explained to you why it was all right to read other people's letters:

'Because we're going to die too. And from the letters' point of view we're already dead. There are no letters that are someone else's.'

Every time you were amazed that he shared his thoughts with you, who couldn't even understand them properly. You simply remembered things.

'In the beginning was not the word, but the drawing – alpha-betical characters are a derivative, abbreviated form.'

Or:

'In his own image and likeness – everyone can do that. Even a cat, even a cloud. The way to paint a forest is not the way the trees see it.'

He hugged you with his hands smeared with pastel and you went out like that, spotted with colour.

During the day you were strong and prepared to defend him against the whole world, but at night you needed to have a good cry in his arms.

All you needed for happiness was to wash the dirty foam from his razor off the sink after him.

You didn't have any children, and he didn't want any.

You fried eggs, breaking the shells against the edge of the frying pan, and a hundred years went by.

You developed an irritation on your upper lip, but he had stopped kissing you a long time ago anyway.

He has others, you don't believe it. As long as it's still possible not to know anything, you need not to know.

The slim, invisible wavy hairgrip suddenly becomes visible.

Someone else's smells.

Lipstick that isn't yours on the coffee table.

'Whose is it?'

'What do you mean, whose? You scatter things all over the flat!'

How does he caress the other one? The same way he used to caress you, or differently?

What words does he say to the other one, as he clasps her in his embrace at their meetings and partings? With you he's broken glass, but with the other one he's a fire-breather with tender hands.

Scrubbing a stain off the floor, you noticed little dents in the parquet. You imagined the other one clattering her sharp heels on the parquet and the drum tattoo excited him.

During your rare caresses in the night, how could you tell if it was really you he wanted in the darkness and not the other one, so inexhaustibly creative at playing 'let's be different'?

In bed you felt frightened that it wasn't you he was holding with his eyes closed like that. You told him:

'Look at me!'

The most hurtful thing was that he brought the other one back to your home. The other one picked up your things, touched everything, grinned contemptuously as if to say: What strange taste your wife has!

You started feeling afraid to go to bed – as if it wasn't your bed any longer. Who had spread out the blanket, fluffed up the pillow?

Your nails are short and scruffy.

You try to imagine his feelings when he comes home, hugs you and feels your stomach pressing against him after he has been smooching with that other, slim one.

He had unhooked the other one's bra and kissed her breasts. What were they like?

When he went out somewhere, you thought it was to see the other one. No matter where he was really going, it was to the other one.

He would phone you to say everything was all right and not to expect him for dinner – while the other one was taking a shower.

You saw every woman he knew as the other one.

You look at what the other one is wearing and think perhaps it's the very dress that he unbuttoned.

You were afraid the other one would say to you:

'You wore him down without love, but I can give him what you can't. He has secrets from you, but he tells me everything.'

What could you say, if that was the way it was?

It was your own fault, after all, you forgot how to be different, didn't you?

He conceals his infidelities, so you have to forgive him, because he's concerned for your feelings, he spares you. That means he needs you, that he values you, he's afraid of offending or insulting you.

A confession isn't honesty, it's cruelty. He doesn't want to be cruel to someone dear to him.

Infidelity isn't the body, the body is always just itself. When people are together, it doesn't matter where their bodies are.

You can't lose him, because you only lose what you don't have.

No one can manage without tenderness and you will never have enough, because the need for tenderness is always greater than any tenderness.

If he has opened a window to get some air, then he was suffocating.

And how can others resist him, if you couldn't?

You said nothing, pretending not to notice anything, that everything was all right. You were afraid of words – words can only destroy. What if he said:

'When the other one touches me, it makes me tremble. But when you touch me it doesn't. I'm unfaithful to her with you.'

Not a single word, reproach or question. It was painful, but you forgave him.

And no bitterness for him – after all, he's in torment too. The feeling of guilt has made him kinder.

When the other one phoned, you called him to the telephone, went into the bathroom and turned on the water so as not to hear.

You were afraid to sniff his things, afraid of finding something in them before the wash – you asked him to look and see if he had left anything in the pockets.

You tried to be light and easy with him – like a sister giving her brother a morning kiss.

'See you!'

Live as if the world isn't falling apart. Don't walk round the place in tears. Wash and iron, because if he goes to the other one in an unironed shirt, she'll take pity on him and iron it.

When the studio appeared, it was easier, he spent the night there on the divan bed.

In the morning, when you don't want to get up and live, smile. Smile again. And again.

Speak words of gratitude to the ceiling that hasn't been white-washed for so long.

After all, children are not from the seed.

A daughter was born, a late child, long-awaited, the answer to a prayer. With a big bruised head – during the birth she tore her mother's flesh to tatters.

A little monkey is born and instantly clutches at its mother's fur, but a child is born and there's isn't even anything for it to hang on to – it's naked, defenceless.

The surge of warmth rising from the infant brought you back together again, in a different way. It became clear again why you were together.

There wasn't enough milk and you felt jealous of the bottle.

He loved changing his daughter himself. He used to say her toes were like little boiled sweets.

After Sonechka was born, you weren't interested in tender caresses, and he didn't insist, and another hundred years went by.

Your little daughter's illnesses consumed you, body and soul, and it became easier to explain his lack of love to yourself. Now you could blame yourself for paying less attention to him because of the child. Your husband had started feeling lonely and abandoned, hadn't he? When the child was ill, that was all you thought about, nothing else existed for you.

When your daughter's eardrum was punctured for otitis, your husband couldn't stand it and left the doctor's office to get away from the screaming. You put your daughter's head on your knees and squeezed it tight in your hands like in a vice. Sonya looked up at you with frightened eyes, unable to understand why the two of you had brought her to this pain, and screamed submissively, without trying to break free.

In front of the mirror you pulled down the skin under your eye with your finger and couldn't believe there were so many wrinkles! You started losing your hair, the plughole in the bath got blocked – you pulled out the wet, matted clumps. You stopped smiling, so as not to show your teeth, eaten away by caries – but that other one yawned deliciously, revealing everything fresh, young and healthy in her voracious jaws.

Behind your back his friends laughed at you, they all knew of course, didn't they?

Sometimes he left a note saying he might not be back for the night. Once he added: 'Once upon a time you married a genius, but now you live with a conceited, aging void. My dear, put up with me for a little bit longer!'

After that you loved him even more.

You often remembered how one day, when you felt you just couldn't go on, you closed your eyes and suddenly felt happy. That was probably the way happiness had to be, momentary, like the prick of a needle: the child is whining, the oilcloth smells of urine, there's no money, the weather's abominable, the milk has boiled over, now you have to scrub the cooker, they're broadcasting an earthquake on the radio, there's a war somewhere, and all of this together is happiness.

Another rainy century. And another.

For a long time already you had shared your table more than your bed, not husband and wife, but tablemates.

You got undressed without looking at each other and each lay down on your own side – a big bed and a rift between you. Your head no longer rested on his shoulder. The distance dividing two frozen creatures on a winter night is negligible, but insuperable.

Suddenly waking up from loneliness in the family bed, you looked at how he was sleeping – his face was really old.

A new sound moved into the home – the slamming of a door.

He was shouting at his life, but you took the brunt, realising that you were his life.

Blazing rows. Long and drawn-out, gruelling, in front of a desperately whimpering child.

One time he was holding a kettle of boiling water and you were scared he would pour it on you, but he restrained himself and poured it in the flowerpot with the aloe vera plant on the windowsill. Afterwards you dumped it in the rubbish, pot and all, and took out the bucket, but the smell of scalded aloe still lingered in the kitchen.

Once when he was drunk he started shouting at you:

'Don't bring me my slippers in your teeth!'

In the bathroom he still hadn't learned to pull the shower curtain completely closed, you had to mop up after him with a rag every time.

And he never cleaned off the streaks in the toilet bowl after himself with the brush.

He despised his friends who had achieved something, and again you took the brunt of it. One day the thought came that your life was blotting paper for his. Destiny wrote something for him and immediately blotted it with you – and then snatches of his life showed through yours.

Clumps of dust gather in the corners, fleeing from the brush like fluffy little animals. You wondered what they fed on and suddenly realised it was your years.

He always threw his socks about. An apple core on the bookshelf. Nail clippings on the table. But the socks were the most important thing. They weren't insignificant or accidental, they were territorial markers. People behave like animals, only they can't remember why. People mark their territory with the smell of their feet, leaving a trail. All animals understand this and they walk barefoot. See how Donka loves to rest her muzzle on feet or slippers and let the smells of her owners tickle her nostrils.

The more difficult it is for people to live together, the more emphatically they mark their territory.

You were always afraid he would say:

'I love someone else. And I'm leaving you for her.'

And then he said it.

He had prepared the words in advance. If you begged him (and you did beg him) to stay for the child's sake, he would say (and he did say):

'The only thing parents are obliged to do for their child is be happy. I'm not happy with you. But I am with her. Unhappy people can't give a child happiness.'

You yourself understood that 'for the child's sake' was only an excuse. You were simply afraid of being left alone. After all, no one would ever love you again.

You told him, not believing it yourself:

'Don't rush things! Let's put it off until summer! Wait a bit! You both need to be sure of yourselves, test your feelings. What if it's just a sudden impulse and it cools off as time passes? Why ruin our life for that? If you really still want to go then, I won't try to stop you.'

He didn't believe it either.

'It's only with her that I've realised what love is.'

'And what about me?

'What do you want me to tell you?'

'That it's a mistake.'

'But it's you, you who are the mistake!'

You grabbed a glass jar of murky water left on the table after Sonya had been using water paints and flung it into the crockery cupboard. Everything is smashed to smithereens, the room is covered in shards of china and dirty water. The child jumped up off her little bed but halted, barefoot, in the doorway.

'Stop! Don't come in here!'

You both went dashing to Sonya. He slipped and hurt his hand on the glass. You grabbed your daughter up in your arms and carried her back to bed. Laid her down, reassured her, walked out, closed the door. Then you started haranguing each other in a whisper.

The blood just wouldn't stop, neither would the hate.

When the words ran out, he smeared the blood from his hand across the chest of your blouse and left, stepping fastidiously over the broken glass.

You collapsed on your bed and broke down in tears, regretting everything but the broken jar. You regretted waiting so many years before you threw it.

You spent half the night clearing up, then took your daughter into your bed. Sonechka tossed and turned, and by morning ended up sleeping crosswise, squeezing you out to the very edge.

The centuries had ended.

The evenings when they collect Sonya are the hardest. You wander round the empty flat, thinking.

Suddenly you realised that you had no women-friends. Over the years they had disappeared, only his friends were left. They spoke to you quite differently now. No one had the time any more. And anyway, you didn't want to look into the eyes of those who had already known everything for ages.

You used to take off your stockings and Donka wagged her tail and licked your toes, but now she licked that other one's feet.

You tried to get drunk, bought a bottle of wine – it was sour and nasty, you couldn't make yourself drink it, poured it down the sink.

Sometimes you try to pull yourself together, sometimes you don't want to. You come across one of his old socks, and the tears are back again.

No one snoring beside you, kicking you in the night, twisting the sheets into ropes.

He has stomach problems. Will that other, young one, make sure he has oat porridge for breakfast and eats less salty food?

You realised what was lacking for him in your life together. A different life was lacking.

But what if he phoned you, drunk and miserable, repentant, and you weren't at home? He will want to tell you that he behaved like a total idiot and ask you to forgive him, won't he? That he loves you and is coming back. He's tired and wants to come and lay his head on your knees. After all, everything in the world has to end like that – after all his trials and suffering, the man comes back to his beloved and lays his head on her knees.

You tried not to go out anywhere, and there was nowhere for you to go to anyway, you drank rowanberry liqueur and kept watch, waiting for the phone to ring. Every now and then you picked up the receiver – a dial tone, the phone's working. One day you flew out of the shower naked in your rush to get to the phone. It was Sonya, wanting to talk about her presents from Daddy.

Sonya came back every time loaded with presents, and you thought that in time he would win the child over to his side entirely.

You lectured him when he brought your daughter back on Sunday.

'So now it turns out that I'm a killjoy all week long, I nag, I forbid, I find fault, I demand, I use discipline – but you're so nice and kind, you're corrupting the child, the word "no" doesn't even exist, you're spoiling her, getting her used to things I can't afford to give her!'

You noticed he still wore the sweater that you knitted for him.

Sonya dances on the bed, boasting:

'Look at the watch Daddy gave me. Can you hear it? Like grasshoppers!'

You shouted at her:

'Go to sleep straightaway!'

She falls asleep with her moulting tiger cub, not her new toys.

He also started sending Sonya postcards with drawings – foxes, bunny rabbits, monsters with two heads, three eyes, one leg, all smiling, waving their paws, calling to her. At first you threw them away, then you stopped when you saw the postcards were numbered. Sonya pins them up on the wall above her bed with thumbtacks. Talks to them before she falls asleep.

Cooking Sonya buckwheat for her supper, you got distracted, gazing out of the window at the dingy colouring of the people walking by. Hurrying along, not realising that they are happy. The buckwheat burned. You sat down at the table, put your head on your bent arm and started bawling your eyes out. Just then Sonya came in.

'Mummy, what's that smell? What's wrong? Are you crying?'

She started consoling her mother like a grown-up, stroking your head.

'Come on, Mummy, it's just silly old buckwheat!'

Sonechka had almost stopped wetting the bed at night but now, since he left, it had started all over again.

You're reading some children's book, and in it a girl is on her way to a flea market where they sell old dolls and suddenly you realise the dolls are little girls who have died. How can anyone write things like that for children?

You were on your way to the children's clinic and Sonechka suddenly asked out loud, so the whole tram could hear:

'Mummy, did Daddy leave us because of me?'

During the school holidays they took Sonya for a week. You almost stopped going outside altogether, didn't throw the rubbish out, didn't wash the dishes, didn't change the bed sheets, didn't iron your clothes. You didn't battle the fluffy little creatures with a rag, you surrendered. It felt to you like revenge. You went off your diet and onto chocolate. That was revenge too.

Your hair hangs down in filthy, tangled ropes and it's so grey, it's frightening.

You looked in the mirror at the wrinkles round your eyes, the dry skin on your cheeks, your withering neck. A woman withers inside first, in her soul, and then on the outside.

You thought: how could it happen – the veins have spread right across my legs like tiny rivulets, my pubic hair is turning grey. And this parting from my body started a long time ago.

You looked at your portraits hung across the walls and remembered how you posed naked and he used to break off to kiss you all over and now you asked yourself:

'Who is that on the canvas? Then who am I?'

You started talking to yourself.

'You have to go into the kitchen, open the little window and put the kettle on. Do you hear?'

'Why?'

'Because. To do that you have to love yourself at least for a moment.'

'Love myself? What for?'

You struck a bargain with fate – if you took a shower now, tidied yourself up, put on nice clothes and makeup and spent your last money on a bouquet of flowers for yourself, then something would happen.

It did.

'Ada!'

The vet you used to take Donka to. Sonechka called him Doctor Doolittle. Doctor Doolittle's the man, he can cure you, yes he can! No one had explained to the little girl that people brought him healthy cats and dogs and took them away castrated, with their claws torn out.

'Adochka, freedom suits you. Just look at you!'

Everyone knows everything. He hugged you round the waist, although he had never permitted himself any familiarity like that before. He grinned brazenly.

'Why don't we have dinner together, now that we've met like this?'

You thought: This is it, the miracle.

'Why not? Take me to a restaurant and order something expensive!'

You sat in a corner, surrounded by mirrors.

The waiter stood beside you all the time, looking at his own reflection, adjusting his bow-tie, tugging down his cuffs.

Doolittle told you funny stories from his practice. You laughed out loud.

The waitress collecting the empty plates leaned down low over the table, offering him a glance into her cleavage. He took a glance and smiled, as if he was apologising and saying: What's a man to do – we're slaves of instinct.

'When you spend your entire life mating animals and putting them down, you can't help becoming a romantic.'

After draining your champagne and putting your glass down for him to pour you more, you asked:

'If you love one person all your life, is it really possible to love another?'

'Why, that's the third time you've asked that!'

'The third time?'

That was when you realised you had been drunk for ages already.

It seemed like everyone there could tell where you were going to go now and what for.

As you were leaving, you saw the waiter lick a plate in the mirror.

When you came out of the restaurant, Doolittle started kissing you on the lips. You hung on his neck and told him:

'Only not back to my place!'

You arrived at his place and as he put on his slippers in the dark, he whispered:

'Don't worry, my wife and kids are at the dacha.'

When Doolittle started pulling off your knickers, you started bawling and told him through your tears that you hadn't slept with any men for years. He thought: 'Good, that means I won't catch anything.'

He heaved away, puffing and panting, but it was all a waste of time.

He went off to the bathroom and locked himself in.

You waited and waited, then got dressed in a hurry and slipped out of the flat.

A thought flashed through your mind – it was winter, you could drink yourself absolutely blotto and freeze to death in the street.

What frightened you was not death, but what would come afterwards. They would inspect you, naked, and slit open your stomach to make sure of something that was obvious anyway.

All you needed was a little dose of powder.

The thought came to you that you were flushing water down the toilet for the last time in your life. You flushed it again.

You gathered up a handful of tablets and started swallowing them. You had forgotten to take something to wash them down with – you went to the bathroom and tried washing them down with water straight from the tap.

But the tablets were so big they wouldn't go down – you had to break them. You sat on the edge of the bath, breaking them.

You remembered that you had locked the front door, you had to open it. While you were walking across the room, you felt yourself staggering already.

You lay down on the bed.

A droning started up in your head. The room started flickering and creeping round in a circle.

You moved the telephone closer. Dialled the number.

She answered, that other one. She was too sleepy to understand.

'Call him, I want to talk to my husband!'

'Do you know what time it is?'

'No.'

He took the phone.

'What's happened? Have you gone crazy? You've woken Sonya!'

'I swallowed a lot of tablets. I'm afraid. I don't want to die. Please come!'

Your speech was already slurring.

'Call yourself an ambulance!'

'Come!'

'Let me call you an ambulance.'

'Please, please!'

'How I hate you! I'll be there straightaway.'

'Only without her!'

'All right. I'll be straight there. And you try to make yourself sick.'

'Wait!'

'What else?'

'I love you.'

'I'm coming, I'm coming.'

She, that other one, wanted to sleep. She had to go to work early in the morning.

■

My Sashenka!

Again I have a sheet of paper in front of me – my link with you. But on the other hand, how can some stupid sheet of paper connect us when everything that separates us seems so insignificant and paltry! How can there possibly be any barriers separating you from me? And you feel that too, don't you?

My dearest darling! If only you knew how much I want to come home!

Probably that's why it's so important for me to write to you. When I write, it's as if I'm on my way back.

Today Kirill asked me to make sure his mother gets his bag if anything happens to him. Then he laughed.

'She won't understand anything in it, of course.'

He talks about her so tenderly all the time.

From here, at this distance, I'm beginning to understand that all my lack of understanding with Mum, my failure to love her, is bunk.

Now I would forgive every time she ever hurt me and ask her forgiveness for everything she had to put up with from me.

And I would start by admitting something that has been tormenting me for all these years, something I simply couldn't confess to her at the time. You see, Sashenka, it's a very stupid story. I was playing with coins on the windowsill. Do you remember our huge, wide windowsill? Or is that just how it seemed to me back then? Well, anyway, I was playing with coins, standing them on edge and flicking one side so that they spun round, turning into small, transparent, ringing spheres. And then my eye fell on a wide crystal bowl with Mum's jewellery lying in it – brooches, bracelets, earrings – and I saw her ring there. The wedding ring the blind man had given her. And I suddenly wanted really badly to set that spinning on the windowsill, like a coin!

The first few times it didn't work, the ring skipped away and hopped onto the parquet floor, but it did work once! It was very beautiful – the airy, transparent little golden sphere jingled as it traced out circles on the windowsill. I especially liked the sound when the ring was spinning on one side and tapping out a rhythm just before it froze. But the next time I flicked the ring with my fingernail, it jumped out of the window.

I ran out into the street and searched and searched, but I didn't find it. Perhaps someone picked it up and took it away.

At first I was going to tell Mum everything, but I didn't, and she didn't even ask. And afterwards, when she did ask, it was too late to own up and I said I didn't know anything. Mum was terribly upset and couldn't stop thinking about who could have stolen her ring. She suspected completely innocent people. I heard her telling her blind man it must have been the woman from the next-door flat, and then she decided it was the doctor she had called when my stepfather had a cold.

I felt terribly ashamed, but I didn't say anything.

But now I would tell her everything.

I think about her and I remember silly little things. For instance, that Mum always slept with a black bandage over her eyes, she couldn't get to sleep if there was any light coming into the room.

When I was little I used to love the smoky smell of her clothes. She smoked a special, fragrant kind of cigarettes. When she was in a good mood she gave in to my pleading and let the smoke out through her lips in rings that passed through each other, and even figures-of-eight.

When the blind man moved in with us, he forbade her to smoke, but she sometimes smoked behind his back, breathing out through the window, and she asked me to keep it our little secret.

I remember once I was ill and she came in from the cold and frost and before she touched me she warmed her hands under her armpits and put her fingers against her neck to check that they were already warm.

Later, when we started doing maths, I thought she was funny, demanding that I do all my homework when she couldn't solve a single one of the problems.

And then, even later, I found a few old photographs in which she was with some man, but not my father, and for the first time I felt surprised at how little I really knew about her. But to ask her about the man with whom she had been recorded for posterity under a palm tree – such a simple thing – was absolutely impossible somehow.

And now I'm amazed at what all our conversations were like. She shouted:

'A great lanky brute and he lazes about all day long!'

'I'm not lazing about, I'm thinking.'

And I used to slam the door in her face.

One day she came into my room late in the evening, she probably wanted to talk about something important. I was lying on the divan, pretending to be asleep. She just covered me with the blanket, stood there for a while and went away.

But the main thing for which I would ask her forgiveness now is the blind man.

One day I came running back from school and found him in my room – he was feeling everything in there. I threw a hysterical fit with Mum, to make sure he wouldn't dare come into my room and touch my things again. And she burst into tears and started shouting at me. Became hysterical too. So we shouted at each other, without listening.

It's only now that I realise how difficult it was for her with the two of us.

The fact that her husband was blind didn't bother her at all. A waiter in a cafe asks her what she wants to order for him – for people who are used to eye contact, it's only natural to ask the guide. But she has learned to laugh and answer:

'Ask my husband, he won't eat you!'

I think, on the contrary, that it made her feel important, being associated with a blind man. I remember the daughter of one of her friends coming to see us, I had seen her before as a very beautiful girl, but then there was a terrible accident. When she was visiting someone, she sat down in an armchair with her hosts' dog and started playing with it, but it wasn't domesticated, it had been picked up in the street. Probably there was some kind of awkward movement, the dog reacted nervously and bit her right in the face. She was beautiful and she became ugly. She came to Mum to ask her to arrange an introduction to some young blind man.

I did my best to spoil their life, but they probably just loved each other and couldn't understand why I was so cruel.

Now I'm trying to recall if he ever shouted at her even once – I can't remember it. On the contrary, in fact, when my mother turned her ankle and sprained her ligaments, my stepfather cared for her very tenderly and brought her food to the bed. I can see it now – her hopping clumsily along the corridor on crutches and him walking beside her, ready to catch her and support her.

I remember Mum was always upset when she looked in the mirror, but he would come up, put his arms round her from behind, kiss her and smile his crooked smile, demonstrating the advantage of being blind – being yourself, just as you are, and not as the mirror wants you to be.

I also remember I was preparing for a physics exam, mumbling something or other, and he suddenly said:

'Light travels hundreds of thousands of miles in a second – just so that someone can adjust his hat in a mirror!'

At that moment it became quite obvious to me too that light didn't really need to be in such a great hurry.

He read a lot. I go into his room, it looks dark and empty, I switch on the light and there he is, sitting in the armchair with a thick book on his knees. He used to take those embossed books for the blind from the library and feel indignant that the pages had been read to tatters. The Braille script letters were all worn away by people's fingers.

And my stepfather used to write poetry too. In the middle of the night he would walk out into the kitchen in order not to disturb my mum's sleep, sit there in the dark and prick holes in paper really quickly with his awl.

Mum often used to repeat his favourite lines.

'Your warmth has become my light in the darkness . . .'

Thick paper pricked all over lay around in heaps in their room. He tried to inculcate a love of numismatics in me. My stepfather collected old coins, he could spend hours on end sorting through them. He had a few rare favourites – he loved the feel of them.

I look at his sunken eye sockets and he tells me about Panticapaeum, the capital of the Bosporan kingdom. I remember those coins with the relief images – a drawn bow with an arrow on one side, a gryphon on the other.

After his hands the coins gave off a sourish metallic smell. I held these light, irregular discs on the palm of my hand and couldn't believe that they were contemporaries of Archimedes and Hannibal.

A little copper coin had an image of King Riscuporidus I – I remember the strange name – and on the reverse side the profile of the Roman emperor Tiberius. My stepfather explained that the Bosporan kings bore the title 'Friend of the Caesars and Friend of the Romans' and minted their coins with images of the emperors of Rome on them.

He especially prized a coin from Utrecht that had no head on it.

He told me that before, when people died, they used to put a coin in their teeth as payment for their journey. And he once joked that when he died they'd have to stick that Utrecht coin with no heads in his cheek.

'I don't want to dodge the fare!'

Just imagine, Sashenka, when I was a child, coins were paper money's little children.

My stepfather sorted endlessly through his worn, flattened treasures with their little bobbles and remnants of Arabic script, and I watched in amazement – it was as if he could see the coins and the past, and who had minted these coins, and what these emperors who had disappeared long ago looked like, but at the same time the cobweb in the corner and the factory chimney outside the window didn't exist for him at all.

Back then I used to feel a kind of superiority over him – there he was, blind, but I, being sighted, could see things that he couldn't. Only now it seems to me that that keen-eyed juvenile observed everything, but didn't see a thing. A blind man should be weak and defenceless by definition. But he was strong, hungry for life, and that was why Mum clung to him. My stepfather didn't seem to feel that he was crippled or deprived in any way. The way he didn't see the light was nothing like when our eyes are blindfolded. He didn't see the light in the same way a sighted person doesn't see it with his knee or his elbow.

My stepfather also had a highly original sense of humour. For instance, he's eating an apple with a knife, paring off the skin, and he holds up a piece he has sliced off on the end of the knife and laughs as he tells us about a young woman out in the street who led him to the post office and when they parted said in a mournfully compassionate voice: 'Better not to live at all than live like that!' My stepfather lost control and hit her with his cane. He told us this story as if he wanted everybody to laugh merrily at it.

And now for some reason I've remembered us living at the dacha in summer, and him walking about in the garden, bending down the branches of the apple trees and touching them. He remembered where each apple was hanging and then every day he felt them to find out how they were growing.

And here's another memory – he was robbed in a shop. He was about to pay and some soft-hearted lady offered to help. All his money was filched out of his wallet. He made a scene and the poor young salesgirl sobbed and protested that she had nothing to do with it.

When I shaved for the first time, my stepfather gave me his eau de cologne. Probably that was the moment when a simple idea first came into my head: he didn't have any children of his own, and all those years he had wanted to feel that I was his son, but I had done everything I could to prevent it from happening.

By the way, I learned that trick from him – if you nick yourself while shaving, tear off a small scrap of newspaper and press it onto the cut.

All those years I used to think about my father too. Why did he leave Mum and me? What happened back then? I dreamed that he and I would meet. For some reason I thought that some day he would simply come to meet me in the school yard after my lessons.

Once I saw a grown-up teaching his son to ride a bicycle – running behind and holding on to the saddle. And I wanted so badly for my father to teach me to ride a bicycle!

And at the end of the school year I remember the entire hall applauding at the gala assembly when the headmaster handed me a certificate of merit. I stand there with my hair already trimmed short for the summer, and I look for my father in the crowd of parents, although I know he can't be here. But what if he has suddenly come back right now? And he's observing my triumph? Feeling proud of me?

Sometimes I used to find things left over from him that Mum hadn't thrown out for some reason. For instance, when I was little I used to play with his slide rule. His old textbooks were still up in the attic, dusty and incredibly boring, full of calculations and formulas. She had thrown out all his photographs and cut the ones where they were together so that even in the photo that showed her sitting there pregnant with me, all that was left of my father were his severed fingers on her plump shoulder.

I once asked Mum about my dad, but the only answer I got was that she didn't want to talk to me about that man now.

'You'll find out everything when you grow up.'

I was afraid to ask about him after that.

It seems to have been this unspent love, reinforced by hate for my stepfather, that my teacher Victor Sergeevich inherited. I'm not really sure if that old crank deserved it.

In class he used to show us the very simplest organisms, protozoa, in the microscope. He tossed his tie back over his shoulder so that it wouldn't get in the way, but it kept falling back down. We couldn't make anything out properly, just some vague blotches, but our teacher assured us that what we were seeing was real-life immortality. And then, to make the point to us, he took me as an example, which delighted the entire class no end, but I felt really hurt, I could have cried, because he didn't understand that he was making fun of me. He started amusing my classmates with the idea of me dividing in two, only both halves are still me, each is a young individual, although it remains old at the same time, and life starts from the beginning – and this carries on for millions of years.

'Just imagine!' he almost shouted in his excitement. 'This infusorian that we are looking at here through the eyepiece of this microscope saw the dinosaurs!'

At the time I was astounded that there was real immortality in the world and that for these protozoa death was not natural, only accidental. But I was even more astounded that Victor Sergeevich, my favourite teacher, had thrown me to the untender mercies of those beasts. I cried bitterly into my pillow at night and decided that he didn't love me any more. Well, then I ought not to love him any more.

Shikra.

But a week after that he had the seizure in our class.

Sasha! I write to you, my little girl, and I forget about everything around me! How good it is!

Here everything is permeated with death and pain and it's absolutely impossible to imagine that somewhere life is carrying on as if nothing has happened. Streets, newspapers, shops, trams. The zoo. Restaurants. People can just drop into the post office. Or call into the confectioner's to buy a little cake.

From here the very simplest things seem strange. Well, isn't it strange that my city is living its own life without me? It has just become invisible to me. It's summer there where you are too. But surely it isn't as airless and sweltering?

How I long for the winter!

To gulp in the frosty air with my mouth. To hear my footsteps crunching across a crust of ice, as if I'm gnawing on dry biscuits as I walk along. To see the icy glacier under a drainpipe. And the early morning snow falling unhurriedly and thoughtfully.

You know, I remember the forest in March, the snow has already gone, but where people walked step-for-step through the snowdrifts in winter, there are still little stumps of ice on the dry leaves. A strange track of dirty, unmelted stumps running through the forest. What did I remember that for?

And I also remember that we left a bottle of water on the balcony – in the frosty night the glass shattered, but the water carried on standing there in a bottle shape.

All this is because we are dying of thirst here.

Sashenka, how many times I have imagined the way I will come back home! And everything there is still in its right place. My room. Books everywhere – on the windowsill, piles on the bookcase reaching up to the ceiling, a stack like firewood on the floor. My old sagging divan bed. My table lamp. No shooting. No death.

Everything in its usual place. The clock ticks, but time has stopped. It's all real, it's home, it's mine.

You know, I dream that I'll get back and simply sprawl there, gazing tenderly at the wallpaper for half a day. It would never even have entered my head before that such a trifle could make a man happy.

Yes, yes, when I get back I'll look at even the most familiar things quite differently – at a tea service, an electric lamp, a soft armchair, a shelf of books. At the factory chimney outside the window. I think that things have acquired an entirely new meaning for me now. If only for that, what has happened had to happen.

Do you know what surprises me about the dead? That they all become like each other. In life they were different, but afterwards all their eyes are the same – the pupils of the eyes are dull, the skin is waxy and for some reason the mouths are always open. It's especially disgusting to look at the hair, I can't explain why. And the fingernails.

And the smell is the same. Not just a smell, of course, but a stink. A stench. The most repulsive smell in the world.

You know, I've seen so many dead fish, birds and animals in my life, but nothing ever stank like human corpses.

And it's impossible to get used to this smell. And it's impossible not to breathe.

In comparison, faecal aromas with an admixture of the quick-lime that they spread over the pits filled with our gastric contents seem like nothing at all. Or the smell of purulent bandages at the dressing station.

But the scent of straw imbued with the smell of horses is one that I just want to draw into myself, to smother the odour of sweat and dirty bodies.

Sometimes I feel I could just cut off my nose.

Really, cut it off and send it home at the first possible opportunity. Gogol's runaway nose didn't sniff at anything. But mine
would walk around and sniff in the familiar smells.

It is amazing all the same that as time passes, the smells I
remember don't get weaker, but grow stronger.

I walk through a park and what the blossoming lime trees exude
is not just a smell, but a vast field of fragrance!

There's our confectioner's shop – vanilla, cinnamon, chocolate.
Meringue, marzipan. Éclairs. Marshmallows. Fruit pastille. Plum
fudge. Halva. My favourite rum truffles.

The green, sappy smell from the flower shop – damp, white
lilies and musty steamed earth.

The smells from open windows – freshly ground coffee. Here
they are frying fish. And there the milk has boiled over. Someone
has taken a seat on a windowsill and is peeling an orange. And
here they are boiling up strawberry jam.

A whiff of an iron, hot material, an ironing board, steam.

Redecorating in progress – the paint sets my nostrils tingling.

And now the smell of leather – shoes, handbags, belts.

Then perfumery – the fragrances of scent, creams, eau de
colognes, powders.

A fishy odour. Fish on crushed ice giving off the fresh smell of
the sea.

Engineering workshops – the smells of rust and grease, kerosene,
engine oil.

From the kiosk on the corner, a whiff of printer's ink on fresh
newspapers.

And here's someone who's come out of a boiler room, he reeks
of sweat, sackcloth, coal.

Flooding out of the bakery – the warm, appetising aroma of
freshly baked bread rolls.

And this is a chemist's! A chemist's smells so much like a hospital!

And further along they're boiling up bitumen and asphalting the road. Everything is drowned out by the smell of hot pitch.

I could walk on like this endlessly, sniffing and sniffing.

●

It will soon be a month now.

More than three weeks have gone by since this thing happened to Sonechka. She still isn't coming round.

And it's not even clear how it all happened at the time. Donka probably set off with a sudden jerk on the lead, dragging Sonya after her, and she slipped on the icy steps and hit the back of her head against the sharp stone edge. She was lying in a puddle under the falling sleet.

I had her transferred to my hospital. What an effort it cost me to make them give her a separate room!

She lies there withered, skin and bone.

Her arms and legs are covered in bluish bruises from the injections.

They bring learned visitors to look at her.

'Now here's an interesting case. The girl that we were talking about. Since the injury occurred she has been in a coma for . . .'

Her parents come to the hospital by turns and sit there for hours.

After all, someone has to take the rags out from under her, drop pure water into her dry eyes. Moisten her parched lips. Turn her over, wash her.

I walk past, glance in – he's looking out of the window and massaging her lifeless feet.

He blames himself for what happened. She blames me.

Ada keeps going to the chief physician, demanding, weeping.

In the corridor I can hear her.

'Well, do something!'

When she's with Sonya, I try not to go in.

When I'm on night duty, I go in often.

The glasses with one lens are lying on her bedside locker. And her watch. I wind it up. There are toys in the bed, brought from home. The tiger-cub with the dangling button-eyes.

Her slippers are under the bed. Waiting patiently.

Once I went in when he was with her and saw him running a squirrel-hair brush along her arm. He saw me, felt embarrassed, put the brush away.

Two of her friends from school came and sat there for a minute, cringing in fright.

He told them:

'Say something, tell her what you're doing in your class now!'

They cringed even more.

For some reason they put an acorn in her fist. When they walked out of the room, they burst into tears.

In the middle of the night he woke up with a shout – he'd dreamed that he trapped Sonechka's finger in a door.

'You know, I'm walking in front and I don't see that she's standing behind me and she's stuck her hand into the opening.'

He's soaking wet, breathing heavily. He tossed and turned in his room until the morning.

We sleep separately.

The first time I went to sleep in the other room because he was snoring and fidgeting and he stuck his hand into my eye in the middle of the night.

But now I understand exactly what he meant that time by a different kind of loneliness. One day I woke up and saw his face beside me on the pillow – old, distant, unfamiliar.

I started noticing things about him that I didn't see before.

In some ways he's incredibly fastidious – in company he puts his glass somewhere up high, on a cupboard, so that no one will take it by accident, but in other ways he's slovenly. When I sort out the clothes for washing, there are always brown stains on his underpants.

I started being irritated by the way he eats. Rapidly, greedily, sloppily.

We leave his old friends' homes and he starts running them down. This one's a third-rater, that one's a bootlicker. He hasn't really got any friends left. Old family friends, or rather, their wives, stopped inviting him after he left Ada, on the assumption that a bad example was catching.

He's getting old and he's afraid of it. And he clings to me even more tightly. And that makes him feel even older.

He has started forgetting everything – important things and insignificant ones. He comes running to me, bewildered, and says:

'Just imagine, I can't remember who painted *The Parquet Planers* in the Musée d'Orsay! It's been bothering me since this morning!'

Sometimes I feel very good with him, so light and easy. But sometimes this darkness surges up inside me.

The two of us are very lonely together.

One day, before all this happened to Sonya, he said:

'But there was a time when we were happy together, wasn't there?'

'Yes.'

'What's happening?'

And he explained it himself.

'You know, you and I are like Fresnel's double mirror. They

took two mirrors that reflect light and joined them together. And at a certain angle two light rays produced darkness.'

Every now and then we have rows, like in a bad film. We wind each other up over trivialities, then shout and slam doors.

Sometimes it's as if I'm watching all this from the outside: Who are these two people in the kitchen? What are they saying? What for?

She's especially irritating. Who is that woman? Could it really be me? No, it's impossible. But then where am I? What's happened to me? Where have I gone to?

'You don't cook lamb right! You know how Ada used to . . .'

The innocent meat goes flying into the rubbish bucket.

'Then she can cook your lamb for you!'

It isn't possible that woman in the kitchen could be me, is it?

After Sonya's accident the rows quietened down, but we still didn't become closer to each other.

He comes back from the hospital and drinks. Once, when he was completely drunk, he muttered:

'You know, Sasha, I've started feeling afraid because I thought: Could you really not be the person I've been waiting for all my life, could this really be another delusion? But if I thought it, it must be true, mustn't it?'

I undressed him, put him to bed and finished off what was left in the bottle.

Another time he said:

'I thought that what we had was the real thing. That when we were together we were real, and with anyone else we would just be searching for each other and never find each other. But it was probably just an illusion.'

The day before yesterday I met Ada in the hospital. She was on her way to her daughter, walking slowly up the stairs, and had stopped by the window on the landing to get her breath back. I had to walk past her. She saw me and suddenly smiled.

I walked over to her.

'Sasha, I know you're doing everything you can for our Sonechka. Thank you. And please don't bear me any grudge!'

She walked on slowly upwards.

That night I simply couldn't get to sleep and I realised from his breathing that he wasn't sleeping either. So we both lay there without sleeping and I said:

'Remember, you told me you made a mistake when you married Ada?'

'Yes.'

'Well, I think you ought to put that mistake right and live with her to the end.'

■

My Sashenka!

How are you over there? What's happening to you?

I know you're thinking about me, waiting for me, loving me, writing to me.

Before I would have crossed something out of this phrase, so that only one 'me' was left, but all that seems so unimportant now!

I miss your letters so very badly! We all wait for the post here, but there isn't any, and most likely there won't be in the near future. Your letters are travelling by some roundabout route. And they will definitely reach me – no matter where they might be. I wait and wait – and I'll wait until they come, no matter what.

I'll get them, probably the whole bundle all at once. They're accumulating somewhere, and later the dam will burst and they'll come flooding through . . .

I've suddenly got a free hour or so – I want to be with you.

We have good news here. There can be good news even here, after all! Just imagine, the diplomatic missions in Peking are still holding out! Everybody thought those people were dead, but they're alive. A messenger broke through from there with a letter, they write that they are besieged and waiting for help. Several messengers sent before him didn't reach us. An expedition to Peking is being planned here, but first the fortified city of Tientsin has to be stormed. We can't leave the Chinese army in our rear.

And here's more news – we have been transferred to the Eastern Arsenal.

Our headquarters has been moved to the facilities of the former military engineering academy and the officers have been accommodated in the same little houses where the German and English professors used to live. I'm writing to you now, seated in the shade of an acacia and swathed in gauze to keep off the mosquitoes. Everyone is still suffering as badly as ever from the sweltering heat. And the sweat's dripping off my nose onto the paper – pardon me for this blot!

When we arrived, everything here was in total disorder. It's obvious that everyone fled at the last moment, after the arsenal had already been taken by the Yihetuan. The rooms and the courtyards were littered with student uniforms and books in Chinese, English and French. It was so strange to leaf through the students' notebooks, with their pages laboriously filled with drawings and exercises. Everywhere there were broken cups, pens, ink, Chinese ink brushes, jade trinkets, caps, Chinese paintings, aphorisms on long sheets of paper, rifled trunks and boxes. Everything abandoned, torn, battered, trampled.

Kirill and I have found a rich European library here. For the most part the books are on mathematics, physics and chemistry. Our soldiers immediately took it into their heads to start ripping them up and burning them – no one tries to stop them any more. It's interesting that all the academy buildings are built in the Chinese style and stand in single file, one behind the other. The first buildings used to house the professors, auditoriums, laboratories and teaching rooms, and the ones behind them were student residences. The various service buildings and the kitchen were right at the back.

A wooden observation tower has been built in the middle of the first courtyard. Today I climbed up to the very top tier, which would offer a delightful view, if only I wasn't thinking about what's going on all around. Directly to the north of the arsenal the Lutai Canal is visible, the Chinese have set up artillery batteries along both of its banks. To the west is Chinese Tientsin, with the western concessions a little further away. The railway line to Tong-Ku runs off to the south-east. And stretching away to the east is a boundless plain, overgrown with kaoliang, with the dark patches of Chinese villages and groves of trees scattered here and there. Somewhere far away to the north and the east, through binoculars I could see the movement of Chinese forces, apparently advancing from Lutai to Tientsin.

Kirill and I wandered round the arsenal and were amazed by its riches. There are armaments workshops, depots and laboratories here. Chinese copper and silver coins used to be minted here too. The immense halls here contain an entire factory in which gunpowder was manufactured and cartridges were produced for the very latest models of Mauser and Mannlicher rifles. The underground depots contain huge stocks of various kinds of grenades, mines and shrapnel. Kirill translated the Chinese inscriptions for me. For instance: 'Vault of underground thunder' means 'Mine depot' and 'Dwelling of the water-dragon' is in fact nothing more than 'Fire-fighting equipment depot'.

Beside the furnaces, large boilers and engines, the Chinese workers had set up images of the patron gods of labour and burned incense sticks to them. Notices in red were stuck on the engines and boilers, with maxims like 'To start an engine is a great happiness', 'To open a boiler means great prosperity'.

This move of ours is a positive one, if only because we are no longer next to the infirmary and do not hear the groans of the wounded by day and by night. Of course, it's bad that I no longer have the chance to drop in and chat with Zaremba or Lucie. You get attached to people very quickly here.

The powder magazines are laid out in an open area in the western section of the arsenal. It's terrifying to walk past them and feel that a single lucky shot will send everything here flying sky-high. And the best thing would be to be killed outright, not maimed.

No, Sashenka, that's what I used to think, but now I think quite differently about that. I used to think that life as a deformed freak or a cripple was a tremendous misfortune, the futile, pointless existence of a worm. I dreamed of an ideal death, so that I wouldn't even notice I had died. Of vanishing in an instant.

But now I want to live. Any way at all.

Sasha, I want to live so much – as a cripple, as a deformed freak! To live! Not to stop breathing! The most terrible thing about death is stopping breathing.

Once in the infirmary I was struck by the following scene: there was a wounded man there with everything smashed – all his arms and legs – waiting for amputation, and some joker was telling a funny story, and everyone in the tent roared with laughter, and this wounded man laughed too. I didn't understand what he was laughing at, I couldn't understand then. But now I understand.

They can wound me, I can become a cripple. But I will live! Hop about on one foot. So what if I only have one foot, I can gallop off anywhere I like on it. Let them tear off both my legs! I'll look out of the window!

If I'm blinded, then I'm blinded, but I'll still hear everything around me, all the sounds, what a miracle that is! My tongue? Let there be nothing left but my tongue – I'll be able to tell if the tea is sweet or not so sweet. If there's a hand left, I want that hand to live! I can touch and feel the world with it!

Sashenka, I'm afraid this letter will seem like delirious rambling to you. Forgive me, my dear one, for all this raving. The raving is not because I'm ill, but because I am who I am.

And the most surprising thing is that everyone here hopes to get back home safely.

And everyone, when he sees someone else whom he knows or doesn't know with dull pupils, waxy skin and an open mouth, thinks joyfully: him, not me! A shameful, insuperable joy: today they killed him, not me! And today I'm still alive!

And I can't rid myself of the thought that any letter of mine, even this one, could be the last. Or might never be finished at all. It's only in operas that everything comes to a meaningful end with the final note of the concluding aria. But here men die at random.

Sashenka, what could be more terrible than to die simply at random?

Every minute and every letter could be the last, so I absolutely must say what's most important and not write about inconsequential trifles.

And precisely because this letter could be broken off at any moment, I have to tell you now everything that I haven't said before or put off for later.

But what can I write about? Everything seems like inconsequential trifles.

You know, there's a story I was going to tell you some time, many years from now, when it will be amusing. But I'll write it now. What if I can't tell you later? It's of no interest to anyone except me. But I need to tell it. It's a short story.

And perhaps, viewed from here, it has already become amusing.

I met my father after all.

Mum had a box that she kept locked in the sideboard. I saw where she hid the key. When there was nobody at home, I opened it. It was full of various documents, papers and receipts. And it turned out that all those years my father had been sending my mum money regularly. I hadn't known anything about that. But the important thing was that I found his address.

I didn't tell Mum anything.

At first I wanted to write to him, but I didn't know what to say. Then I decided to go to see him. One night in a train, and there I was standing outside his door.

I stood there and couldn't bring myself to ring the bell.

Imagine it – living for years and years, thinking about this meeting. And now I couldn't explain to myself what I wanted. What did I need this for? I hadn't slept a wink all night in the train. I wasn't some naive adolescent, to go thinking I would finally acquire the loving and beloved father I had dreamed about so much. I knew I would meet someone who was a stranger. And that he didn't need me at all. After all, he had abandoned me. And he hadn't enquired after me once in all those years. Maybe he wouldn't even let me inside the door. What was it I wanted? Finally to receive the love of which I had been deprived all my life? That wasn't possible. I had already lived the part of my life when I really needed him, without him. Perhaps I was an avenger? Come to wreak vengeance on the scoundrel who had abandoned his wife and infant child? To spit out my backlog of hatred? My righteous wrath? Someone had to punish him for his villainy, didn't they? To punch him in the face? Humiliate him? Perhaps what I needed was his repentance, his pleading for forgiveness?

Strangely enough, I felt hate for my mother and stepfather, rather than for this man, about whom I knew nothing.

What if he feels frightened that I want something from him? I don't want anything from him. If he tries to give me anything, I won't take it.

I felt uneasy. And the longer I stood in front of that door, the more obvious it became that I no longer wanted this meeting that I had been dreaming about since my childhood. And I didn't want him.

I was already on the point of leaving, but just then the door opened. He must have sensed that there was someone standing there.

A flabby, wheezing body. He drew the air into his blocked nostrils noisily. I hadn't been expecting to see an obese old man with puffy circles under his eyes and flabby cheeks. It was him. He looked at me without saying anything.

I said:

'Hello! I'm here to see you.'

I was astounded that he realised who I was straightaway, as if he had also been waiting for this moment while he lived through all those years.

The confused expression on his face lasted only a brief moment, then he raised his eyebrows, sighed and simply said:

'Well, come in. Are you hungry after your journey?

It was a strange feeling, as if all this wasn't happening to me, it was all so impossible and so commonplace at the same time. He introduced me to his wife and children, saying that I was the son of his first wife, Nina. Everybody felt awkward – nobody had been prepared for anything like this. Nobody said anything. His wife spoke for everybody, but she spoke in a hoarse, strangled whisper. She explained that nervous stress had triggered a growth on her thyroid gland and it pressed on her windpipe. Strangely enough, she reminded me of my mother somehow.

My sister turned out to be a young maiden of vast proportions. She sat down and the armchair was instantly overflowing with her. She glared sideways at me, as if I wanted to steal something from her.

But the little boy, on the contrary, really took to me. It obviously tickled his fancy that an older brother had suddenly appeared out of nowhere. He asked straight away if I knew any combat holds and was disappointed when I said no. Probably in his boy's world the presence of an older brother who knew some combat holds would have made his life a lot easier.

They were my brother and sister, but I didn't feel anything for them – and why should I feel anything?

My brother dragged me into his room and started hastily showing me his riches – models of ships, toy soldiers, a cardboard fortress – and he told me his sister didn't go to the grammar school because they were boycotting her there, no one wanted to sit with her in the classroom or the dining hall. And so she hung about at home all the time, since she didn't have any girlfriends, let alone boyfriends.

It was strange suddenly to find myself in the middle of someone's life.

When she and I were left alone together for a while, I had no idea at all what to talk about and I started asking what she read. I had absolutely no intention of offending anyone, but she suddenly declared in a resentful tone of voice:

'A woman knows that men who look at her make no distinction between herself and her appearance.'

I was glad when we were called to dinner.

Nobody said anything at the table either, only my father's wife asked me in her strangled wheeze about my plans for my life.

The poor girl took the lid off the tureen to pour herself more cabbage soup, but our father admonished her:

'Perhaps you shouldn't have any more?'

Her face immediately turned scarlet, tears spurted from her eyes, she jumped up from the table and ran off clumsily to her room.

Our father heaved a sigh, crumpled up his napkin and went after her, but he came back empty-handed. She wouldn't open the door for him.

After that everyone finished eating in silence, staring at their plates. I sat there and thought: 'What am I doing here? But everything in the world happens for some reason, doesn't it? Surely there must be some kind of sense to all this?' That sense refused to reveal itself to me. How could I ever have imagined that my meeting with my father would be like this?

I sat with my little brother for a while, helping him solve problems about trains and pedestrians and feeling astonished that he could be so backward at his age. Our sister looked in and tossed a scarf that had been dropped in the corridor onto the bed.

He pulled a face at her back as she left and whined:

'Barrel-belly, wobbly jelly!'

I put my hand on his neck.

'Don't talk about her like that.'

He twisted up his face.

'She's my sister! I talk about her any way I like.'

I squeezed his neck. I could see from his face that it hurt.

'She's my sister! Don't you dare talk about her like that again! Do you understand?'

He squealed that he understood and I let him go. His glance made it clear that he didn't like having an older brother at all any more.

In the evening my father and I were left alone together. He kept sipping tea from a large cup – he said he had kidney stones.

I asked what he did. It turned out that my father was an architect. I hadn't even known that about him.

I enquired what he was designing at the moment and the answer was:

'The Tower of Babel!'

Then he told me they had been commissioned to design a new prison.

He sat there, shoulders hunched, one leg crossed over the other. Just like me. Only now did it strike me how alike we were. I started noticing my inflections, gestures and grimaces in him. My nose was his, too, and the shape of my eyes, and my lips.

I asked if my father remembered me being born. He livened up at that and started telling me about the first time he saw me. He said that immediately after I was born my little face was like an Egyptian bas-relief, but the next day the depth of everything had increased – my nose was more convex, my eyes were more deeply set, my lips were lips. I was carrot-coloured from infantile jaundice, and he was also amazed that I appeared in the world with fingernails that were already long.

I asked if he remembered how we went to meet Mum at the railway station, and he sat me on his shoulders so I could look out for her. He nodded uncertainly.

He asked me about Mum, about her blind husband, about my universities. But I could see that he wasn't very interested. Neither was I. We were both yawning. I'd had a sleepless night in the train before all this.

They made up a bed for me in his study, on the divan beside the bookcase.

I kept waiting for him to say something important to me. But all I heard was:

'Goodnight, we'll have another good talk tomorrow.'

There was something pitiful about him.

Before I went to sleep I took down a book at random from the shelves to read, it was some old work about types of building stone. Apparently 'sarcophagus' was the name of a type of stone quarried in Troas that possessed the property of annihilating the body of a dead man, including even the bones, without leaving a trace, so they made tombs out of it. Flesh-devouring. It was strange, stone absorbing a human being.

I woke up early in the morning, in the dark, when everyone was still asleep, and went to the railway station without saying goodbye to anyone. I left on the first train.

Before I left I had lied to Mum, saying that I would stay overnight at a friend's place, but after I got back, as we drank tea I told her I had gone to see my father.

She didn't speak for a long time, clinking the spoon in her cup. Then suddenly she said:

'What for? He's not your father.'

I was dumbfounded.

And then Mum told me that when she was young this architect had wooed her for several years, but she had never loved him.

'He invites me to a concert and we walk along the aisle in the hall, everyone's looking at us, and I'm dying of shame for him – scruffy and crumpled, smelling of plain soap.'

He asked her to marry him – she refused. But when she became pregnant with me, she remembered about him and agreed. She said that at the wedding she tried to pull her stomach in, but nobody noticed anything anyway.

It was as much as I could do to mumble:

'But that means you used him!'

'Yes, I suppose I acted meanly. Perhaps. But for your sake I would have done anything. I told myself: the child has to have a father. I thought it would be possible to love him. It didn't work out. I told myself I had to! But in the end I realised I couldn't carry on. I tried to persuade myself to be grateful to him, but when it came to it I was almost sick every time he touched me. It wasn't a family, it was torture. And the moment came when I exploded. It was a difficult time for him – a bridge he designed had collapsed. And then I told him everything as well.'

When I recovered my wits I asked:

'Then who is my father?'

She took out a pack of *papyrosas* that she hid from my stepfather and lit up at the window. I waited.

Finally she answered.

'What difference does it make? Perhaps you never had a father. From the moment you appeared in my stomach you had no one else but me. Consider it a virgin birth.'

And she gave a bitter laugh. She never said another word about it.

There, my Sashenka, I've told you.

Do you know what is really amusing? At the time I wanted to write a serious story or even a novella about this: a youth searches for his father and finally finds him. I didn't understand that it is really a very funny story. Good Lord, and I wanted to be a writer! To be a writer is to be no one.

Sasha, I find that me, the old one, funny and repulsive now. I have crossed him out. I'm so old already, and I still don't know anything about myself. Who am I? What do I want? I'm still no one! I still haven't done anything in this life! I could find any number of excuses for that, but I don't want to look for them. I'm starting all over again from the very basics. I know, I can feel, that someone different, someone real, is growing inside me. And he has so much strength and desire to do something important! When I get back, I'm not going to waste a single minute. Everything's going to be different. I shall have time to do so many things, accomplish so much! I shall even look at the sky quite differently.

I know, you read these stupid lines and you thought: He can look at the sky anyway . . .

No, Sashenka, that's not right, not right!

Do you know what idea has just come into my head? You'll laugh. Please don't laugh, my darling!

When I get back, I could become a teacher.

I imagine that now you'll recall how the ancient Greeks chose their teachers. A slave breaks his arm or his leg and becomes useless for any kind of work, and then his masters say: 'That's another pedagogue we have!'

I don't know what sort of teacher I would make, but somehow I have the feeling that it's for me. In any case, I could give it a try.

Yes, somehow I have the feeling that I could make a good teacher. I could teach literature. Why not? What do you think?

In general, thoughts keep coming into my head now that were

completely impossible before. For instance, I want us to have a child. Are you surprised?

I was surprised at myself. And for some reason I want it to be a boy.

But I imagine him already grown up a bit. I don't know anything at all about babes in arms and I'm probably afraid of them. I think, for instance, about how we'll play chess – and I'll play without a queen, to encourage his love of the game.

I'll record his height by putting a book on his head.

We'll draw together, make things. I'll show him how to make a whistle out of an acacia pod.

I imagine myself teaching him to ride a bicycle, he weaves all over the place and I run behind, holding on to the saddle. But that's after he grows up a bit.

We'll have everything, Sashka, my darling, believe me!

And I also imagine that you'll go away somewhere and we'll wait for you and go to meet you at the railway station. There'll be heaps of people there. I'll sit him on my shoulders and tell him to look out for you, or else we'll miss each other. He'll see you and shout:

'Mum! Mum! We're here!'

●

Yesterday I had night duty. I dropped into the children's ward and showed them a slide strip on the wall about little Tom Thumb. He threw his crumbs to the hungry birds, as if he knew from the very beginning about the ogre's castle he had been brought to with his brothers and sisters and he didn't need bread any more.

Then I get to Sonechka's room.

She's still lying like that with the acorn in her little fist, still absolutely doesn't want to die, although nothing at all can be done.

I stroked her gaunt arm.

Wound up the grasshopper-watch.

Snow falling outside. Quiet, slow. Soft, fluffy, mute.

I lay down on the edge of the bed and hugged her, pressed her against myself. Started whispering in her ear:

'Sonechka, listen to me. I'm going to tell you something very important. Try to understand. I know you can hear me now. In one book I read about death that it's like when you're a child playing outside in the snow, and your mother watches you through the window, and then she calls you. You've just been out playing for long enough and it's time to go home. You've tumbled about in the snowdrifts, you're wet, your felt boots are full of snow. You'd like to go on and on playing, but it's time. And it's no good trying to argue. You're stubborn, and that's really great. There's only a little handful of you left, and you're still clinging on to life. You don't want to go. You're a great girl! Such a tiny little girl, you're really great! But you have to understand that you can't live, you know. It's all the same to you, but you've worn your parents ragged. They love you so much! They've been told there's no hope. The doctors who looked at you and wanted to help you very much, they can't do anything. Don't feel hurt about it! Perhaps they might not understand some other things, but they know all about this. They seem like big, grown-up, clever people to you, but they really can't do anything. Believe me, if you could just look at your body, you'd realise straightaway that it's no use to you any more. You shouldn't cling to it any longer. Do you understand that if you let your body go, you'll be helping your parents – you love them very much too, don't you? They're worn out.

Even just a little drop of hope could give them the strength to carry on, despite everything. But when there's no hope left, it just hurts really, really badly. They'll feel better if you die. It's hard to understand, but try, my skinny little honey-bunny. Just look at this body, it's absolutely no use to you now. It can't dance any more, it will never be able to curtsy, or run, or skip about, or draw, or go outside. When it dies, that will be great. You know, life is a lavish gift. Everything in it is lavish. And your death is a gift. A gift to the people who love you. It's very important for people when their dear ones leave them. That's a gift too. It's the only way they can understand anything about life. The death of the people we love, people dear to us, is a gift that can help us understand the important reason why we are here. And then, just imagine, you're a little girl who really doesn't know anything yet, not even why a light bulb shines, not to mention things like Fresnel's double mirror, but when this happens, you'll learn something that none of the grown-ups here, not even the wisest ones, know – it will all be revealed to you. If you like, I can take your acorn, bury it in the ground in spring and it will grow into a little tree. Now you tell me, what can an acorn, living its little acorny life, know about the life of an oak tree? A body is just a body. You grow out of your ballet shoes, don't you? It's just that you've grown out of your body too. And here's the most important thing: don't be afraid that you'll suddenly be alone. Remember, you drew the way a tight little thread runs back from every object to a single point? That's the way the world is. In the beginning we were all together, a single whole. Then everything was scattered, but that little thread pulling us back was attached to every one of us. And afterwards the whole world will gather back together at that single point. Everyone will go back there – first you, then Donka, then your mummy and daddy – it's doesn't matter who goes first. Some people call it the vanishing point, but its best name is the convergence point, because that's the place where we'll all be together. Even railway tracks come together there. And all the trams go there. And the kite that you and your daddy launched was flying back there to that point, only it got tangled in the wires. Just imagine, it's still hanging up there. It waved to me today as I was coming to work. But it's late already. Outside the window the snow's falling, thick and white. It's quiet. Everybody's sleeping already, they've run themselves to a standstill. My little girl, this body of yours can't do anything any more, but you can do everything. Now curl up tight and warm!

Sasha, my odd-eyed love!

I dreamed about you today!

Would you believe, I can't remember the dream exactly now, but we were going somewhere together. Then for some reason you disappeared and I ran after you, but I couldn't run, all my movements were as laborious as if I was up to my chest in water. Why is it that dreams are forgotten straightaway? Never mind, it's not important. The important thing is that I dreamed about you, and we were together.

And perhaps you dreamed about me too? Imagine that my dream met your dream somewhere, they kissed, put their arms round each other and hugged each other tight.

My little girl! My love!

Tientsin will be stormed in two days. At least, that's what they say. Everyone here is expecting it, but no one really knows anything for sure. We're preparing for the expedition to Peking, but then again they say that we'll have to wait until the rainy season — where are those rains now? — and it's unlikely that we'll be able to set out before then. Rumours, rumours and more rumours. That's all that keeps everyone going here.

I'm alive and well, although I've lost a lot of weight and all my clothes are falling off me. For the last few days I've been having stomach problems again. I went to the doctor, but Zaremba only advised me not to eat anything for the time being. I haven't developed lice yet. Like most of us here, I wash and shave only occasionally, I'm all shaggy. Today I decided to have a shave and spruce myself up. I sat on an empty shell crate and scraped off my five-day stubble. A scrap of bandage served as a shaving brush. I don't have a little mirror to shave with — I broke mine and had to borrow Kirill's. I may not shave regularly here, but every now and then I have to, otherwise I'd go completely to seed.

You know, I looked in the mirror when I was shaving and suddenly saw myself with my mouth open. You understand — I saw myself dead. I've started seeing everybody as they will be after they die, including myself.

But I try to drive away thoughts like that.

Today Lucie left for Tong Ku with a group of wounded. They were sent off down the Pei Ho on a barge. What joy I saw in the eyes of those men who were finally being carried away from Tientsin, away from the bullets, grenades, operating tables and agonising torment, and what envy in the eyes of those staying behind!

When Lucie was saying goodbye to our men, she burst into tears and kept putting her hand over the mole on her neck. Our new colonel, Stankevich — I haven't told you about him, but I will later — gave Kirill leave to see her off, he's there now, at the quayside, but he should have been back ages ago. I hope nothing has happened to him.

I feel so glad for their happiness! They searched all their lives and then found each other – here and now! Kirill has confessed that they have decided to marry. She's going to wait for him in Tong Ku.

Although, of course, I don't really understand what Glazenap sees in her. She's a sweet person, but too simple – I think that's it – for him. And a lot older. But that's not important. How does Ovid put it? The girl herself is only an insignificant part of what you like about her.

Kirill has come back now. Flopped onto the bed, turned to face the wall. He didn't say anything at first, then he said:

'Now I absolutely have to go back alive.'

Sashenka, in places where there is death, where they send men to kill, there is always so much falsehood. Do you know what I think about all that now? Winning or losing really isn't important, because the only victory in any war is to survive.

But apart from the lies about the struggle between good and evil and the beautiful, false words about immortality, in all this there is still some very important truth, and I can sense it. Probably that is why I'm here, to understand it.

People grow coarser here, but they also become gentler. Something that was hidden before is revealed in them. I've noticed that even the soldiers I saw as coarse beasts start writing tender letters home. He probably used to get drunk and beat his wife there, but now he writes to her: Yours with kisses and hugs, your loving Petya. Wasn't it worth sending him here for that alone?

And me? Without this experience, would I really have understood that I am scrambling my way through life from the complicated things to the simplest? The very simplest of all?

Yes, here there is so much evil all around, so much crude, sense-less, ugly cruelty, but I only cling all the tighter to what is human in myself and around me. It is all the more important to preserve the small grains of humanity within me and around me. For instance, I never really had any friends. But here I share what could be the final days and hours of my life with a man, and all my human warmth flows into him, like into a funnel.

Kirill is as dear to me now as a brother, and this awkward man in thick glasses becomes ever dearer to me as the roll-call of killed and wounded grows longer. At this moment he doesn't even suspect that I am writing to you about him. He has taken off his glasses in order to wipe them, and the gaze of his vulner-able eyes with the puffy eyelids is completely, childishly help-less. Now he has turned back to face the wall. He even sleeps in his glasses.

He and I have shared the same thoughts and fears – how close that brings us together! The same thought constantly in mind – let nothing happen for one more day, and another! And another! And another!

I remember him looking down at his feet and sighing:

'How ugly they are! But it will still be a shame if they're blown off.'

Kirill has an ingrown toenail on one foot. He joked that he will probably be identified by that toenail if he is left without a face when he is killed.

For the first time I have experienced that remarkable feeling about which so many lies have been told – male friendship. It really doesn't require very much. Simply to know that he won't abandon you and you will help him in every possible way you can. There's always something miraculous in meeting each other alive and well.

And now I feel real joy that Glazenap is here and nothing has happened to him. I think he has fallen asleep. Nestled down on his little Chinese cushion stuffed with tea. I can hear husky breathing and babbling. He's muttering something in his sleep. Probably dreaming of his beloved. Lucky man! Ah, no, he's not asleep, he was talking to himself. Now he has got up and walked out.

The cicadas are already chirruping in the poplars, setting my ears ringing.

For some reason I've remembered Kirill telling me that he used to play at barbers when he was little, and he once trimmed a cat's whiskers. Afterwards the cat used to bump into chair legs and thrust its face past its food.

I've started feeling differently about the men as well. The more of them that are killed, the more strongly I feel my closeness to them. Writing out the lists of the dead yesterday, I suddenly, for the first time, called this battalion my own in my heart and felt myself a part of it.

I used to think life was a preparation for death. You know, there was a time when I felt that I was some Noah to whom it had been revealed that sooner or later a flood would come and the life of everyone on earth would end. So he had to build an ark in order to escape. Noah no longer lives like everyone else, all he does is think about the flood. I also built my ark. Only my ark was not built of wooden beams, but of words. And so everyone around me was living in the present day, rejoicing in the fleeting moment, but all I could think about was the inevitability of the flood and the ark. They seemed wretched to me, and I probably seemed the same way to them.

I thought I had to write down all the most important things. All the creatures two by two. Events, people, objects, memories, pictures, sounds. Look, a grasshopper has flown in and nuzzled against my knee. And it's entirely up to me to take him with me or not. I'd been through something similar in my childhood with the tin buried under the jasmine bush. Only now I could take absolutely everything with me.

Noah's work is a deliberate, wise acceptance of death.

I make a rather useless kind of Noah.

Sashenka! This is all nonsense, there never was any Noah. And my ark of words will sail away, and I'll be left here! And we have to prepare ourselves, not for death, but for life! I'm still not ready for life, Sashka!

There I was, the Noah of Noahs and fool of fools, looking for something important, big, unachievable, and I had to end up here to understand that I have you. That I already have something big and important – you. Death is all around, but I can feel the deluge of life within me, it seizes me, lifts me up, bears me along towards you.

At night such anguish surges over me, and the only salvation I find is in us, for after all, what happened has not gone anywhere, it is still here, alive, it is in me and in you, it is our substance.

Do you remember, in winter I came to our monument after the hairdresser's, I had stabbing pains in my back and my ears froze at once in the unaccustomed cold, and by evening a hard frost set in and we strolled about, both of us wrapped in your scarf. I can see that scarf now – the large, loose stitches of the knitting. We got frozen stiff, went to your place, got undressed and lay under the blanket with our teeth chattering – you took my icy hands and put them between your legs to warm them up.

Or do you remember how we went riding on a bike at the dacha and your skirt got tangled in the wheel?

These are little pieces of our life, after all. How many of them there are, Sashenka! Or rather, how few there still are!

When I stayed with you the first time, I went to the toilet at night and in the darkness I couldn't see anything, I fumbled my way along the walls, knocking my knees against the chairs, and woke you up.

And when a speck got into my eye, you licked it out with the tip of your tongue.

Tell me, do you still bite your hangnails? Don't do it, my darling, don't gnaw on your fingers, you have such beautiful fingers, so delicate!

Once you started thinking about something and walked round the flat with a toothbrush stuck in the corner of your mouth.

And do you remember, you came to me, I put the coffee pot on the stove – and forgot to pour any water into it? I had to throw it out.

And another time we forgot about the kettle, it boiled away in the kitchen, turning it into a steam bath. Afterwards you took a sip of tea and then, staring at the light reflected in your cup, you suddenly said:

'Look. I've got tea with a ceiling lamp and sugar!'

Your feet wouldn't fit into your new shoes – you stretched them on with a tablespoon.

And your conch! *Strombus strombidas*, always stuffed full of cigarette ends! Knobbly, with horns. How is it? Where is it? Is it waiting for me?

My love, you and I parted so long ago, but I still feel you as if only a few days have gone by.

I close my eyes and I see you sitting there on the bed, as you did that time, in my shirt, with your arms round your knees and your chin resting on them, just out of the bathroom, you'd been washing your hair – you made a turban out of a towel. Your ankle with a scratched mosquito bite is right there in front of my face. I kiss your ankles.

I shall definitely feel the pulse in your neck, the way I did then. I really like the way it beats in that precise spot. I love that hesitant little bounce under the thin skin.

I'll see your chapped lips, I'll kiss them and kiss them. They change colour round the edges. And there's a delicate crust in the middle.

I'll be flooded with such love for you, for your lips, your ankles, for all of you! At night in the darkness I'll whisper tender words to you, kiss you, caress you, make love to you!

You're mine, I won't give you away to anyone!

And I want you so frantically. I need your body so badly!

After all, I'm alive, Sasha.

●

A tram morning. There are so many of them.

Outside the window it's still dark, and in the dull light of the bulbs inside the tram everybody has the blue faces of drowned people.

Some are dozing, some are soiling their eyes with newsprint.

On the front page – war, on the back page – the crossword.

From the major cities they inform us that people should not sit in a public library with a leaky ceiling that has green blotches on it – homeless people go there to catch up on their sleep, lying there, stinking, with their faces nestling in a binder of magazines.

They write from Gaul that in the evening, in the dense rays of the sunset a fine skin grows on the cobblestones of the street.

They write from Jerusalem.

Science news: scientists have calculated that for the last five thousand years most people have grown close not by choice, but like trees, which do not choose either their neighbours or their pollinators, but simply intertwine their branches and roots because they have proliferated.

It has also been demonstrated experimentally that there's something funny going on with time. Events can take place in any sequence and happen to anybody at all. It is possible to play a comb and tissue paper in the kitchen so that it tickles your lips and at the same time, in an entirely different kitchen, read a letter from someone who no longer exists. There you are at the dentist's, they're poking the needle into your root canal, twitching the nerve, and then eight centuries later the fringe on the tablecloth flutters. And in general, as the ancients observed, as the years go by the past does not recede, but moves closer. And all the watches can only chirp like grasshoppers, showing different things to different people, when everyone has already known for ages that the time is ten to two.

As a result of barbaric over-catching in the Alps, butterflies have almost disappeared.

Tea rolled up in newspaper can replace a cigarette.

By evening it might perhaps turn a bit fresher.

Breaking news. There she was walking along, not knowing that life is shorter than a skirt.

Readers' letters. How great it is when you're expected back for dinner.

A snow woman laments, wondering why everyone pities the *Titanic* and no one pities the iceberg.

Wanted – a stamp with an image of a pigeon-fancier who is waiting for his pigeons to come back and not looking up into the heavens, but into a basin of water – he can see the sky better like that.

Single, nobody's fool, brown-haired for ages already, no bad habits, well, maybe I smoke sometimes, a sister to myself, in the Druidic horoscope a Mustard Seed, height – fit under your arm, no volume to me at all, eyes like the pools in Heshbon, by the gate of Bath-rabbim. Fairly well-off. Used to work in a hospital behind a high brick wall with broken glass stuck on the top to scratch the wind. The children there were afraid of jabs, not cancer – it took a long time to find a free spot on a pincushion arm.

Now the Empress of Life. The message and the messenger.

I weave the fine threads of justice and mercy.

I scrape with the curette. A little arm and little leg lying on a little tray, I look to see what's still missing – before I scrape everything out.

I come home tired after work and it's a non-home.

At night I toss and turn on the battered old divan bed and it mutters something in Old Divanic, full of sibilants. The tap in the kitchen is a scatterbrain. I bought a new pillow and I'm tormented with it – it smells of something chickeny. Nocturnal cries, strange and foreign, drift in through the window – I live opposite the zoo now. By the time I gather myself to go there for a walk, it's winter again already. The cages are empty.

Once I go, and no proper snow has really fallen yet, nothing but dandruff. They've drained the water out of the pond, there's lots of rubbish on the bottom.

I went into the monkey-house, it's overheated and it stinks. I watch them rubbing urine on their palms and fur. It's their words.

Then I tagged on to some school children, and they led us all off to the far end of the zoo, where there's nothing but chickens. Perfectly ordinary, domesticated chickens. A whiff of my pillow. And that's where they started telling us that when a chicken is incubating her eggs, she keeps turning them all the time so that the life-giving maternal warmth of her body reaches all the parts of her child, and therefore, when a healthy brood hatches out it's the result of her persistence and concern. But then it turns out that this is not an example of conscientious motherhood at all. What actually happens is the following. The chicken's stomach gets hot. Driven by her discomfort, she looks around for a suitable object to cool her own inner heat. The chicken sits on the eggs because they are cool. After a while they warm up, so she turns them over to position the cool side uppermost. After she has repeated this for a sufficient number of times, the young hatch out and, to her great surprise, she finds herself faced with a clutch of chicks. There, children, see how nature has thought of everything for us!

I left the chicken house and saw a wintry she-elephant, a solitary lost soul. Freezing outside while her non-home is being cleaned. Swaying to and fro in the early December twilight. Stepping from one foot to another. Feeling the chill. Steam coming out of her trunk.

Suddenly I feel like the same kind of wintry elephant. I stand there and sway to and fro with her. How did I end up here? Why is it so cold? What am I doing here? I need to go home! I need warmth!

After Daddy left, Mummy was lonely and she got a cat that had kittens regularly every year and Mummy gave them away for free to the dealers at the pet market, anything so that they didn't have to die. Her health had deteriorated very seriously in the last few years, and every time I came to see her, all she ever talked about was the cat and her kittens. Every time she tried to persuade me to take one, and I kept refusing. But now, after the she-elephant, I've agreed. I live opposite the zoo now anyway, I'll set up something like a local branch.

I didn't spend a long time choosing, I took the one who crawled over to me. I called her Thumbtack – for her nose.

I carried the kitten home inside my coat and she kept trying to crawl out. I blew in her face, she crinkled it up and hid away again.

Thumbtack played all the time and it was so wonderful to watch her. The first time she saw herself in the mirror she started attacking her reflection, with her fur bristling and her claws thrust out. After banging her nose a few times, she lost any interest in the mirror once and for all, but she could hunt a piece of string for hours. Or after she'd had a good sleep, she could tear round the room for hours like lightning – from the bed to the armchair, from there to the curtains, from there to the sofa and round and round like that until she knocked something over. Then she would hide under the sofa, and had to be lured out with a skipping, dancing piece of paper.

I decided to teach Thumbtack to use the toilet, but she fell into it and after that she was desperately afraid of water.

For some reason she didn't want to go in sand, but she liked a box with rustling scraps of newspaper.

She wasn't ashamed of anything, a child of nature. There I am eating, and she could sit herself down on the table in front of me, knot herself into a pretzel with her back leg pointing up at the ceiling and lick her little pink anal orifice. It really is strange that for the Egyptians my Thumbtack enjoyed the status of a god.

She scratched the armchair to ribbons until I got the idea of dragging an entire log back home for her. She loved to sharpen her claws on it. It was impossible to imagine that my Thumbtack was an animal, that she could tear someone apart with those claws.

Somehow Thumbtack grew up without me noticing and became Button.

I heard somewhere that it's all the same to cats whether their owner is at home or not. Rubbish. Button was always delighted when I arrived. When she saw me, she got up, arched her back, stretched sweetly and came to be fondled. I would take a shower, put on my warm towelling bathrobe, plaster cream on my face and settle down on the sofa with a book, putting my feet on the cat like a hot water bottle. I read and stroke Button with my foot. She purrs deliciously.

The only horrible thing was when she came into heat. Poor Button rubbed herself against the furniture, rolled around the floor, crept along on her belly, started wailing desperately. Mummy told me to take the cat to the vet and have her spayed. But I felt sorry for her.

Poor Button, I wanted to comfort her, to fondle her, but when I started stroking her, she immediately assumed the mating position. She kept trying to run outside into the street, I had to lock her in.

At night it was impossible to get to sleep, watching the way she writhed and wailed for attention. I lie there with my eyes open, covered in moonlight, and think that my cat is part of some gigantic mechanism that includes the moon and spring, high tides and low tides, days and nights, a wintry elephant, and in general all the cats and non-cats who have ever been born or not been born yet. And I started feeling that I, like her, was a part of this mechanism, this order, established in some incomprehensible fashion, that required touching. I felt like howling too. Over all the millions of years, how many there have been like me and Button, with or without a coat of fur or scales, who have suffered the same torment and could think of only one thing – how they long to be caressed!

During the day I assist nature, rummaging in other people's

reproductive organs, but at night Button and I will shrink down to a single body and wail together.

After all, moonlit nights were specially made to torment us.

And someone yells in the open window, so loud the entire Universe can hear it:

'Yes! Yes! Yes!'

Then Button disappeared, she couldn't bear it any more.

I dashed outside without my coat, ran round all the nearby courtyards, called, shouted, asked chance passers-by. She didn't come back. Perhaps someone took her in. Perhaps she got run over. My little Thumbtack.

At work they consoled me, told me that some people they knew were always getting a cat, but it always ran away, then they got a new one and gave it the same name. So they had the same Pussy in a new skin. Feline immortality.

Mummy suggested I should get a new kitten too.

But I didn't want to do that again. I get used to a cat and then the parting hurts. And I decided I'd rather get myself a wintry she-elephant. She wouldn't run away.

I always agree to work on holidays, so I won't be left alone with myself so much. It's not so bad during the day, but in the evening I come back to this strange place where my bed is and drink a little glass of liqueur before I get into it in order to get to sleep quicker and escape from myself.

And I'm glad when Yanka asks me to go round on Saturdays and sit with her children.

I like going to them. Before I can even take my coat off at the door Kostik, their eldest, is dragging me into his room by the hand. He takes toys out of a huge basket and presents them to me. And I stand there with my outstretched hands piled high with little cars and animals, and they're already tumbling onto the floor, but he keeps piling more on.

I once talked to him with the nutcracker – now every time I come, the child shoves the nutcracker into my hand and asks me to make it talk to him again.

And now they've had Igoryok.

Yanka didn't want to know in advance what she was going to have, and she was hoping for a girl, but it was a boy. She was upset. The midwife joked about it, clicking the scissors she had just used to cut the umbilical cord and asking:

'Well then, shall we snip it off?'

After the birth the entire flat was turned into a child factory all over again, everything scattered all over the place, baby weighing-scales on the writing desk, piles of clean nappies everywhere, reeking of lavender, heaps of baby jackets, the kitchen muggy with steam, like a bathhouse – the rubber teats are boiling in a saucepan.

Yanka in a bathrobe over her nightdress that is wet with milk, talking to me and knitting a tiny little sock, just like a doll's. And so quickly. She knitted one and started on another. Her husband dropped in – he put the finished sock on his finger and started walking it, skipping across the table on one leg, he jumped across onto his wife, skipped along her arm, onto her shoulder, onto her head. Yanka laughed, took it from him, drove him out, said go on, you're stopping us talking.

Yanka is upset because after the second birth her figure has changed, she's blown up, her face has turned plainer. Her milk is boiling over, her breasts are covered in lumps, her nipples are cracked.

She said the only reason she liked being pregnant was because she could indulge any whim she fancied. She invented a desire, and it was accepted that her husband would set out in the middle of the night to look for a pineapple.

She can do anything she likes with him. That's what everyone calls him – Yanka's husband.

But if anything serious needs to be done around the home, Yanka tackles everything herself, he's a dental technician, he takes good care of his hands.

He has the annoying habit of sticking out his lower lip and plucking at it with his fingertips.

In general he's a wonderful father, always fussing over the children. But he's funny. When the older boy was still in his cradle, he talked to him, repeating a single word:

'Daddy! Daddy!'

He wanted his son's first word to be 'Daddy', not 'Mummy'.

But the child said quite clearly: 'Give!'

Yanka's first birth was very difficult and I remember her saying then:

'Never again! Sashka, never have a child!'

But later, when she got pregnant again, she said something quite different, that you forget all the terrible parts, with all the pain, and you start wanting to live and have children again:

'What a clever idea that is of nature's – forgetting! You know, the horror is forgotten, but how can you forget holding a newborn baby in your arms? The back that fits in the palm of your hand, the velvety skin, the little pot belly that bulges out at the sides.'

When the three of us went out walking with the pram, Yanka's husband pompously explained that the agony of birth is necessary to arouse the maternal instinct. He'd read somewhere that experiments had been carried out and monkeys who gave birth under anaesthetic bit through the umbilical cord afterwards and ate the afterbirth, but they refused to feed their children.

'So pain is necessary. It's been proved scientifically. There is no life without pain.'

I feel good with my Yanochka. We're always reminiscing about something or other.

Once she spent the night at our dacha. How old were we then? Thirteen? Fourteen? Mummy sent us to hang out the washing on the line between the birch trees and we started slapping each other on our bare legs with the wet towels for a joke. First for a joke, as a game. Then viciously, until the tears came.

How lucky I am to have Yanka! And her Kostik. And now Igoryok as well.

The baby's chest measures two centimetres more than his head – a sign of good health. He sucks eagerly.

There's more than enough milk. Yanka doesn't know what to do with it all, she lets her husband suck it out.

When I stay to sit with the children for the evening, Yanka expresses a bottle of it.

As she leaves, she stuffs cotton wool into her bra.

'It's a nightmare. I'm soaking wet every time. Why couldn't woman have been created with a built-in tap?'

They go, and I love feeding the baby so much. While his older brother plays with his bricks on the floor, I warm up the cold bottle in water on the cooker. I settle down in an armchair with the hungry little miracle. I sprinkle a few drops on the inside of my elbow, lick it off myself, then start feeding him carefully. He pulls touching little faces, blows bubbles and I feel completely happy. Something's wrong, he's whimpering. It's not flowing out of the bottle properly. I go to the kitchen and try to widen the hole with a hot needle. Now it flows too freely. I have to change the teat. Then I walk round the room with him over my shoulder, patting him on the back to make him burp. I fondle this tiny creature with its pungent scent of milk and urine.

Then I put Kostik to bed and read to him before he falls asleep.

The last time I was reading I lay down beside Kostik, put my arm round him and felt him move away from me.

'What's wrong?'

'Your breath smells bad.'

I know. There's something wrong with my stomach. I should go for a check-up, but I'm afraid. What if they find something?

And then I go back home at night. I blow a kiss of greeting out of the window to the invisible she-elephant, climb into a cold bed, wake up in the morning several minutes before the alarm clock rings, look at the ceiling and it's covered in blotchy yellow patterns. It looks like a newborn baby's nappy.

There is no life without pain.

What a clever idea that is of nature's — forgetting!

But this Sunday I slept to my heart's content and was woken by bright sunlight. And coming in through the open window from across the street were the cries of the animals — squawking, roaring, lowing. The squealing of life.

I stretch sweetly and listen to the unintelligible voices. Piercing screams, someone screeching gleefully, perhaps birds of paradise? As if I've woken up in a tropical forest. Or in paradise. And they're all clamouring in rapturous delight at this sunny morning. They can't contain themselves. And those who couldn't howl with happiness, they simply froze, dumbstruck in their rapture — the tree, the window, the glint of sunlight on the ceiling.

Sashenka!

I'm not feeling too well today.

Dysentery is running amuck here, and yesterday typhoid fever was found.

It's barbarous – they forbid us to drink the water and no one drinks it, but they still wash the cooking pots and crockery with it. There's a genuine epidemic starting up here – the soldiers are stuck in the latrines all the time.

The most terrible thing is when the wounded have diarrhoea, and to make things worse, there's nowhere to get any hay or straw.

It's still as hot as ever here, my head hurts, my thoughts are confused.

You know, it's a long time since I wrote anything properly, that's why my letters are such a mess. And the worst thing is, there's absolutely no way I can be alone. That's what exasperates me most of all.

And, of course, the heat is wearing me down – in all this time there hasn't been a single rainy or cloudy day. My head's buzzing, I can't gather my thoughts, but I need to think about something real at least sometimes, not just diarrhoea and lists of casualties.

All morning I've been writing letters and numbers – that's what men actually turn into.

I need silence and solitude, but here I'm surrounded by hustle and bustle – noise, crude jokes, stupid laughter, swearing, idiotic conversations, reports, statements, orders.

I want to get as far away as possible from all this and stroll about on my own for a while. The impossibility of being alone is oppressive.

I quarrelled with Glazenap today – he kept pestering me to talk, not realising that sometimes I simply need to think, to listen to the silence, to be alone. Now he's walking sullenly to and fro across the room, like a pendulum.

Sometimes I have to write a lot – like yesterday. My hand gets tired and starts hurting, the joints in my wrist ache. I tried writing in smaller letters, in order not to get so tired, but they shout at me to make my writing bigger. And on top of all this, the sweat drips onto the forms, blurring the letters. The papers stick to my hand. If I smudge the letters, I have to start all over again. More swearing.

Another annoying thing is that writing in the dark – and I have to write a lot in the evenings, when it's dark already – makes my eyes ache really badly. I write by the light of a candle stub, straining my eyes, everything starts flickering and I start seeing double. When I come back I'll have to go to the doctor, he'll probably prescribe some spectacles for me.

And I still absolutely cannot get used to these lists. I write out the names and imagine their families, their mothers. No one will be able to explain to them what it was all for.

All that's left behind from wars are the names of the generals. But no one will ever remember about these men, my men.

I once read the correspondence of Abelard and Héloïse, and it struck me for the first time that there are known victims and unknown victims. Abelard suffered a great misfortune, he was castrated by crude, cruel people. Ever since then, for hundreds of years, the whole world has pitied him. And they'll go on pitying him for hundreds more. But in the same letter he says that those who mutilated him were caught, and one of them was his servant, who had lived with him for years. Just imagine how swinishly he must have treated his servant for him to take his revenge like that! Well, those men were not only castrated in reprisal, they were blinded too. And no one pities them or remembers about them, although they suffered even more than he did.

I write out these lists and I think – no one will ever pity these men either.

Do you remember what Héloïse and Abelard called their son? Astrolabius.

And what became of that Astrolabius later? His story would probably have made another whole *Hamlet*. But no one will write it. Who needs him? Who will ever remember him?

I've just remembered my grandmother. She always used to get distressed like this about people who died. When she was told that someone she knew, or even someone she didn't, had died, she always wanted to find out exactly how he died – she wanted him to have had a painless, easy death, she wanted him to have suffered as little as possible. That seemed funny and stupid to me then: the man had already died and now, God knows how long afterwards, here was someone wishing him an easy death.

Glazenap really got my back up today. When you're drowning in a dysentery-ridden pit and your head could be blown off at any moment, isn't it ludicrous to be pondering on your own immortality?

He sits there, trying to convince himself.

'So, I didn't exist before – and that wasn't death, but something else. And afterwards I won't exist either. And that won't be death either, but that same something else again.'

But I said:

'A slap round the ears!'

He didn't understand a thing, of course, and I didn't try to explain. He wouldn't understand anyway.

He doesn't understand that all the religions and philosophies in the world only try to charm away death, the way village women charm away the toothache.

It's probably like this: the body fights against death with pain, and the brain, the mind, fights it with thought. Neither of them will save you in the end.

And the most important thing, something that I know now, is that Christ and Siddhartha of the line of Gautama both had their mouths open – like all dead men. I can imagine them dead very clearly now. It's no problem. I can imagine the flies walking about in their mouths too. All their lives these wise men taught that death does not exist, they taught resurrection and reincarnation, and they got slapped round the ears! The Saviour can't save anyone, because he never rose from the dead and he never will. And Gautama rotted like everybody else, he didn't become anybody – not any kind of Buddha! And he wasn't anybody for thousands of years before that. The world is not a dream, and my self is not an illusion. My self exists and it needs to be made happy.

Today there was a scraggy horse standing tethered by the kitchen. Waiting to be slaughtered for meat. It fanned itself with its tail and shook its head about. Its eyes were all flyblown. An animal tied to the door of the kitchen doesn't know how much longer it has to live. That's the difference that makes a man a man: we are the only living creature that knows death is inevitable. And that's why happiness must not be put off for the future, we have to be happy now.

But how can I be happy, my Sashenka?

I shall have to break off at any moment now – we're going on a reconnaissance mission, the plans for attacking Tientsin have been changed again. They change everything here all the time, we can never be certain of anything. But if the assault has been postponed, it means someone has had the good fortune to live for a day or two longer. If only I knew exactly who. Never mind, we'll soon find out. And what are they doing anyway – delighting in the two days of life they have been granted? It's unlikely. Everybody's hoping for something.

The surgeon and his mate have arrived, they're going with us too, they want to look at the area from which the wounded will have to be brought back. I can hear Zaremba telling some funny story and everybody laughing.

There, you see, I have no quiet time to do a bit of thinking. But how I long to think about something far away, as far away as possible from all this!

What am I talking about? The fact that there's no such thing as time.

Oh yes, there are hours and minutes, but time is us. Does time really exist without us? I mean, we are merely the form of time's existence. Its carriers. Its agents of infection. So time is a kind of disease of the cosmos. The cosmos will eventually overcome the infection, we'll disappear and the recovery will begin. Time will pass off, like a sore throat.

Death is the cosmos's way of fighting against time, fighting us. After all, what is the cosmos? In Greek it means order, beauty, harmony. Death is the defence of universal beauty and harmony against us, against our chaos.

But we resist.

For the cosmos time is a disease, but for us it is the tree of life.

Only it's strange that the cosmos flowers were called that – such mundane flowers, nothing out of the ordinary.

My stomach's churning, forgive me for these details. I'm afraid I might be coming down with typhoid fever. And my head is splitting.

There now, they're calling me. I'll finish writing this evening. Sasha!

I'm back. It's night already.

My hands are still shaking, forgive me. I simply can't pull myself together. And my ears are still ringing from the blasts.

I shouldn't tell you all this, but I can't help myself. I've been through too much to keep it all in.

There was our new battalion commander Stankevich, deaf Ubri – I told you about him – our surgeon Zaremba, his assistant and another officer, Uspensky, very young, the order for his promotion to warrant officer arrived only today. And several staff officers and privates as well.

That Uspensky prattled away without a break, but he stuttered all the time. A garrulous stutterer. He was bursting with happiness at having been promoted. Even Stankevich ordered him to shut up.

I got a cramp in my belly and moved away from them a bit into a small ravine. I squatted down, and that was when the bombardment began. A shell fell right on the spot where they were standing.

I ran to them. I can't tell you here what I saw.

Forgive me, I'm starting to shake again.

I see Ubri lying about ten steps away, closest of all to me. His arms and legs seem to have been amputated. They're not there! A boot with the remainder of a leg is lying beside him, his face is covered with grey soot. I leaned down and he seemed to be still alive. His mouth was open. As I watched, a kind of curtain descended smoothly over his pupils. He died at the very moment that I leaned down over him. I don't know why, but I realise what I should do – reach out my hand and close his eyes. I do reach out, but I can't touch them.

I walk on. Around me men are screaming, groaning, writhing about in blood.

I see Stankevich, our commander, lying in the grass. I get the impression that he simply got tired and decided to lie down for a while. I run over to him. His face is calm, his eyes are open slightly, as if he is peeping. But his hands look as if they have been put through a meat grinder. I take him by the shoulders and try to lift him up. His body yields to me easily, but the back of his head stays on the grass.

A wounded horse is jerking its hind legs close by, behind it is our surgeon's mate, Mikhal Mikhalich – with no face. A bloody mush of teeth, bones and cartilage.

I hear groans and run towards them – it's Dr Zaremba. He's still alive, looking at me, bleating something and gurgling blood. His stomach is ripped open and a pile of intestines has tumbled out onto the dust of the road. Zaremba is lying in a puddle of black blood, groaning, and I can't understand why he's still alive and what I can do. I shout at him.

'What? What shall I do?'

He can only bleat, but eventually I understand what he wants. He wants me to kill him.

I hear more screams, jump up and walk on.

I see one of the staff officers – dead, with his legs doubled up under him like a circus acrobat. And his mouth – again, like all of them – is open. The eyes look, but they don't see. There are thick gouts of blood on his beard.

Finally I find one person alive – the stutterer Uspensky. I can't tell where he's wounded, but blood is gushing out of his throat. The uniform is smoking on him, his eyebrows and hair are scorched, through his tattered breeches I can see bloody abrasions on his legs.

I lost my head completely, I didn't know what to do. I sat beside him, trying to reassure him.

'Hold on, everything will be all right!'

Some other soldiers came running up, medical orderlies. I helped them carry Uspensky to the infirmary. On the way he started choking on his own blood and an orderly stuck his fingers into his mouth so that the blood could flow out feely.

At the infirmary I sat with him for a whole hour, I just couldn't leave him. He was conscious and I kept repeating over and over:

'Hold on! Everything will be all right!'

It was very hot in the tent: sultry air, clouds of flies, odours of putrefaction. I fanned him and drove away the flies. There was nothing more I could do for him.

But when he died, I reached out to his face and closed his eyes. It's not really all that hard, after all.

He had to be moved and I helped to lift him. A dead man is much heavier than when he was alive. I'd heard about that before from the other men.

Sasha, I need to be with you very badly, right now!

I'm very tired.

I need to come and lay my head on your knees. You'll stroke me and say:

'It's all right, my love! Everything's all right now! It's all over. Everything will be fine now, now that I'm with you!'

●

As I got ready first thing in the morning, I already knew I would stay at this stargazer's place. My nostrils recalled the tantalising scent of his eau de cologne.

I looked in the mirror and didn't recognise myself. A grey face, black circles under my eyes.

My body is turning drab.

I sorted through my hair and pulled out a few grey ones.

The eyes are still the same: the left one blue, the right one brown, but the eyelids are a bit swollen.

The skin on the neck is starting to wrinkle.

I leaned down over the washbasin, washed my breasts with cold water. They dangle, gelatinous and dismal, covered in little blue veins.

I pulled out the hairs round the nipples with tweezers.

The toes are gnarled.

Over coffee I started filing down my nails, but I need to file down my life.

We met at the entrance to a park strewn with poplar fluff. An old woman there was playing an accordion.

We walked for a little while. Then I took him home.

On the way I lingered for a moment in front of a shop window with a mirror displayed in it. I simply tidied up my hair, and suddenly I caught the glance of a young girl walking by, looking at me. And in her mocking eyes I read who I was for her – an old, fading woman, whom no hairstyle in the world could help any longer.

A telescope on a tripod by the window.

A candlelight supper. Music. *Don Giovanni.*

He lists the moons of Saturn.

'Titan, Iapetus, Rhea! Dione! Mimas! Hyperion! Phoebe!'

I smile admiringly, although he has forgotten Tethys and Enceladus.

He laments the fact that it rained during the last lunar eclipse.

He closes the window so the mosquitoes and the poplar fluff won't fly in. A moth kept fluttering against the window all the time.

He started telling me about his telescope, stroking it affectionately on the back.

'This, by the way, is the only real time machine. And mine is six times more powerful than the one Galileo had!'

Then the promised performance – he took the telescope and we went up onto the roof.

As we were walking up the stairs, he leaned down to tie his shoelace and suddenly I could see that he had a bald patch.

On the top floor – the door to the attic. He unlocked a huge padlock with his own key. We clambered out onto the roof. A warm wind. The bottom of space awash with lights, the top spangled with stars. The fluff is lying in snowdrifts even on the roof.

'There, I have my very own sky up here.'

He started showing me the constellations.

'Look – the Pleiades. And over there,' – he put his arm round me – 'Alpha Tauri. It's cool, sure you won't catch cold?'

He hugged me more tightly.

'But in actual fact all the constellations are nonsense. Fleeting juxtapositions that mean nothing. Might as well call people passing by in the street or birds flying past constellations. Giving names to the stars is actually like keeping an inventory of the crests on the waves in the sea.'

He explained that it was all a matter of the time discrepancy. Those stars passing by have one time, and we have another.

'Do you understand?'

'Yes, I understand.'

'All these globular clusters and diffuse nebulae are like snapshots for us, click – and it's for ever. Once upon a time there was a big bang. Boom! And everything went flying apart. But it flew apart for us. In actual fact it rapidly flew apart and rapidly gathered itself back together again. Another boom, and it flew apart again, gathered itself back together again. Another boom. How can I explain this more simply for you? Well, say, it's like a child that takes a piece of plasticine and makes little animals, people, trees and houses out of it. Then he rolls it all up, scrunches it all back into one lump. But the next day he starts modelling again. Or this is better: remember the old woman by the park? For us it's eternity, but it's really just like a chord on an accordion – pull your hands apart, squeeze them back together. Apart, together. Understand?'

'I understand.'

While he set up the telescope on the tripod and lingered over adjusting it, wispy clouds piled up in the sky. When I glued my eye to the eyepiece to take a look at the moon, he started stroking my head.

'You've got fluff in your hair.'

We went down. The wardrobe in the bedroom was open and I was amazed at the number of suits and pairs of shoes hanging and standing in it.

On the wall there are photographs of his children, a boy and a little girl, twins: in a pram, then going to school, then graduating from it.

Everywhere in the flat there are traces of other women. They probably mark their territory deliberately. On the shelf in the bathroom there are panty liners. And hair lacquer. Among his eau de colognes – a lipstick. In the waste basket, on top – a clump of black hairs. And on the dark armchair in the sitting room my eye was caught by an obvious long ginger hair.

I asked:

'Do you have a lot of women?'

He laughed.

'One. And she loves me. Have you heard of metempsychosis? The woman who loves is a single being. She dies and is transformed into a woman who doesn't love, and her soul migrates to another woman, who loves. It's one woman who loves, with different bodies.'

I thought I would be undressed, the way it supposedly ought to be done, but he disrobed deftly first, lay down and put his hands behind his head. The light in the corridor was on, and in the semi-darkness of the room he could see everything. I felt embarrassed about my breasts and didn't take my bra off.

He fumbles and fusses about on top of me and I ask myself a question that I can't answer: Why am I sleeping with a man I don't love?

I remembered the parable about the sage who instructed his companions to do strange, inexplicable things. But afterwards profound meanings were revealed for their stupid actions, meanings invisible to them but intelligible to the sage. First he instructed them to make holes in a boat belonging to poor fishermen and it sank, then he ordered them to kill a traveller they met on the road, and finally, without taking any payment, he restored a ruined wall in a village where the people had refused him shelter and food. And then he explained the meaning of these actions. They sank the boat so that it would not be seized by a tyrannical king who was pursuing them and confiscating all the boats, the traveller was on his way to kill his son, and the wall belonged to orphans, and there was buried treasure there, which they would discover later.

I remember that one day I met a man with a bucket of snow in the street. I was surprised and wondered where he could be taking a bucket of snow, when there were snowdrifts all around. But the sage who had sent him no doubt knew why it was necessary. That same sage has sent me to this stale, musty bed, but not yet revealed the meaning.

The stargazer was still beavering away, he'd come out in a sweat.

Afterwards he flopped over onto his back, lit a cigarette and asked in a complacent voice:

'Well, how was it?'

I replied:

'Like Donna Elvira, who realised it was Leporello.'

'What?'

He didn't even understand.

He deftly tied the condom in a knot before tossing it into the waste basket. Grinned with a yawn.

'A teaspoon of that fluid tyrannises a man – makes him do what it wants! What humiliating enslavement!'

He started snuffling almost immediately.

I tried to get to sleep, but I couldn't. The bed's uncomfortable, soft, like a feather bed. I sink into it. And what about these sheets? Who has slept here before me?

That mocking glance in the mirror kept creeping into my mind. That girl's eyes repeated again and again that no hairstyle would do me any good now. And if that was how people saw me, it was how I really was.

And all night long the moth fluttered against the window.

I suddenly felt frightened of seeing this man in the morning. And even more frightened of seeing myself with him. I got dressed quietly, picked up all his things, his trousers and shirt, off the floor, arranged them neatly on a chair and left.

It was already getting light. The city was quiet, empty, with a hollow echo. Even the deposits of poplar fluff had frozen motionless along the edges of the pavements.

I walked through a formation of trams that had spent the night at the depot.

As I approached the zoo, I was presented with a scene out of a parable. My she-elephant was being led along the tramlines. She was walking somewhere, in no hurry, swaying and flapping her ears, sniffing at the road surface and the rails with her trunk, raising swirls of fluff. The sage knows where she's being taken to and what for.

I got back home and felt a desperate desire to get washed. First I took a shower, then I filled the bath and lay down to soak.

I lay there watching tiny bubbles appear on the little hairs all over the skin of my body.

Suddenly I wanted to slip completely under the water, head and all. Become a water monkey.

I took the snorkelling tube out of the cupboard, the one I'd bought once upon a time and never used. I submerged and froze.

The silence underwater is so strange, more like a noise. I can hear everything, even things I don't normally hear. Only everything comes through some kind of thick membrane. And my pulse beats loudest of all.

It occurred to me that this was probably how it was in Mummy's stomach.

I don't know how long I sat under the water with the tube in my teeth, perhaps ten minutes, perhaps an hour, until the water went cold. I was chilled right through.

I climbed out, slipped on my bathrobe, went over to the mirror and looked at myself for a long time.

Then I puked all morning long.

■

Sashenka!

Tientsin has been taken.

I've just finished the lists.

We have only 150 men killed. There are three times as many wounded. Our brigade commander, Major-General Stessel, is wounded too, but he returned to headquarters after being bandaged up.

In all the allies lost more than 800 men. The Japanese got the worst of it. They launched straight into a frontal assault and blew up the city gates. The Americans' General Butler was killed.

The allies attacked the Chinese city from the west, while our detachment attacked from the east, by the Lutai Canal, and stormed Li Hunchan's fortifications. Part of the Chinese force scattered, part withdrew towards Yantsun and Beitsan.

And so I wrote a victorious communiqué. Everyone here is rejoicing. All the staff officers are walking around as if it's their birthday.

Those who have become my letters and numbers are probably especially delighted.

That was yesterday, and today we went to look at the captured city.

Here is my victorious communiqué for you, Sashenka.

On the way we first stopped at the *impans* – the fortifications taken by our men yesterday. The Chinese camp had been abandoned, together with all its contents. I saw a scattered deck of Chinese playing cards, and I was going to take them as a souvenir, but I changed my mind. Why would I want to remember this? The bodies of Chinese soldiers that had not yet been cleared away were lying nearby, already fly-blown and gnawed on by dogs.

Peasants under guard were clearing away the bodies. They caught hold of them with hooks and dragged them into large pits. The sun rose and started beating down and the stench from the dead men became unbearable. The peasants worked with bunches of grass stuffed into their nostrils.

Fire had raged all night in the city, and now the ruins were smoking. It was impossible to believe that this had been a living city of a million people. There were battered and broken wagons, handcarts, rickshaws, dead animals and people lying everywhere, and a smell of smoke and scorched fat.

We came across dead people every step of the way, some of them still dressed, but most naked, for some reason. One old woman was lying on her back and her breasts had slipped up along her sides towards her armpits. In some places they were already raking the bodies together into heaps and carting them off somewhere. Everywhere there were swarms of vicious flies that couldn't tell who was already dead and who was still alive.

We had to clamber over heaps of debris. At one spot my foot slipped on something and I almost fell. Under the rubble I glimpsed a scorched, twisted face.

A dog growled at everyone passing by. Its front legs were sound, but the back ones were broken, and a wound in its side was teeming with maggots and flies. The dog couldn't bark any longer, it could only try to crawl with its front legs. It growled hoarsely at us too.

Everyone walked by. But I stopped and shot it.

There, Sashenka, that was my first killing, I make a poor soldier.

At the site of the fire, pigs smeared with ashes were rummaging under the smoking beams and rafters, among some scorched and burning timbers – I didn't realise straightaway that they were charred bodies. I saw the fingers of a smouldering hand crumble at a jolt. And all of this gave off an appalling stench. A thought flashed through my mind: I've just seen pigs eating roasted people, why did I have to see that?

One charred body astounded me – either the person had shrivelled up like that in the fire, or it was a child.

We came across that American with the camera again.

The surviving part of the city has been taken by the Japanese. There are Japanese flags on the houses and shops. The prudent Japanese had laid in a huge supply of flags and, on taking Tientsin, they handed them out to the inhabitants straightaway.

The Chinese city itself is hideous. The Chinese pave and sweep their courtyards, but for them the streets are cesspits. They are narrow and dusty, probably impassable with mud in the rain. We walked along winding laneways, sometimes completely deserted, which made me feel uneasy. All the doors of the houses smashed in and things tossed out into the street everywhere.

The Chinese had fled or hidden, and the ones we came across went down on their knees at the sight of Europeans, holding out pieces of white material with some kind of hieroglyphs on them, shaking them at us. There were the same hieroglyphs on the walls. Kirill explained that they said 'shun man' – 'peaceful people'.

The banks and shops have been plundered and gutted. There is smashed furniture underfoot. Every now and then we met soldiers and officers of the allied forces, loaded down with plundered property. The city is being completely devastated. What cannot be carried away is torn, trampled and smashed.

We saw our men too – a soldier walks along with a bundle, gathering up furs, silk, figurines. He goes into the next courtyard. Finds something much better there. Shakes everything out into the dust and stuffs new things in.

Screams and shots on all sides.

We heard a woman's shriek, wild and bloodcurdling, very close by. We dashed into the yard, but met several Sepoys already on their way out, loaded down with sacks, and one of them was pulling up his trousers as he walked. They gestured to indicate that there was no point in going into that house any more. There was no one screaming now, anyway.

When a crippled beggar sitting in the middle of the street saw us, he started bowing and repeating:

'Katoliko – shanga, katoliko – shanga!'

Teams of allied soldiers are searching for Yihetuan and Chinese soldiers who have changed their clothes and mingled with the local population. A brief investigation is followed by an execution. The investigation consists of tearing the man's clothes off – the mark left on a shoulder by the recoil of a rifle butt is sufficient reason for the execution. The men are shot on the spot. Several Chinese were executed in our presence. First they cut off their pigtails, then beat them to a pulp with rifle butts. And only after that did they shoot them.

I have read this over again and asked myself: Why am I writing down all these horrors?

In actual fact the only thing I want is to forget them as soon as possible. But I shall still write down everything that happens here anyway. Someone has to preserve it, don't they? Perhaps that is why I am here, to see everything and write it down.

If I don't write down what I've seen today, there will be nothing left. As if it never happened.

Or perhaps I shouldn't write anything down? What for? Who needs it?

My heads aches terribly now. It's splitting apart.

Sashenka, I don't understand who I am and what I'm doing here any longer.

●

I had a dream. I'm at the seaside with Mummy and Daddy. The beach. Mummy's going to swim. She puts on her rubber cap, tucks her hair into it. I suddenly realise that she's naked and I shout:

'Mummy!'

She laughs.

'There's no one here!'

I look around and the beach really is empty, there's no one apart from us. She walks into the sea and calls us to follow her into the deep water. Daddy and I stay in the breakers. She swims easily, cutting through the water with powerful movements, with only her white cap bobbing on the surface of the waves.

I was woken by a strange, dry sort of sound. Lying there in the remains of my dream, I can't understand what it was. A glass sphere has fallen off the dried-up New Year tree.

I come to my senses and remember – Mummy is dead.

At night everything's quiet – I can even hear the dry fir needles showering onto the floor.

There's a tickle in my throat. I'm falling ill. It hurts to swallow. My nose is blocked, I can't smell anything. My head's full of thick mush.

The third time already this winter.

And I'm tired of getting up in the dark.

I'm tired in general.

Mummy was celebrating her birthday then, I just dropped in for a minute, she had guests and I didn't want to stay for long. In recent years she had been working at the opera house, selling programmes, she had acquired new friends, I didn't know them. She asked me to go into the bathroom with her.

'Take a look at what I've got here! Do you feel that lump? Sashenka, my daughter, I'm afraid!'

She had a nodule in her breast.

'Mummy, people get all sorts of lumps.'

'At first it was small, like a carbuncle. But now it's started growing. Or am I just imagining it? And the glands have swollen up under my arms. Can you feel the bump? And on my head behind my ears.'

'Mummy, we all have any number of little tumours from the day we're born. It's nothing to worry about. All women have the same sort of thing. You just need to get a check-up. Does it hurt?'

'No, not really.'

'Don't worry, everything will be fine!'

It wasn't. She turned out to have a malignant tumour and her ovary was affected. The disease generally develops very rapidly.

Mummy's round of hospitals and operations began.

I went to see her almost every day.

She found it hard being in hospital, she wanted to go home, she said the walls in the ward were coated with sickness, like the soot and grime in a kitchen.

At the first clinic she shared a ward with an old woman who was completely withered. She had clumps of hair sticking up on her bald cranium. She was always putting on makeup. The worse her condition got, the brighter her makeup became. She had almost no lips of her own left, and she drew huge fat circles round her sunken mouth. Her groaning prevented Mummy from getting to sleep all night long. When I came to see her, she begged me:

'Sashenka! Take me away from here! I can't get a wink of sleep. I won't survive this!'

'Mummy! You have to be patient! They're treating you here!'

She started shouting at me, saying I wasn't interested in her and I didn't give a damn that she was going crazy there. Mummy always used to be so restrained, but the illness has changed her completely. She thought the doctors were all incompetent specialists, or they were prescribing the wrong tests and the wrong diet. The nurses got the worst of it. Mummy complained that they never came when she called, that they were all rude and couldn't care less about the patients' suffering. She expressed her outrage so loudly, she could be heard out in the corridor.

'They don't do anything but take money! All they think about is running off home as soon as possible and enjoying life!'

But the nurses complained to me about my mother, saying she wouldn't let them do their job. The moment they walked out of the ward, she pressed the bell to call them and when they came back, she'd already forgotten what she wanted and abused them for not giving her a moment's peace.

It hurt me and made me feel ashamed every time I heard all this.

Her exasperation and rage were vented on me. As if she waited for my arrival to pour out all the bitterness and resentment, as if I was to blame because she was the one with cancer, and not the nurses, or the man walking by outside the window, or me.

After that she would calm down and then we would sit there in silence, I would stroke her hand and she would suddenly start to cry.

'I lie here and think: there's that old woman washing the floors, so strong and wiry, she'll be washing floors for another twenty years. Why me and not her? And I'm surprised at myself: how could I get ideas like that into my head? Forgive me! Sometimes

I get the feeling that I'm not me any longer. I'm turning into someone else here.'

Mummy was suffering serious pain already, and she was always asking for injections to relieve it.

'They can't even give injections properly! I'm black and blue all over!'

And she would show me her arms and legs, covered with needle pricks.

I gave her the next injection myself and she calmed down.

'Sashenka, you do a jab properly, it doesn't hurt at all.'

Then she sank into unconsciousness.

I got terribly tired – I used to come after work and care for Mummy, help her get washed, brush her hair, trim her nails, massage her back to prevent bedsores, apply cream to her legs, push the bed over to the window so that she could look at the trees. But it wasn't the work that tired me most – it was hard for me to be there with her thoughts, her words, her silence. Her fear at the end.

After the first operation the surgeon told me:

'We haven't got it all out.'

But I tried to convince her that she was on the way to recovery.

Sometimes instead of Mummy's hospital I stayed at Yanka's place with her children, that was my lifeline, I seemed to become myself again, restore what Mummy and her cancer took out of me.

I call them that – Yanka's children. They like it.

And I'm constantly amazed at how quickly they grow – only yesterday Kostik was standing in an upended stool, then he kept wanting to go to the bridge to watch the choo-choo, and now he's gone to school already! It's terrible! I went to buy him exercise books, a pencil case, pens, pencils, a satchel. Yanka was glad to be spared all that.

They love me. One time Kostik gave me a matchbox.

'Only be careful opening it!'

'What's in there?'

He held it up to my ear. Something was scrabbling about inside. He had caught a beetle for me.

'Aunty Sasha, take him home with you, he can live with you, so you won't get bored on your own!'

My little wonder! He's concerned about me being lonely.

While I was with them I forgot about everything: Mummy's illness, the clinic, the very fact that cancer exists in the world. I take the groceries out of my bag, put the milk, juice and biscuits on the table, and they shout:

'Hooray! Milk! Hooray, juice! Hooray, biscuits!'

And I start shouting with them:

'Hooray! Ryazhenka! Hooray! Condensed milk! Hooray! Bagels!'

And we are simply happy, for no reason at all.

I set up a little bench in the toilet for the older boy, so he didn't have to pee in the potty. He was terribly proud of peeing in the toilet, like a grown-up, going up on his toes and flooding the floor for me. Now the little bench has been handed down to the younger brother. Apart from all the other childhood ailments he has phimosis – a tight foreskin. For a long time we hoped no surgery would be needed, but it's impossible to watch the child going through that agony every time.

I love to wash them, especially in summer, when they come running in from the street all dirty and sweaty. I rinse them off in the bathroom, sponge the dirt off their feet – sunburned, with white strap marks from their sandals. They fool about, throwing foam all around the bathroom and splashing. I'm wet through. We laugh. I wash their hair with shampoo, they squeal, their hair is silky under my fingers. I rinse it with the shower.

After the bath I scrub them with the towel and we laugh at the way their clean hair squeaks between my fingers.

When I get tired, I lie down for a rest and then Igoryok settles in beside me and drives a little car around on me – up and down the mountains. He growls, making the sound of the motor. It's really lovely!

Of course, there are arguments and tears and shouting. They quarrel and fight over any little thing. It always ends with victory for the older boy. One day they both wanted the same toy, I said Kostik should let his younger brother have it, but a minute later the little boy came running to me in tears.

'Igoryok, what's happened?'

He's choking, he can't say anything.

I call Kostik, who spreads his arms wide in amazement:

'You told me to let him have it, so I did!'

And Igoryok says:

'Yes, but first he dipped it in the toilet!'

One time I caught them playing doctors – taking each other's temperature with a finger up the bottom. Now what am I supposed to do about that?

Yanka has got pregnant again too, although she said she didn't want to have any more children. She complained:

'What sort of breast is this? Like a soft-boiled egg! But it used to be a hard-boiled one! And the skin on my legs is like a map! Look, rivers running all over it!'

I looked at her breasts – transparent, covered in blue veins, with dark-brown nipples – alive, working, needed – and I envied her.

Yanka was thinking seriously about having her tubes tied.

'Why would I want any more?'

I remembered what Yanka told me about Kostik when he was told he was going to have a little brother – his childish horror at not being unique in the Universe.

'Why do you want a boy? You've already got a boy!'

But when Igoryok was born, Kostik was so delighted by the appearance of a baby in the house that he wasn't even jealous. One day he asked me to wrap him up in a blanket and carry him around like a newborn infant. I wrapped him up and started walking round the room with him. He stuck his thumb in his mouth and closed his eyes. Then he burst into laughter and started struggling.

'Let me go! Let me go!'

But I didn't want to.

Everything had started falling apart in Yanka's family, and I thought this child might help bring them back together again.

Before the pregnancy I used to hear this:

'He lies there, saying nothing, with his face turned to the wall, then gets up, comes into the kitchen and throws his supper on the floor!'

She complained about her husband, saying that he was his mother's only child and now he was acting like a spoilt brat – picking on trifles, yelling, apologising, throwing hysterical fits.

'And he's never washed the dishes even once!'

I try to reassure her.

'But you have such wonderful children!'

She replied:

'Sashka, believe me, children are no substitute for love.'

Once she said bitterly:

'I've finally understood what a family is – living in hell and hiding it for the sake of the children.'

They had started quarrelling a long time before. After one of their rows, Yanka came running to me with the children and stayed for the night. In the morning her husband came to apologise: he rang the bell, banged on the door and threatened to break it down, Yanka didn't want to let him in, but the children started howling. When I unlocked the door, he was already furious again because we'd refused to open up. More yelling. The poor boys! They dashed at their daddy and then at their mummy, waving their little fists. It all concluded with an absolutely farcical scene of reconciliation and the family setting off home, leaving me lying down with a migraine.

And then Yanka started feeling sorry for me.

'Sashka, I'll find someone for you! You need to get married!'

'What for?'

'You don't know why people get married?'

'No.'

'To fill the void. Look, we quarrel, even in public, we yell and slam doors, smash the dishes, he waves his fists about, I burst into tears. But afterwards, after we've let off steam, we both love each other. I couldn't live without all this frenzy.'

Now that Yanka was expecting another child, they seemed to have settled down. When I went to see them, he hugged his wife, put his hand on her growing stomach and smiled.

'There now, at last I'm going to have a daughter. We tried really hard, didn't we?'

Yanka examined her stomach in the mirror, pulling up her blouse, and all of us – me, the children and her husband – looked at it, and we all wanted to run our finger down that vertical brown line and press that protruding belly-button like a doorbell. And we did press it, taking turns.

'Zing! Zing! We're waiting for you!'

When the first snow fell and the entire city was smothered, we went out into the yard to make a snow woman and rolled huge balls of snow. And when the snow woman was ready, Igoryok walked up to her, stroked her bulging snowy belly with his mitten and said:

'Like Mummy!'

After her second operation, my mummy spent a month at home, and I had to take time off work to look after her.

I made her herb teas and cream soups.

I caught myself feeling afraid of drinking out of her cup, although I realise that cancer isn't catching, and deliberately made myself try the soup with her spoon.

Gradually, imperceptibly, Mummy had turned into an emaciated, sick old woman. It was painful to watch her get out of bed, grope so long for her slippers with her feet and then slowly shuffle her way to the toilet, holding on to the wall with her withered hand. And when she spoke, her voice was withered too.

I remember her brushing her hair in front of the mirror, picking the hairs that had fled from her out of the brush and sighing.

'What's left of me?'

I washed her in the bath and was amazed: this couldn't be Mummy, surely?

She hadn't dyed her hair for ages. It was chestnut on top, but all grey at the roots. Huge, monstrous scars instead of breasts. And down below, between her legs, lifeless wisps of grey. Swollen varicose veins protruding from her legs in strings of purple and blue knots.

Now she often remembered things from her childhood and youth that she had never told me about before.

She said that when she was a little girl she dreamed of long, white opera gloves.

'You know the kind, close-fitting kidskin gloves right up to the elbow?'

Her dream had never come true.

When Daddy was still courting her, they strolled round the streets until late. When the tram they had to take to get home arrived, they took turns saying to each other:

'Let's miss another one, shall we?'

And so they missed the last one and had to walk halfway across the city.

Mummy sighed.

'Well, who could have thought then that life would slip by like all those trams we missed and this would be left?'

She hadn't told me anything about her parents before, but she started talking about them now – 'your grandfather' or 'your grandmother' – although I'd never seen them in my life, they died long before I was born.

Mummy started remembering her first child, my older brother, all the time. A photograph I had never seen before suddenly appeared on her table – a pudgy, plump-bottomed little baby smiling with his toothless mouth.

One day in her reverie Mummy started calling out:

'Sasha! Sashenka!'

I walked over to her.

'I'm here, Mummy.'

She opened her eyes and gave me a strange kind of look.

I realised it wasn't me she had been calling.

For her, life had started to contract, everything she had lived through was turning transparent, one thing showed through another.

I was wiping Mummy dry after a bath and she remembered that when I still used to play with dolls, I once told her:

'When I grow up, I'll be big and you'll be little!'

She smiled, as if apologising for something.

'And that's just what's happened. We've swapped places.'

I needed to escape from her illness every now and then, and Mummy understood me, she used to drive me out so that I could go somewhere and unwind, not stay with her all the time.

'But Mummy, you'll be bored. What will you do?'

'You know, I've got so many things to remember!'

In the evening I used to go to Yanka's place, where I watched her husband put his hand on her stomach and wink at me:

'Now this time it's a little girl! I ordered one!'

But I knew something that he didn't.

I'm Yanka's close confidante, I know all her secrets, although sometimes it would be better not to know.

Yanka thought she had got pregnant and when her husband was away, she didn't bother to take any precautions with her lover. Then afterwards she realised she had got the days mixed up and the date of conception fell during the time when her husband was away.

Yanka was unfaithful to her husband almost from the very beginning. Often, while I sat with her children, she was in someone's bed, and if her husband asked, I was supposed to tell him some lie. He didn't ask.

Yanka took her second lover to forget the first. And the third to forget the second.

It seems to me that she was always that way, even in her young days she never loved anyone, but she liked making men fall in love with her, driving them crazy, and then watching them go wild and fight over her.

Her latest lover was a musicologist. Apart from their secret rendezvous, they sometimes ran into each other at parties held by people they both knew.

'Just imagine, we were sitting beside each other on the sofa and

I got carried away by the conversation and started tousling his hair the way I always do! It was a good thing nobody noticed!'

She laughs at her lover's absolutely childish jealousy of her husband.

Once, putting on her lipstick in the mirror before she leaves the children with me and goes to her musicologist, she says:

'My husband doesn't understand anything about my body! But he does!'

That time she had a head cold with a sore on her lip and a cough.

I asked:

'Yanka, why all the rush, with your nose running like that? Get well first!'

But she laughed.

'Ah, but he likes it when he's inside me and I cough. He says everything in there suddenly tightens right up!'

I asked Yanka how she could go with two men in the same day. She replied that it used to bother her a lot until she learned to separate them, draw a symbolic line between them – take a shower, wash her hair with a different shampoo, shave her legs, put on a different perfume.

'I don't know how to explain it. You see, Sashka, it's the only thing that keeps the family going. I come back home from my lover feeling easy and relaxed. After I've been unfaithful, I'm tender and loving with my husband again. I have the strength for the housework and the children again, for his favourite stuffed peppers. And my husband thinks: "What a wonderful wife I have!"'

Her musicologist struck a false chord with me from the very beginning. I couldn't understand what Yanka saw in him – he always reeked of sweat, with a hint of decay. And I didn't like the way he looked at me. One day during the summer, they turned up at my place late in the evening, both hungry, and the table was bare. Yanka went off to the kitchen to cook something, he put on some music he had brought with him and started pestering me to dance with him. Squeezing up close, rubbing himself against me. His hands start wandering. He keeps squinting at the kitchen door in case she comes out.

I dragged him out onto the balcony and there in the darkness I wound my arms round his neck and started kissing him on the lips. And he snuffled as he started kissing me back hard, but all the time he was on his guard. Where was Yanka? Could she see us?

I pushed him away and laughed.

He asked in a frightened voice:

'What's wrong?'

'Nothing, it's just that I like everything to be light-hearted and jolly, delicious and beautiful. That's what I was born for! But your nose is too long, your eyes are set too close, you've got gap-teeth and your stomach looks as if it's been buttoned on.'

I didn't mention the smell.

He probably hates me now.

From Yanka's place I used to go back to Mummy, to her cancer.

I couldn't bring myself to do it for a long time, but finally I asked her:

'Mummy, why were you unfaithful to my father?'

'Can't you forgive me?'

'No, it's not that. I realised a long time ago that I have no right to accuse you of anything. And I have no right to forgive you. I just think it must have been hard for you, being devious and telling lies all the time.'

'I didn't tell lies. It's not a lie. You just come home, forget one truth and remember another. Change from one woman into another.'

'Did you fall in love with them? Like with Daddy?'

'I fell in love before I was married and afterwards – it has nothing at all to do with marriage. Sometimes you can fall in love overnight. You wake up and realise you fell in love while you were asleep. But the way you love your husband is quite different.'

'Did you hide everything from him?'

'Why hurt him and torment him? He's near and dear to me, after all. Why make someone dear to me suffer?'

Afterwards she tried to continue the conversation several times. I felt that she wanted to justify herself to me, and I interrupted.

'Mummy, you don't have to explain anything to me.'

'No, listen. A man makes a woman different. I saw myself with their eyes and felt the way they felt about me. With one I was tired, lethargic, no good for anything, and with another I was real, I was desired. A woman has a need to be generous, and if you're not given the opportunity, that generosity looks for a way out.'

One time, after a long silence – I thought she had dozed off, but she was back there, in the past – Mummy said:

'You know, I always used to cut your daddy's hair for him. And it wasn't until I cut the other man's hair that I really felt I was being unfaithful to my husband.'

She waited for me to say something. I didn't.

'And anyway, what a stupid word that is – unfaithful. You're not taking anything away from anyone. It's simply something different, something else that you need. And this something else doesn't take anybody's place. This something else wasn't in your life before, it fills a vacuum that would have remained unfilled. Without it, you go around feeling as if someone has taken a huge chunk out of the world and out of you. It helps to make you feel complete, real, alive. With the others I was happy as a woman, do you understand? And they said all kinds of things to me that your father never said.'

And then she added, embarrassed:

'I'm an old fool, right? I should just keep quiet?'

'Mummy, talk to me about everything. You never talked to me about this before, did you? Don't be ashamed!'

'I'm not ashamed. And I'm not making excuses, I've got nothing to be ashamed of or make excuses about. What's really terrible is not that it happened, but that it's impossible to tell the people closest to you – your husband, your daughter – about your inmost feelings, what torments you and what makes you happy.'

And then out of the blue she started telling me, as if it was something very important, about the time in her childhood when she stole a beautiful doll's blouse from her friend at the dacha. The other girl cried her eyes out and Mummy wanted to give it back, but she knew she couldn't do that now, and she helped her friend search for the blouse, which she stuffed into her knickers and then threw into a tangle of nettles when nobody could see.

'Mummy, have you carried that around inside yourself all these years to tell me about it now?'

'I never took anything that didn't belong to me ever again.'

'My mummy, how I love you!'

At moments like that I felt so warm and cosy with her again, as easy as once upon a time long, long ago, when we used to pull our feet up onto the sofa and whisper about everything in the world.

If not for Mummy's cancer, I would never have felt that closeness again.

Mummy was at home, but then in late autumn Yanka ended up in hospital. She was walking along the corridor in her school during the break, when the junior pupils were dashing about, and one rammed his head into her stomach at full pelt. She was frightened at first, but then everything seemed to be all right after all.

A little while later Yanka told me that she couldn't feel any more movements in her stomach. Her husband took her to the hospital and I stayed with the children. He came back alone, despondent.

'I ask the doctor: "Is it dangerous?" And he tells me: "If the foetus is alive – no. But if it's dead and has decayed, then it is. But don't you distress yourself!"'

He just couldn't understand how his long-awaited daughter could suddenly be called a decayed foetus.

Yanka lost her baby, complications set in and she had to be kept in hospital.

During that period I was torn between Mummy and Yanka with her children. Mummy understood that I was needed more there, and I had to move into Yanka's place to look after the boys. I took unpaid leave.

Those few days when I lived with them were difficult and wonderful at the same time. It was wonderful to feel that I was needed. I slept on a camp-bed in the children's room. In the morning I rose early in order to tidy myself up and not wander round the flat with a sleepy face and tangled hair. I made breakfast. Yanka's husband went to work. I took the older boy to school and the younger one to the kindergarten. I went round the shops, came back and did the cleaning, the washing, the cooking. Everything I hated doing so much at home was a joy here. Then I collected the children, fed them, did various things with them, including Kostik's school work. Yanka's husband came and I fed him. He praised everything I cooked. That was really lovely.

Yanka's husband started looking at me quite differently. I felt it. Before, he didn't seem to notice me at all. But now he helped me with the housework and washed the dishes without a murmur. Once when he saw I was sitting slouched over, he gave me a back massage. He has very gentle hands. Another time he gave me flowers for no reason at all. He hugged me and kissed me self-consciously.

'Thank you! What would we have done without you?'

I was as if I was playing a game – this is my family, this is my home, this is my husband, these are my children. And they all played along with me.

Almost every day we managed to visit Yanka in the hospital – it's very close by.

As we walked along the street, all four of us holding hands, anyone looking from the outside might have thought that we were together, we belonged to each other.

Yanka looked very poorly, with sunken cheeks and bright red eyes from crying. She was running a temperature.

She told her husband:

'Don't look at me: it'll give you a fright!'

She really did look terrible with her rabbity overbite, lop-ears and strands of greasy, unwashed hair.

She told me:

'Sashka, you've really blossomed!'

They'd explained to her that she couldn't have any more children.

I didn't know what to say to that.

'But that's what you wanted, isn't it?'

'Yes, that's what I wanted.'

And Yanka burst into tears again.

We sat beside her bed and she saw the boys keeping away from her, with her frightful, tearstained, sickly face, and snuggling up close to me. She saw her husband behaving quite differently with me from the way he did with her. One time she asked with a bitter laugh.

'Having a good time without me are you, then?'

Then Yanka was discharged, my game came to an end and I went home.

Mummy had a second operation.

I remember the conversation with the doctor who took away my last hope.

I asked:

'Tell me, how much longer has she got left to live? A year?'

'Oh no! Everything will move quickly now.'

'And there's nothing else that can be done?'

'No.'

He apologised for having to go and added:

'Tell her about it. I always think it's best if someone close tells them, not the doctor.'

I went back to the ward, knowing that Mummy was waiting for me there and she would ask:

'Well? What did he say?'

Before going to her, I went down into the courtyard, to gather my strength. I wanted to take a gulp of fresh air, with no hospital smell. Outside, light snow was falling and the yard keeper was scraping it into heaps with a spade. A cat ran by and for a moment I thought it was my Thumbtack, I called her, but it was Thumbtack in a new skin.

I remember I thought about the doctor who had given me the news:

The message and the messenger.

He could have suggested that I sit down, told me the same thing in a different tone of voice, let me hear at least a little bit of sympathy.

It's probably his defence against news like this – that cold, dry tone.

The yard keeper smiled at me and blew his nose as if he wanted to boast: Just look how much snot there is in this nostril, and now look how much there is in this one!

An old couple walked by, talking.

'In that sense liver cancer's better than the others . . .'

I don't know why all this has stuck so clearly in my memory.

When I went back to the ward, Mummy asked:

'Well? What did he say?'

'Everything's going to be all right.'

Mummy dozed off after she was given a dose of painkiller.

I sat beside her, looking out through the window at the snowflakes, black against the bright background of the sky. Mummy fell asleep, but immediately gave a shudder and opened her eyes. She gazed round the ward, saw me and said:

'I kept on believing that a miracle would happen. And you know, I think a miracle has happened. I'm ready for this. I'm not afraid of anything any more.'

Mummy's illness entered some new stage. She had suddenly found peace and acceptance. She used to be afraid of being left alone, but now she seemed to be afraid of any intrusion into her narrowed world. Before, she used to ask me to phone her friends and get them to visit her in the hospital more often. She complained that when someone is ill, people start avoiding them.

'If you have nothing more to give people, they go.'

But now she asked me to make sure there were fewer visitors. And if someone did come, she said nothing most of the time, waiting for her visitor to leave.

During the final days she and I didn't talk, just spoke a few insignificant words to each other now and then.

One time she handed me a sealed envelope and said she had thought out all the arrangements for her funeral and written down what I should do.

'Only promise me you won't spend money on anything unnecessary! Don't waste your money on me. Do you promise?'

I nodded.

Mummy's appearance had changed a lot. She was being consumed by the cancer. She dried up, shrivelled away. It became easy to turn her over in the bed. Her eyelids turned black.

She was tormented by hunger, but she couldn't eat anything any longer, every time she took food her body sent it all back. At first Mummy was ashamed of these fits of vomiting and didn't want me to see her like that, but later she didn't have the strength to be ashamed. I sat beside her and stroked her shoulder, and she groaned from the pain of the nauseous spasms that had just ended and the fear that she would start vomiting again soon.

I tried all the time to keep her hopes up, assuring her that everything would be all right, and she seemed to me to be clinging to this hope. But one of her friends met me in the corridor and said:

'Sasha, your mum knows all about herself, she knows she hasn't got long left to live, and she asked me not to tell you, so you wouldn't be upset.'

She burst into tears:

'Poor thing, she's suffering so much. Oh, let it be quick!'

Mummy complained:

'If death comes to everyone, what did I do to make mine so painful? Why do I have to suffer so much? I'd like to live out my last days with dignity, but what dignity can there be with pain like this! And the most terrible thing is not that I don't even look human any more, but I've stopped caring.'

She was afraid of the nights and demanded a double dose of painkiller. Sometimes she asked for more medication only half an hour after her regular injection.

I wanted so much to do something for her, but there was nothing I could do, apart from insignificant little things: adjust the pillow yet again or warm the cold bedpan before slipping it under her.

Afterwards I went home and left her alone.

One day, only just before the end, Mummy started asking me to stay with her that night. She'd heard a conversation in the corridor and thought they were talking about her, saying she wouldn't last until morning. She pleaded so desperately that I arranged it with the duty doctor and stayed with her, although in the morning I had to get up early and go to work. They made up a creaky old bed for me, one that a perfectly healthy person couldn't get to sleep on, let alone a sick patient.

Mummy was restless, she couldn't lie still, and I gave her cold compresses all the time.

She was suffering badly, I squeezed her hand and remembered how we had her cat put to sleep. The cat had been ill for a long time, and when we brought her to the vet, he looked at her and said:

'Why are you tormenting a dumb animal like this?'

There was no hope of recovery and we decided to have the cat put down. Mummy took her in her arms, and she was given the injection. The cat curled up and started purring. I could see how fine and cosy she felt, falling asleep in loving arms.

And even then I thought how strange it was that we pity cats and help put an end to their suffering, and we pity people but do everything we can to prolong theirs.

It seemed to me that Mummy and I ought to say something important to each other that night, but we only said the usual things.

I was feeling very sleepy.

So we didn't say any of the most important things to each other then.

They were giving her strong injections to help her sleep, but they had stopped working.

She had already lost her voice and she whispered:

'When the pain is this bad, I'm not human any more.'

I saw the nurses leaning down, trying to understand what she was saying, but then drawing back from her breath, as if they could breathe the cancer into themselves.

Mummy whispered more and more often:

'Let it be soon.'

The last time I saw her she was in a very bad way, she was groaning, her mouth had gone dry, beads of sweat had sprung out on her forehead. Nausea and vomiting even from a sip of tea. Hoarse, laboured breathing. The tumours were squeezing her out of her body.

They called me at work and told me to come, my mother was dying. I called my father.

He didn't pick up the phone for a long time. When he answered, I realised at once that he was drunk, although it was only midday.

'Bunny! Guess what I found yesterday!'

'Daddy, listen, this is important!'

'Felt boots! With galoshes! Like brand-new!'

'Daddy, Mummy's dying!'

I told him to come to the hospital. He mumbled something.

There was no tram for a long time. I had to wait and then take one that was packed.

At the railway station my father clambered into the tram, he didn't notice me. I almost called to him, but he was already arguing with someone. I felt ashamed – I didn't want everyone to know that he was my father.

It looked as if he had drunk more after our conversation on the phone.

I hadn't seen him for a long time and was amazed at how much he had aged and let himself go. Sunken, unshaven cheeks, sprouting grey stubble. An absurd knitted cap and a dirty coat with one button torn off. And all the time he kept repeating, loudly enough for the whole tram to hear:

'So she's dying, is she? Well, aren't we dying? Riding along in a tram! But where are we going? The same place, that's where! Big deal, she's dying! The swimming bunny!'

Then he accosted someone:

'What are you looking at me like that for? The felt boots and galoshes? Aha, really practical, they are! Old tat, of course, but the frost kills the stink!'

He started gabbling something about galoshes and chocolate.

I couldn't bring myself to go over to him. He noticed me after we got off at the hospital. Dashed towards me and tried to kiss me. I shoved him away.

'Just take a look at yourself!'

He plodded after me, muttering something resentfully under his breath.

We were too late, Mummy had already gone.

I felt as if something had happened that I could never put right. Not because Mummy was gone – during her illness I had been prepared for that.

For all those months I had felt guilty about her, I don't know why, perhaps because she was going and I was staying. And I thought this feeling would pass off if I was with her at the moment she died. I wanted to be with her and hold her hand. But I got there too late.

She was with me all the way through her illness, but she died all alone. That was what hurt me most of all.

For the first time in many months her face looked calm and at peace. Her suffering was at an end.

My father stood over her and cried, with his hands over his face. I noticed that they were covered with pigment spots and thought his liver must be in poor condition.

It was good that I had to deal with the documents and the funeral arrangements – all that business connected with a death takes your mind off things.

In the evening I sat by the phone with Mummy's address book and called her friends and acquaintances to tell them she had died. It was a strange feeling, every time I called someone new, she seemed to come back to life again and only die after I said:

'My mother's died.'

It was all so strange. The wreath, the ribbons, the coffin. The motionless body, out of which I had appeared in the world. Once upon a time I was inside her, and I wasn't anywhere else. And now she was inside me. And she wasn't anywhere else.

When I was getting Mummy ready, I sprayed her perfume on the body and put the bottle in the coffin.

It turned out that Mummy had paid for everything in advance. She already had a place in the cemetery. It was her mother's old grave, and her first child was buried in it too. For some reason she had never taken me to the cemetery. Now she wanted to lie with them. She had chosen an old photograph for the headstone, one in which she was young and beautiful. That's the advantage parents have – they leave without seeing their children in old age. Mummy will never see me as a tearful, irritable old woman, the way I have seen her.

I also recalled how we used to quarrel when I was a spiteful, heartless young baggage and once even wished that she would die – and now look, it had happened.

On the day of the funeral, thick snow fell from early in the morning and turned the cemetery into a world of snow statues – the trees, bushes, fences and gravestones stopped being themselves.

Everyone kept brushing the wet snow off their coats and caps, Daddy wiped his bushy eyebrows with the end of his scarf.

On the way there we ran into another funeral at the entrance and we had to wait. There was a beard covered in snow protruding from the coffin. It stopped being a beard and turned into a little snow statue as well. The other funeral had music. The musicians shook the snow off their instruments, knocked the saliva out of the mouthpieces, huddled up discontentedly, stamped their feet under the falling snow. One of them furtively sipped cognac from a little bottle.

Fires were burning here and there in the cemetery, to thaw out the ground. The smoke drifted to us through the wet flakes as they fell.

I had the strange feeling that we weren't burying Mummy, but someone else.

I knew it wasn't her, that the body in the coffin was empty, that Mummy couldn't be lying there, piled over with snow in an uncomfortable wooden box, with bare, blue hands crossed on her sunken chest, but there were moments when the similarity of this dead woman in the coffin to my mother became unbearable and the tears started pouring from my eyes. Especially because the snow didn't melt either on her hands or her face and I had to brush it off with my glove.

When I leaned down over her, just before they closed the coffin, I sniffed her for the last time – the aroma of the perfume mingled with the smells of the upholstery in the coffin, the snow, the fires, the flowers, the dead body. But all that wasn't Mummy's smell.

My father leaned down and pressed his forehead against hers.

Then he came over to me, with droplets dangling on the hairs sticking out of his nostrils. He was going to say something, but just shook his head, as if he was swimming and water had got into his ears. I wiped him under the nose with my handkerchief and hugged him, pressed my head against his wet hair.

'Daddy, put your cap on, you'll catch cold!'

A workman was shoving a rope though under the coffin to lower Mummy into the grave. It seemed as if everybody wanted to hug someone at that moment, and he hugged the coffin.

I was surprised that, apart from her closest women friends, some other people I didn't know at all had come to the funeral. As one woman kissed me, she said:

'Sasha! How much like your mother you've become!'

We went back along the path between the dead cemetery, where nobody had been buried for a long time, and our living cemetery, and the thought came to me that now I could never hug Mummy again, but some tree could hug her with its roots and snuggle up to her.

Yanka didn't come to the funeral, although I was expecting her. Something had happened to her in general, after that time she was in hospital and I stayed at their place. We used to be best friends, but now she didn't call, didn't come round, didn't ask me to sit with the children. I lugged a tree home for the New Year, decorated it and bought presents for the boys, I wanted to invite them over, have a party for them and me. But Yanka wouldn't let the children come to me, she said they'd both caught a cold. Only I could hear them shouting into the phone that they wanted to go and see Aunty Sasha.

After Mummy died, I sorted through all her papers and photographs, and met my father to give him some of them. He announced that he had started writing his memoirs and all this could come in useful. I asked him to give me something to read but he refused.

'All in good time.'

We talked about Mummy, about how hard it was for her to die.

'You're still young, bunny, you don't understand anything about this life! Illnesses are necessary – they help! When the suffering's that bad, it's not so frightening to go.'

He drank a little bit, got drunk quickly and started exclaiming indignantly:

'They go sticking rags in a dead man's mouth to give him plump cheeks like a little baby, pomading his hair and painting a happy smile on his face! When I imagine them putting that clown's makeup on me at the end, I feel sick! And I can't imagine myself in the ground at all. I don't want that! I want to go like a sailor – splash into the ocean!'

'Daddy, you ought to get married again!'

The exhausting trips to the hospital were over, it should have been easier without the cancer, injections, bedpans, vomiting and groaning, the odours of a decaying body, but I found myself thinking that I'd got used to going to see Mummy in the evening and thinking on the way how I would tell her about my day, the good things and the bad things, all the walking about and standing in queues and worrying, how hard it had been for me – and how I managed it all in the end.

I sorted through Mummy's things. The combs, powder compacts, little mirrors, scent bottles, hair pins, little jars, tubes, tweezers, pairs of scissors, brushes – everything that can't exist without a woman – went into the rubbish bag.

I came across her old dresses in the wardrobe. As I sorted them out I recalled where and when I had seen her in this dress or that one. Sometimes I couldn't remember anything, but sometimes a living picture appeared in my mind's eye immediately: there was Mummy in her blue velvet dress, getting ready for the theatre, combing her hair, talking on the phone in front of the mirror and assuring the receiver that no one wore their eyebrows that way any more. And then I found her Chinese robe with the sky-blue dragons – I scrunched it up and plunged my face into the flowing silk, but it only smelled of old laundry.

Little paper envelopes. All accurately labelled.

'Sashenka's first tooth'.

I think: Is that mine or his?

'Sasha's hair – one year and three months'.

And again I can't tell if it's mine or not.

I found a home-made cardboard fan that I made for her some time at the dacha when I was little, to drive away the wasps. She had kept it for some reason.

I looked through the photographs and was amazed – in her young days Mummy really did look very much like me. Is it possible that if I live to be old I shall be exactly like she was during her illness?

Some of the photographs had dates on them in Mummy's writing. In one photo Daddy is hugging Mummy somewhere surrounded by snowdrifts. It's strange that there are snowdrifts already in October. They're both wearing old-fashioned skiing outfits, but there are no skis to be seen. I checked the date and calculated – it turned out that they had been photographed exactly at the time when I was conceived. Although Mummy's smiling, her eyes are serious somehow. But Daddy's laughing with his mouth wide open. He still didn't know anything about himself then, or about Mummy, or about me. Generally in old photographs nobody ever knows anything about themselves.

Mummy once told me the kind of precautions they used to take: they put a metal cap smeared with petroleum jelly on the neck of the womb. But during menstruation it had to be taken out. Mummy didn't always put the cap in and she protected herself with acid tampons instead – before she went to bed with Daddy, she diluted some citric acid, moistened a piece of cotton wool with it and tucked it inside herself.

But that night they wanted me.

Somehow I can picture that night, my night, very clearly.

They got back late in the falling snow, like the snow that fell on the day of her funeral, and Mummy hung her black astrakhan coat up to dry.

I see Daddy trying to take off Mummy's stockings and she whispers:

'Careful! You'll ladder it like that!' Mummy told me there used to be a little repair shop at the railway station for fixing ladders in stockings – there was always a queue of women standing there.

Daddy probably kissed her impatiently while she neatly rolled off her stockings, then stuck them in the gap between the mattress and the headboard of the bed. And then she still had to lean backwards and curve her back to pull off the belt with the rubber bobbles. Or did her punctilious attention to detail not extend to lovemaking?

I don't know anything about her.

But I do know that afterwards, when I had already begun, Daddy got up for a smoke and opened the window that hadn't been papered shut for winter yet.

'Look, the snow's teeming down again! Come here!'

Mummy threw her astrakhan coat on over her naked body and walked across to him barefoot, holding the collar closed at her neck. Still hot after making love, she leaned out of the window, scooped up a handful of wet snow off the windowsill and started munching on it.

They stand in the dark at the open window and watch the snow falling.

Daddy puts one arm round her, moves the *papyrosa* in his other hand as far away as possible and blows a stream of smoke out sideways from the corner of his mouth. In her wet winter coat Mummy snuggles up against Daddy and runs the handful of snow over the inflamed skin on her neck, and in the snowy light from outside the window her arm, naked to the elbow, is as white as white, as if she's wearing a long opera glove.

My Sashenka!

Rain has set in here. It's pouring down almost without a break.

We're back at the camp. At this moment it's drumming on the roof of the tent above my head. I'm watching yellow mud creeping along the path. And there are bubbles on the puddles.

Everything in the tent is damp and unbearably dirty. But, by contrast, on the outside the canvas is clean and white, all the dust has been washed off.

At first everyone was delighted when it started lashing down, they put out cooking pots and buckets to catch the rain, took their clothes off, had a wash, ran around naked, washed their uniforms and underwear. The rain here is southern, steamy, strong.

We've washed everything, but there's nowhere to dry it – now it's hanging up all round the tent and it smells of mould.

That drumming on the canvas is driving me demented.

And I've been shivering since the morning too. It looks as if I've picked up a fever. A strange kind of sensation. I seem able to see and hear everything, only from the outside, somehow.

And sometimes the connection is suddenly lost, that is, I stop understanding obvious things. For instance, I don't understand how all these people around me appeared in my life. Or why I'm here with them now in this damp, smoky tent as they chortle loudly, taking off their shoulder belts, smelling of *huang jiu*: one of them has blown two fangs of smoke out of his nostrils, another has a red stripe on his forehead from his forage cap, and another doesn't have a single hair on his cranium, his skin glistens like thin cigarette paper. And now they're swearing as they discuss the action of melinite shells.

Or do I simply have a temperature? I must have fallen ill, that's why the flow of life is such a messy jumble.

The cook complains that without any butter he has to fry everything in soya bean oil.

I walked past the admiral's tent and there were cages with wet chickens. I don't understand.

What is there to understand? Chickens, cages, rain, an admiral – but even so I don't understand a thing.

An inspection was arranged for Admiral Alexeev's arrival – the men prepared, smartened themselves up, polished their forage cap badges bright and shiny, everybody was lined up in the rain early in the morning, they waited for two hours, the corps commander arrived, saluted and looked at one infantryman's rifle, it was dirty and he gave everybody an earful. But what have I got to do with all that?

I don't understand who we are, where we are and why we're together. This rain and the shots somewhere in the distance are inexplicable. These documents I have to copy out interminably are inconceivable. It's not possible that the same hand that is writing this letter about my love to you will later trace out the lines that bring grief into someone's home, as if I'm a messenger bearing bad news. I'm not a messenger.

Kirill found an amulet on a dead Yihetuan – a piece of yellow paper in a little bag on a string round his neck. A note with an incantation written in red that was supposed to make him invulnerable. Kirill hung it on his own neck. I don't understand.

He and I have quarrelled again. I understand that even less.

The soldiers have never read Shakespeare and they never will, but they know they shouldn't eat a lot before a battle, it complicates their condition if they get a stomach wound. They know that a dirty wound can be washed with urine or disinfected by cauterisation – as a last resort the powder from a cartridge can be used. What do they want with the monologues of the Prince of Denmark? To be or not to be. Absurd. Impossible to understand.

The water has gathered into little puddles on top of the tent and Kirill is draining it off by pushing a stick of bamboo up into the canvas where it sags under the weight. Why am I writing this? I don't understand.

The depredation in the city is unrestrained and insatiable. They loot everything. The Englishman Captain Bailey was appointed commandant. In order to stop the pillaging, he promptly had one of the English soldiers, a Sepoy, shot. Our superiors decided not to let themselves be outdone and ordered two Russian soldiers to be shot. They grabbed the first two who came to hand and shot them. When he learned about this, General Fukushima ordered three Japanese soldiers to be shot.

I drew up the documents about those two soldiers. Vasilii Alexandrovich Zimin and Alexander Mikhailovich Loktev. One was twenty, the other twenty-one – incidentally, his birthday was only three days ago.

I saw the firing squad cleaning their rifles with expensive silk textiles. I don't understand any of this at all.

This rain is enough to drive me insane.

And I knew that Loktev – pale eyes and white hair, almost no eyebrows.

While I was writing just now, Glazenap ran to get some boiling water in the rain, and on the way back he slipped in the mud and scalded his left hand. He's sitting there, howling quietly, the skin has come up in red blisters. Everybody's pestering him with advice. Now he's run off to the infirmary.

The day after tomorrow we set out for Peking, despite the rain. Today I copied out the plan of march onto clean paper. There was water dripping from the ceiling of the staff HQ tent. I had to take care all the time that drops didn't fall on me.

What do they mean, Peking? Does it exist anywhere on the face of the earth?

And how can we walk anywhere through this impassable mud?

I find it hard to concentrate. My stomach's in a terrible state. When I don't eat anything, it's not too bad, but when I do eat, the diarrhoea and vomiting are instant. They gave me some kind of powder in the infirmary – it doesn't help.

I feel hungry all the time.

It's a good thing you can't see the way I am now, unshaven and barely alive. Everyone here is the same. And covered in mud. All our tents are smeared with yellow clay, and our beds, and our clothes. But I think I've already written to you about that. I can't understand if I have or I haven't. And if so, what for?

What do people write for? As long as they write, it means they're still alive. If you've read these lines, it means death's been postponed. I'm a match for Scheherazade and her stories! Only she's a rich woman compared with me. A thousand nights, just imagine it — it's an entire eternity! But how many more nights have I been granted? That number exists somewhere, it's out there waiting for me, like an undiscovered America.

Sometimes I'm not myself, my darling, and I need you to find myself again, to rediscover and restore myself. I have to cling to something real, and I cling to you.

If I am writing to you, it means that everything is all right, I'm still alive. I write therefore I live. Strange, that's exactly what I wanted to escape from. But I can't.

Sometimes what's happening seems like a dream in which everything is inexplicable, absurd, but painfully real, with sounds and smells. I probably just need to wake up into reality, but where can I wake up to get away from this ragged dripping of water all round the tent and the smell of mould on clothes that aren't drying out?

I tried to do the opposite — if not wake up, then at least fall asleep. But I couldn't. My head's too thick and heavy.

I drank some water — the sand's grating in my teeth.

Glazenap came back with his hand bandaged. He sat down on his bed, admired the fresh white dressing for a moment and said thoughtfully:

'Everything in the world is a sign of something, isn't it? Everything has a meaning, it tells us something. Maybe this is a sign to me that everything will be all right?'

It's a good thing no one but me heard him.

If only I could believe stupid Glazenap that I can fall asleep and wake up living in a different time, with all this forgotten, like a bad dream.

And finally, what death is, I absolutely cannot understand. And I probably never will.

Will I ever understand anything!

I'm must be asleep after all, dreaming. I'll wake up some time. I will wake up. If only I could wake up!

I can't take any more of it.

Now some men around me are drinking tea.

I don't know who these men around me are. I don't understand what they say to me.

I don't understand what I'm doing here – why aren't I with you?

My Sashenka! I think I've already understood everything I was supposed to understand. That's enough for me. I want to come to you.

But they'll drive us off to somewhere or other along impassable muddy roads.

Sasha, every step I take here has meaning only because it's a step towards you. My love, whichever way I walk, I'm walking to you.

I listen to the rain drumming, beating my brain out of my head, and I remember the way the rain used to patter at the dacha – what a sweet sound that dacha rain made, whispering on the roof of the veranda in the morning!

How I loved those rainy days when I could lie on the divan, listen to the rustling of the wet leaves through the window and read.

And now I'm amazed that I couldn't feel happy that summer.

Of course I was happy, only I didn't know it. But it seemed to me that I knew everything and understood it all.

I remember reading in *Hamlet*: 'The time is out of joint'.

And it was all clear to me. What's so difficult to understand?

But I've only really understood here. Now I know what he meant.

Do you know what Shakespeare was really writing about? About the fact that the time will be back in joint when we meet again and I put my head on your knees.

●

My love, my only one!

It's such a long time since I wrote to you.

Everything's all right here.

Only I get very tired.

Don't think that I'm complaining. I'm strong. Or rather, my sister is, she's the strong one, but I can just burst into tears for no reason at all. You know how easy that is for me.

There I go again, making things up, some sister or other.

I just can't get used to myself. I've been trying all my life and I still can't. And I can't get used to life either, although it's high time I did.

It's very hard sorting out the fine threads of justice and mercy. I know everything, I understand everything, but it's hard.

And getting up every morning in the dark. And then coming back alone and in the dark again.

But she's not like that at all, everything's easy for her. She sees everything and feels everything differently. It's impossible to explain this to anyone, but you'll understand. For instance, say I'm going to work in the morning. I'm waiting for the tram, the icy wind has brought tears to my eyes and my cheeks are scorched by the cold. The frozen crowd at the tram stop is sullen and silent. Not quite shadows, not quite people. The tram still doesn't come, perhaps it won't come at all. They jig up and down, hawk and spit, catch up on their sleep standing. I close my eyes too, so as not to look at all this.

But she looks, and she sees something different.

Snow-powder slithering slantwise over the ground. Little stars on the snow. Overnight the trees and wires have sprouted furry hoarfrost as thick as a finger. Even the rubbish tip is dolled up like a bride.

And thick, steamy clumps round the crowd at the tram stop – the soul scattering as it self-seeds. The tram comes rumbling up, listing over and jangling. Rasping sparks off the wires.

The shadows at the stop start stirring and make a dash.

We've squeezed in somehow. The conductress abuses us, shaking her satchel of change. Her glasses have steamed up.

I've grabbed a strap, I'm swaying about. The leather loop smells sour. The tram churns its human contents on the points.

In the dull light of the little lamps, the paper of yesterday's *Evening News* looks like a drowned man's skin. War on the front page, crossword on the back page. We have been treacherously attacked by the kingdom of Prester John. The convergence point of lines in perspective, the navel of the world, a handful of letters.

The news is still the same. Some have been stabbed, but these were trampled to death. Pharaohs' tombs ransacked while they're still alive. Lambing proclaims the end of winter. You went sinister, but we went dexter. Right now, at this very moment, a gondolier is pushing off with his foot from a slippery wall covered with mould and waterweed.

Scientists inform us that our warm-blooded breathing is why it's getting warm and damp in the tram. But at every stop the frosty chill from the door creeps in under my skirt.

And the researchers are still obsessed with time. After all, they discovered experimentally long ago that it doesn't just fill space up to the edges, like thin porridge, it's heaped up, like thick porridge. But now a problem has arisen with the way it's stored. According to the latest data, it can only be preserved by chrono-graphiclers, and only consecutively, one thing after another, in a line that runs back to where the tramlines go, where it joins up with them, but for convenience this linear time, like an infinite string of macaroni, has been chopped into handy snippets of words.

Readers' letters. There's a game for very young children — a board with a circle, a square, a little house and various objects cut out of it, and these shapes have to be inserted into the correct holes. If you lose a piece, there's nothing to cover the hole with. No little house, just a gaping void. And I have the feeling that my life is a similar collection of gaping voids: house, husband, love, this evening — and nothing to fill them with. Holes in the universe, they let in a draught. And more and more of these holes as the years go by — as more people leave.

The weather overseas: sunny, warm.

Tomorrow's horoscope: crooked and twisted.

Wanted.

Lonely, happy despite everything, sick, red eyes, couldn't get to sleep last night, kept gasping and panting, blocked nose, slept with her mouth open, woken again and again by her own snoring, walks around all day long with a nose full of snot and head full of lead, blows her nose hard enough to burst her nostrils, dries her hanky on the radiator, the hanky gets harder every time, it crunches when she picks it up. Sees everything and knows about everything. Was given her serving of happiness and keeps asking for more.

I'm lucky, I'm already at the window. I grab my mitten with my teeth, breathe on the glass and rub a cavity in the crust of hoarfrost with my fingers. The tram jolts over the points, rumbles across a bridge.

I put my eye to the spy hole and watch the river-dawn, ruled across with the lines of ski tracks. We used to have P.T. classes here too. I recall the strange sensation when I passed under the span of the bridge on my old skis – rusty railway structures above my head, an invisible tram rumbling, and I'm soaring above the void, there's an abyss below my skis. It's so wonderful moving clumsily along above the water, thrusting with the little poles.

Every time we rumble across this bridge, I remember the squealing bundle on the ice. Perhaps this is the very same river?

I look into the cavity and there's a lunastice in it. The wintry smoke above a factory looks brainy. Gasholders drift by for a long time, crowned with signal lamps, then it's the school stop – in there behind the hoarfrosted windows the first lesson has already started and the sleepy yawners are being told that you mustn't gaze at the moon for a long time, or you'll turn into a lunatic, that little boys are future soldiers and little girls are nurses, and that a caterpillar's self and a butterfly's self are quite different, but still the same.

I have to go almost all the way to the final stop, the tram empties and loads up with frost again.

I get out. Hoarfrost like untrimmed velvet on the bushes, squiggly golden monograms in the snow by the fence. Canine? Human? I'm constantly amazed by the things that pass through my mind.

A woman wearing an orthopaedic shoe limps down the steps of the porch, screwing her leg into herself at every step. She works in the library and loathes the readers because they take out a book and bring back a flat greasy pancake with its pages falling out, and in revenge she writes who the killer is on the first page of the detective novels.

At the records office an invisible person behind the little window jabbers away, nibbling the words like a rabbit nibbling on a carrot.

I go up to my place, turning right on the second floor, there's a sign on the door of the office: So-and-So Such-and-Such, Empress of Life, Mistress of Women. And they sit in a queue, all full of their winter crops, conversations about cloudy urine, one child more – one tooth less, a cantaloupe stomach is a lad, a watermelon stomach is a lass.

And I know everything about all of them.

For this one the nights are endless, but the years are jogging past. And life curls on like an endless potato paring.

This one would like to have everything like everyone else: husband, child, breakfast together in the morning, but she doesn't know how. Last year she bought a river cruise, decided this is it, nowhere to retreat, I'll sail off into my holiday alone and come back happy. And there she is on the last evening, sitting on deck and looking at a seagull that's sitting on the handrail, looking at her. And the seagull thinks: 'We're sisters, aren't we? You, me and that landing stage over there that no one ever lands on.'

And this one here, with the languorous sheep's eyes, is an absolutely hopeless painter who gives her paintings to all her friends for their birthdays, and they don't have a clue what to do with them and last year this couple – he's a big-mouthed dope and lucky devil, when they ask 'which hand is it in?' he always gets it right, and she works in a dog parlour, washing and clipping dogs, it's hot and everything's closed up tight, because after the bath a little doggy could catch cold, and so she runs outside for a smoke all sweaty, covered in dog hair – well anyway, they hung the artist's gift up in the dining room when she was there, then took it down and forgot to put it back up the next time she came. She arrives, and there's a clock hanging where her still life used to be. Now she's sitting on the little bench by the window, lost in thought and counting something on her fingers.

I walk in, take my dress off, hang it on the hanger behind the door, put on a crisp white coat.

And it begins.

'Next!'

She takes off her warm leggings and panties, wiping her runny nose on her wrist, and clambers onto the cold chair. Goose bumps have spread across her blue, skinny thighs and her buttocks with the red stripes from the elastic. Curling ginger.

The fine threads of justice and mercy.

And this morning, when the snow and the half-light were still a single whole, there was a girl with a cold at the tram stop, sniffling snottily.

I was standing beside her. There was no tram for a long time. Then someone gasped:

'It's coming!'

The tram stop started shuffling and rustling.

'Number five? Or number twelve?'

'A five!'

The tram came closer and closer, but the girl suddenly skipped away from it, darted behind the shelter, and started choking as she leaned over to vomit. Her granny's salted cucumber saw the light of day again, along with something chopped fine, like vinaigrette.

Before she could get her breath back and spit out the last bits, the tram was long gone. I went too.

I stayed.

I'm riding in the tram and standing at the stop.

Steam hovers over the blob of vomit. A jackdaw has flown in and hopped up lopsidedly. It pecks at this hot dish.

I walked right up close to her, our patches of breath meshed and crumpled together. I ask:

'Are you all right?'

She wipes her lips with snow and squints sideways at me, as if to say: Get lost.

I:

'How old are you?'

She:

'That's none of your business.'

I:

'Of course not. It's just that once upon a time I didn't have a daughter. I looked at you and suddenly thought she could have been like you now.'

She:

'What do you want from me? Who are you?'

I:

'What difference does that make? I'm just waiting for a tram. In short, I'm the Empress of Life. The message and the messenger. It's not important. Don't be afraid of me.'

She:

'I'm not afraid.'

I:

'I know everything.'

She:

'You don't know anything.'

I:

'Conceived without sin and no one believes you?'

She:

'Mind your own business!'

I:

'But where did it come from then? Just went for a swim in a pond, did you, and there it was?'

She:

'But I never did anything wrong! I swear I didn't!'

I:

'Well now, my little girl, all, sorts of things happen. You could have picked it up on your finger and stuck it in. Birds manage to introduce the sperm on the wing.'

She:

'What have birds got to do with it?'

I:

'Birds don't have anything to do with it. But a human being, as you don't know yet, is completely alone. The only state in which a human being is truly not alone is when a woman is expecting a child. Be happy, you stupid fool! Do you think you're the only one? What's the big deal? All sorts of things happen! You're not the first, you won't be the last. Children aren't from the seed. So consider it a virgin birth.'

She:

'I'm afraid.'

I:

'Everything will be all right. You'll see. Don't take on so! You're healthy and beautiful, you'll manage. And you'll have a healthy, beautiful child.'

She:

'I don't want to. I've decided I'm not going to.'

I:

'But that's not for you to decide, if you want to or not. Who's asking you? You think about that stomach of yours. A watermelon's a lad, a cantaloupe's a lass. Whatever way it turns out, basically.'

She:

'No!'

I:

'Calm down, there's a clever girl! Go and thank that pond for the present and, like Alyonushka at the millpond, ask for the child to be born normal and with eyes as huge as possible, and for it to have everything in the right place – arms, legs, head, you know, all sorts of things happen!'

She:

'I'm not going to have it anyway!'

I:

'Yes you are!'

She:

'No I'm not!'

I:

'Yes you are! Pull yourself together! Here, take my handkerchief, blow your nose. And listen. Once upon a time there was a little girl, just like you, with the same kind of head cold, she blew her nose just like you, and she conceived without sin just like you. No one believed her. And what was in her girlish head was the same as in yours. The ice on the river had just started to break up. She went down there one night and put her little bundle on an ice floe. The child floated off downstream. Weeping bitterly, she walked away from the river, back to her non-home, but she realised there would be nothing but non-life there. She wandered round the streets until morning. The milk flowed from her breasts, because when woman was created, they forgot the tap. The child's cry was ringing in her ears all the time. Eventually she couldn't stand it any more and went back to the river. The child's cry came closer and closer. And then she saw her little bundle on an ice floe that was slowly drifting along the other side of the river, from upstream. She threw herself into the river and ran over the ice, falling through into the water all the time, grabbed the child and clambered out, barely alive, onto the bank. She sat down in a snowdrift, freed her hot breast and stuck it in the child's mouth. The child fastened on it and slurped greedily. And life began – clamorous, fragrant, and imperishable.'

■

My Sashenka!

We've been on the march for several days now.

There are only snatches of things in my head, so I'll write to you in snatches.

The rain has stopped, we've managed somehow to light campfires. The night is thick all around, I can't see anything, only the faces are lit up.

At night everyone's different somehow, unfamiliar. Everyone's tired and bad-tempered.

Sometimes the campfire flares up, and suddenly I can see a cart and a horse's face, then once again the darkness closes in from all sides.

I do have a fever after all. Inside my head as well there are glimpses of light, then darkness all around. Then thoughts appear, but very remote somehow.

Remember, you asked what I thought about the Mona Lisa? Now I know for certain what she's smiling at. She's smiling because she's already there, and we're still here. She's smiling at us from over there. And it isn't a smile at all. She already knows what we don't know yet. We all hope that there might be something there, but she already knows there isn't anything, so she's grinning at us for being so foolish.

I'm feverish, everything gets jumbled up together in my head! A day's gone by, it's raining again, and it's windy too. It's lashing down harder than ever, and the flap of the tent is snapping. My head's hot, but my feet are cold.

Everybody walks about wet all day long, and there's nowhere to dry ourselves.

Something bad is happening to me. Every now and then I stop understanding where I am and what's happening to me. Is this me?

Darkness all around, then sudden glimpses of light.

The wet canvas flutters, but somehow I don't have the strength to do anything about it.

The mosquitoes have appeared again with the rain. My face and hands are swollen all over from bites. At this moment I have to write with my eyes screwed up, constantly shaking my head.

The roads have been washed away, in the ruts the water is up to our knees. The sticky mud hangs like heavy weights on our feet and coats the wheels, it's very hard for the horses.

I'm unbearably thirsty. I've drunk water from puddles several times, although I realised I was only upsetting my sick stomach even more. But I was tormented by thirst.

The paddy fields are flooded with water, there are lots of snakes in them. They weave along right at the surface and their tracks can be seen on the water for a long time afterwards.

As I walk along, the grass always seems to be stirring nearby, and I hear rustling sounds.

Yesterday they arranged a midday halt and everybody was so tired, they collapsed where they were standing. Afterwards one infantryman showed everyone a dead snake that he discovered he had been sleeping on.

'And I was wondering what that rope was, irking me under my side.'

Total confusion. Units fall behind and get mingled together. Men get frightened and start shooting at each other. Yesterday the English thought that some Russian infantrymen who had captured a village off to the side of the road were Chinese, and they started shelling them. Several men were wounded and one died on the way to the infirmary, he'd lost a lot of blood.

The plans for the offensive keep changing endlessly. Right now the Japanese are at the front of the advance, we're behind them, the Americans are behind us.

Today we passed through several villages abandoned by their inhabitants and devastated by the Japanese.

From one village they started firing at our extended column. General Stessel ordered a battery to be deployed – in a few minutes there was nothing left of the village.

We are advancing along the right bank of the Pei Ho. The Chinese army is withdrawing in total disarray. At the villages we come across the sites of their halts, abandoned all higgledy-piggledy: they leave everything behind – crates of shells, cartridges, rifles. Where the Japanese have passed through, the villages are totally devastated. They take everything edible and force the remaining Chinese to go with them as porters. They shoot some to intimidate the rest. There are many bodies of local people killed like that scattered around the villages.

The pillage is continued by our men, although they can't carry much away with them. They prowl round the villages and lug off watermelons, cantaloupes, vegetables, chickens.

The Chinese don't have bread – instead they eat boiled rice and pancakes, all without salt.

The soldiers have stopped eating the pigs, of which there are huge numbers everywhere – they devour the corpses that litter the villages around here now. There's no one to clear the dead away.

All the detachments have many stragglers. We keep coming across Japanese trailing behind their forces in an endless procession or on their way back to Tientsin. And everybody, regardless of nationality, is suffering from dysentery. Everywhere men sit along the sides of the road with their trousers lowered and agony on their faces, whether Japanese or Russian. Our men pick up the weakest of the Japanese stragglers and sit them on their two-wheeled carts, infirmary wagons and big guns.

It's a hot day, not a breath of wind. But the road still isn't drying out, although it runs along an embankment built to separate the fields from the Pei Ho when it floods. There are puddles of stagnant water everywhere, and a terrible stink rises up on all sides. Traces of matter regurgitated by sick stomachs are ever-present.

Everyone is afraid of being ambushed. From time to time shots ring out from the thickets. The kaoliang is impenetrably thick and so tall that it can easily conceal a man on horseback. Sometimes the soldiers' nerves give out and they start blazing away wildly at the thickets. All the time it seems as if there's someone skulking in there.

I've set my hand to writing a few more words. The same villages, the same kaoliang. The thickets are so dense that a man disappears in just a few steps. The soldiers have been forbidden to run in there to relieve themselves. There have already been several cases of men being found with their stomachs slashed open.

Forgive me, my dear Sasha, it is so long since I have been able to write you a real letter, a good one. I write down whatever comes into my head at the halts.

Right now, I want to hide from everything that's going on here, but I still write anyway – what if my letters are useful to someone some day?

Perhaps someone will want to find out something about us. About what I saw today. About how we marched until late and slept the rest of the night on the wet ground, without pitching the tents. Everyone just toppled over anywhere at all. The rains have transformed the clayey road into liquid mush. The wagon train and the limbers of the guns sank up to their wheel hubs and the soldiers dragged them out with their bare hands. Today I pulled my foot out of the liquid clay and left my boot there.

But who could possibly be interested in my boot?

All the same, I'm going to write anyway.

Night again. We've settled into a ruined village. Our under-wear and tunics are so wet, you could wring them out. There's no chance of drying our puttees. We've stuck a candle stump in a Chinese paper lantern, it's barely even glimmering. And we're gulping down a murky, perfumed substance – Chinese green tea, brewed up in a soldier's billycan. I made myself eat three eggs. Mosquitoes, sweltering heat, stupefying vapours from the puddles and ditches.

The men are afraid to drink from the wells, they make the Chinese drink the water from them first – the old men haven't fled from the abandoned villages. The water's brownish, thick as pea soup.

I've already told you that the Japanese are marching ahead of us – we've just passed a tree on which men are hanging by their own pigtails, knotted round their necks.

During the day either it's scorching hot, so there are men sprawling about with sunstroke again, or a tropical downpour floods the whole area in about an hour. The water doesn't soak into the clayey ground and it forms entire lakes in the hollows, while ditches and streams are transformed into unfordable rivers.

Men collapse, exhausted, and are dragged aside, onto the high, dry spots, otherwise they could choke on the puddles and the liquid mud.

The commander of the advance positions has just been setting out his company in a sentry-line. The rain was lashing down and the sentries had to stand up to their ankles in water. The posts are deliberately set up on low ground – at night there's a clearer view looking upwards.

Clumps of trees above the kaoliang – either burial grounds or villages.

An overnight halt under the open sky. Everyone bunched together, on their guard. The murmuring of the kaoliang is like the rustling of someone creeping up on us.

The moment there's a brief halt, the column lies down instantly. The men get so tired that they fall asleep on the bare earth in all sorts of positions.

We walked all night, the nearby villages were burning all around us. In the glow we could see everything in the sky. Then the rain started again, but the glow forced its way through it. A reddish kind of rain, that sort of thing doesn't happen.

The road is as impassable as ever, from time to time we have to help the horses drag carts that have got stuck out of the mud.

I was so tired that I collapsed in a heap and slept like that for a while, without getting undressed, in my dirty boots. We crammed into some kind of mud hut and the soldiers fell asleep on the floor, using each other as pillows. They all smell of mould, sweat and ingrained dirt.

My own smell is quite unbearable.

It was quiet outside, but then we heard either shouts or groans coming from the fields. Kirill asked:

'Is that a bird?'

'No. They probably haven't picked up the wounded.'

We weren't allowed to sleep. Early in the morning the sentries imagined they saw someone and opened fire. It turned out to be a dog. Men's nerves give way, they fly off the handle at the least little thing and shout at each other.

Everybody is so embittered that they're turning savage. There are atrocities on all sides.

The Chinese soldiers shoot from ambush, concealed in the kaoliang thickets, and when there's danger, they take off their jackets, fling their guns away and creep out, bowing, pretending to be peaceful civilians. The Japanese and the English and our men now kill everyone they meet.

In my presence Cossacks hacked to death several men they came across in a field. Perhaps they were peasants hiding from the troops passing by, but who's going to investigate now? And who's bothered anyway? No one will ever find out about those people's deaths, or their lives.

I have seen a man being stabbed with a bayonet and still grabbing at the bayonet with his hands, trying to turn it aside.

In one village they captured a young man and interrogated him in my presence, and Kirill interpreted. The captive sat on the floor with his head thrown back, because his hands were tied behind his back with his own pigtail. Skin and bone. Eyes full of hate and fear. A gaunt, dirty face. To all the questions the young man answered 'miu', which means 'no'. They shot him in the foot, he squealed and spun round on the floor, spraying blood, but still kept answering 'miu'. They dragged him outside and threw him down the well.

Sashenka, I'm tired, deadly tired.

The only thing that gives me strength is that you're waiting for me.

I'm writing this the next day. Kirill has been killed.

This is how it happened. Several of our soldiers were sent to a village nearby, Kirill went with them. They were gone for a long time. More men were sent, they came back and said there had been an ambush in the village. We dashed over there.

I didn't understand immediately what I'd seen.

That is, I understood immediately, but I didn't want to understand.

They had all been killed. But first they had been tortured. The bodies had been mutilated. I don't want to write about what I saw.

Our men tried to set fire to the houses, but in the rain nothing would burn.

At the far end of the village they found an old man and dragged him back by his ankles. He was covered in yellow mud. When they dropped him, he stayed there like that, lying face-down, but he was alive. They turned him over onto his back with a boot.

An old man with a long grey pigtail wrapped round his neck.

They started beating him with their boots and rifle butts.

I intervened, tried to hold them off, but they shoved me away so hard that I slipped and fell in the liquid mud.

Someone stepped on his Adam's apple with their heel and I heard his throat crunch.

Now we're drinking tea. It feels good to have a hot drink.

What was the meaning of this day? What a stupid question. All my life I've been asking myself stupid questions.

The meaning of this day, if it has one, is probably only that it has passed.

Another day has ended and brought our meeting closer.

●

Volodenka!

I need you very much, because I am only real with you.

And you understand everything in me, even when I can't understand something myself.

I'd really like to share only the good things, only it's so important for me to share everything with you!

But I wasn't intending at all to complain, on the contrary, I need to share my happiness with you.

I felt happy at the very moment when others feel grief.

I'll never be able to explain this to anyone. Only to you. You'll understand.

Well, I've learned what déjà vu is: it seemed like I'd only just been handed Mummy's death certificate, and I was already going through the formalities for my father. The same documents, the same words. The same fuss and bother over the funeral, the strange, unnecessary rituals, the unreal ceremonies that have nothing at all to do with my real Mummy and Daddy.

Daddy died at home. That was what he wanted.

The funeral was rather absurd.

The lift was too small and the stairs were narrow, so the porters had a really hard time getting Daddy down from the fifth floor. The sides of the coffin kept banging against the walls and railings. The porters shouted to each other and the noise brought our neighbours out, peering through open doors. Several women stood at the entrance with their hands over their mouths.

Little boys playing football out in the yard shouted and came running to watch the funeral. The ball shot up in the air and bounced right up to the coffin.

We set off to the crematorium.

Daddy lay in the coffin with his arms folded like a real goody two-shoes. I stroked his chest, which was calm, not heaving wildly like it did during the last few minutes before he died.

I pushed a lock of hair back off his forehead and on the cheeks that I had shaved clumsily I saw tears – my tears.

It was hot, flies landed on Daddy and I drove them off.

In the crematorium, while we were waiting on the bench, all I could see were his knuckles. Daddy's stomach had swollen up from all the tablets, it towered up above the sides of the coffin. As I looked, I automatically compared the hands folded on his chest with the window catch behind them and suddenly I thought that Daddy was breathing.

The people who came included some women I didn't know. Lovers? Cohabitants? Did he love them? Did they love him? I don't know anything.

When I kissed Daddy for the last time, I noticed that a lady-bird had landed on his shoulder. I brushed it off, or it would have burned up.

I overheard someone enquiring what the temperature in the furnace was.

When they closed the lid, I saw Daddy smile.

Now I'm sitting and reading the exercise book in which he was writing something at the end but never showed me.

My father had been saying for ages that he was going to write his memoirs. Perhaps he really wanted to. But all that was left was a skinny exercise book with more pages torn out than written on.

He used to joke that he was writing the book of life.

'This is my pamphlet of existence, bunny. When I've written it right to the end, to the very last full stop, then you can read it.'

After his stroke I spent a lot of time at his bedside. His right side was paralysed. One side of his mouth and the corner of his eyelid were twisted, there was mush instead of words, but I learned more or less to understand him. Even before he started getting up again, he was already jotting things down in the exercise book with his left hand. I offered to write for him – he wouldn't let me.

In general, he recovered rather quickly. He didn't spend much time at all in the hospital – he didn't want to stay there. He said the nurses were ugly, they hardly ever looked in and only did what they were required to do with the seriously ill patients.

The district nurse who came to do his remedial exercises with him at home complained indignantly to me that he grabbed at every protruding part of her body with his good hand.

I replied:

'Well, that means he's on the mend.'

'But I can't do anything, because your father keeps grabbing my breasts!'

'Slap his hand! It's not sick.'

I told my father:

'What do you think you're doing? Can't you be patient for a while?'

He mumbled something with his crooked mouth.

And now here I am, leafing through his notes – and there's nothing there. That is, nothing that I wanted to find. Almost nothing about me, about my childhood. In fact, there's only one mention of me.

'*Sometimes I think about my life: Well, that's all down the drain. But sometimes I think: No, I made Sashka, didn't I. She's the one who'll save my soul. Maybe my entire crazy life can be forgiven for her sake?*'

I was probably expecting to find out something about myself, about the side of life that was hidden from a child's eyes. Instead of that, there were fragmented jottings about everything in the world and about nothing.

'*At night I listen to the clock, taking my life away from me. Loneliness* is when you seem to have everything not to be lonely, but you don't really have anything. And so, in the middle of my insomnia, I stand there in the bathroom, naked and aging, in front of the mirror. I look at my body — it's betraying me. Puffy bags under colourless eyes, clumps of hair sticking out of my ears. I scratch between my shoulder blades with a toothbrush and I think — I'll die soon. How did it come to this?'

'I should take death lightly: once you're ripe, up you come, like a carrot in a vegetable patch. But I can't do it.'

'The time has been changed again. Seems like they only just changed it the last time. I'd better get a move on and write something, or they'll cancel it altogether.'

'In my youth I used to think about how some day I'd grow old and write my memoirs, so I used to note down in my diary things that might come in handy later. And now here, at the other end of life, after all these years I remember that youth writing the diary that was supposed to help me remember the important events and experiences of my life now. But now it turns out that what seemed important then is all nonsense. And I didn't take any notice of what was really important. And that means that to write now about myself then would be a lie.'

'I've just remembered that when I was a child my father bought me a tortoise in a pet shop. I was happy. It was a cold winter day and I hurried home, because I was afraid my tortoise would get cold. The pet shop's still there, in the same building, half a century later. I was walking past it and dropped in for a minute. What did I want? To catch my old, happy self? What does that boy, whose father tried to din into him why Achilles could never catch the tortoise rustling in the box, have in common with this sullen and not entirely sober passer-by? Why, nothing!'

'I read about reincarnation, then decided to have a shave. I look at my grey stubble and realise that the transmigration of souls goes on all the time, we simply migrate into ourselves. There was a boy who became an old man, and his soul migrated from body to body a countless number of times

*— every morning. The body becomes a different one overnight without our noticing.'*

I remember my father young and strong, doing his exercises. We used to play at swings — he held out his arm and I clung to his wrist and swung on it. But now, after the stroke, it was terrible to look at him. He expressed himself in half-words, his right arm didn't work, he'd lost weight, the skin on his neck had sagged.

Daddy had been ill earlier, but he had never told me. He was probably afraid of appearing weak to me. Once he even went into hospital for an operation on a stomach ulcer without saying anything to me. He didn't phone. He only told me he had been ill after he recovered.

But this time he had to accept his own weakness.

The first few days were especially hard. I'd only just finished with all the worry and strain of Mummy's illness, and now I had to go to see my father every day.

He lived in a complete mess, without any household things at all. There was no trivet, so he put the frying pan on an ashtray. He wiped his hands on the curtains. I had to buy everything or bring it from home.

Back to the bedpan, the massages, the bedsores, the spoon-feeding. Immediately after the stroke he was incontinent. I put nappies under him, as if he was a small child.

Afterwards, on the contrary, he developed constipation, and I had to give him enemas regularly.

Once, when I cleared up the contents of his stomach that had flooded across the sheet and changed the bed, wrinkling up my face at the stink, he mumbled something.

I don't understand.

'What, Daddy? What do you want?'

He was apologising to me.

'Oh, don't be silly, Daddy! You wiped my bottom, didn't you?'

And at the same time he acts like a child. While I'm washing him, he starts acting up – the water's either too hot or too cold. I lather him up with children's soap on a sponge and he starts whingeing – the sponge is scraping his skin. I have to lather him with my hands. His skin dangles flabbily, as if it's slipping off his body. I wash all his folds and wrinkles.

I massage his disabled arm and wonder what happened to the strong, muscular arm I once used to swing on like a monkey. Arms must be reincarnated too, if it has taken up residence in this length of limp, paralysed rope, covered with flabby fibrous veins and brown spots.

I cut his hair and his nails. I soaked his feet in hot water, steaming the calluses, the yellow nails that had grown into his toes, the gnarled excrescences on his bumpy heels. In his old age the second and third toes on his left foot had crossed. He joked, saying that was for good luck.

I washed him everywhere – his skinny thighs with dangling buttocks and his crotch. Could I really have been in there once upon a time – in that crumpled, wrinkled thing lost among the tufts of grey hair?

He was afraid that he had cancer too – of the prostate. I felt his prostatic gland.

'Daddy! You'll recover and give me brothers and sisters yet!'

My father started reading medical books and arguing with the doctors, explaining to them how they ought to treat him.

They told him not to smoke – he carried on puffing away as if nothing had happened. I gave that up as a bad job.

I cook him semolina – he turns sulky, clatters his spoon resentfully, sniffs, prods feebly at his plate, clears his throat, wrinkles up his face.

'A bit of herring and some onion would be good!'

'Eat it, or I'll tip it over your head!'

He remembered how he once poured kefir over me and started chewing his semolina obediently. I sat by his bed, and enjoyed remembering my childhood with him. It was strange that he didn't remember at all some things that stood out so clearly for me.

But he did remember the Hawaiian dance – with our hands in our pockets.

Once he brought me a Japanese print as a present. Before I could even get a proper look at it, Mummy saw it, flushed scarlet and took it away from me. So I never did see what was in it.

I remembered the wonderful smell of leather when he was an Arctic pilot and he put his helmet with the huge goggles on me and I climbed into his high fur boots.

When I watched that film afterwards I was surprised or, rather, very upset. Not because the film was rubbish, but because I realised for the first time that Daddy was a bad actor. Not real.

But when he tied a turban round his head and sat with his legs crossed and the kingdom of Prester John stretched out all around, as far as the eye could see – he was real then.

And just what were all those white and black lions, gryphons, metagalarinariae and lamias?

And there was something I remembered and told him that he couldn't have known.

'I went into your room, and you were asleep. Curled up tight and warm, like a child. I was so amazed then that my daddy slept like a child!'

And I also asked him to forgive me for the years when I spurned him and humiliated him, as if I was taking my revenge for something. Why was I taking my revenge? Because he turned out not to be the Ruler of Rulers or King of the Naked-Wise or Lord of All

Lords? Because he didn't live in the Capital of all Capitals, the para-mount city of all lands, inhabited and uninhabited? Because he didn't travel across his lands in a small tower on the back of a she-elephant?

Why did I say that I despised him and Mummy? Could it really be true that I despised them?

'Daddy, forgive me for the way I behaved then! And for every-thing I said that hurt you! I'd ask Mummy to forgive me, but there's no one to ask now.'

Daddy answered:

'Oh come on, Sashka! I forgave you then already. It's just a way people have of growing up.'

I took a book to leaf through off the shelves, opened it, and there were clippings of hair between the pages. I realised it was probably from when Mummy was cutting Daddy's hair all those years ago and he was sitting there reading.

Among all the clutter on the cupboard I found a box of chess pieces.

'How would you like to play, the way we did back then? We haven't played for a thousand years!'

We started playing, and I suddenly won.

'Did you lose on purpose?'

He smiled, but I realised that he hadn't lost on purpose, he'd simply lost. He was a poor chess player.

*'You know, I started recognising my father in myself a long time ago. I can feel his movements in me, his wry smiles, his gestures. How did he get inside me? There was a time when what I wanted more than anything in the world was not to be like him, then suddenly bang – take that! He outwitted me, even in this I lost to him.'*

Daddy had never told me anything about his parents. He only said that they had gone somewhere far away and died there. So I grew up without any grandmothers and grandfathers.

One day he said:

'What actually happened then, nobody knew at the time. It only became an event when someone wrote it down in his memoirs. And you know what's most important about memoirs? What you don't tell!'

He threatened to take revenge on his enemies and those who had done him wrong by not mentioning them at all.

'Not a single word! As if they never existed! Cross them out of life! Tell me now, Sashka, isn't that just the perfect murder?'

On the day he first went outside with me and we walked slowly round the building, step by little step, he noted down in his exercise book:

*'How much I've shrunk! The collar of my shirt is too big for my tortoise neck. I just couldn't understand about Achilles and the tortoise back then. But now I understand. I'm the tortoise and Achilles will never catch up with me.'*

And here are some old entries:

*'Wisdom should accumulate with the advancing years of life, but what have I accumulated, old fool that I am? I've accumulated answers to all the questions that were so important once upon a time, but have now become absolutely unimportant. Even the incontestable fact that soon I won't exist is something that I'm only vaguely aware of.'*

*'They were talking on the radio about plants and birds that are threatened with extinction. Some unfortunate animals are on the point of disappearing. But that's me, I'm an animal on the point of disappearing!'*

And then this, when he started going outside on his own:

*'I went down in the evening to take a stroll round the block. How good it is, simply to take a stroll on my own! Get shafted by a stroke and you soon wise up to what's good. I stopped to catch my breath and saw something on the asphalt, reflecting the light of the streetlamp. A worm or a slug had crawled across and left its mark in life, only not in its own, but*

*mine. It even got onto this page. And it will never find out about it. For some reason that really cheered me up. I felt like springing up onto a bench and doing a tap dance the way I used to. What a young dope, how old was I then?'*

I thought I would find something in his exercise book about Mummy, but there's nothing about her. I only found one phrase on the family, which seemed to have been copied from somewhere:

*'A family is the hatred of people who can't manage without each other.'*

I once asked Daddy if he regretted leaving Mummy when he did.

He answered:

'No. We were like two wild animals grappling, tearing each other to pieces. Once you lose your dignity as a human being, it's time to say goodbye. Can you believe that after one quarrel she leaned out of the window to get her breath back, I was walking past on my way to the kitchen, and I could hardly stop myself grabbing her by the legs and shoving her out!'

One time my father asked:

'Do you want to know why your mother and I separated?'

'No.'

And another time, out of the blue, he started telling me about how he once assured Mummy that it was all over with some other woman, and she believed him, but it wasn't over at all.

'I looked her straight in the eye and felt terrible, like some kind of executioner!'

'Why are you telling me this? You ought to have told Mummy.'

'That's exactly why I'm telling you, because I didn't tell her.'

'So what do you want?'

'I don't know. For her to forgive me?'

'For that especially?'

'For that and for all the rest. But above all, yes, especially for that.'

'It's all right. Everything's all right. She would have forgiven you for that. And for all the rest too. What a thick-headed couple you are, even after death you can't agree about anything without me!'

'*I woke up in the morning, but forgot why. Then I remembered. I'd started wondering what death really looks like. Not a skeleton with a scythe, is he? Once upon a time I asked my father why he lied. He answered: "When you're grown up, we'll talk about it." But now that I've been all grown up for a long time, and I'm even growing backwards already, I'd ask him something quite different: "Father, what does death look like? Tell me; you know!" Death probably looks very simple – a ceiling or a window. A pattern on the wallpaper. The face that you see last.*'

He joked with me and tried to be cheerful, but in the exercise book he was talking to himself, preparing.

'*After death people probably simply go back, become what they always were – nothing.*'

'*Somewhere I read a description of how when they burn someone on a funeral pyre in India, the skull cracks like a chestnut. Somehow I don't believe it. But then an acquaintance of mine told me that his mother was one of the first to be burned in a new crematorium that had just been opened. And back then the relatives could watch the body burning through a window. I don't really understand why – to make sure it hadn't been swapped with something, or what? And he saw his mother sit up a bit in the flames.*'

Daddy often told me he didn't want to be buried in the ground.

'Where's the pleasure in knowing I haven't disappeared completely, but I'm lying somewhere under two metres of sand and rotting bit by bit? And with a stone on top of me! They used to put stones on graves so the dead wouldn't climb out!'

He didn't go to Mummy's grave with me even once, he said he couldn't stand cemeteries. But I discovered from his exercise book that he had been there in spring after all.

'*I wanted to buy flowers for my bunny, they're selling tulips everywhere and I never gave her any bouquets when she was alive. But then I thought they would only get stolen from the grave anyway. Our daughter ordered a stupid stone. But then gravestones are probably never very smart. I sat down and remembered. It was good — quiet and sad. Almost no snow left. The smell of last year's leaves. I ought to put up a little railing, but that's terribly expensive these days. I got there late and I was the last one back out, they closed the gates behind me. As I walked along the fence I saw some old men and women climbing out over it. That's funny — runaways from a cemetery.*'

He asked to be cremated and have his ashes scattered somewhere in the countryside.

'Daddy, what are you saying?'

'What's wrong with that? I'm not asking to be buried standing upright, like Nostradamus! I just want them to cremate me and scatter the ashes. I want to disappear, dissolve. Sprinkle me somewhere on a vegetable patch! Do you promise?'

'All right.'

'*Who was the bright spark who said that suffering is uplifting? What bullshit. Suffering is degrading.*'

He often used to tell me that he didn't want to go as painfully as Mummy. He wanted to do it himself.

'*After all, I've thought about this so many times before. What's wrong with it? Only not in the flat — there'll be other people living here, it would be upsetting for them. One fine day simply tell the woman next door that I'm going on holiday — and disappear. The only thing that stopped me was the thought that I'd have to say something to my daughter. And what could I tell her?*'

He'd been clinging to me, and for months I wouldn't even talk to him on the phone.

After the stroke he said to me:

'Sashka, if I'm suffering really badly, promise you'll give me a jab of something? You know what's needed.'

'Are you out of your mind?'

He started drinking again, deliberately bringing his own end closer, I couldn't do anything about it any more. He got drunk while I wasn't there and then suffered, he said it was indigestion and drank glass after glass of water with bicarbonate of soda. I tried to make him see sense several times, but he only swept all the little bottles and boxes of medicine off the bedside locker.

In late May he suffered a second stroke, from which he never recovered.

He once wrote in his exercise book:

*'It's just annoying that on the day of my death nothing will change and nothing will happen, they'll carry on selling roasted sunflower seeds at the station in the same old way, taking the little heaped glassful out of the sack and pouring them into the pocket that's held open. They'll carry on drinking beer at the corner, sucking the foam off their moustaches. A woman will stand in a window, washing the frame. And the most interesting thing of all is — that day already exists, it comes round in the calendar every year, it can be commemorated. It already exists, only it hasn't been revealed to me yet, like some law or some island.'*

I've just read that and thought that Daddy died in early June, on the fifth, that's the day of his death now. But that means the fifth of June was the day of his death before, it always was. The day existed, but the death didn't. Only I can't remember what happened on that day last year. The same as always — sunflower seeds, beer, a woman in a window washing the frame.

I stroked his yellow hands with tarnished nails, they were already leaving.

During the final days we hardly talked at all, just exchanged a few meaningless words, exactly the way it was with Mummy.

I come in from the kitchen. He whispers:

'Have you been drinking coffee?'

He smelt it.

I pick at my hangnails, that annoys him:

'Stop it!'

He wanted persimmons, I went to the market for some and cut them in half. I feed him with a spoon, but he doesn't eat.

'I don't want it.'

It's hot, but if I open the window, it lets in even more sultry heat. He asked me to put my cold hands on his hot forehead. I held my hands under icy water from the tap to make them colder.

The day before, he sensed everything. I could barely make out what he said:

'I'm dying, childy.'

'So he's dying, is he? Well, aren't we dying? Riding along in a tram?'

He screwed his face up. That was a smile. He whispered:

'Sashka, how I love you!'

Mummy died without me, and I can't explain why, but it was very important for me to be holding his hand at the moment when it happened.

I told him:

'Daddy, I want to hold your hand when you die. Do you promise not to die without me?'

He lowered his eyelids.

Then his final minutes arrived. Daddy breathed so hard that the bed shook about under him. He couldn't talk any more and he kept his pleading eyes fixed on me. I knew what he was pleading for.

I wanted to hug him, I lay down beside him on the bed, snuggled up against him, looking into his eyes all the time. The look in his eyes changed. He was looking at me, but his eyes weren't pleading. There was a kind of astonishment in them.

He was going. He was still with me, but he had already peeped over there. He stopped, lingering for just a moment at the boundary line. He had seen what I couldn't see from that room.

Daddy was struggling to tell me something.

'What, Daddy, tell me! What?'

Gurgling sounds poured out of his throat.

And I suddenly realised what he was trying to tell me after he had peeped over there. He was trying to tell me there really were imperishable people and mute cicadas living there.

Daddy told me several times that he already knew what would be the final phrase in his memoir. Somewhere he had found an ending that scribes used to round off their books – about a ship and the depths of the sea. But the final entry in his pamphlet was quite different.

'*Apparently, according to the latest data, a dead man can hear even after he's dead – of all the functions, hearing is the last to leave. Sasha, my daughter, say something to me.*'

I'm writing all this to explain an amazing feeling: I held his hand at the moment that is probably the most important one in a person's life, and I felt happy.

Sashenka!

My darling!

Tell me, could it be that everything around me really doesn't exist?

Rain again. Falling all day long.

Can all this possibly be reality, and my reality? Of course it can't.

Well, all right, rain, but it could be a quite different rain, couldn't it? There are all kinds of rain. Not every one of them is real, is it?

Perhaps it's that dacha rain. It set in first thing in the morning. And in that place everything's real. The buzzing of the mosquitoes on the veranda. The leaky roof, the drip-dropping in the basin. Windowpanes covered with dust-spots left by raindrops. The garden rustling through the half-open window. The saturated lilac has a special rainy smell. On the path in front of the porch the puddles are alive.

I recline on the divan with a volume of Shakespeare on my knees and write in this same notebook. Composing things. How good it is to compose things! About love, death and everything in the world. Afterwards I can take everything I've written and burn it, can't I? How wonderful that is!

I've just lain down with the notebook and started pondering, then I glance at my watch and it's already ten to two! You're waiting for me. Now I'll slip into my rubber boots, put on my old raincoat and set off – along our path. First to the corner, where my neighbour cultivates his tea roses behind the fence, then through the forest to the bridge over the ravine, and from there I can already see the roof of your dacha. I'm particularly fond of that path through our forest. I love the way you're amazed every time I know the names of the plants. What's so special about that? Anyone can do it.

My love! Wait a little bit longer!

I'm coming!

●

My love, my dearest, my only one!

I woke early and lay there, thinking about you.

My darling, this will be a very joyful letter.

But to begin with I have to tell you everything in the right order – and first of all that the whole city has been smothered in snow.

I woke up in the middle of the night and remembered that I didn't have to go to work today and could carry on calmly wallowing in bed. And it was only then I felt how tired I had become over the last days and weeks. And years. But there was a strange glow outside the window. I glanced out – everything was covered in snow. I lay down again, wrapped myself up like a chrysalis, the way you like, and looked out through the hole at the snow outside the window. And then how sweet it was to go back to sleep again!

When I woke up out of habit early in the morning, while it was still dark, I heard the spades scraping outside the window and remembered that snow had fallen, and again I was deluged with such great happiness! I fell asleep again, this time until midday, I slept to my heart's content.

I sat down to breakfast facing the falling snow.

Afterwards I just sat there like that in front of the window, as if it was a stage, and watched the wet flakes striking against the glass and slowly slipping down.

I brewed myself some strong tea. No need to run anywhere. That's so good!

The winter outside the window somehow makes the reddish flush of the tea in the glass especially warm.

I couldn't wait, I went for a walk. I tumbled out into the falling snow.

I walk along and the fresh clean smell makes me crazy.

The day has gone crazy at the smell too, as if it has forgotten its part and is ad-libbing wildly.

And the entire city is completely out of its mind.

The road junction has snow porridge in its mouth and it's mumbling something.

The statue used to have dark hair, but now it's an albino.

They wondered where the Abominable Snowman lives, and here he is in our little garden square.

The heavy branches sag down, trying to grab people by the scruff of the neck, everyone has to stoop.

How wonderful to have winter and snow! Especially the snow! It's come to create everything anew.

The park was hollow, bare and open for half the winter, but now it's palatial architecture in snow — arches, towers, domes. The trees hang down so low over the road that the cars seem to be driving in through snowy gates.

And in general the snowfall transforms everything into a single whole. There was everyone in the world all living on their own, but now every bench and pillar, not to mention the postbox, understands the plenitude and seamless unity of existence.

A passer-by hides from the snow under his umbrella. The only wise guy around. All the others simply dust themselves off and pat themselves down with their mittens, but on their shoulders and caps the snow rises like yeasty flapjacks.

In every courtyard children are rolling big balls of snow and making snowmen.

The snow is wet and sticky. I scooped some up in my fist and couldn't resist it − I bit off a little chunk.

The snow skips about lightly and impetuously as it falls. It infects the entire city, but especially little boys and dogs. In the school yard the senior pupils fight snowball battles, thrust handfuls of snow into each other's faces and down each other's necks. Scarves and caps lie about on the ground. A mongrel dog barks and chases the snowballs, snorting and biting at the snow.

I stood there, watching the dog dash joyfully backwards and forwards, spraying saliva about. Suddenly it stopped right in front of me and glanced up at me in surprise, as if to say: Don't just stand there, come on! − then it yawned, snapped its jaws together loudly and went dashing off, felling snowflakes with its tail and barking resoundingly in its happiness.

I walk on, without knowing where I'm going. What difference does it make, when it's tumbling down so thick?

Herringbone prints from shoes on the pavement − like New Year trees.

Black clearings thawed round the manhole covers.

The street name signs have been plastered over.

The snow flies raggedly, on a slant, and builds up unevenly at an oblique angle on the windowsills.

And the wet snow only sticks to the trees on one side, they look like they have white trouser stripes.

Some bush with beetroot-red withies comes creeping towards me out of the snow-swirl. You know what it's called.

And there's a cyclist, defying the winter. The sticky snow coils onto the tyres of the bike. Now he's jumped off to push it by the handlebars.

I walk past a building site – the dirty, wet planks of the board-walk under the awning spring pleasantly as I walk on them, tossing me up at every step.

A hairdresser has slipped out for a smoke, she catches the snowflakes with the glowing end of her cigarette, and there are white flakes in her hair already. Someone came out and a cloying whiff of hairdressing chemicals escaped through the door. How can anyone breathe that all day long?

Then I walked past a kindergarten and glanced in through the window.

I stand and watch mums and grannies unfolding costumes and dressing up children – rabbits, snowflakes, foxes, bears. One boy has put on a wolf mask and he's scaring everybody. A little girl pulls on a long white sock, hopping about on one little foot.

In another window there's a huge festive New Year tree, flaring up brightly, then fading away. In the corner presents are being stuffed into a sack.

And in the last window Grandfather Frost is fastening the hook on the back of Snow Maiden's dress. She's gazing into the mirror and putting on her lipstick. Alive, even though she was sculpted out of snow. But nobody's surprised.

I went home.

I was sorting out papers and started thinking, flapping the pile against my lips. And something really stupid happened – I cut my lip on the edge of one sheet. A nasty little cut, very painful.

In the evening I decided to go to a concert. I'm not very fond of the Scandinavian composers, but even so.

I can't live without music. Everything superficial and superfluous is blown away, like a dry husk, only what's real is left.

But this time for some reason I couldn't concentrate, everything around me interfered and distracted me.

In the cloakroom people stamped their feet, brushed themselves down, wiped off their plastered spectacles.

I went into the ladies' room, with women putting on powder and makeup and a bathhouse noise echoing in my ears. I took it into the concert hall with me.

I try to get into the music, to be alone with myself, but I can't do it. It's as if the music has hangnails.

I sit there, seeing the peeling gilt on the circles and boxes, the threadbare velvet.

Someone rustles a sweet wrapper, a cloakroom tag is dropped. From out in the street I hear a fire engine's siren or an ambulance wailing.

I keep touching the cut with the tip of my tongue.

I think about the music, but my thoughts are worn into holes.

For some reason I remembered you repairing a bicycle at the dacha and standing it in the middle of the veranda with the wheels upwards. The tools were lying on newspaper. I accidentally caught my hip on a pedal and the wheel started turning with a soft rustling sound.

The woman in front of me kept fingering the coral beads on her neck all the way through the first part of the concert, and when she got up at the interval, her seat couldn't resist it and tried to hoist up her skirt.

I left at the interval, before the second part.

Even more snow has piled up. It keeps teeming down, insatiable.

Cars glide soundlessly through the falling snow, driving round in a circle on the square – they've arranged a quiet merry-go-round for themselves.

Snowflakes swarming under every streetlamp. And I can see their shadows.

Even without the streetlamps everywhere is bright from the snow.

And at the crossroads the snow-white light means I can cross the street.

I stopped at a shop window. Children's warm elephant-slippers. I look at them and they stare back at me.

I went home.

I had gone to bed already, then I got up again, dressed and went outside.

Quiet and blank, nothing but snow. It makes breathing easy, delicious.

I've decided to sculpt a little girl for myself.

I'm going to have a daughter.

I take some snow and it's pliable and plausible. Everything turns out well – little arms, little legs.

When my fingers freeze, I warm them up in my pockets and carry on sculpting.

Little cheeks and little nose. Little fingers, little toes. A smooth, firm little bottom. A navel.

She turned out a wonderful little girl!

I picked her up carefully and carried her home.

Put her to bed and tucked her in.

I touched her feet – little icicles, I started warming them up, breathing on them, rubbing, kissing.

I put the kettle on to feed her raspberry tea.

I warm up her little feet and tell her there's a country where people with one leg live and they skip about on it faster than people with two, and their foot is so huge that in sultry weather they shelter behind it from the hot sun, and there are other people there who live on the smells of fruits, and if they set off on a long journey they take these fruits with them and sniff them.

As I tell her this, I rub her little heels and look in the mirror, and it reflects the window, and I can see the snow falling.

The little feet warmed up, and I thought she had already fallen asleep.

I leaned down to kiss her goodnight, but she said:

'Mummy, what's that?'

'I cut it on some paper, it's nothing to worry about, go to sleep!'

I wrapped her up tight, tucking the blanket in from all sides, and was just going, but she said:

'Mummy!'

'Now what?'

'Will you buy me those slippers that are elephants?'

'Yes, yes, I'll buy them! Now sleep!'

■

Sashenka!

My love!

There's nothing here.

Where's the helleborine? Where's the wood sorrel?

No marsh marigold, no meadow gentian, no sow-thistle. And no lovage or tansy.

Where's the buckthorn? And the orchis? Where's the field scabious?

Why isn't there any willowherb?

Where's the bearberry? And the broom?

And the birds? Where are the birds?

Where's the yellowhammer? Where's the black woodpecker? Where's the gannet?

And the chiffchaff, where's the chiffchaff?



●


My love!

My Volodenka!

Every day you're closer and closer to me.

Just a normal day.

I try to wake her up, but she starts kicking out and hides her head under the blanket.

'Bunny, it's time!'

But she burbles:

'Oh no it isn't! It's still night. I'm dreaming you.'

Well, what can I do with her? And it's the same with everything.

I go to bed very late and fall asleep as soon as my head touches the pillow, although it sometimes seems to me that I fall asleep on the wing. But even so, I set the alarm clock for early. It's very important for me to get up so that I have a few minutes to myself.

Outside the window – darkness, endless winter, frost.

I brew myself coffee and think about the day that's just beginning. And about you. And about everything in the world.

I run to the shower and wake up my little bunny on the way. It's a whole ritual. I start playing Sleeping Beauty with her – muffled up in the blanket, she's the forests and mountains through which the prince gallops in search of his beloved, and now I – that is, he – have galloped up and start kissing her. She snuffles contentedly, quite clearly waking up, but she won't admit it. And how fragrant the nape of her neck is before the other smells of the day have attached themselves to it!

But when even the prince is no help, a hedgehog creeps in under her blanket. My little bunny jumps up with a joyful squeal and throws herself on my neck. The day has begun.

I come out of the shower and she hasn't got dressed yet. She's putting on her tights with the heels on top of her feet, they won't pull up. She's chilled through and shivering, but not doing anything to get dressed more quickly – she'd rather sit there and play awkward.

And she's got a wobbly tooth too, she keeps touching it with her finger. I slapped her hand and she scowled.

I'm making porridge in the kitchen – we both love to watch the oats in the pan smacking their lips. I call:

'Come on, where are you?'

She comes, pulling on her jumper, waving an empty sleeve in the air, pretending she has one arm missing, giggling.

'Stop fooling about! Sit down, will you!'

A new game begins – she smears the porridge round her plate, drawing something on it.

'Bunny, it's late!'

She declares solemnly:

'How can it be late, when it's still only morning?'

She huffs and puffs over her porridge, but the moment I sink into thought and look at the window overgrown with hoarfrost, I get a slap across my hands.

'Mummy! Don't nibble your fingers! How many times do I have to tell you?'

I go back into the room, pull my dress on in a rush, come back – she's pinched the crumb out of a crust of bread and informs me gleefully:

'Mummy, look, the crust's yawning!'

Mooncalf raptures.

We're already late, we pull our coats on at the double, but the things that were got ready and gathered together the evening before are playing hide and seek. Everything disappears – mittens, cap, scarf, spare shoes and socks. I muffle her up and fasten my own coat on the stairs. In the entrance hall the cold already takes my breath away. We tumble out into the freezing darkness.

We hurry to the stop. Dense gloom. Ringing footsteps on frozen-over pavements. Ice everywhere – I just hope I don't take a tumble!

We walk by the rubbish dump, I usually try to run past here, but today even the smells are frozen.

Bunny keeps trying to resolve various important matters as we walk along, but I don't hear anything she mumbles, I can only see the little white cloud emerging from her lips.

There are still lots of stars in the sky, but tears have sprung to my eyes in the frosty air and the stars are all fluffy.

We're only just in time for the tram. We're lucky, there are actually two places together. As we ran the last stretch, we thawed out our cheeks and now they've gone numb.

Bunny promptly starts breathing on the frosted-over window and rubbing a spy hole in it.

Just a normal tram. Clattering along in showers of sparks. Passengers catching up on their sleep, muffling themselves in scarves, huddling up to keep warm.

We've got a talkative conductress.

'Well then, warm-blooded creatures, frozen stiff, are you? Never mind, you'll soon breathe the place warm!'

Someone has opened a newspaper above my head. War on the front page, the crossword on the back.

'Mummy, Mummy, an elephant!'

'What elephant?'

'An elephant, there! We drove past an elephant!'

'There aren't any elephants in winter.'

She pouted and turned away. Put her eye to the peephole again.

'But there was an elephant! I saw it!'

She can't calm down.

'It's true. They were leading it along and we drove past it!'

I pulled down her hood and kissed her on the nape of the neck.

It occurred to me that I would have to wash her today. It's always a joy to do that. And she loves the bathroom too, she can play in there for hours. She's always thinking up something new, for instance, she'll start drawing on the steamy tiles of the wall. Or launching little soap-dish ships. Or playing uninhabited islands with her knees sticking up out of the water.

I love going in to join her in the overheated, muggy bathroom, I make sure to shut the door quickly and not let any cold air in. The gas column drones, the hot shower pricks her with its slim little needles, she squeals and splashes.

I wash her hair until it squeaks.

She always pulls on the chain and opens the plughole herself, and then helps the whirlpool swirl round with her finger.

I take the warm towel off the radiator, wrap her up in it, sit down on the toilet and sit her on my knees. I rub her little back, little tummy, little legs. We both like the way the last dribbles of water glug and gurgle out of the bath into the drain – we wait for that growling moment.

She inspects her crinkly fingertips, trying to spot when they turn smooth, turn back into her. I remember how frightened she was the time when she first noticed this, she wailed that she was still little, but her hands were like an old woman's. She couldn't calm down until she saw her fingers five minutes later.

Sometimes I look at her and see myself when I was little. Once upon a time I used to munch an apple just like that and walk to and fro along the strip of light on the parquet from the chink in the curtains. I loved the milksop my mummy used to make, just like her: now I cut the bread up into little cubes and toss them into the bowl of warm milk, then sprinkle them with sugar from a teaspoon. Mummy also taught me to make the bed – I showed my bunny once how to make the pillow's ears stick out from under the blanket, and now the bed is always made up.

But some things are all her own. For instance, she plays with an invisible animal that no one but her can see. He lives in her conch shell. That same *Strombus strombidas* of ours, which has now become someone's home.

I really love to watch her playing with this invisible creature, feeding him, giving him tea. I still don't know what kind of beastie it is. Bunny considerately blows on its saucer, so it won't scald its mouth. Nags at it not to swill the tea round its mouth before swallowing it. Moistens a handkerchief with saliva, wipes the dirt off its face and scolds it in my tone of voice. And when it falls ill, she treats it with a special medicine – the smell of chocolate, which she keeps in the big box from the New Year sweets.

Sometimes I can't stop myself, I grab her up in my arms and kiss her here, there and everywhere – on her little neck, her cheeks, the top of her head, and she tries to break free, no more mummy, she says, let me go!

Once when I was putting her to bed she suddenly asked:

'Mummy, where did I come from?'

'I sculpted you out of snow.'

'Not true! I know where children come from!'

She's funny.

At the station my father climbs into the tram, there are lots of people, we're sitting at the back and he gets in through the front door, I wave to him, but he doesn't see. I only hear him speaking loudly, as if he's on a stage – he's already had a drink first thing in the morning – telling the entire tram about how they bought him new galoshes when he was a child.

'Those galoshes made the day a real celebration! Soft crimson baize on the inside! And that delicious smell of rubber! And I just can't wait to go outside in them, to where the fresh snow has fallen, because the prints from new galoshes are very, very special – like chocolate bars! We pretended that was our chocolate. I took my mitten off, picked a bar up carefully with my fingers and munched on it. And we used to gorge ourselves on that snow chocolate!'

'Mummy, is there still a long way to go?'

'No, we'll be there soon.'

The conductress's glasses have steamed up, she's pushed them up onto her forehead and she's counting the change in her satchel, examining the coins with no heads minted in Utrecht.

'Mummy, is there still a long way to go?'

I hug her to me and whisper in her ear:

'Listen, there's something I've got to tell you. There'll be someone there, don't be surprised when he lays his head on my knees.'

'Why? Does he love you?'

'Yes.'

'I love you too. Lots and lots!'

And she laid her head on my knees.

■

Sashenka!

My love! My darling!

I'm on my way to you. Only a little bit further to go.

Something amazing has happened to me.

I suddenly hear this:

'Right then, show me your muscles!'

I don't understand a thing and I ask:

'Who are you?'

He says:

'Who am I? Can't you see? I'm Prester John, and everything round here is my kingdom – clamorous, fragrant and imperishable. I am the Lord of Lords and the Ruler of all Rulers. In my kingdom everyone knows his own future, but he still lives his own life, lovers love even before they find out about each other, get to know each other and get talking, and the rivers flow one way during the day and the other way during the night. Tired?'

I:

'Yes.'

He:

'Have a seat. I'll just put the kettle on.'

I:

'I can't. I have to be going.'

He:

'I know.'

I:

'I ought to hurry. The point is . . .'

He:

'I know, I know everything. She's longing to see you.'

I:

'I don't have any time. I've got to go to her. I'll be off.'

He:

'Hang on, you won't find her without me. I'll show you the way. Sit for a while, take a breather. I've just got one thing to do, then we'll be going. I'll be quick.'

I:

'Tell me, that picture on the wall . . .'

He:

'Well, go on, go on! Don't worry about me writing. I've got to finish this off, there's only a little bit left. I'm listening.'

I:

'Where did you get it?'

He:

'What?'

I:

'That cross-section plan of a steamship. The one with the sailor drawn in on the anchor, there he is, with a bucket and brush.'

He:

'You've got to take that with you. Take out the thumbtacks and roll it up into a tube. And by the way, don't you know that the anchor is the only thing on a ship that they don't paint? Well, all right, that's a mere trifle. You've got to take everything important with you, not forget anything. Have a think, get yourself organised.'

I:

'But I haven't got anything. I don't need anything.'

He:

'Have you forgotten, or what? You said yourself that the unnecessary things are the most essential. There, hear that?'

I:

'A stick clattering along a fence?'

He:

'Yes. Everyone who fancies the idea clatters it as they walk by, some with a stick, some with an umbrella. And now, do you hear that – grasshoppers, as if someone's winding up a little watch? And that's a tram rumbling over the points in the distance.'

I:

'And what's this?'

He:

'Those? Prickly burrs. You threw them in her hair. Then you pulled them out again, but they clung on tight. You've got to take all that. And the smells! You can't possibly leave the smells behind! Remember the sweet aroma from the confectioner's shop? Vanilla, cinnamon, chocolate, your favourite rum truffles.'

I:

'Look, there's the list from my herbarium, with "Ribwort, *Plantago*" written in painstaking childish writing. Are we taking that too?

He:

'Naturally. And the wood-pile of books from the floor of your room. And your mum's ring, which is still spinning and jingling on the windowsill, skipping about like a transparent little gold sphere. And the way a certain person used to polish his glasses with his tie.'

I:

'And the scrap of newspaper stuck to a shaving cut?'

He:

'Yes, of course, after all, every scrap of paper like that has its own person, unlike all the others, and he feels with his fingers for the hands on his watch without any glass on the dial.'

I:

'It's time we were going.'

He:

'Yes, yes. We'll be off in a moment. Wait just a little bit!'

I:

'And where's the round pebble that's eternity?'

He:

'Ah, I threw that away. Stuck it in my pocket and went for a walk. There was a pond there. Eternity skipped on the water a couple of times, then went plop, and there was nothing left behind but circles, and then not for long.'

I:

'Let's go!'

He:

'Hang on! Just a moment. There was something I wanted to tell you, but I can't remember what now. Ah, that's it – don't listen to Democritus! Bodies can touch, and there isn't any gap between souls either. And people become what they always were – warmth and light. Now let's go. It's time. Check to see you haven't forgotten anything. I'm just finishing up. That's it. The pen squeaks across the paper like clean-washed hair between fingers. My weary hand hastens and lingers, tracing out at the last: Happy as the ship having passed over the depths of the sea is the scribe on reaching the end of his book.'